Misfortune

NANCY GEARY

WARNER BOOKS

An AOL Time Warner Company

WARNER BOOKS EDITION

Copyright © 2001 by Nancy Whitman Geary
All rights reserved. No part of this book may be reproduced in any form or by any electronic or mechanical means, including information storage and retrieval systems, without permission in writing from the publisher, except by a reviewer who may quote brief passages in a review.

Cover design and photo illustration by Shasti O'Leary

Warner Books, Inc.
1271 Avenue of the Americas
New York, NY 10020

Visit our Web site at
www.twbookmark.com.

 An AOL Time Warner Company

Printed in the United States of America

Originally published in hardcover by Warner Books
First Paperback Printing: June 2002

10 9 8 7 6 5 4 3 2 1

Grace

ACCLAIM FOR MISFORTUNE

"Few writers succeed in describing the world of the American aristocracy or how they truly live. But Nancy Geary has an authentic voice. She knows this world. What a great first novel!"
—**Olivia Goldsmith, author of *The First Wives Club***

"A shrewd and entertaining mystery."
—*American Way*

"An irresistible read, both because it takes you behind the hedges of blue bloods in the Hamptons and because it's a compelling mystery that keeps you guessing whodunit and whydunit until the final page. A stylish and expert debut."
—**Jane Heller, author of *Sis Boom Bah***

"A stunning debut which should be subtitled *An Un-Hampton Novel*. Nancy Geary, like Richard North Patterson, writes brilliantly about the world of old money, manners, and mores."
—**Nelson DeMille, author of *Up Country***

"A riveting tale of privilege, prejudice, and violent death. Haunting, compelling, and beautifully written, Nancy Geary's astonishing first novel reads like a cross between Scott Turow and Edith Wharton. I couldn't put it down."
—**Amy Gutman, author of *Equivocal Death***

For Gordon

Acknowledgments

I feel privileged to work with Jamie Raab at Warner Books and appreciate her wonderful suggestions and help in shaping this book. I thank Maureen Egen for her belief in my work. Also thanks to Sona Vogel for her careful copyediting and attention to detail.

I could not have written *Misfortune* without the encouragement of my family and friends. I owe them a great deal. I wish to thank Gordon Walker for sharing his critical eye and logical mind and for his constant support during the writing of this book; Natalie Geary for her advice and love, as well as her assistance with medical information; Lisa Genasci for her eternal optimism that my work would one day appear on a bookshelf and for her help in leading me to my agent; Marc Glimcher, Isabelle Glimcher, Lily Glimcher, Juliana Hallowell, and Mark Phillips for reading the early chapters and urging me to continue; Christof Friedrich for his patient explanation of hair sample analysis and Patrice Milley for checking my gardening and floral details; Aliki Nichogiannopoulou and Missy Smith for their friendship and for ensuring that

I never felt isolated; Carlos, Jack, and Fanny, my dogs, for making work at home a constant adventure; and Diana Michener, my mum, for her inspiration.

I am very fortunate to have had the help and guidance of all those at Nicholas Ellison, Inc., especially Alicka Pistek, and of Carol Frederick at Sanford J. Greenburger Associates. I appreciate their work and efforts on my behalf. I am forever grateful to Nick Ellison, an extraordinary agent and invaluable friend.

Misfortune

I couldn't have picked a better day for her to die. I like the idea of July Fourth, the Day of Independence. Tonight, fireworks will explode against the blackened sky in bursts of green, red, blue, and gold. Sparklers will sizzle while I celebrate in private the true liberation. As years pass and I advance toward my own death, the anniversaries of this day will sustain me.

I wonder if she will know it is her last breath. I wonder whether she will experience the agony of dying, of squarely facing her own mortality, of realizing what she has done, what pain she has caused, or whether it will all be over so soon that she will remain in ignorant bliss. I'll never know, but I will forever wonder what she feels as she collapses. Does she have a single regret?

I've never seen the inside of a morgue, that place where she'll be stored along with all the other unlucky souls. She wouldn't like the motley company, but death is democratic. It doesn't much care who you were, where you came from, or what you did. No one gets to be special.

There will be an autopsy. Certainly her death is a surprise. But if I've done everything right, the medical examiner will be disappointed. He'll find no poisons, lesions, evidence of violence. Her death will be declared an accident. Only I know otherwise.

Alone, I content myself with the knowledge that I am right to have done what I've done. I know that. My hatred is unambiguous. The depths of my pleasure at her death are unfathomable. The world is a better place without her.

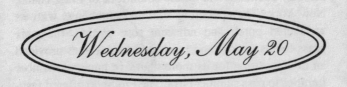

Wednesday, May 20

*W*hy am I the only one willing to admit what we're all thinking?" Clio Pratt's voice filled the rectangular sunroom. The afternoon heat through the rows of mullioned windows baked the terracotta tiled floor. She leaned forward, rested her elbows on the tabletop, and clasped her fingers. Her eyes scanned the faces of the five men and women seated around her. "Henry Lewis does not belong here."

Gail Davis, a middle-aged woman with platinum hair tied back from her face with a grosgrain bow, averted Clio's gaze. Gail played with the clasp on the shell-shaped earring that she had removed from her left earlobe. She looked out the window at the expanse of grass tennis courts and listened to the spray of the sprinkler system watering the acres of green. Her pulse rose by several beats per minute.

The six people seated around the table constituted the Membership Committee of the Fair Lawn Country Club, a private tennis establishment situated on twenty-six acres in Southampton, on the south fork of Long Island, New York. The sprawling shingled clubhouse with its weathered porch and adjacent rose garden, thirty-six grass tennis courts, and renovated health club provided an idyllic setting for its more than five hundred member families to pass summer days. The Pro Shop offered fashionable tennis attire emblazoned with the club's logo, an interlocked monogram, for which the only acceptable method of payment was a house charge. Less athletic members could play croquet or run up healthy bar tabs from Pimm's Cup with celery or vodka Southsides mottled with mint.

On this particular Wednesday, the Membership Committee gathered for the last time before the official start of the summer season, the Memorial Day holiday weekend.

Gail looked down at the stack of folders in front of her, material that she had distributed to members of the committee well in advance. Each one represented a family, couples who had spent all winter lobbying other members for approval, gathering recommendations, and endearing themselves. Gail knew that many would be disappointed with the outcome of this meeting and would have to reapply the following fall, if at all.

"Henry is a respectable man. He and Louise come with impeccable credentials," George Welch, the committee's vice president, countered. "If I could be so bold, I might add that Louise's parents have been members here for longer than you." He shifted in the wicker armchair.

The overhead fan slowly circulated humid air.

"I tend to agree with George," said Wallace Lovejoy,

revealing a hint of a British accent. Wallace ran his fingers through his shock of white hair as he glanced down at the pages in front of him filled with personal information on Henry Lewis. "Look, Henry's mortgages are low on both the house here as well as the city apartment. His girls are in private schools." He lifted his eyes and removed his half-glasses. "He's a first-rate cardiac surgeon. His wife couldn't be more gracious, or pleasant to be around. I've never heard one word of financial instability, marital infidelity, anything unsavory. What more do we want?"

The room was quiet.

"And how many times have you and Maggie included the Lewises in your summer entertaining schedule?" Clio asked. It was no secret to the assembled group that the Lovejoys socialized with a more diverse crowd than most. They had been known to attend at least one Greek Orthodox wedding, as well as several Bar Mitzvahs, to travel as far as East Hampton for a lively cocktail party, and even to mingle with the new money, those who had gravitated to eastern Long Island in recent years complete with armed security guards and indoor media centers.

"That's not the point," George said, defending Wallace.

Wallace inhaled, looked down, and appeared to search for a crack in the tiled floor. "We haven't had the pleasure, but I've run into Henry at numerous professional functions."

"I see," Clio said.

"But I expect this summer to be different. We really do

like the Lewises, would like to see more of them, socially, I mean."

"Why don't we vote?" Gail spoke up. "We've all had ample opportunity to review his file, to meet with him. What else is there to do?" Gail glanced at her thin gold wristwatch. As secretary to the Membership Committee, it was Gail's job to move through the entire agenda in a timely manner, count and record the vote, and issue notifications of the committee's decision. In situations like this, she wished she had never been appointed to the position. She liked neither dissension nor debate. At the time of her appointment, though, the committee considered only females appropriate for the position, and of the women members, she was an ideal candidate. She had built a successful interior design business, personally selecting tissue box covers, coordinated bed skirts, coffee mugs, and other intimate details of most homes in the area. Her social calendar was filled months in advance. She was a lively conversationalist, never burdened a dinner companion with bad news or complaints, and remembered promptly to write thank-you notes.

"A vote is premature. Henry Lewis hasn't even had the benefit of a thoughtful debate." George's voice sounded nervous, slightly hysterical for a man practiced in maintaining composure. Beads of perspiration glistened on his sunburned face. He reached into the back pocket of his khaki slacks for a handkerchief and patted his forehead.

"I don't care how charming, how intelligent, or how perfect Henry Lewis is, he doesn't belong here. He doesn't fit in," Clio said.

Gail couldn't bear to hear the words that she knew

were coming. She looked again at the time. Nearly five. She needed a drink. For a moment she allowed herself to imagine the taste of a gin and tonic, the feel of a crystal tumbler, the smell of lime.

"What more do I have to say?" Clio continued. "Henry Lewis is black."

"I can't believe I'm listening to this." George rested his forehead in the palms of his hands.

Clio tucked her long dark hair behind one ear. "Oh, please. Don't act so appalled. You don't want a black member in this club any more than I do."

"Henry's race may raise several issues of concern." Jack Von Furst, the committee president, spoke with deliberate calm. An elderly man with a full head of salt-and-pepper hair and deep walnut eyes, he exuded the charm of a diplomat. Despite the heat, the creases in his linen pants remained crisp. "But I don't think any of us wants this conversation to become inappropriate."

"Inappropriate?" George bellowed. "Is that your characterization? This is the worst prejudice I've ever witnessed. It may come as a surprise to you, but the rich aren't only white and Protestant anymore. Broadening the scope of the membership here is long overdue."

"Let's not get carried away," Jack replied. "The only issue for debate is the eligibility of Henry and Louise Lewis for membership, nothing more. We don't need global condemnations of this committee, or the club."

"Henry is only one example of what's been going on since this club's inception. We exclude everyone who isn't exactly like us. God forbid our worlds wouldn't be as insular as we'd like."

Wallace nodded. Even Gail, who shied away from politics, had to concede that members of the Fair Lawn Country Club came from the narrowest stratum of society. She tried not to admit to herself that she liked the homogeneity, but it did insure a certain decorum, a similar frame of reference. It made her feel safe. True, she experienced occasional pangs of conscience when people she otherwise respected were turned down, most often because they were in the entertainment industry, a euphemism, she knew, for the fact that they were Jewish. In fairness, though, she reminded herself of the changes that had occurred over the last decade. Several second-generation Catholics had children in the morning tennis clinic. An Asian woman, a former model, had been accepted when she married a member. Wasn't that progress?

Besides, Gail reassured herself that the Fair Lawn Country Club's membership simply reflected the demographics of the area. Southampton lay ninety miles west of New York City. A summer bastion for Wall Street tycoons and their families; most flocked to the area surrounding the club, the several square miles between the south side of Montauk Highway and the Atlantic Ocean. Gail decorated houses with names, By the Sea, Seven Maples, Point Ashore—all twelve-bedroom homes with wraparound porches that sprouted from manicured lawns. These were people who referred to their rooms as the "great room," the "upstairs drawing room," the "solarium," the "butler's pantry." They communicated by intercom with their guesthouse, poolhouse, and children's wing. Few people cooked their own meals, and nobody did their own dishes. These same people belonged to Fair

Lawn. The club's parking areas, like the members' own raked gravel drives, were lined with imported automobiles.

"Louise Lewis's mother and father have been important sponsors of our Fourth of July tennis tournament. They host several of the guest players. They throw the opening reception," George pleaded with the group.

"The tournament, yes. Didn't Louise win one year?" Peter Parker righted himself from his slouched position in an armchair by the window. Round bellied and red faced, he resembled an aging Humpty-Dumpty. Gail, like others who had known him for more than the last decade, remembered his lively sense of humor and boisterous personality, but his heavy drinking now kept him quiet and passive. He rarely had opinions on any of the applicants for membership and tended to vote with the majority. Mention of the summer's showcase event, the Fourth of July member-guest tournament, prompted his interest, perhaps because cocktails flowed earlier than usual on the spectator-filled porch. "She had a great partner, guy from Piping Rock. Can't remember his name."

"Henry is the Bancrofts' son-in-law. Let's not forget who we're talking about." George's voice steadied momentarily. "Louise breezed in as a junior member when she turned twenty-five. I don't remember that there was a single voice of opposition."

"That was before she chose her spouse," Peter muttered, more to himself than the assembled group.

Custom, as well as practice, dictated that children of members became junior members when they attained the age of twenty-five. Junior membership gave them all the rights and privileges of membership at a slightly reduced cost. When junior members married, the newly constituted family had to apply on its own.

"No juniors have been turned down when they came up with their own families, have they?" Wallace turned to Gail as if she might keep track of such statistics.

Gail couldn't be certain, but if her memory served her, no grown children had been denied other than one young man who, as a teenager, had destroyed the men's locker room and been arrested twice for minor drug charges. "I can review the files if you think it matters," Gail replied.

"Wally's point is that we're sending a very clear signal that Henry, and Henry alone, is the problem." George clenched his fist.

"So what?" Clio replied. "I don't want him around. Make him a member, and it won't stop there. We'll have no way to limit whom he brings into the club."

"We could impose specific limitations on his guest privileges," Jack suggested.

"There are considerable restrictions already," Gail offered. "The same person can't come more than twice in one month, or three times in a season. These limitations safeguard against abuse."

"You know as well as I do that Henry is prominent among his people. He'll have friends. We'll be opening the floodgates," Clio replied.

"There is a legitimate issue of whether Henry will be welcome. He is different, and we certainly don't want him to feel isolated," Jack remarked.

"Henry and Louise aren't going to be isolated unless you force them to be," George countered.

"Do we need to consider the possibility of a lawsuit?" Gail tried to remember an article she had read about an all-male undergraduate social club at Harvard University. A woman had sued the Fly, as it was called, claiming that its failure to admit women deprived her of important contacts in the business world. Gail couldn't remember how it had been resolved, but she thought it might be relevant to the discussion.

"Henry doesn't strike me as the type to sue. He's not"—Jack paused to select his word—"militant."

"He bloody well should be." The anger in George propelled him to his feet. "What are we doing?" He looked around for the answer that no one would provide.

"Sit down, George," Jack instructed. "You're not suggesting that Henry be exempt from discussion because of his race, are you?"

George did not reply.

"Perhaps we should follow Gail's suggestion and take a vote." Jack exhaled. "Let the majority of the committee determine the outcome, as we always do."

"A vote won't be necessary," Clio announced. "I'm throwing a blackball."

Gail gasped. A blackball trumped any legitimate vote and prevented the candidate from ever seeking membership in the future. That act created a permanent scar that no amount of support could undo. Although the official club rules gave each member of the committee one blackball to cast per year, in the three years Gail had served as secretary, and for as long as she could remember hearing leaks of the supposedly secret Membership Committee meetings, no one had received such treatment. Even a candidate who had been indicted on charges of tax evasion at the time of his vote was deferred, not blackballed. He pleaded guilty and ended up in prison, a two-year sentence, if she remembered correctly. For a brief moment, Gail's mind wandered, wondering if he would reapply upon his release.

"This is outrageous. You're not even a member of this committee." George's already red face seemed to explode with rage. "Richard would never do such a thing."

This mention of Clio's husband silenced the group. Richard Pratt had been a member of the committee for more than twenty years. Gail, who served with him for his last two, admired his natural graciousness, his gentility. In retrospect, even his more draconian choices seemed well reasoned.

Gail looked across the table at Jack's pensive expression. She imagined he was racking his brain for snippets of conversation, if any, that he might have had with Richard over the years about race relations, about the issue of whether the Fair Lawn Country Club should be integrated. It was unlikely. Richard was a private man, that Gail knew. In the myriad charitable lunches, cocktail parties, and dinners where their paths had crossed, he rarely gave opinions or discussed personal matters. No one knew why his first marriage to Aurelia Watson, the mother of his two daughters, had ended. He never uttered a bad word, or even a snide remark, about his ex-wife, and rumor had it that his generosity toward her far exceeded his court-imposed obligations. He had been a bachelor for several years, longer than most men of comparable wealth and stature, before he met Clio, his second wife, to whom he had been married now for nearly thirty years. His devotion to her had been apparent from the very start, after they met at a brunch arranged by Jack and his wife, Constance. The look in Richard's eye when he spoke of Clio, the gentle way that he rested his hand on the small of her back when they stood together, the quiet smile that crossed his lips when she entered a room, served as windows to his adoration.

Gail hadn't seen Richard since his stroke the year before. She had heard reports that it had physically incapacitated him almost completely and that his mental acuity remained unpredictable, with periods of lucidity followed by moments of disorientation. Because of his condition, Clio stood in for him on the Fair Lawn Country Club's Membership Committee and its Board of Governors. The allowance of a proxy was an unprecedented gesture. It served as a living tribute, a sign of the deep respect and fondness for Richard that was nearly universally shared.

"I spoke to Richard about it this morning. I'm simply exercising his choice," Clio clarified.

Could Richard Pratt actually have directed such a course of action in the state he was in? If so, did he appreciate what he was doing? Gail looked around at the group of baffled faces.

"Shall we move along?" Clio asked, glancing at her gold wristwatch.

The bang of George's fist on the table reverberated, sending a chill down Gail's spine. She flinched.

George rose from his chair. "I have greatly misjudged you," he said, looking Clio straight in the eye. His voice was low. He appeared to be struggling to steady its quiver. "I urge the members, in light of this development, to abstain. Henry is too good a man to fall victim to your small-mindedness. Abstention of a vote on his application to membership at least gives him an opportunity to reapply. Give Henry Lewis the decency he deserves."

"You are assuming I'll change my mind next year."

"No, I don't expect miracles." George spoke slowly, each word articulated. "I'm merely hoping you won't be here next year."

Clio laughed.

After a few moments of awkward silence but for the creaking of wicker seats as their occupants stirred, Gail spoke. "Do I hear a motion to abstain on the application of Henry and Louise Lewis?" She tried to sound official.

"Yes," George said.

"I'll second," Wallace added.

She sighed in relief. "All right, then." She wanted a gavel to punctuate the decision, but her job as secretary came with no such trappings. Instead, Gail flipped open the next folder in her pile. "Bruce and Nancy Sullivan."

From opposite sides of the table, George and Clio settled back in their chairs, their stalemate permeating the air. The remaining business transpired quickly. At half-past five, Gail reviewed the accepted applicants, recorded the time, and dismissed the group. There had been no further dissension, no mention of Henry Lewis. She hoped that the entire incident would disappear quickly from the collective memory of the committee.

George Welch stood first. "Good evening, all," he declared as he headed toward the door. Then he stopped and turned to face Clio, who still sat in her chair. "I won't forget this," he warned, hovering above her. "I just hope Henry Lewis can wait long enough to see you gone."

Clio smiled a truly beguiling smile of white teeth and full lips. "And I thought you liked me."

Paul Murphy opened the screen door to the pub at the Fair Lawn Country Club and stepped inside. He surveyed the rectangular-shaped room with its green-and-black-plaid carpeting, fieldstone fireplace at the far end, and polished wood bar along one side. Three women Paul knew sat at one of the many square tables.

"Hi, Paul," said a thin, freckled thirty-year-old with a long red ponytail.

"Hey," Paul muttered, trying to remember her name. He had given private lessons to her, and each of her three children, once a week for ten weeks last summer, but despite the $6,000 bill he sent, he could recall only her account number: 327.

"When are you starting the ladies' clinic?" she asked.

"When do you want it to start?" He flashed his cater-to-the-clientele smile.

"We'll be out for good at the end of June."

Typical, Paul thought. Fair Lawn Country Club wives and their children moved out from New York City to spend the summer in Southampton once the private schools closed. They left their husbands behind with the choice of a lengthy commute or long weeks alone.

"Well, I guess that's when we'll begin, then. Ladies' clinic wouldn't be the same without you."

"And we want you to give us a real workout," another

of the women interrupted. Paul remembered her: Shelby
Mueller, with her four-carat yellow diamond ring and ruf-
fled tennis panties. Watching dozens of women in short
pleated skirts with tanned legs crouch in the ready position or run after balls had its moments, but he could have
gone without the sight of Shelby, one of the few women
at the Fair Lawn Country Club who hadn't found some
way, whether a personal trainer, an annual month at
Canyon Ranch, or liposuction, to get rid of cellulite.

Despite his repulsion, though, catering to Shelby was
in Paul's best interest. Last year he had made a quick
$20,000 when Frank Mueller, a forty-two-year-old
founder of an Internet company, gave him stock shares as
a tip for teaching him top-spin and an effective slice
backhand. "You gotta have a hundred million to be a
player," Frank, a short, balding fellow with thick glasses
and a stomach that hung over his monogrammed tennis
shorts, had remarked. "Here's a start." The price per share
had risen several hundred points by the end of October,
allowing Paul to cash out and splurge on a long-awaited
trip to Australia.

"Really make us sweat," the red-haired ponytail remarked. The women giggled.

They got up from the leather-upholstered chairs. "See
ya," they chimed.

Paul sighed. Another summer in Southampton.

He pulled himself up onto a bar stool and, instinctively, rubbed at his muscular thighs. He had spent the
better part of the day checking net heights and line spac-
ings, then unpacking the boxes of inventory that filled the
Pro Shop. As of this Memorial Day weekend, the Fair

Lawn Country Club would be swarming with people once again, a sea of starched white sportswear, V-neck cotton sweaters, Tretorn sneakers, and color-coordinated tennis peds.

"What can I get you?" asked Arthur, the bartender.

"Transfusion." The quick fix of grape juice and ginger ale would get his juices flowing. Although, given his fatigue, he craved a beer, club policy prevented employees from drinking on the premises, and he couldn't afford to get in trouble with management so early in the season, when there still was time to find a replacement.

Arthur set the glass of purple bubbles in front of him.

"You're the man."

"Any time."

The screen door slammed, and Paul turned to see George Welch enter the bar. He had known George for years. A reasonably skilled athlete, he was much in demand as a doubles player because of his strong serve, aggressive net game, and constant humor. George seemed to regale his partners and opponents alike with stories, jokes, and witty remarks.

George took a seat without acknowledging Paul's presence. His face was red. He unbuttoned his collar and barked, "Get me a vodka. Straight up."

"The Membership Committee meeting's over?" Arthur asked.

"In more ways than one," George replied. His subsequent silence made clear that he did not intend to elaborate on his oblique comment.

Paul took a long sip of his transfusion, then smacked his lips. "So, will this season be the best ever?'"

Arthur wrinkled his forehead. "Economy's booming. I don't see why not. What do you think?" he asked George, obviously trying to engage their sullen companion in the somewhat idle conversation.

"I don't give a shit, is what I think." George tilted his head back and drained his glass. Then he pushed the empty tumbler toward Arthur, indicating he wanted a refill. Arthur obliged. "Hypocrites. All of them. All of us. I don't know who we're trying to fool," he muttered.

"The meeting went that badly? Who got axed? Don't tell me. Some poor schmuck whose net worth dropped to only ten million." Paul tried to sound clever, but he knew his attempt was feeble. George glared at him. "What's the news from the winter?" he said, changing the subject.

Arthur jumped in a little too quickly. "Barry Edwards died. His wife donated a marble fountain in his memory for the rose garden. There'll be a dedication in June." He paused, appearing to consider what other information he could share. Although George stared at the bottom of his glass, seemingly not to hear the conversation, Arthur had to avoid gossip in front of members. "Dave Flick bought a yellow Lamborghini. He's driven it over here a couple of times, but no one's been around to see."

"Except for you," Paul said.

"Right." Arthur removed several lemons from a drawer under the sink and began to slice them into thin wedges. "Same old, same old, I guess you could say, huh, George?"

George didn't respond.

"What about Richard Pratt?"

Arthur shrugged. "Not much news from what I hear. I

guess he's hanging in there." He wiped off the far end of the bar with a damp towel. "Mrs. Pratt's around, though. I saw her earlier this afternoon. Nice lady."

George looked up at the mention of Clio Pratt's name. "She's not," he said matter-of-factly. "And don't let anyone tell you otherwise."

Paul was surprised. Although he didn't know Clio Pratt well since she hardly ever took a tennis lesson and didn't come to the ladies' clinic, she seemed friendly when she frequented the Pro Shop. At least she didn't order him around like some of the women did, demanding sizes and service as though he were the hired help. He wondered whether he should come to her defense but decided against it. It was too early in the season to get embroiled in disputes between members.

Arthur surveyed the bar in search of something to do.

"I could use a change of pace," Paul remarked to fill the awkward silence.

"Couldn't we all," George echoed.

Arthur swept the two empty glasses off the bar and began to rinse them in the sink. "Every summer's a little different," he said without looking up from his task. "And the great thing about unexpected events is that you never know when to expect them."

Frances Pratt heard three honks outside her bedroom window. She glanced in the mirror, ran her fingers through her thick brown curls, and grabbed the cabled cardigan from her bed. Pressing her face to the screen, she called down to Sam Guff, who waited in his blue Jeep Cherokee with the engine idling. "I'm coming."

Keys, lights, money, she reminded herself of what she needed. Plus water for the dogs. As she stopped to flick the switch at the threshold, she remembered her lucky gold hoop earrings. Couldn't leave without them. She retrieved the jewelry from a small box on her bureau.

"Bye, guys," Frances said to Felonious and Miss Demeanor, her black mutts, as she quickly rubbed each one behind its ears. As she did, she noticed a slight graying around Felonious's muzzle, a sign of age that she didn't want to see. She had rescued both dogs from the Orient Point animal shelter at four weeks and bottle-fed them for the first month after their mother had been the victim of a young boy's target practice. They had grown to look more like Labrador retrievers with broad faces and square noses than the scrawny puppies she had first brought home. She couldn't imagine life without these dogs, her only roommates.

Frances greeted Sam as she climbed into the seat beside him.

"Feeling lucky?" he asked.

She smiled but said nothing.

Patsy Cline crooned on the radio as they drove the three miles of back roads into the main street of Orient Point. On the north fork of Long Island, a sliver of land jutting out into the sound toward Plum Island, Orient Point was best known for its ferry service to New London, Connecticut. Frances liked its relative quiet. "It's where real people live. People with the same concerns as me. People who do their own laundry." She remembered the speech she had given to Blair, her younger sister, as she justified her decision to settle herself just outside of town in a farmhouse surrounded by potato fields and vineyards. "Orient Point is a great place to live, lots of open space, a four-dollar movie theater, a strawberry festival, a Woolworth's. What more do I want?" Besides, Frances liked the distance from her family. Forty-five miles from Orient Point to Southampton gave her the space she needed. She was alone, but not too far.

As Sam turned the truck into the expanse of concrete that formed the parking lot behind Our Lady of Poland Church, Frances could see that the crowd was bigger than usual. The summer was coming, and with it, Wednesday night bingo grew in popularity. Frances checked her watch: ten minutes until the first game began.

For the past seven years, the entire time she had lived in Orient Point, Frances had been coming to the Catholic church on Wednesday evenings to play bingo in the basement. It was her only foray into any house of worship, but she couldn't resist the game. Grand compared with most of the architecture in the surrounding areas, the square brick building had white columns and a marble statue of the Madonna set inside a carved arch to mark its entrance. Since the previous week, Frances noticed that the planters had been filled to overflowing with fuchsia geraniums.

"Mary on the half-shell must like pink," Sam observed under his breath as they approached the Madonna.

"Quiet," Frances whispered back, anxious lest they offend any of the many people who took great pride in Our Lady of Poland. She had heard the parish included more than two hundred families.

They followed the hordes inside, waited in line to pay

a five-dollar admission fee and purchase one-dollar cards, then settled themselves at one of the many folding tables laid out in rows across the basement. Frances scanned the numbers on the four cards she had bought. Too many duplicates, the cards are too similar, she thought as she glanced over to see if Sam suffered the same problem.

"I'm not trading," he said without looking at her.

"I wasn't asking you to."

"But you were thinking to ask." He smiled.

Frances had met Sam, a forty-three-year-old widower, the first night she had come to play. Sitting beside him, she couldn't help but notice his hazel eyes, pronounced cheekbones, and thick wavy hair. Nor could she avoid staring at his left hand, the thumb, index, and little fingers with two stumps of flesh in between, as he rolled the bingo chips in circles on the table with his palm. At the brief intermission before the final blackout game, she had introduced herself and, exaggerating her reach toward his right side, extended a hand. He hadn't hesitated to shake it.

"Sam Guff," he said, looking her straight in the eye.

By coincidence, he turned out to be her neighbor from across the street. The following week he had offered to drive her. After that their routine was established. Frances now looked forward to their Wednesday evenings, as much for the time spent with him as for the bingo.

"Everybody ready," the master of ceremonies shouted from the podium at the front of the room. Tonight the numbers would be drawn by Abby Flanagan, an elderly woman with thick black glasses and a mole on her cheek that was prominent even from the back of the room. She wore a printed sundress, rolled nylons, and white nurses' shoes.

"Game one is a square. All the B row, all the O row, and the top and bottom of the card."

Frances watched Abby's underarm jiggle as she spun the wheel. The room was quiet.

"B nineteen!"

"N forty-three!"

Sam placed a chip on his card.

Frances felt her heartbeat quicken as the wooden, numbered balls spun in their metal wheel. Why she loved bingo, she could not say, but she justified the hours spent in this windowless basement as a harmless indulgence.

"B seven!"

Richard Pratt had introduced his daughters to bingo thirty-one years ago when he took Frances and Blair to a Sunday night game at the Fair Lawn Country Club. It was one of the many family events offered during July and August. The main room of the clubhouse was emptied of its wicker couches and chairs and replaced by round tables covered in cotton cloths with floral centerpieces. Children between the ages of five and fifteen, the young ones accompanied by parents, the older ones left to their own devices, ate fried chicken, overboiled corn, sweet-potato rolls, and coleslaw off china plates. Frances hadn't been able to eat, her stomach queasy with excitement for the waiters to clear, then distribute bingo cards and ice cream in Dixie cups.

The first time she won, she remembered weaving her way through the tables to the front of the room, then waiting, legs trembling, as the caller checked the numbers on her card against those called. She knew that all eyes were upon her, each child in the audience hoping that she had placed a chip on the wrong number, misheard, so that the game could continue and they still would have a chance. There was no error. The prize, a gift certificate to Lily White's, the only toy store in Southampton, was hers.

"Fanny, she just called G eighty-four." Sam leaned toward her. "You've got it on both cards. One's in the square."

She focused her attention on the caller as the game progressed.

"*Bingo!* He's got bingo," a woman shouted from the back corner of the room. A black woman in a green dress with a white lace collar pushed a wheelchair with an elderly man in it. He wore what appeared to be a flannel bathrobe and carried his winning card on his lap. Although his head hung forward, shaking slightly as the woman maneuvered him around the tables and folding chairs, Frances could see his smile.

May 20. She suddenly remembered.

"Frances, it's Clio," the voice at the other end of the telephone had said. It had been nearly three in the morning when the ringing pierced her sound sleep.

"What happened?"

"Your father's in the hospital. He's had a stroke."

She drove the two hours to New York University Medical Center in the foggy darkness, her eyes transfixed on the windshield wipers sweeping rhythmically back and forth over the glass in front of her. Clio waited in the visitors' lounge for the intensive care unit, sitting with her feet tucked under her and a cashmere blanket draped across her lap. Her dark hair was pulled back from her pale face, and her eyes looked sunken. Frances could see her hands tremble as she held a paper cup of tea that had long since cooled.

"How is he?"

"I don't know." Her voice was flat, soft but steady. "They still don't know."

"Have you seen him?"

"Yes. Briefly."

"Was he conscious?"

"I'm not sure he knew I was there."

"I should let Blair know." Frances remembered for the first time since Clio had called that her sister was on a business trip to Japan, selling art to Honda executives for their headquarters.

"I spoke to her. She'll be on the first flight back."

Frances could think of nothing else to ask or say. She settled herself on the opposite couch to wait, glancing periodically at a well-worn copy of *People* that someone had abandoned. The articles on movie stars, rock singers, and celebrity models blurred into a sea of triviality. Clio stared ahead blankly, moving only slightly if voices were heard in the hall. Hours passed.

"We've got a winner," Mrs. Flanagan announced. The crowd clapped politely, then cleared their cards for the next game.

"Are you all right?" Sam asked.

"Yeah. Why?"

"Just wondering. You seem kind of quiet."

"Well, this is hardly the place to chat. This is serious competition." Frances tried to sound lighthearted.

The waiting had stretched for hours. At one point, sometime late in the afternoon, Dr. Handley had appeared. He'd removed his glasses and rubbed his eyes.

"Richard's had what's called an intracerebral hemorrhagic stroke on the left side of his brain. A blood vessel ruptured and there's been extensive bleeding in the brain tissue. He's still in surgery."

Afterward Richard Pratt remained in intensive care, heavily medicated and sedated. He didn't move or speak and opened his eyes only for a second every so often. Clio stood sentinel, rubbing his hand, wiping his face with a warm washcloth, whispering words Frances couldn't hear, kissing him gently on the cheek. Although Frances offered to spell her, Clio left the hospital for only the briefest intervals to shower and change, returning quickly to resume her post. Frances managed to walk around the block, to stop at a nearby delicatessen for a tuna salad sandwich wrapped in waxed paper along with thick slabs of pickles, to call into the Suffolk County District Attorney's Office to check her messages.

Seated in a vinyl chair by the window, Frances watched as Clio hummed Frank Sinatra's "Come Fly with Me," massaged Richard's feet, and refluffed his pillows several times each hour. Although Frances was moved by Clio's affection, the intimacy she shared with Richard even though he was too ill to notice, her attentiveness left little room for Frances or Blair, who returned from the Far East. Only when Clio left for a brief moment to summon a nurse or make a cup of tea could Frances approach her father's bedside. She stared down at the veins in his eyelids, the gray at his temples, the collarbone protruding from his loosely tied hospital gown. She rested her hand on his shoulder, leaned over close to his ear, and whispered that she loved him. Whatever else had passed between them, in the few moments she had alone these words seemed the only ones worth speaking. The rest didn't matter.

After a week the three women met with Dr. Handley at his office across the street from the hospital. "There's widespread damage to the brain tissue surrounding the site of the rupture. He has virtual total hemiplegia, or paralysis on the right side of his body, his face, his arm, his leg. His motor skills, coordination, and speech are certainly impaired and, I expect, his brain function is, too, although we haven't completed all of our testing."

"Is the damage permanent?" Frances asked.

"It's too early to say what improvements he might make with proper rehabilitation." Only time would tell.

"Fanny, Fanny, you've got a bingo." Sam tapped her arm.

Frances looked down at her card where chips made an X through the free space in the center. She forced a smile.

"Pretty great given the odds. Look at the size of this crowd." Sam's face was animated with excitement he assumed she shared.

"Do me a favor?" Frances asked.

"What?"

"Take it up for me."

Sam looked confused.

"Please." Frances couldn't explain to him that the thought of being watched by this crowd was unbearable. The rush of memories brought on by the anniversary of her father's stroke made her feel vulnerable. At least for tonight, she wanted to hide among the other nonwinners.

"Whatever you say." He nodded, then stood up. Before leaving his place with her card, he bent over and murmured, "Maybe this will be your lucky summer."

Blair Devlin stretched her lean legs on the chaise longue, wiggled her toes, and flopped her head back on the blue-and-white toile pillow. "So, what is it you needed to tell me?" She yawned and twirled a strand of straw-colored hair around one finger.

Jake, her husband, sat at a mahogany captain's table in the corner of their bedroom. An array of papers, spreadsheets, and inventory lists covered the polished wood surface in front of him. He couldn't bear to face his wife. He looked again at the ledger numbers in front of him, wishing somehow that they would change, that he had made an error, that the debt would shrink. He prayed for a miracle.

Although the last ten years of Jake Devlin's life had been spent building the Devlin Gallery for Modern Art in Chelsea, the gentrified neighborhood of former warehouses on Manhattan's Lower West Side, he recognized with a mixture of reluctance and pride that Blair was the gallery's biggest asset. She had an eye, a talent for separating mediocre work from true inspiration, and an ability to understand artists. She had been right about their last undertaking, a woman whose odd assortment of oil paintings looked to Jake like the work of a deranged adolescent, a single dried leaf on a silver plate, an assortment of sheet music burned at the edges with a fish skeleton strewn across them, an apple core underneath a wooden table. Blair made sense of the images. "It's a new approach to death, death in its simplest, purest form," she explained. *The New Yorker* coopted her clever perceptions in a positive review. The show sold out.

Even more important than her interpretive talents, public relations savvy, and social flair, Blair's specialty was sales. She charmed cash out of clients' pockets. Jake chuckled, remembering last Tuesday's $50,000 sale to the plastic bucket manufacturer from North Attleboro, Massachusetts, in town for a hardware convention. The overweight man stuffed into his Nantucket red khakis could hardly stop from drooling as Blair explained the subtleties of an artist's lateral brush stroke by running her fingers across his thigh. Jake might have been jealous had he not loved the money as much as she did.

Although the paperwork in front of him documented every step of the gallery's financial downfall, Jake still couldn't accept that it had happened. He rested his forehead in the palms of his hands. Where had all the money gone? He had taken out a second mortgage on their Central Park West apartment, withheld money from artists whose pieces had been sold months before, and still there wasn't enough to cover the bills. Worst of all, Blair had no idea. At first he convinced himself that he could rectify the problem, but no amount of juggling could remedy the acute situation. Then, he couldn't bear to confess.

Each time she took a potential client to the Four Seasons
for lunch, sent a bottle of Perrier-Jouët to an interested
curator, bought an Armani suit for an opening, he wanted
to explain that sales had been less than anticipated, that
he had cut deals to move inventory, that the expenses of
their lives couldn't be sustained. Each time he failed. Her
anticipated reaction seemed far more ominous than financial ruin would ever be. That he could not give her
everything she wanted negated all that he had accomplished.

Jake Devlin took a deep breath and turned to face his
wife. He was struck, as always, by her beauty, her shiny
hair now billowing over the pillow, her pale complexion,
the hue of her full lips. The slightest shift of her toes, their
pale pink polished nails wagging back and forth, was
enough to arouse him.

What would she think of him now?

Jake had waited until the last possible moment. In
thirty-six hours, with the start of the Memorial Day
weekend, Blair planned to settle herself for three months
in Sag Harbor, Long Island, in a cottage on the water they
had rented for the past several years. Although Sag Harbor on the Peconic Bay lacked the panache of the ocean
side, it was a charming town built around a lively marina.
Most important, it was still affordable to wannabes who
cherished its proximity to the artery of the Hamptons:
Route 27.

The Devlin Gallery's best clients summered in the
Hamptons, and Blair was unwilling to let them slip far
from her sight. That left Jake to run the business alone
and commute back and forth amid the traffic of the Long

Island Expressway every weekend. The Devlin Gallery faced the summer season, historically its slowest time, with a large inventory, little cash, a default notice on its operating loan, a stack of unpaid bills, and several unhappy artists threatening to take their work elsewhere. Tonight was Jake's last chance.

"Well, are you going to say something, or are you just going to sit there?" Blair asked. Her voice teased. "Because I wanted to talk to you about Marco. He's agreed to have us represent him."

Marco, an Argentinean sculptor, was Blair's recent obsession. She first had heard of him when the *Chicago Tribune* reviewed a show of his eight-foot bronze nudes. The article reported that Marco remained unrepresented by any gallery because, according to his interview within, he "failed to find spark, someone who really understands me or my work completely." That had been enough bait for Blair. After their initial contact, she had gone to his Brooklyn studio. Alone. Upon her return, Jake listened to her animated stream of accolades. Blair's mind was made up to lure Marco to the Devlin Gallery.

"Marco says he needs a hundred-thousand-dollar advance, as a show of our commitment to him," Blair continued. "I said that wouldn't be a problem. My concern, though, is that we need more space, probably two thousand square feet, minimum. His work is so gloriously big." Blair seemed oblivious of the rising barometer of her husband's anxiety.

"What do you expect for selling prices?" Jake tried to sound calm, but his voice seemed timid. He wanted to be distracted by indulging her schemes.

"He's still unknown, though that'll change." Blair furrowed her brow. "Maybe seventy-five, eighty thousand."

An $80,000 sales price meant the gallery could take forty in commission minus advertising and other related expenses, Jake calculated. He turned back to his papers, momentarily absorbed in the possibility of a new success.

"Anyway, I invited Marco out to Sag Harbor next week—Tuesday, I think it is—to go over details."

"Tuesday? But I won't be there."

"Did you want to be? I never expected you would."

"You were planning to negotiate his terms without me?"

"Well, I suppose we can rearrange, although with his schedule, it might be difficult."

"Forget it."

Blair ran her forefinger along her bottom lip.

Jake forced himself to continue. "We have to talk. I have a bit of discouraging news. Discouraging isn't accurate. I have bad news." He exhaled, relieved that the words hadn't stuck in his throat. "It's about our finances, or rather the gallery's finances."

"What about them?"

"We don't have enough money."

She laughed and waved a hand toward him. "That's what you always say. Don't be such a worrier."

"Listen to me." The raised volume of his voice surprised him. He took a breath, not wanting to sound panicked. "We have a very real, very large cash shortage. This is serious."

She sat up.

His voice softened. "I don't know how to explain this

to you, except to say that our profits don't cover our expenses, not the gallery's expenses and not our living expenses."

"What?"

Her harsh tone triggered a raw nerve and radiated down his spine.

"I'm saying we need a substantial infusion of cash, and we need it soon. We're behind on the lease, our mortgage, our taxes, our bills, you name it." He paused, trying to compose himself. The articulation of all his worries left him with an odd feeling of euphoria and despair. "I'm sorry."

"Arrange to borrow more," she ordered.

"I can't. Believe me, I've tried. The bank won't extend our operating loan. We don't have anything as collateral. Everything is borrowed against alr—"

"That's ridiculous," Blair interrupted. "We've got plenty of equity in our apartment. A second mortgage is tax-deductible anyway." She seemed to dismiss him as an idiot for not thinking of such an obvious solution.

Jake felt sweat moistening the front of his shirt. "I did that already," he almost whispered.

"You what!"

He felt himself gasping for air. "I did that already," he repeated.

"How could you?"

Jake's throat burned. "Blair, listen to me. I had to. Before year end, to pay our taxes."

"I own our house, too. How could the bank agree to loan us money?"

"I signed your name to the application."

"You forged my signature?"

"I assumed it would be short-term, more like a line of credit that I could repay. I didn't want you to worry. I didn't think you would ever have to know." He wanted her to hold him. He needed to feel the touch of her skin, but he didn't dare move. He had never seen her this angry.

"It was my down payment. The equity in the apartment is mine."

"Blair, please."

"What else haven't you told me?"

Jake was silent.

"Well, Mr. Money Manager, Mr. 'You don't have to worry about the business end of things, dear, I'll take care of it,'" she mocked, "what do you propose to do now? Are you telling me we are going to lose our house, the gallery? Is that what you're saying? Have you thought of a solution, or should I just start packing?"

"I thought maybe you could talk to your father."

He watched the rise and fall of her chest as she breathed. When Blair finally spoke, her voice was low. "You want my father to bail us out again?"

The Devlin Gallery had relied on Richard Pratt's extraordinary wealth and generosity before. The year Jake and Blair married, Pratt Capital, the privately held venture capital firm that Richard had built over four decades, contributed $170,000 to cover the first year of a long-term lease for a new showroom. Six months later the company guaranteed Jake's $5 million operating loan to allow for their considerable expansion. Then, two years ago, Blair asked again. That time Pratt Capital came up with $750,000, enough to pay back taxes and renovate their apartment with state-of-the-art lighting, marble bathrooms, and a new kitchen with soapstone counters and German appliances. They were even featured in *Architectural Digest*, a photo shoot of their designer apartment accompanied by a story on living with contemporary art.

Richard had never lectured Jake, never doubted his business skills, never asked for an explanation or accounting. He wrote checks without question and was gracious enough not to mention the money again, as if the transaction had not happened. Richard Pratt made it easy.

"Not a bailout. More like an investment." Jake tried to sound cavalier. "We could offer a generous return, especially once Marco gets off the ground."

"What are you suggesting, exactly?"

Jake was silent.

"Are you wanting me to talk to Miles about a deal?" she asked, referring to Miles Adler, Richard Pratt's long-time employee and adviser, who had bought 43 percent of Pratt Capital after Richard's stroke the year before. "I hardly know him."

"I thought you could talk to your father."

"My father doesn't make decisions on his own anymore, in case you hadn't noticed."

She was right. Since Richard's illness, Clio seemed intimately involved in his financial affairs. At the very least, nothing could be done without her approval.

"You could still talk to him, make him understand our situation. It's not like he wouldn't understand. He could convince Clio that it's the right thing to do. Or maybe you could talk to Clio directly. They could loan us the money personally. Pratt Capital wouldn't have to get involved."

"I suppose."

Blair closed her eyes. Jake knew what she was thinking. Asking her father had been one thing, but the idea of begging Clio for help was entirely different.

"If he had never married that . . . that bitch . . ." Blair's voice drifted off.

Jake had heard the story of Richard and Clio's wedding, now nearly thirty years ago, more times than he could recall. Blair had been five, her sister, Frances, eight. Blair's eyes sparkled as she recounted how handsome her father had appeared, his lean frame outfitted in a morning suit.

"Mom dressed me and Fanny in floor-length pink taffeta. I don't know why she went to such an extravagance, given that Dad was marrying someone else, but even Clio had to admit she did an exquisite job," Blair explained whenever the subject of Richard's second marriage arose. "Mom painted white baskets and filled them with rose petals. We dropped the petals along the aisle." At this point in the storytelling, Blair would smile as she remembered her role as a flower girl. "It was a fairy-tale wedding," she said, describing the tented ceiling of white-and-gold fabric, the table arrangements of white lilacs and deep pink peonies, the tiered cake filled with marzipan cream. Jake had heard the story so many times, he almost felt he had been there.

During the reception Richard had lifted Blair snug into his arms, twirled her about the dance floor, and whispered in her ear that there was nobody prettier than she.

According to Blair, that day, spent in the glow of her father's affection, had been one of the best of her childhood. She had no premonition of what was to come.

"Do you think he loves her more than me?" Blair gazed absentmindedly at the opposite wall.

Jake sighed. Blair's chronic rearranging of relationships, her attempts to place love in a hierarchy, amazed him. He wanted to reassure her. "Your father loves you as his daughter. She is his wife." He felt like a nursery school teacher.

"She's the second wife, though. That matters. I would never agree to be second."

He said nothing. Then, after a moment, he added, "Clio would want to do what would make your father happy." He regretted that his words seemed to defend Clio, but they needed help.

"Maybe. A half million would make no difference to her."

"Right." Jake felt encouraged. "Remember, your father would do it. He has been generous before. He believes in us, in what we're doing. Why wouldn't she do the same?"

Blair didn't appear to be listening. She rubbed the back of her neck with her long fingers. "Did I ever tell you what she did to my kittens?" she asked as she massaged the base of her skull.

"I don't think so." He tried to check the impatience in his voice.

"I had this incredible cat. Seaweed. She was part tabby and part Persian with long orange hair. It was always a big deal whether or not I would be allowed to bring Seaweed when we went to visit Dad and Clio. I remember begging Dad, over and over, trying to explain that Seaweed was my best friend and I couldn't leave her behind, but Clio was allergic, or so she claimed. She didn't like pets of any kind and didn't want them in the house. One fall . . ." Blair paused to think for a moment. "The November that I turned twelve, Seaweed got pregnant. The vet told us she would be due at the end of December. It was quite possible that she would have her babies when Fanny and I were supposed to be with Dad at Christmas. I couldn't bear not to watch her have her kittens. Dad finally agreed that I could bring her, but I had to promise not to let Seaweed out of my room while she was pregnant and I had to make sure I moved her out to the garage before she delivered her kittens. All month I was getting ready for those kittens. I don't ever remember looking so forward to anything. Fanny got excited, too. We would watch Seaweed's belly move and imagine the tiny kittens inside. We built a whelping pen and, when we got to Southampton, set it up in a corner of the garage with towels around it. Two days after Christmas, Seaweed went into labor in the middle of the night and had her kittens under my bed. There wasn't time to get her outside to the garage."

As he listened, Jake marveled at the intensity of Blair's memory. She had the ability to conjure up the vivid details of a scene or a moment from nearly twenty years earlier. Today was no exception.

"At first, I panicked. I knew Clio would be furious. But Seaweed was very clean and left barely a mark on the carpet, which was under the bed anyway. Besides, she had these four beautiful, tiny kittens. Their eyes were closed and they hardly moved, but they made this incredible mewing sound. Fanny and I stayed up all night just watching them. The next morning, I invited Clio to come and see. It was stupid. I think at the time it never occurred to me that she wouldn't think they were adorable. But sure enough, she was livid. She told me I was irresponsible. That I had no respect for her home or her rules. She insisted that the kittens be moved out to the garage immediately. I just remember crying and crying because I had read in a book that you couldn't touch newborn kittens. If they get a human scent on them, the mother rejects them. I tried to explain that to Clio, but she didn't believe me. She said it was absurd, an old wives' tale, whatever that meant. She said Seaweed would be a good mother and take care of her kittens even out in the garage. I begged her to let them be. They weren't hurting anything under the bed. Fanny even offered to pay to get the carpet cleaned with her baby-sitting money. Clio wouldn't listen. She sent the maid up to get them. Oh God, that woman was dreadful. Her name was Marion, and she had thick fingers and ankles and wore orthopedic shoes. I tried to block Marion from getting at the kittens, but she grabbed me by the wrist and pulled me away." Blair rubbed her wrist, as if experiencing the pain all over again.

"What about Fanny?" Jake asked.

"She sat in a corner of our room perfectly still, like she was in shock and couldn't move. She didn't cry or anything. She had this blank expression on her face. Seaweed was hissing and obviously scared. Clio stood in the doorway telling Marion to hurry up. Marion just reached under the bed, shoved the kittens into the box, and marched out. Oh—" Blair gasped. "It was a nightmare."

"What happened?"

"Fanny and I were punished and had to stay in our room. We weren't allowed to go out to the garage. That night, Clio didn't come downstairs for dinner. Dad said she wasn't feeling well. He told us how disappointed he was in us for not respecting the conditions he had imposed on Seaweed's visit. We had been selfish. We ignored Clio's allergies. We needed to remember that we were not the only ones living in the house. That's what he said. Typical. He always takes her side. But I had been right. The next morning, when I went to check on the kittens, they were dead. I guess Seaweed had abandoned them. They didn't really have fur at a day old, and the garage was damp. They must have gotten cold. Plus, they weren't fed. All it took was twenty-four hours because they were so young. I felt awful for the kittens and for Seaweed, too. Seaweed wasn't a bad mother. That's just what cats do if you touch their babies. It's instinct. Clio killed them." Blair's voice cracked, and she covered her eyes with the backs of her hands. "I don't know why I just thought of that now."

The two were silent. Jake rearranged the papers on his desk and wondered how to redirect Blair's attention back to their financial problems.

"And here's the icing on the cake," Blair said after a moment. "About three years later, Justin got a kitten, a little white one, that was allowed to be loose in the house."

So that was part of the story, the horrific memory, Jake realized. Justin, Blair's half-brother and Clio and Richard's only child, was allowed to do, and to have, what Richard's two daughters could not. Jake got up from his seat and moved over to where Blair lay on her chaise longue. He took her hand and rubbed her palm.

"So think of the money we need from Clio and Richard as restitution."

"For Seaweed's kittens?" Blair smiled. "I'll see."

Jake exhaled. Maybe he would survive this crisis after all.

Friday, May 22

$\mathcal{F}$rances Pratt checked the gas gauge. The needle hovered near the red empty indicator, but the warning light hadn't illuminated. Frances calculated that she had more than thirty miles remaining in the tank, enough to get to Southampton without stopping to refuel. She hated to be late, especially for her father, who had come to expect her six o'clock arrival each Friday night. "My reliable daughter," he said, these words replacing a more traditional form of greeting.

"You chose Friday nights as a way to perpetuate your solitary existence," her sister, Blair, had criticized her many months ago when her scheduled visits first began. "You could visit Dad anytime. It's not like he has other plans."

"I don't consider the time wasted." Frances's comment had ended the debate. Friday nights worked well for her. She ran little risk of seeing Clio, who had a massage therapist in at five o'clock and then could be relied on to go out, usually to a cocktail party. Frances had no intention of changing her routine.

Frances pressed the accelerator lightly with her bare foot. Traffic was light along Route 25 West, the single-lane road between Orient Point and Riverhead. Her mind drifted away from static-filled talk on the National Public Radio station. She focused on the speeding landscape, barking Rottweilers tied to chain-link fences, wild daisies growing amid cars propped atop cinder blocks, whirligigs spinning in front yards. Gradually these familiar objects gave way to hedges and well-kept homes as she turned onto Route 24 and crossed from the north to the south fork of Long Island.

The evening light had settled over the cedar-shingled roof of Treetops, Richard and Clio Pratt's estate on Ox Pasture Road, so named for the well-placed, majestic oak and maple trees that shaded the plush lawn. The recently completed single-story addition, a rectangular structure with a vaulted roof and ramped entrance, made the house asymmetrical but more interesting architecturally. It accommodated Richard's limitations well. Clio had done a good job, Frances thought. Except for the neat line where new shingles met the older ones of weathered gray, the flow of the magnificent structure had been maintained.

Frances pulled her pickup truck around to the side normally reserved for service vehicles, landscapers, pool cleaners, garbage collectors, electricians, and now the constant stream of medical personnel and suppliers. She shut off the engine, adjusted her rearview mirror to catch her reflection, and frowned in disgust. She hadn't had time for a shower that morning, and the usual sheen of her brown curls was dulled by dirt. She opened the glove compartment and sorted through papers and candy wrappers until she found a rubber band, which she used to pull her hair back. Then she pinched her cheeks, a poor substitute for makeup, but something that she learned from watching *Gone With the Wind*. She grabbed her knapsack and got out.

"Hello, Frances." Lily, one of two live-in nurses, issued a greeting as she opened the door. Pale but for dark circles under her vacant eyes, Lily looked sicker and weaker than the myriad patients for whom she had cared over the course of her professional life. Her voice remained cheery.

"How's Dad?" Over the past year of weekly visits, Frances realized how hard it was to predict her father's frame of mind. Sometimes he seemed completely engaged, limited only by his physical disabilities. Other moments Frances wasn't at all sure that he was even aware of his surroundings.

"Pretty good today." Lily smiled slightly, revealing her nicotine-yellowed teeth. On more than one occasion Frances had seen her cowered behind the trash bins, trying to sneak a cigarette on grounds that Clio had declared "smoke-free."

Frances forced a grin. She didn't like conversations with people like Lily, with whom she shared nothing but the tragic connection of a disabled family member. Unlike her sister, who delved into the personal lives of all three of Richard Pratt's nurses and who remembered to inquire about a date, an infirm relative, the outings on a day off, Frances had no interest in establishing more intimate connections with these caregiving strangers. Nonetheless, through her sister, Blair, Frances had learned that Lily had been a nurse for seventeen years, first at a trauma center in Brooklyn and then at a private psychiatric facility somewhere on Long Island. One of eight children, she had never married. She spent her hard-earned money on Club Med package tours to the Caribbean. Salt and pepper shakers marked "Welcome to Martinique," a shot glass stenciled with flamingoes, several teddy bears with "Club Med" emblazoned on their bellies, and other cheap souvenirs covered every inch of the three windowsills in her bedroom, and a wall calendar counted down the days until her next vacation. Other than these paltry facts, Frances knew little about the person with primary responsibility for her father's daily care.

Frances looked past Lily into her father's spacious living area. It had wide-pine floors washed in pale cream and few furnishings to block the movement of Richard's wheelchair. A set of French doors at one end opened onto a deck, partially shaded by a green-striped awning, which overlooked the driveway and front lawn. Through an arched door to the right of the sitting area, Frances could see Richard Pratt's "gym," as Clio called it, complete with a heated lap pool and an odd assortment of machines, colored balls, mats, and small dumbbells for use in his rehabilitation. A ramp led down to his bedroom. Frances had never seen where her father slept in his new living arrangements, but she imagined it was similarly spacious and cheery.

The living room was quiet.

Richard Pratt sat by the window, a crimson blanket draped over his withered legs, a book resting on his lap. He stared out at the lawn. Hearing her footsteps on the floor, he looked up and issued his usual greeting.

"I thought I might not be so reliable today," Frances responded. "I almost ran out of gas."

"But you didn't." He smiled. "That's what matters."

"How are you feeling?"

"Better for your arrival." His words came slowly, slightly slurred. "Today has been quiet. No physical therapy. I can relax."

"Rest up. You may be getting visitors. Remember, it's a holiday."

"Ah, yes." Richard's lips parted in a crooked smile. Like the distortion of a circus funhouse mirror, his facial paralysis had turned his grin into a demented leer. Frances remembered a childhood story about Alexander, a crocodile, who tried to warn the mayor that the rising river would soon flood his town. The crocodile smiled in an effort to get attention from the people on the street. Instead they fled in horror, thinking that his toothy grimace was a precursor of their demise. Frances wondered how much of her father she misunderstood.

"What are your plans?" Richard asked.

"Plans?"

"The weekend."

"I haven't gotten that far. I was supposed to go to trial on Tuesday and thought I would be working, but the case got postponed." She paused, trying to gauge whether her father wanted her to continue. He closed his eyes, but his head bobbed slightly, an indication that he was listening.

She pulled a Windsor chair up next to him and sat down. "The defendant, who happens to be a lawyer himself, claims to have a new witness, some expert psychiatrist from California who will testify that he embezzled funds from his clients because he suffered from battered men's syndrome."

"Hmm," Richard mumbled.

Frances thought for a minute. "What I can't figure out is why the judge is willing to go along with it. You should see his wife, the frailest thing in the world, scared of her own shadow, following her husband around like she is attached to his butt by a rope." Frances checked herself. Crude imagery might work with police, other assistant district attorneys, those engaged in the rough-and-tumble of solving life's crimes, but she didn't like it to spill over into the rest of her life. Fortunately her father didn't seem to notice.

"I actually like the idea that she is supposed to be the batterer. I expect the jury will find his theory as incredible as I do, if we ever get to trial. This is one of the oldest cases on the docket, but the judge gave him a month continuance anyway to prepare his expert." Frances rolled her eyes. "Ugh. Why am I boring you with work details? I'm sorry." She crossed her ankles and settled back in her chair.

"You're not boring me."

Frances looked at her father, watched as he extended his shaking arm toward her as if to hold her hand, then brought it back to rest on his lap. They hadn't touched. Frances scanned the room for signs of Lily. They were alone.

"And the man, that man who stole from the older couple?" Apparently Richard recalled details of her most recent trial, a two-week-long prosecution of William Howard Avery III, who had stolen more than half a million dollars from a retired couple. The money had been virtually everything they had. She could not recall mentioning the Avery trial, but in her search for conversation to fill each visit, it must have come up. Her father's memory surprised her.

"The sentencing is not until July."

"Oh."

"Can I get you anything? Water? Tea?" Frances asked.

"No. I'm fine."

"Do you want me to read to you? Didn't we leave Inspector Dalgliesh on the brink of a major discovery?" She forced a smile. Many of her visits over the past months had been spent reading mysteries aloud to her father. They shared a passion for uncovering facts, for unraveling the intrigue and getting at the truth. Frances remembered the times, years ago, when her father read Agatha Christie novels aloud to her, changing his voice for each character, squeezing her arm as the suspense grew. Her father liked Hercule Poirot, the debonair Belgian with his twisted mustache, but she preferred Miss Marple, the detective who rode about on her antique bicycle. Miss Marple struck her as a cross between a crime-solving cleaning lady and a penny-candy store owner.

Now, their roles reversed, Frances tried to read P. D. James with some of her father's dramatic flair.

"Not today. Tell me about . . ." Richard paused. Frances had learned to be patient as her father spoke, to let him finish each thick, deliberate word even if she knew midsentence what he would say. "Your sister. Any news on when she'll arrive?"

"I assume she and Jake are driving out tonight. I'm sure the traffic will be bad."

"The traffic on the Long Island Expressway is always bad." He looked up. "Sometimes she calls from the car. She talks. I can't hear anything. Cellular phones are full of static."

Frances nodded. She remembered the pocket telephone that her father had carried everywhere, even to the tennis court. "I'll see Blair tomorrow. I'm having dinner with them. I'm sure she'll come by on Sunday."

"I hate for her to spoil what little free time she has coming here. You tell her not to worry about me. She should be with that husband of hers."

Frances felt a surge of anger. Blair's weekly visits in the summer were seen as herculean efforts, gestures of unmatched kindness and loyalty, even though the trip from her house in Sag Harbor to Southampton took no more than twenty minutes. During the winter, if she and Jake came out for the weekend, they could stop by on their way back to Manhattan Sunday nights with only the slightest detour to the house from Route 27. Frances spent almost an hour in travel each way from Orient Point fifty-two weeks a year. Although she wanted to visit, and made the journey out of her own desire to see her father, not a sense of familial obligation, she would have appreciated some recognition. She wondered whether her father praised her efforts to Blair, whether it was easier for him to point out one daughter's virtues to the other.

"Is it a party?"

"What?"

"Blair's dinner. Is it just you?"

Frances smiled. Her father never stopped trying to turn the conversation to her social life or lack thereof. He seized on any opportunity to extol the virtues of marriage, of settling down, and pried her for information on the status of men in her life. Discussion of a dinner party inevitably would lead to whether Frances was bringing a date, a subject Frances didn't care to discuss. She hadn't had a date in over four months, unless she counted bingo with Sam or a late night coffee with Detective Meaty Burke, a former FBI man who'd been happily married to his high school sweetheart for more than forty years. Meaty was her friend. They worked together. Socially Frances didn't spend much time with anyone. She could never explain to her father that she actually liked being alone.

"I'm sure it's a party, although Blair knows better than to tell me so." She paused, then added, "Don't worry, Dad. I'll go."

They sat in silence, staring out the window at the pink light permeating the sky.

"How's Clio?" Frances asked.

"Busy," he said. "Standing in for me takes up her day, or so she tells me." Richard's tongue seemed too large for his mouth, and it drooped over his lips as he spoke.

"I haven't seen her in a while," Frances remarked more to herself than her father.

A moment passed. "You should."

Right, Frances thought, remembering her only impromptu visit to see her stepmother. A month after her father's stroke, while he was still in a rehabilitation facility, Frances had been in the vicinity of his Southampton home, or at least close enough to Ox Pasture Road that a stop wasn't too obvious a detour. She had felt especially emotional that day, thinking about her father, Clio, the shock of their leading separate lives after such a long time. There was a difference between building a life alone and having solitude arrive unexpectedly. For a moment Frances forgot her past, her relationship to Clio. She just thought of Clio's loss.

Perhaps I'll be offered an iced tea or asked in for a swim, Frances had thought when she arrived at the house. The round-faced girl in a gray starched uniform with a white collar and apron pinned to her chest answered the door. She took Frances's name and disappeared into the house. Frances waited on the doorstep, no more welcome than a census taker or encyclopedia salesman. When the girl returned she announced that Mrs. Pratt was not receiving guests at the moment. Frances would have to come back another time. It would be best if she called first. She could leave a message if she wanted. "Just tell her I was thinking of her. It's not important."

Frances had done her best to avoid Clio ever since.

She could think of nothing to say to her father and searched her memory for pleasantries, news, even gossip, to keep him entertained. Frances admired her sister's ability to make small talk. Blair always had an anecdote to share, a tale from the glittering art world in which she and Jake mixed, a comment on local politics or zoning issues, an uncanny interest in the weather if all else failed.

Unless Richard wanted to hear about larceny trials, a businessman who altered his company's financial records, a real estate broker who embezzled a down payment, a lawyer who double billed, Frances had nothing to tell. Criminal justice in Suffolk County moved at a relatively lazy pace.

Frances shifted in her seat, recrossed her legs, and stared at her feet.

"How are the dogs?" Richard's speech broke the silence.

Frances looked up. "They're good. Bigger than ever, almost ninety pounds. I think maybe too big, but I can't bear to put them on a diet. I can't manage to put myself on one, either." Frances tried to sound funny. She knew her humor was a poor attempt to have her father reassure her that she looked fine, but he didn't respond. He knew she had at least ten pounds to lose, and he wouldn't lie even to make her feel better.

Richard slumped forward in his chair. Frances watched his eyes droop, his head fall forward from his shoulders. Often drowsy, he could fall asleep only to awaken moments later. Perhaps a few minutes of peace was all he needed. She did not want to move, did not want to disturb him.

When he opened his eyes, he looked startled. "Was I asleep?"

"No, Dad," she lied. The urge to embrace his frail body overwhelmed her, but she remained still for fear her unexpected touch might startle him. Since his stroke, her father seemed uncomfortable with physical displays of affection. She couldn't remember the last time she had hugged him. "How about a few pages? See if we can figure out who did it."

"All right."

Frances removed the P. D. James volume from her knapsack. "Do you remember what's happening?" she asked, wondering whether her father would like a synopsis.

"I think so, yes."

"Okay, then. We're at chapter fourteen . . ."

Her voice echoed against the walls of the empty room. She had spent so much time over the past year reading aloud that it hardly required concentration anymore. She let her mind drift away from the words on the page to images flicking before her like a slide show. She saw her father's smile as he stood knee deep in water, supporting her round belly to keep her afloat, advising her to keep her mouth shut. She was three and just learning to swim. She felt his firm grasp, tasted the salty ocean, heard his encouragement, "Kick, keep kicking, don't stop, you can do it." Excited, she ignored the cold, until her lips turned blue and her teeth chattered. "That's enough for a while." Back on the beach, as her mother wrapped her in a towel and rubbed her dry, her father praised her efforts. "Well done. She's a born seal."

She stopped reading. Her father had fallen asleep. His head fell over to the left, and his mouth was open. Frances dog-eared the page, tucked the book back into her knapsack, and replaced her chair where she had found it against the wall. She looked at her father. Drool ran from the corner of his mouth and down the side of his cheek. Gently, so as not to disturb his slumber, she wiped the moisture from his face with a tissue. Her hand trembled slightly, but he didn't stir.

Frances watched his eyelashes flutter. Satisfied that he remained asleep, she held her breath and bent over to kiss the translucent skin of his right cheek. It felt cool on her lips. She lingered no longer than a moment, then turned hastily toward the door.

The luminaries on the verandah added a subtle light to the evening sky. As Beverly Winters steadied herself on the arm of an oversize wicker couch, she watched through the rows of French doors. People moved about the chintz-covered furniture, gathered in clusters of three and four for conversation, sipped glasses of wine or tumblers of gin and tonics. The cool air had driven most of the partygoers back inside to lean against the white marble fireplace, sit on plush cushions, and immerse themselves in the glow of votive candles arranged on tables throughout the living room and adjacent library. Only Beverly remained outside, along with two heavyset men smoking cigars and interrupting each other, arguing over Alan Greenspan's latest pronouncement on inflation. Beverly hadn't said a word in over twenty minutes. Her neck hurt from nodding her head in feigned attention.

Beverly watched Clio Pratt enter the room and dole out kisses, greetings to acquaintances aimed more at the air than anybody's cheek. Beverly admired Clio's style, the pale blue silk dress with a similarly colored cardigan sweater draped casually over her shoulder. Beverly compared herself, inevitably, with Clio, who seemed comfortable socializing without her husband in a world where singles, especially single women, were not exactly welcome. They were the same age. Beverly was a widow, Clio soon to be one, according to what Beverly had heard of Richard's health. While Clio exuded charm, Beverly found herself wanting. She knew she could be crass, even vulgar, when she drank. Years of cigarette smoking had left her with yellowed fingertips and a permanent hoarseness to her voice. A pack a day, probably more, she had lost track since she started buying her cigarettes by the carton. Varicose veins wove their way through her thin thighs. Several liver spots dappled her hands, and a bunion on her left foot prevented her from wearing high heels.

Beverly swallowed the remainder of her Chardonnay and made her way back inside to the bar for a refill. She watched Clio settle into conversation with a couple she didn't recognize.

"What can I get you?" the bartender asked.

"White wine. Thank you." Relieved of her glass for a moment, Beverly searched through her sequined clutch for her cigarettes, removed a Marlboro from the box, and looked about for a light.

"Here you go." The bartender held her filled goblet toward her. He watched her scan the room, her unlit cigarette dangling precariously from between her thickly painted lips. "Can I get that for you?" He smiled as he reached into his pocket and produced a pack of matches. Beverly leaned toward him, accepted the light, and drew a long inhale.

As she exhaled she looked again for Clio, who had moved to the bar and stood beside their host, Jack Von

Furst. Clio ordered a glass of Perrier with lime and smiled appreciatively at the bartender. Then she turned her attention back to Jack. Beverly could hear the spirited conversation about an author whose book was a *New York Times* best-seller, someone Clio had met recently at a benefit for underprivileged boys in New York City. "After reading his book, all of that obsessive detail about Hindu ritual, I didn't know what to expect, but he couldn't have been more normal." Clio laughed and rested her hand on Jack's arm.

"I've heard his book is quite good."

"It's educational, certainly, if you're interested in Eastern customs. I'm not particularly."

"All I know is that the Hindi are missing out on one of life's great joys, a steak dinner at the Palm." Jack chuckled at his own humor.

Clio smiled. "I suppose it should interest us, make us more worldly." She cocked her head.

"Why? Why should I be driven by some need to understand other cultures? I have a hard enough time understanding our own," Jack said.

"Jack, I haven't had a chance to say hello, or to compliment you on another wonderful season opener," Beverly interrupted, trying to sound witty. "Clio . . ." She nodded and forced a slight grin.

Jack greeted her with a loose embrace. "Getting something to drink, I hope," he said with a smile.

"Beverly always manages to find the bar, don't you?" Clio's sarcasm seeped through her ostensibly sweet tone.

Beverly gripped her glass, willing herself not to throw it. Why waste such a good wine? she thought. Courton-

Charlemagne went for $32.99 a bottle the last time she checked. "I see you're on the wagon," Beverly said, nodding toward Clio's sparkling water.

"Oh yes." Clio's laughter seemed forced. "I guess you could call it that."

"That, my dear, is why you're the picture of health." Jack put his arm around Clio's slender waist and gave her a slight squeeze.

"What a wonderful outfit," Clio exclaimed as she pulled gently away from him. She stood back and surveyed Beverly's taupe pantsuit. "You know, I think I saw that in Paris. I can't think now when, it must have been when Richard and I were last there." The obvious reference to outdated fashion was not lost on Beverly. "It suits you." She smiled.

"Thank you." Beverly decided to treat Clio's remark as a compliment in the hope that Jack would do the same. He did not appear to be listening.

"Have you been over to Fair Lawn yet?" Beverly asked. "I hear the bar was redone over the winter."

"I didn't notice," Jack remarked casually.

"Yes. Gail Davis did it. There's a Scottish pub feel to the place. It's cozy," Clio said.

"Gail's a great decorator," Beverly added, realizing as she said it that she hardly knew what homes Gail had done.

Then, as the conversation came to a standstill, Jack turned to Clio. "How's Richard?"

"Well, all right, I suppose. His spirits are good, as always, but that's just the way he is. Never a complaint."

"I must visit," Jack remarked.

"He would love that."

"Has he improved?" As she said this, Beverly regretted her choice of phrase. Richard's condition interested her. He had been a friend. She was concerned for his health, but her motives were selfish as well. She wondered how long before Clio, like herself, would be a middle-aged woman in search of a mate. Nervously she twirled the Bakelite bracelet on her left wrist.

"I don't know that I can honestly say improved, but he doesn't seem worse, thank God. He's an avid reader. I buy him books all the time and he just absorbs them, seemingly overnight. It's deceptive, really. At times his mind seems as engaged as ever."

Beverly thought for a moment that she could see tears forming in Clio's eyes. It must be the wine, she decided.

"His physical therapy is slow, though. He's discouraged, but he can't see the progress he has made. The therapist loves him, as you might expect. Says she has never seen anyone more determined. That's Richard, I guess. That part of him will never change." Clio looked wistful.

"How are you holding up?" Jack laid a hand on her shoulder.

"It's hard, impossible, really, not to have what we had." Clio stopped, looked up at Jack. "What am I saying? I'm fine, absolutely fine. You must think me a terrible person to complain."

"Not at all, my dear. It's an unfortunate situation."

Clio nodded knowingly at Jack. "The addition is a huge improvement," she said.

Beverly had heard of the Pratts' recently completed construction project, a separate wing designed for

Richard that had nearly doubled the size of the already opulent Pratt residence. Rumor had it that Clio had hired a construction team of nearly forty and overseen personally every detail.

"Because of the ramps, Richard can get everywhere," Clio continued. "The architect did a wonderful job. He actually got in a wheelchair himself to make sure that Richard's access would be perfect." She paused for a moment before continuing. "It's a much better setup. His nurses even seem happier now that they have their own living space. I guess everyone needs privacy." She paused and sipped her water. "I must confess I sleep better knowing they are right near Richard. I'd lived in such fear that something would happen, something that I wouldn't know how to handle. I'm sure you would understand." Clio addressed this last remark to Beverly.

"I'm sure I would." Beverly regretted her defensive tone. Dudley Winters, her only husband, had been dead for nearly three years. He had committed suicide while she slept in their bed. Clio's thinly veiled reference made her uneasy.

"Any exciting summer plans, or will you be here like the rest of us, puttering around?" Jack, ever the perfect host, turned to Beverly to change the subject.

"I'm renting the house for August. Otherwise, I'll be here."

"Do you mind having strangers in your home?" Clio tossed out her remark.

"Oh, it's not that bad."

"I just couldn't imagine it."

Beverly wished she had the luxury of staying in her

house all summer. Accepting renters was tantamount to erecting a "Cash Needed" sign for all to see. Worse than an embarrassment, it was a humiliation, but the month of income paid most of the house expenses and property taxes for the whole year. She could not manage without it.

"Who are you renting to?" Jack asked.

Clio laughed. "Since when did you take an interest in the transient population around here?"

Beverly ignored her. "A nice couple from Manhasset. He works for an investment bank, Morgan Stanley, I think. They have several small children and an au pair."

"Good. Sounds good." Beverly couldn't tell whether Jack had paid attention.

"You'll have to excuse me," Clio said. She squeezed Jack's hand. "A dreamy party, perfect as usual. I would love to stay, but I'm already late for the Bancrofts' dinner."

"Yes, I'm sorry we can't make it, but people are bound to hang on here," Jack replied, glancing at Beverly. "Give my best to Marshall and Beth, won't you?"

Clio smiled. "Of course. Love to Constance. I'll call her tomorrow." She embraced Jack.

"She'll want to know all the details, I'm sure."

Beverly watched her depart. Her lithe body slid across the polished hardwood floor. She knew without looking that Jack was watching Clio leave, too. Clio inspired such glances from other women's husbands.

Beverly imagined Clio's call to Constance Von Furst at nine the next morning, the earliest civilized hour to start phoning. Clio would sit at the antique farm table in her sunny breakfast room and gaze out over her expansive lawn as she finished a bowl of raspberries and sipped iced cappuccino. Beverly could hear their polite chatter, Clio thanking Constance again for a lovely cocktail party, filling her in on the details of the Bancrofts' intimate dinner for thirty-eight of their nearest and dearest, the menu, the seating arrangement. "The Bancrofts are such lively hosts, even at their age." Then Clio would reassure her, "You were positively missed." Constance, relieved that her absence was noticed, might ask whether cigars were offered after dinner or who wore "Oscar" or "Calvin," shorthand references to designers so patronized by these women that there was no need for formality. Clio and Constance shared criticisms of unsuspecting people, women mostly, who could never have imagined that their actions and appearance were monitored so closely. Constance, listening, would sip herbal tea sweetened with one teaspoon of clover honey out of a hand-painted porcelain cup. Beverly wished that she could start her day this way, wished that she could be included, once again, in the inner circle.

Jack interrupted her musing. "Excuse me, won't you," he said. "I'd better see how the Champagne supply is holding up."

"Yes. Yes, of course."

Beverly's gaze remained on Clio. More than a dozen people stopped her on the way out for a final comment. Each one appeared more interested than the last in establishing a connection before she disappeared into the night.

Life is easy for some people, Beverly thought as she

emptied her wineglass. The oaky alcohol soothed her hot throat. She nodded at the bartender for a refill.

"I don't understand why you spend any time at all with that woman." Valerie Moravio's Texas drawl startled her.

Beverly turned to face her friend and smiled. Valerie, a former Dallas Cowgirl, had a flair for the dramatic. Tonight was no exception. A fountain of blond curls cascaded from the top of her head. Heavy makeup accentuated her blue eyes. She wore a yellow sleeveless dress that clung to her ample bosom. Her neck and earlobes dripped gems. A diamond ring, easily five carats, dwarfed her long-nailed fingers. This farmgirl had struck gold when she married Luca Moravio, a sports agent, whom she met at the Super Bowl in 1978. When the Dallas Cowboys defeated the Denver Broncos, Luca turned his attention to the nineteen-year-old cheerleader performing her synchronized splits, jumps, and cartwheels. Valerie was set for life.

Despite the fact that Luca and Valerie didn't belong to a single country club, Luca's outrageous humor and endless anecdotes about major sports figures ensured that they were included on every guest list. Beverly admired the fact that Valerie, easily bored by most of the cocktail parties, actually turned down invitations. That took confidence.

"How are you?" Beverly asked.

"Clio Pratt has done you wrong, and you're the fool if you waste time on civilities."

"What are you talking about?"

"Don't play dumb with me, sugar. Maybe this soiree is not the time for conversation. I can respect that. God knows I should learn to be as discreet as you, but I can't stand to see a woman humiliated, especially by another woman. It's not right."

"I don't know what you mean."

"Clio Pratt is playing you for a fool." Valerie put her hands on Beverly's shoulders and turned her slightly. "You listen to me. That woman's told everyone who would listen to her that you were responsible for Dudley's death."

"Dudley committed suicide." Beverly coughed out the words.

"May he rest in peace." Valerie looked upward, seemingly to the heavens, crossed herself, and then returned her gaze to Beverly. "Clio says you drove him to it. She told me just the other day that you planned to leave Dudley, for another man, maybe, she didn't know, but leave him nonetheless. That set him off. Made him do it."

Beverly couldn't breathe.

"Apparently, Dudley told Richard that he couldn't stand the thought of getting sicker, dying, alone."

Valerie's words stung. Dudley's debilitation, his protracted, worsening emphysema, had consumed their lives, but they had kept their problems quiet, or so she thought. Beverly was stunned to hear that Dudley had confided in Richard, a friend to be sure, but hardly to that degree. As if the humiliation of his suicide had not been painful enough, Beverly now felt her wounds reopen.

"When I saw you being so sociable and all with Clio, well, I just thought I should let you know."

Beverly felt dizzy. Why was Clio circulating such a rumor now, three years after Dudley's death? She reached for the edge of the bar for balance. "Look, honey, Luca and I are leaving for dinner. He's had enough of all this finger food hors d'oeuvres stuff. He says that itty-bitty bites of nothin' just make him hungrier for a meal. A nice fat sirloin, although tonight I may be able to get him to settle for a veal parmigiana. You want to join us?"

"No. No, that's okay."

Valerie leaned forward to kiss her friend. "Oops, sorry." She wiped red lipstick from Beverly's cheek. "You watch yourself. Call me tomorrow."

Beverly turned away from the house and walked across the lawn. Rage ripped through her. Nearly three years of trying to put Dudley's death behind her, to resurrect the semblance of a life for herself, had been undone in a moment. She had lived through the whispering, the gossip. She blamed herself for his death because she'd wanted a divorce, but no one understood that their marriage had fallen apart long before Dudley ever grew ill. She had nursed him, washed him, and comforted him even after she'd stopped loving him, only to be subjected to insincere condolences upon his death. She knew that most people would have preferred that she, not Dudley, had been found at the bottom of the swimming pool strapped into a wheelchair. But she had survived. She wouldn't go through all of that again.

Dew seeped through her sandals as she stood on the lawn trying to collect her thoughts. The cool air stung her flushed face. She had to confront Clio. She had to stop the rumors. She had to shut her up.

Sunday, May 24

$\mathcal{G}$eorge Welch, vice president of the Fair Lawn Country Club's Membership Committee, turned the leather-covered steering wheel to the left. As his silver Mercedes pulled into the driveway, its tires crackled on the broken shells bleaching in the sun. He pressed the power button in his center console to lower the window and inhaled the smell of the ocean. There is nothing like it, he thought, relishing the moist, salty air in his nostrils. Proximity to the water invigorated him. Each morning he drove from his house on South Main Street to the end of Dune Road, parked at the landing, and spent the next thirty-eight minutes walking, a mile with the water on his right, then a mile back, retracing his steps. These beach walks did more for his mental health than years of counseling had begun to do. His anxiety and aggression shed as he dug his heels into the sand. He returned home relaxed, tranquil. Some might even call it happy.

George pulled up to the shingled home and turned off the engine.

The cloudless sky accentuated the edge of the gambrel roof. Trimmed in white with navy blue shutters, the house looked well maintained, especially for one exposed to the battering of sea winds. No paint peeled. No shutters hung askew on their hardware. The glass in window after window sparkled in the sun. The landscaping was similarly meticulous. Surrounding the house in beds mulched with cedar chips, rhododendrons bloomed cottony white flowers. Between each shrub grew clusters of purple iris and pale pink peonies. The lawn had been recently mowed, leaving neat lines in the grass. Not a single weed marred the brick walk. Picturesque, George thought.

Standing by the entrance, George could hear the ocean, the sound of the surf just on the other side of the house. He had dreamed of living right on the beach, watching the Atlantic from every room, hearing the rhythm of the waves. George remembered the sound machine that he had bought for his daughter, now so many years ago, when she was just a baby. The small box had several natural noises selected for their soothing qualities, the ocean, the rain, birds, a fire. He had used it to help put her to sleep, especially when her mother wasn't around. Like most things in his life, it had been a success.

His wife hadn't wanted to live by the ocean. "It's a maintenance nightmare. You think upkeep is expensive now," she'd warned. "All of the furniture will have to be reupholstered every three years. We'll have a constant mildew problem. Plus, I've read that excessive moisture is bad for the trachea." That was Mary. Economical, orderly, she ran the house much as she had run her second-grade classroom: tidy, punctual, planned. Their neighborhood near Southampton village had the characteristics of an affluent suburb, not the windswept feel of a coastal town. They could be anywhere. Mary's idea of a water view was a glance at their gunite swimming pool.

Although the front door was slightly ajar, George Welch rang the bell. Almost immediately Henry Lewis opened it. Trim and athletic, Henry looked younger than forty-three. He had cocoa-colored, smooth skin, high cheekbones, dark eyes, and close-cropped hair. He wore beige linen pants, a green polo shirt, and loafers. George fought back the urge to think Henry handsome. He had always believed it was inappropriate for men to notice other men's looks.

Henry extended his hand. "George, good to see you."

George shook hands and felt Henry's grip tighten around his.

"Come in, come in. Is Mary with you?"

"No. She's at home, straightening up from the weekend. She cleans before the cleaning lady arrives. Don't ask me why. She sends her best." He hoped the nervous edge to his voice did not reveal his anxiety.

"This way." In response to Henry's gesture, George stepped forward into the living room. Two taupe couches straddled the fieldstone fireplace. A slab of glass on a chrome stand formed a table in between. George looked around for the customary clutter, the figurines, magazines, and knickknacks of people's lives. The room was spare. The breaking surf appeared to roll in through the far wall of glass.

"Pretty dramatic views you've got here," he murmured.

"Thanks. It's a nice change from Manhattan. Have a seat. What can I get you? Iced tea? A beer?"

"Oh, nothing, really. I'm fine." George perched on the edge of one sofa.

"Okay, then. I'll just get Louise. Make yourself comfortable." Henry turned to leave.

"Actually, I thought we should talk for just a moment. Alone."

Henry stopped. His gaze mixed curiosity and concern. George hadn't meant to sound an alarm, but the firmness in his voice gave him away. He had been dreading this meeting all weekend. Although the Lewises would receive official notification from Gail Davis that the Membership Committee had declined to act on their application for membership to the Fair Lawn Country Club, George had wanted to tell Henry in person. It seemed like the right thing to do. He now had the sinking feeling that it would be far worse than he had anticipated.

Henry sat opposite him and crossed his right ankle over his left knee. George couldn't look straight ahead. He let his eyes drift to the end table and focused on several pictures of the two Lewis girls. Their teeth-filled grins jumped from the silver frames. The images of two children in bikinis with a sand castle in the foreground, of one pushing the other on a swing hung from a tree branch, of both with arms wrapped around their beaming father, were familiar, timeless. No different, these girls are no different from my own, he thought.

"They're good. Both of them. We feel very lucky," Henry said.

"How old are they?"

"Eliza is seven and Madeleine will be four in August."

"They must like it out here." George stumbled over his own small talk.

"We all do."

Silence passed between them. George could feel Henry's gaze fixed on him.

"Are you staying out through Monday?" George searched for conversation. He wanted to ease into the discussion, backtrack from the clear indication he had given moments earlier that something was wrong.

"Louise and the girls are going to stay, but I'm heading back to the city tonight. Memorial Day doesn't get much observance where I work." He smiled. "Actually, a transplant candidate is being transferred from a hospital in the Midwest."

A heart transplant, somebody flown in from halfway across the country to get another man's heart; the concept was hard for George to imagine.

"Wouldn't it be easier to bring the heart to him?"

"To her," he corrected. "But to answer your question, she's been my patient for quite some time. Her husband wasn't happy with the care she got in Chicago, and brought her to New York last February. He wants us to see her through."

"Do you actually do the transplant?"

"I'm part of what's called a transplant team. I'm one of several surgeons involved, each with a specific role. Let's say it's a group effort." He paused. When he spoke again his voice was matter-of-fact. "Despite my pleasure in seeing you, George, I'm quite confident that you did not give up a Sunday afternoon to come chat about organ transplantation. What's on your mind?"

George felt his heartbeat quicken and wondered whether Henry's cardiac perceptions were astute enough to notice. Apparently Henry wouldn't tolerate further delay. "As you probably know," he began, "the Membership Committee met last Wednesday."

"I see."

"Yes, well, we had to act on a number of applications. It really was a startling number, more than I've seen in years." He couldn't look at Henry. "Sometimes, I wonder to myself why people are even interested in joining Fair Lawn. I ask myself that question when I'm faced with folder upon folder of people, all really nice, decent people, knowing they may be rejected." George's words gathered speed as he rambled. "It's so hard to make decisions. Many of us wish that we could just admit everyone, open it up to all the wonderful younger families like yourselves wanting to come in."

"Just say it, George. We weren't accepted." The words fell flat.

George inhaled deeply. "Henry, if it had been up to me, you know it would be different, but I'm only one of six. People are very reluctant to let in anyone new, complaints of the club being too crowded, parking problems, you name it." He hoped that he sounded sincere. "You know how people are. Figure they're in so they pull the ladder up behind them. In fact, there was a concerted effort to admit only legatees, given the numbers." As the words escaped from his mouth, George realized his mistake.

"Louise's parents have been members for years."

"Yes, yes, that's right. What am I thinking?" George mumbled. Then he changed his tack. "The issue, Henry, is that Louise is well-known. She grew up here, has been a junior member. People don't know you in the same way."

"Come on, George. Don't bullshit me."

"I'm not, really," George pleaded. "I'm optimistic about your chances for admission next time round. You know politics."

Henry stared down at his folded hands.

"We both know that there are six very different people on the committee. You had Wally, Wally Lovejoy. He's crazy about you both. You had me. Of course you had me, but for people like Jack Von Furst, Gail Davis, you're just a name on an application." George could not bear to identify the true source of the problem. "Maybe Louise could work on Gail, play a little ladies' doubles, have a drink afterward, you know how it is, talk charities. Isn't Louise involved in . . . what's that charity? YOUTHCORE, that's it, I knew the name would come to me." Henry didn't respond. George continued, "I'm pretty sure Gail volunteers there. Anyway, next time the focus has to be on gathering momentum, getting a real show of support across the board."

"There won't be a next time."

"Oh, come on, that's ridiculous, lots of members have to go two, three years—"

"Let's cut to the chase," Henry interrupted. "I'm a

black man, a black man married to a white woman, and that won't change. Not next year. Not any year."

George sat without moving. He felt numb.

Henry's voice, low and controlled, resonated. "I shouldn't be surprised, now, should I?" He leaned back in his chair and crossed his arms across his chest. "In fact, as I think about it, Louise and I must have put you all in an awkward position. Here we are, a decent, successful, some might say prominent family, and for you to refuse us, you'd have to admit to yourselves that race is still an issue. That couldn't have felt too good, now, could it?"

"It wasn't like that," George tried to reason, although he knew his efforts were futile.

"What I wonder is, who was willing to admit that? Were you? Were you at least honest?"

George didn't reply.

"It's not as if I hadn't imagined it could happen this way. In fact, if I let myself, I can hear the conversation. 'We'll be filled with coloreds before we know it.' " Henry mocked imitation. "Was that it? What did they say about Louise, George? Were you all sorry she married me? What did they say about my girls? I want to know what was said about Eliza and Madeleine."

"Nothing. Not a thing. The girls weren't discussed."

"Well, then what happened?"

"There wasn't a vote," George whispered.

"What?"

"We abstained. We moved to abstain. So that you could reapply next year."

"I'm not a fool." Henry knew the procedures.

George looked down. He hadn't wanted to explain

about the threatened blackball or any other details of the deliberations. He already had breached etiquette by breaking the news to Henry himself. "It wasn't going that way."

"Who kept me out?"

"I—I can't tell you," George stammered. "The meetings are secret. You know that. My hands are tied."

"Tell me!" The words seemed to boil in Henry's throat. He had gotten up from his seat on the couch opposite George and walked behind him, out of George's sight. George wanted to turn around, but his shoulders froze. His torso wouldn't move. "Tell me who it was."

George felt his nerves crumbling. He reminded himself that he had been angry. Anger still burned in him over how Henry and Louise had been treated. It wasn't fair, wasn't right. He felt ashamed. "Clio, Clio Pratt, Richard's wife. She was going to blackball you. There was nothing for the rest of us to do." There, the words were out.

"What's going on?" Louise Lewis appeared in the doorway. She looked frightened.

"Please, leave us alone," Henry instructed.

As Louise moved toward her husband, George could hear the pad of her bare feet on the floor. She reached for Henry's shoulder, but he twisted away, out of reach. He paced the room, seemingly oblivious of George's presence, immobile and mute, on the couch.

After several moments Louise turned her green eyes to George. "We didn't get in," she said.

"I—I," George stammered again. "I was just in the process of explaining to Henry that it often takes a couple of years, that you shouldn't be discouraged. I'm sure your parents can tell you that. There's still plenty of time."

Louise shook her head.

"You and Henry need to meet people."

"Don't patronize me with your strategy for next year." Henry turned and glared at George.

"Henry," Louise interjected. "We knew this could happen."

"We'll talk about it later," Henry said.

Louise looked at George, then back at her husband. "We were hopeful, especially given Mum and Dad's history with the club." Her eyes welled with tears. "Both of us really wanted it for the girls. You know, it's a great place for kids. It was for me. Eliza loves tennis already. She's quite good."

George smiled meekly.

Louise turned away. When she spoke, her words seemed directed at some distant point beyond the room. "I wanted others to see us as we saw ourselves. That's all. Just another family." Her mouth quivered, and she raised her hand to cover her lips. "But we should have known. I should have realized."

"It'll happen for you. Don't give up," George said.

"Please, stop this. George, I want you to leave. Leave us alone," Henry's voice trembled slightly.

Louise exchanged a bewildered look with George.

"I mean it. Now."

A tear ran down Louise's cheek, but she stayed silent.

"I'm sorry, Henry. I truly am. You've got to know that. I did everything I could," George almost whimpered.

"I don't care what you did, or what you claim to have

done. How dare your committee sit in judgment of my life, of my family, of me?"

"Stop, Henry," Louise begged.

"Let me help."

"I don't need your help, George," Henry continued, his voice lowering. "I can handle this myself." With that he turned his back to George, walked over to the wall, and propelled his fist directly into the plaster. George heard the crack of his knuckles, but Henry didn't flinch.

George rose cautiously to his feet, wondering for a moment whether they would support him, and walked out. At the door he turned to face Louise. Behind her he could see Henry in the distance, a silhouette in front of the windows to the sea.

Louise pressed her hand into George's. He felt a slight tremble in her palm. "I thank you for trying. Henry does, too. He just can't do it right now."

George wanted to hug her, to make some physical gesture that would indicate how sorry he was. He wanted her to understand that he wasn't like the others, but he felt paralyzed. He walked slowly to his car, unwilling to contemplate what Henry might do under the circumstances.

As he got into the driver's seat, George felt sick to his stomach. Perspiration soaked his shirt, and he wiped his brow with the back of his hand. A painful throbbing behind his eyes intensified as he pulled the car out of the driveway. Glancing in the rearview mirror, he saw Louise, her lanky body leaning against the door frame, the folds of her skirt swaying slightly. He looked away.

As George turned onto Gin Lane, his vision blurred. The pounding in his head prevented him from focusing on the road, and he was forced to pull his car onto the grassy curb. He activated his hazard lights, then leaned forward over the leather steering wheel to rest his head. How could this have happened? What would he do if he were Henry? He couldn't bring himself to answer.

Aurelia Watson examined the corrugated cardboard box. It had no markings, no indication of when it had been packed, what it contained, or even with what move, out of many in her life, it could be identified. She remembered nothing about it and apparently had not missed its contents. Only the sagging sides, dust, and collection of debris on top revealed the passage of time. It had sat untouched for years.

Aurelia couldn't explain to herself why she had chosen this beautiful May afternoon to clean out her attic. The idea simply had come to her like forwarded mail as she drank her morning coffee. Holding the warm green mug in both hands, she rocked back and forth in her porch chair, listened to a creak in the floorboard, stared out at the village of bird feeders in the corner of her garden, and felt compelled to purge herself of accumulated odds and ends.

Plus, she needed space. Twenty of her best oil paintings, landscapes on canvases as large as three feet, were arranged on the floor and propped against the furniture in her living room. The day before, her exhibit at Guild Hall, the prestigious East Hampton gallery, had come down after three weeks on display and not a single sale. "It's a bad time of year. The season hasn't really started," the gallery's director tried to console her as she stacked the colorful array of potato fields, dunes, trees, and flowers into her minivan. She chauffeured them back along Montauk Highway, through Bridgehampton and Water Mill to Southampton, then onto Halsey Neck Lane and into her own driveway. Her tears stopped only when she displayed the images in her home showroom. Then Aurelia surveyed her array of work and felt proud, whether the rest of the world noticed her or not.

At some point, though, the paintings would have to be put away. The living room, her only sitting area, was unusable in its present arrangement.

Light through the circular window cast odd shadows in the attic as Aurelia moved about, crouching. She knew that organization and decision making were not her strengths, so she forced herself to choose what to keep, what to throw away, and what to give to the thrift shop at the First Congregational Church. She did not attend church, never had and never would, but it seemed as good a cause as the next. Sleeping bags, a tricycle, assorted baskets and vases, and a needlepoint bench she designated for the Congregationalists.

The moth-eaten rug, chipped pink teapot, and yellowed newspapers would go to the dump. The aluminum pan would, too. She had read that cooking with aluminum caused Alzheimer's disease.

The children's clothes were more problematic. As she unwrapped smocked dresses, white lace-up shoes only four inches long, a pair of velvet-collared coats with brass buttons, she tried to remember how Frances and Blair, her two daughters, had looked in each outfit. It was hard to imagine them young and small. Three years apart, she'd insisted they dress as twins, but early on they had minds and wills of their own and refused to be treated as dolls. Richard Pratt, then her husband, had laughed as he'd watched her wrestle with the toddlers. "You should feel flattered. Your daughters are just like you. Nobody will ever tell them what to do."

The clothes had been packed carefully in white tissue to preserve them for a future generation, although so far grandchildren remained nonexistent. Aurelia had almost given up hope for a second generation, or her redemption as a doting grandparent. Frances, her eldest daughter, had passed up her opportunity for motherhood when she broke off her engagement to Pietro Benedetti, the handsome Italian who had been her beau since her first year at law school. Aurelia had liked Pietro. He seemed like the gentle sort, soft-spoken and modest, despite his financial success and somewhat flashy clothes. She never understood what the problem had been. Frances didn't share, and Aurelia knew better than to pry. Now, at thirty-eight, Frances appeared to have no prospects for a family.

The marriage of Aurelia's youngest daughter, Blair, to Jake Devlin held faint promise. Aurelia had heard nothing of their plans for children. They seemed consumed with their Manhattan gallery and had such busy social lives that Aurelia often wondered if her daughter and son-in-law had to pencil in time with each other around the various dinners, meetings, charitable events, and art openings that filled their schedules. Besides, if a junior Devlin ever did appear on the horizon, fashion-minded Blair would spurn recycled clothing.

Aurelia concluded that the miniature wardrobes should go to the church.

She rested her palms on the small of her back and glanced around the attic. All that remained was the unidentified box. As Aurelia separated the interlocking flaps, dust filled the air. She coughed, removed her tortoiseshell glasses, and rubbed her eyes. When her vision cleared she looked inside at hundreds of letters bundled in batches held together by rubber bands. Aurelia closed her eyes, remembered the grab bags of her daughters' birthday parties, and reached in. She removed a handful of correspondence. The elastic snapped and broke against her thin fingers as she tried to stretch it loose. A sheet of folded crepe paper topped the pile. *Happy Birthday, Mom*, block letters in red surrounded by yellow crayon sunbeams, jumped out at her. She could still see a ruled pencil mark underneath the letters to keep the lines straight. Inside, Blair had written, *Don't be sad your 35. Someone will marry you soon.* Aurelia laughed, as much at her nine-year-old daughter's spelling error as at the sentiment. Each "o" had two eyes and a mouth smiling back at her.

Aurelia spread the assorted correspondence on the floor. Stationery, notebook paper, thin sheaths of airmail dimpled by the pressure of a ballpoint, greeting cards for birthdays, Mother's Day, a few anniversaries, her hip surgery, these documents marked her life's major and minor events. The penmanship varied, but she recognized most, including her own, a small, neat script perfected in secretarial school. Aurelia opened the creased page.

March 27 1966, it read in the upper-right-hand corner. She continued:

> *My dearest Richard,*
>
> *I am ill equipped to explain my feelings or why I think it best for us to part. You have been a good husband to me, and a wonderful father to the girls. I cannot ask for more, but I realize, as the ritual of our life together becomes ever more complicated, that I feel increasingly stifled, weary of the obligations imposed on me by the life we have built, threatened by a domesticity upon which other women seem to thrive. Don't misunderstand me. I love to watch our beautiful daughters run across the lawn, or make angels in the sand dunes. I love to feel their small hands around my neck, to hear the sounds of Frances's voice. I relish the day that Blair too may speak fully so that we may know what is behind those expressive eyes and garbled sounds, but I don't want my time spent buying school uniforms, coordinating ballet and piano lessons.*
>
> *You deserve better, a wife who will care for you, who will live up to your expectations, who can be the joy in your life, who will make sure that the doormen are adequately tipped at Christmas, who will not bring vagrants into your elegant world. I have not meant to hurt you, have not meant to do anything wrong, but I seem to cause nothing but aggravation. I want so much to be different, but I cannot will myself to change.*
>
> *I love you. I do now as much as ever, but I sense*

that we both recognize that our lives, our priorities,
have drifted apart, yours into a world grounded in
work and a society that I find alien, mine in a cre-
ative chaos that you label destructive. Our shared
love for Frances, Blair, and the safe haven of our
home in Southampton cannot hold us together.
These are common loves. They do not make us a
couple. I will miss you. I hope that we can stay
friends, for the girls, but also for us. I am sorry.

Aurelia reread the letter through several times. She remembered preparing drafts, changing the words and
phrasing to try to capture her emotions, her sense of loss,
her compassion for the man whom she honestly did love,
but she couldn't remember what had ultimately made her
decide not to send it, especially since it contained
thoughts that she had expressed to Richard many times
before, and after, that date. Perhaps it had seemed too formal, or too irrevocable.

The vagrant, though, she remembered well. That was
Albert.

It had been Christmas, she presumed 1965 given the
date of her letter. There was a timelessness to the holiday
season in New York City, the Salvation Army bell ringers
outside of Bloomingdale's, fake garland and colored
lights lining the small shops along Lexington Avenue,
carols piped through outdoor speakers into the streets,
filling the frigid air with familiar tunes. Piles of snow
laced with soot and dirt obstructed pedestrian traffic.

She encountered Albert by accident, nearly stumbling
over him lying across a grate as she came out of the 59th

Street subway station at Lexington Avenue. Her packages showered over him as she lost her balance and let go of her shopping bags to free her hands. She managed to avoid falling, but only barely. As she straightened herself, she looked down and noticed a bearded face peering out from amid a heap of glittering gift-wrapped parcels. He accepted her apology without a note of hostility or resentment in his voice.

"It's my fault for being in the way," he replied.

She gathered up her purchases, reaching across his bundled stomach for a blue box that had fallen behind him. She could smell a stale, acidic odor on his clothes and a mixture of fried potatoes and whiskey on his breath.

"What are you doing here?" The words spilled out, and she stood up, embarrassed. She, like most New Yorkers, generally avoided interaction with strangers. "I beg your pardon," she said quickly. "It's none of my business."

"That's all right. Don't worry." His voice was soft, and she found herself staring into his dark eyes. She knew that she should move along, get her merchandise home, wrapped, and strategically placed under the eight-foot blue spruce that she and the girls had decorated. Instead she found herself listening.

"I ask myself that question all the time. Why are any of us where we are?" He ran his dirty hands through his hair. Aurelia noticed his unevenly bitten fingernails, his soot-stained wrists. He continued, "I suppose it's a mixture of circumstance, luck, and willpower, an odd combination given that only one is in our control." He folded his hands in his lap. "Did you actually want an answer to your question?"

Nodding, Aurelia lowered herself onto his worn blanket. Her black cashmere overcoat spilled over the curb, and she could feel the hot fumes of the passing subways wafting up through the grates. The crowds hurried past her. Several people cast perplexed stares her way, but as she listened to Albert speak, she became oblivious of the noise, the hundreds of booted feet slogging past, the frenzy of rush-hour traffic. Before long she had learned that Albert had been a stockbroker. "I was reasonably successful, not super-rich, but I made ends meet. I lost my job when I started showing up drunk. Everybody understands a hangover. Half of Wall Street shows up hung over, but I was drinking on the job. There's no way to excuse that."

"Did anyone offer you help?"

"Sure. Yeah, my boss discussed some program he said I could get into through our firm. A colleague offered to take me to an AA meeting, but I declined. What you're calling help is the kiss of death in my profession. Makes you seem weak. Besides, I thought I could handle things on my own."

Shortly after he was terminated, Albert's wife returned to her parents' ranch in Wyoming with their son. For all Albert knew, they were still there. By the time the divorce papers were filed, there was virtually nothing left to divide. He took several changes of clothes, a pipe, and a duffel bag.

"What do you plan to do?" Aurelia felt the urge to caress his whiskered cheek.

"Well . . ." He paused. "I have to figure out if I should sit for my recertification exam." In response to what must have been her surprised look, he added, "My broker's license is up for renewal next month. If I don't take the test, I could miss out on some great opportunity."

Aurelia lost track of time as they sat on his blanket discussing his future, debating the merits of returning to a life on Wall Street. As the gray sky further darkened, she realized the need to return to the home that awaited her. Reluctant to part company, she invited him home, offered him a warm shower, a meal, and a chance to sit with his feet up in the library. He accepted. Back in their apartment, he played Go Fish with Frances and shared her bowl of pretzels.

As the afternoon passed, Aurelia knew that she should telephone Richard at work to tell him about Albert. Richard didn't like surprises. In retrospect her silence was idiocy, but each time she looked in on Albert and Frances absorbed in their game, she convinced herself that his presence was harmless. Richard and Albert could be introduced when Richard returned home.

She had been naive.

"What are you doing?" Richard asked that evening. Aurelia, speechless, stood against the wall of the kitchen, hugging herself. "This is insanity. He has to leave."

"Why?"

Richard looked at her quizzically, as if she had left her mind on the subway that afternoon. "If you won't tell him to go, I will."

When Albert departed, Aurelia gave him a small oil painting of the ocean off Montauk Point. She had painted the seascape the summer before and framed it in gilt. "To hang over your fireplace, real or imaginary," she said, embracing him quickly by the elevator. As he tucked the image into his bloated duffel bag, she reached out to touch his arm. "Where will you go?"

"I'll be all right," he said quietly.

"Please," she begged, "I need to know where you'll be."

The red indicator button on the wall lit up with the elevator's arrival. A bell rang as the door slid open on its tracks.

"I need to know."

Albert smiled and licked his lips. As he held her hand for a moment, she could feel the callus of his toughened skin. "Off the west side entrance of MOMA. There is a subway grate there. The steam's warm." He stepped into the elevator without looking back.

Aurelia watched the door shut behind him and listened to the rumble of the cables as the elevator descended. She felt a palpable emptiness. When she turned around, Richard stood on the threshold. Behind him their Christmas tree glittered with glass ornaments and small white lights.

"Are you all right?" Richard said. She didn't respond. "What were you thinking, you and two little girls alone in the house with a total stranger?"

"Albert is harmless. He entertained Frances for most of the afternoon. Blair was asleep. Apparently she skipped her morning nap, so went down promptly at three. Besides, Bea was here for a while when we first arrived." Aurelia tried to sound calm, organized, as if the afternoon had been planned perfectly.

"A twenty-year-old baby-sitter is hardly adequate defense," Richard admonished her, referring to Bea. He moved toward Aurelia and reached out to touch her forehead, as if feeling for a fever. "Maybe we should get a housekeeper, someone to live with us, to help you," he said patiently, his voice calm. "You need some time to yourself, for your painting."

"I thought you of all people would appreciate my efforts to provide a moment of comfort to someone in need."

"Don't do that, Lia. I am not attacking your sentiment, only questioning your common sense."

"Well, I think I'm perfectly sensible. It's important to meet people, to experience the world, to get out of this Park Avenue apartment. We miss things up here on the fifteenth floor, stuck in our routines. Albert has lived through hell. All he needed was someone to talk to, to treat him like a person."

"Why did that duty fall to you?"

"It didn't fall to me. He didn't harm anyone. I enjoyed talking to him. I admire his introspection."

"What does that mean?"

"It means that he's not like the people I spend time with. He's open. He examines his own faults. His universe is so unlike our insular one. It's good for me, and good for our daughters, even if they're too young to realize it."

"I doubt what's-his-name would appreciate being the guinea pig for your social expansion."

"That's not fair, Richard. We were talking, that's all. He seemed lost. Perhaps I did, too."

Aurelia had often wondered whether these words, her admission of her own troubles, had been Richard's undoing. Thirty-four years later that fateful conversation rang in her ears, each word, Richard's tone of voice and facial expression ingrained in her brain. Richard had turned and walked out of the room. Lying in bed that night, she had wanted to leave, to run to Albert, to huddle under a mildewed blanket on the concrete pavement by the Museum of Modern Art, to smell him, even to taste him, but she didn't move from between her flannel sheets.

Within the week Richard hired Mrs. Bassett, a heavy-set woman of fifty-eight with big forearms, who wore her red hair in a bun at the base of her neck, a black uniform, and hooked boots. "Marriage isn't perfect. You've no business expecting it to be," she chastised Aurelia on more than one occasion. Loyal to Richard from the very beginning, Mrs. Bassett stayed in his employ even after Aurelia left with the girls.

Aurelia refolded her letter and stuffed it into her pocket. She eased herself onto the floor, sitting cross-legged to scan the patchwork quilt of correspondence in front of her. She ran her hands over the piles of letters, feeling the varied textures of paper. Her eyes rested on an envelope covered in the rounded cursive letters of Frances's hand. It was postmarked July 22, 1972, more than six years after she and Richard had separated.

July was Richard's chosen month with the girls under the terms of their separation agreement. He took them to

Southampton, to the home he and Aurelia had shared during their marriage. That left Aurelia at liberty for thirty days each summer. She traveled, exploring cities in Europe and South America, always alone, unscheduled. Only rarely did she make any effort to meet up with friends or acquaintances; instead she ambled unfettered.

The summer of 1972 found her enrolled in the American Academy in Rome, taking a painting course entitled Luminosity and Color. Days spent watching the light move across a porcelain pitcher, nights engrossed in spirited conversation with a fellow student ten years her junior, carafes of Chianti and plates of prosciutto-wrapped breadsticks, had rejuvenated her. She even flirted with changing her name to Venus, Juno. A goddess.

Aurelia removed a single sheet of cream-colored paper from its envelope. It had a sunflower in each corner.

Dear Mom, an eleven-year-old Frances had written in black script. *Dad says you are going to be a great painter. Is that true? I hope so. Blair does, too.*

Aurelia felt a laugh spill out as she imagined her two young daughters discussing their mother's artistic portent. The letter continued with details of Frances's day, tennis clinic, a play date to the pizza parlor. As she flipped the page to read the back side, Aurelia felt her heartbeat quicken. *When are you coming home? I don't like it here anymore. Clio is weird. She pats my behind when I come inside after swimming to see if my suit is still wet. I don't like it. Dad says Clio doesn't want us to ruin the furniture, but I'm careful. I really am. I dry off out-*

side. I don't even sit in the living room. I'm not bad. She just says I am. Please hurry back.

Aurelia felt a tingling behind her eyes as she stared at the paragraph. Despite the passage of time, her daughter's plaintive words resonated anew. How many times had Frances begged her not to go away, begged not to be left with Clio? How many times had Aurelia issued the same insincere instructions: "She is your father's wife, and he loves her very much. You must do your best not to upset her." Aurelia could see Frances's face clearly, her round cheeks streaked with tears, her hazel eyes rubbed red. She had expected Richard to remarry, had wanted him to find someone else. She just hadn't expected Clio.

Aurelia replaced Frances's letter in its envelope and repacked the correspondence. No good could be gained by reliving the past. Aurelia needed no prompting to draw on her well of memories, the consequences of her selfishness. She closed the box, pushed it under the eaves, and left the attic.

The late afternoon light cast a gray pallor through the house. Aurelia rubbed at the cramped muscles in the back of her neck as she made her way to the bathroom. Her legs hurt, too, her body's way of reminding her that she had aged. She turned the chrome faucet of the tub, waited a few moments for the water to run hot, and added liquid lavender suds, swirling her hand in the water to stimulate bubbles.

She pulled her white smock over her head and hung it on a peg behind the door. As she moved she caught a glimpse of herself in the floor-length mirror. She stopped and turned to squarely face it. Why did her appearance surprise her? The mirror never seemed to reflect what her mind told her should be there. Folds of white skin streaked with purple veins hung from her stomach, behind, and legs. She ran her hands along her flesh and squeezed the fat of her upper thighs. In another era she might have been considered voluptuous, an erotic Aphrodite, but her physique was incompatible with late-twentieth-century visions of beauty. There were times when her body distressed her, when its shape compelled her to lie on the floor and lift her legs in endless repetitions of ineffective exercises, but most often she could not be bothered. She had grown comfortable moving in a larger frame and failed to think of herself as heavy, until the sight of her nakedness reminded her.

Aurelia turned off the water. Steam clouded the mirror, which she rubbed clear with a hand towel. She sat at her vanity table and removed a red lip-liner pencil from the top drawer. She stared at her face, the crow's-feet around her eyes, the crevices on either side of her thinning lips, the deep lines in her forehead. Then she began to draw, marking each wrinkle on the mirror, first with tentative lines, then bolder and thicker, accentuating the epithelial ravines. Her reflection became mutilated by red. When she sat back her face disappeared from view, but the lines remained, an abstract self-portrait.

What had she done? Richard had survived, had found Clio and been given a second chance. Even with his deteriorating health, he would look back on a good life, one that he had enjoyed. But Blair and Frances had grown up desperate to forget their childhood. Her girls remained scarred by her decisions. Unless she could think of a way to make amends, her cavernous corpse would be buried with the pain she had inflicted. She wished more than anything that there were some way to undo the past.

$\mathcal{I}$ hope you like sashimi. I couldn't remember," Clio said as she pushed the black-lacquered tray toward Blair.

Blair looked down at the well-arranged assortment of raw fish. "I love it. I didn't know there was a good place to get Japanese food around here."

"There isn't." Clio picked up a small piece of raw tuna with her chopsticks, dipped it into a shallow porcelain dish of soy sauce, and ate it. "Hannah took some lessons and makes it herself. She gets great fish out here, as you might expect, but we bring the seaweed, wasabi, that sort of thing, out from the city."

Blair liked that people from Manhattan referred to it as "the city," as if there were no other place in the world that qualified as such and that she, as part of an elite group, knew what the reference meant. Blair looked at the pickled ginger, arranged carefully into the shape of a rose. "Hannah is a great cook."

"She is. We're lucky to have her."

Blair liked Hannah. Unlike most of Richard and Clio's servants, who came and went before Blair even learned their names, Hannah seemed a permanent fixture, having been in the Pratts' employ for the last twenty-two years. No more than five feet tall, she looked nothing like an established cook in an affluent household, capable of tending to the culinary needs of the Pratts and their many houseguests. She wore her blond hair in a ballerina's bun, tight at the back of her head with each stray wisp rendered immobile from hairspray and styling gel. She had bony hands, a thin nose, and a pronounced clavicle that protruded through her cotton uniform, leaving Blair to wonder whether she ate a single one of the delicious meals she produced.

"You're very kind to invite me over. When I called, I'd intended to take you out." Blair played with the corner of her starched linen napkin.

"I can't think of any place in town where I'd want to eat. Practically nothing but potato wedges and oversize hamburgers. The restaurants cater to the tourist palate."

"This is much nicer," Blair agreed. She swallowed hard, trying to rid herself of the lump building in the back of her throat. She diverted her gaze from the well-laid table in front of her and looked about the Pratts' oak-paneled library. Double-lined damask drapes partially covered the arched windows and spilled onto the floor. A pair of love seats covered in chintz, and two Chippendale armchairs formed a seating arrangement around the fireplace. Over the stone mantel hung an oil painting of Clio that Richard had commissioned shortly after their marriage.

The round skirted table where the two women sat could fit up to six for family meals and intimate, informal dinner parties. Blair remembered evenings seated in the very same chair, staring through the twin flames of the candelabrum at her father across the table. Clio sat to his right, Frances to his left, Justin, Blair's half-brother, next to his mother. The light flickered off the King George–patterned Tiffany silverware as her father ate steak au poivre and creamed spinach. "My family all together in this wonderful spot with delicious food, what more could a man want?" Richard asked this rhetorical question more than once. Each time Clio smiled as if she had everything in the world to do with his state of bliss and rested her hand on his. He turned, looked at her, and smiled back.

To Blair, this repeated interchange seemed deliberately intimate, an effort to distance his two daughters. Watching their obvious affection, Blair had the overwhelming urge to shout, *You could ask for a lot more. Just because someone looking through the windowpanes might see a scene of apparent domestic serenity, looks are deceiving. You could ask for your daughters to be well treated. You could ask that they be given privacy, that your wife not rummage through their drawers looking for God only knows what kind of contraband stashed away in their Carters cotton underwear. You could ask that she treat your daughters as well as her own son, that she recognize that we are all equally your blood. The fact that we sit here around your stinking table should not give you comfort. We're here only because we have no other choice.*

Blair hated her rage, a feeling well buried in the cemetery of her past but so easily resurrected from a memory such as the one she experienced now seated at this table, staring at Clio. Blair tried to distract herself. She cast her eyes toward the floor-to-ceiling bookshelves illuminated by seemingly invisible lights. How many times had she climbed the library steps and run her fingers over the rows of leather-bound books, reading the gold-engraved titles out loud? The library made her think of Henry Higgins in *My Fair Lady,* her favorite movie, about a gutter-dwelling flower girl transformed into a magnificent woman by the tough love of an aristocratic professor. Higgins had moved gracefully around his library, removing books from shelves, opening and shutting them as he pondered, "Why can't a woman be more like a man? Men are so honest, so thoroughly square, eternally noble, historically fair . . ." Despite Higgins's lyrics, the men Blair knew hardly earned such esteemed titles. Even her father, so well suited to life in a smoking jacket, failed to insure even the most basic fairness in the treatment of his children.

"Did you visit Richard this past weekend?" Clio asked, ending Blair's reverie.

"Actually, I thought I'd stop in after lunch. I meant to come by on Sunday, but the day just slipped away."

"That happens." Blair couldn't tell whether Clio's words were intended to reassure, or chastise her. Clio often masked her pointed comments by appearing to muse out loud.

"How is Dad?"

"You'll see for yourself, I'm sure."

"You've been great to him. None of us thanks you enough." Blair's flattery was genuine, at least with respect to Clio's handling of Richard's stroke.

"Your father is an extremely brave man. There aren't many of us who could endure what he has to every day and remain eternally optimistic. As for me, I do what any wife would do, or should I say what any wife should do." Clio looked up from her food and stared at Blair. Then she smiled slightly and returned to her meal.

Was this a veiled reference to the first Mrs. Pratt? When Aurelia left Richard, he had been in the prime of his life. She never would have deserted him because of an infirmity, would she? Blair wanted to think not, but wasn't sure.

Blair fingered her tapered chopsticks, letting the comment pass. The continuing silence felt awkward, as if a warm towel at the base of her neck had grown cold. Blair knew better than to raise the subject of her own mother. Clio had made perfectly clear from the moment she'd moved into the house at Ox Pasture Road that there was to be no mention of Aurelia's name, no reference to her in any way. Occasionally Blair slipped. She remembered the day she asked to use the telephone to call her mother or when she admitted that Aurelia had given her a new tennis racket. Clio's focused glare made clear that these comments, innocuous to the outsider, were blasphemous. Any relationship between Blair, Frances, and their mother was nonexistent in Clio's household.

Clio balanced a piece of yellowfin tuna adroitly in

front of her and remarked, "So, are you out here now for the summer?"

"Pretty much, yes. I may have to go back to the city once in a while to check on things at the gallery."

"How's your business doing?"

Blair coughed and reached for a sip of water from the goblet in front of her. "Fine. Pretty good, really, better than I hoped," she lied. "Actually, I wanted to talk to you about the gallery." She tried to relax back in her chair, but her legs seemed to stick to the cushion, making it impossible to shift her weight without a major movement, a disruption she didn't want. Blair thought she detected a slight smirk on Clio's face but decided to ignore it. "Sales are going well. We have a wonderful collection of artists doing a range of work, not like a lot of downtown galleries where everything feels the same, but, as I'm sure you know, it's a competitive business."

"I haven't been to galleries in the Village in I can't tell you how long. Richard and I used to make a point of going several times a year, just to keep up with what was being shown. You're now in SoHo?"

"No. We're in Chelsea. Rents in SoHo have gone through the roof, and more and more dealers are moving to our area."

"A little off the beaten track, wouldn't you agree?"

"I guess it depends on whose track you want to be on." Blair tried to sound clever, but her tone was defensive. "We've got great space, it's just a little small for our current plans."

"And what are those?" Clio rested her chopsticks on

the porcelain holder to the right of her plate. Her erect posture seemed impossible to sustain.

"Well, we've had an exciting recent discovery. A sculptor from South America. Argentina." She tried to sound professional, distant, but felt a bubbly excitement at the mention of his name. "Marco does wonderful bronze nudes."

"I'll have to come and see." Clio sounded distinctly uninterested.

Blair stared at the oil painting on the wall in front of her of a haystack in a field that Richard and Clio had loaned to the Metropolitan Museum of Art for its show on van Gogh in Arles. The canvas emanated a haunting light. This piece was part of the Pratts' impressive art collection, paintings and sculpture acquired over the years at auction or from the well-established midtown dealers that remained a league above the Devlin Gallery. On the walls of Clio's bedroom and study hung early Italian religious art, Masaccio, Gilberti, in ornate gilt frames. Downstairs, a pair of Dubuffet figures graced the entrance to the dining room. Several Picasso drawings as well as a "blue" period self-portrait hung in the living room along with portraits by John Singer Sargent, James Whistler, and Winslow Homer. In addition to the van Gogh haystack, a Georges Seurat park scene and one of Monet's smaller images of a London bridge in fog filled the library. Even the downstairs powder room contained a Renoir oil of a fruit plate, worth more than the entire inventory of the Devlin Gallery.

"We were lucky to get Marco. He had an extremely successful show in Chicago. Several New York galleries went out to have a look. When he and I met, he said he wasn't represented because he had never found a dealer 'whose vision he admired and whose heart he trusted.' Those were his words exactly. He's really a poet as well as an artist. He wants me to represent him."

Blair realized that the mention of Marco's name had made her blush. Tilting her head down so that Clio wouldn't notice the sudden flush to her cheeks, Blair mentally replayed the past twenty-four hours. Marco's visit to her house in Sag Harbor seemed like a dream. It had been scheduled for only a few hours, a lunch meeting designed to clinch the relationship, but his jitney had departed for the city without him. How long he could stay without arousing suspicion was the more pressing question, although in truth, at this moment Blair didn't care whether their budding romance was discovered. Marco's magnetic narcissism drew her to him. Blair liked to imagine him at just this very moment lying nude on the weather-beaten deck, reading *Art News*.

"What does Jake think?" Clio asked.

"About Marco?" She paused but caught herself from hesitating too long. "He's thrilled." Despite her husband's repeated telephone calls over the last day to determine whether Blair had yet asked for money, she had tried her best to put Jake and his managerial ineptitude out of her mind.

"Is he out here this week?"

"No. He went back Monday night."

Clio cocked her head slightly and appeared to eye Blair all over. "It must be hard to be apart so much in the summer."

"It is." Blair tried to sound sincere. "But there is the old adage: Absence makes the heart grow fonder."

"Is that right? I never found that to be true." Blair sensed that Clio's words dangled in front of her, teasing. Then Clio abruptly changed the subject. "So, what is it you wanted to discuss?"

"Well, as I mentioned . . . ," Blair began, pushing her chair back from the table and crossing her legs. She felt beads of perspiration run down the front of her chest and hoped they would not show on her lilac T-shirt. "Marco's work is enormous, too big to properly display in our current space. We need an additional showroom. Fortunately, the floor below us is vacant, and would be perfect." She paused. Clio said nothing. "How should I say this?"

"What?"

"I was wondering . . ." The words felt heavy in her mouth. "There are some significant expenses associated with signing Marco. He wants a financial commitment from us, an advance. It's standard, really, but we just don't have the available cash. We're waiting on checks, customers who've been slow to pay, and we've had quite a number of bills come due." Clio looked bemused by Blair's ramblings. She knows what is coming, Blair thought, and she isn't going to make it easy. My entire life, she has never made one goddamn thing easy. She sits there flashing her perfectly manicured fingers at me, comfortable in her Jil Sander pants, a woman who spends more on a pair of summer sandals than most people spend in a week, who thinks nothing of a thousand-dollar dry-cleaning bill. Now she wants me to beg. This is Jake's fucking financial mess, anyway. He should be here, groveling at her feet.

Blair had the urge to abandon this plan, but the memory of Marco kept her from a hasty exit. Her skin tingled remembering his fingertips touching her lips, holding a strand of her hair. Would he walk away without the advance? As much as she hoped their attraction was mutual, she couldn't take the chance.

Blair cleared her throat. "I want to make you a proposition." She was surprised at how authoritative her voice sounded. "Would you and Dad consider an investment in Devlin Gallery?" Her teeth pinched the sides of her cheek as she tried to keep her mouth from trembling.

Clio laughed. "Haven't we made a number of them already?"

"Excuse me?" Blair feigned ignorance, but her astonishment must have shown on her face. Her throat felt hot.

"Did you think I didn't know about the money your father has given you and Jake?"

Blair was speechless.

"We have no secrets, Richard and I. There was, there is, nothing your father and I don't share. He would never have given you money without my consent."

"But it's his money." Blair looked around as if the words had come from a source other than herself.

Clio appeared to ignore her comment. "Now you want more, do you? Would this be another so-called loan, or would it be simpler to call it the gift that it really is?"

"We're perfectly prepared to pay you back, with interest. We're not looking for a handout, only an investment in what promises to be a winner."

"The winner being this sculptor fellow?"

"Marco. Yes. His pieces will command substantial prices. I'm sure we'll be able to repay you in full after just a few months, certainly by year end."

Clio sat silent. Blair tried to calm herself by eating, but her chopsticks shook in her hand. She put them on the edge of her plate and interlaced her fingers in her lap. The silence seemed interminable.

"I'm sorry," Clio finally said. "It's just not possible."

"Why not?"

"With your father in the condition he is, we need to be more prudent about investments. I don't see how a loan to the Devlin Gallery fits that criterion."

"I said we'd pay you back."

"I know, and I'm sure your sentiment is sincere, but given your track record, I don't think we can rely on that."

"What's that supposed to mean?"

"Your father has tried to help you, has given you substantial sums on multiple occasions. It's apparent to him, and certainly to me, that there is poor management somewhere, either that or a poor selection of artists. Otherwise you wouldn't have been here again and again."

"Dad believes in us, in what we're trying to build. His prior investments were to help us to get up and running, the initial lease, our working capital, that sort of thing. Any new business needs funds. Our gallery is still young by New York standards." The words felt like cotton stuck in her throat.

"As I recall, the most substantial, and recent, gift was for home renovations."

"That's because, I, we . . ." Blair stumbled. What was going on? How could this be happening? "Jake has poured our profits back into the business, but we needed a place to entertain clients, somewhere people could see how to live with the art we sell. Our apartment renovation was for marketing."

"That may be, but the point is, the money was spent, and it did not come from the business's profits. Look, Blair"—Clio leaned forward—"my number one concern is your father. Our investments, personally and through Pratt Capital, need to carry less risk now."

"I'm telling you that there won't be any risk."

"If that's the case, you should have no difficulty getting a commercial loan from a bank."

Blair felt tears begin to well in her eyes, a mixture of humiliation and disbelief. This was all Jake's fault. She had swallowed her pride and come to her stepmother for help, that was bad enough, but she never expected to be criticized, ridiculed, or, worst of all, denied. She wasn't prepared to lose her business, her home, her newfound attraction. Apparently she had underestimated Clio and overestimated herself.

The memory of the previous day burned in her mind. She and Marco had walked the beach holding hands. She'd rested her head on his arm for a moment, feeling the hard curves of his muscles. As they'd dragged their bare feet through the soft sand, they had discussed his future at Devlin Gallery. "I will make you a household name," she had said.

Laughing, he'd replied, "Very good, but I haven't even seen my first hundred thousand."

"I know. It's coming. The money will roll in."

Then he'd kissed her, his warm lips pressing onto hers. "Are you this ambitious for me alone, or is it for yourself?" he'd asked afterward.

"For both of us."

Now, all she could think was that Marco would leave. If the lack of money didn't drive him away, the inadequate show space certainly would. He would be a fool to stay. She couldn't fault him for finding another dealer under the circumstances, but the thought made her desperate.

"Please, can you at least talk to Dad?"

"Frankly, I don't see why I should."

"Dad would want to help."

"I know he would. He is the most generous man I know, and thinks of everyone before himself. That's why I've gotten more involved in his business affairs. In the condition that he's in, and with the needs that he now has, I've got to make sure his financial best interest comes first."

"But he cares about my best interest."

"He certainly does. Blair, you are thirty-five years old, and he has looked after you your entire life. Now it's time for you to think about him."

"Him or you?" Blair twisted her napkin.

"Our interests are the same."

Although uttered with the utmost sincerity and tenacity, Blair doubted the truth of Clio's words. Clio was hoarding the money for herself, for her house, her clothes, her car, and her causes. Her concern was life after Richard, not life for the duration of his existence.

"Well, I'll talk to Dad. I think the decision should be left to him."

"He already knows what you want."

"What?" Blair consciously closed her mouth.

"I'm not as naive as you may think. Didn't you think that when you called to invite me to lunch, I would understand your agenda? I've been your stepmother for nearly thirty years, and you've never called me before, let alone wanted to do anything with me socially. It was logical to assume you wanted something."

"And you talked to Dad then, before you even knew what I was going to say?"

"I told him that we had spoken, that we were going to get together, that I assumed you or Jake or the gallery needed money, and that I was inclined to say no. He agreed."

"I don't believe you." Blair hadn't meant to speak her mind.

"You don't have to. He'll tell you the same thing. It'll break his heart to say no to you, but he understands he should. Go ahead and discuss it with him. But let me assure you, if you prey on him, I'll intervene. I won't let him be badgered."

"How dare you accuse me of something like that?"

Clio ignored her. "You can't avoid me. I'm here for better or worse. You may not like it, but that's the way it is." She wiped her mouth, then lifted a silver bell to the right of her place setting.

Hannah, the cook, appeared a few moments later and began to clear the dishes.

"Would you care for dessert?" Clio asked as if nothing untoward had transpired between them.

"No. Thank you. I've had quite enough." Blair's tone was low. She wondered how long she could stay seated, looking at her stepmother, without screaming. "I had best be going."

"Aren't you going to see your father?"

"Another time would be more appropriate," Blair replied. "I can let myself out."

Clio remained in her chair.

Blair stood in the driveway and felt the late spring sun through the cool breeze on her cheek. She gazed at the long railed ramp leading from the gravel drive up to her father's entrance and regretted that she hadn't been to visit several days before. She could have explained the situation to him before Clio poisoned the well, explained that the money was a loan, that the gallery really needed his help, that this would be the last time she would ask for anything. He wouldn't question her business acumen or her aesthetics. Clio had to be lying about his wishes.

How dare Clio accuse her of mismanagement? She was more than competent to run the gallery and had done a good job. Hadn't she built its reputation? Hadn't she attracted new artists, some of whom left more established dealers to come with Devlin? She would like to see Clio try to do better, a woman whose only accomplishment was her marriage. Clio had never worked a day in her life.

Perhaps she should go to see her father after all. She needed to feel his strong arms around her, to hear his soothing voice telling her that all would turn out right;

but she knew this comfort was a thing of the past. He was weak now, could hardly lift his arms, let alone embrace anyone, and his often inaudible words lacked the authoritative tone upon which she relied. Besides, she knew that Clio would be with him at this moment, reporting on their lunch together, laughing smugly at how well she had foretold the purpose of Blair's visit. She felt a wave of exhaustion wash over her.

Blair had just driven out of the drive when her cellular telephone rang. She knew it was her husband before she lifted the receiver.

"What did she say?" he asked.

"She said no."

"What?" The crack in Jake's voice made her cringe.

"Didn't you hear me? Clio told me to get a commercial loan. She won't give us the money."

"It's not possible. What did you say? How could you not convince her?"

Blair felt the sparks of her anger begin to flame. Jake, not she, was responsible for this mess, yet once again she was supposed to solve their problems. "Look, I did the best I could, and I don't need you to second-guess how I raised the issue."

"But how could this happen? They've never said no."

"*They* didn't say no. Clio did. But apparently she had already spoken to Dad."

"I . . . I . . . ," Jake stammered.

Hearing her husband on the verge of tears made Blair nauseated. She hated weak men. Her husband was a coward who had spent his adult life hiding behind the Pratt family name and their money. That was the difference between him and Marco. Marco needed no one. "Pull yourself together. The point is that neither Pratt Capital nor my father is going to come up with the money to bail you out, so I suggest you figure out an alternate plan. I refuse to lose Marco."

"I don't know what to do."

"Think fast." Blair wanted to hang up on him.

"Do you think if we could get by Clio, your father would give it to us?"

"It doesn't matter. The pure and simple fact is that we're getting nothing if Clio has anything to do with it. This is your problem now, and you better solve it."

"Clio? It's Miles." Miles Adler had never known Clio Pratt to answer her own telephone and was slightly startled to have gotten her directly, and after only one ring at that. Rather, he had grown accustomed to expecting the singsong sound of a maid's voice, "Pratt residence, good day," then several minutes on hold to gather his thoughts. Now Miles adjusted his grip on the receiver, leaned back against his black calf's leather chair, swiveled it around 180 degrees, and focused his gaze out the window behind his desk. From the twenty-first floor he had a commanding view of the treetops of Central Park, the Sheep Meadow in its constant state of reseeding, and, beyond that, the skyline of Manhattan's West Side.

"I meant to call you."

"Quite frankly, I wish you had. I just got off the phone with Randolph McDermott." Miles paused to give Clio a chance to interrupt, but she remained quiet. He ran his finger along the rounded edge of his polished granite desk. The three-inch-thick slab of stone felt cool and smooth. "Randolph tells me you called off the Pro-Chem deal."

"That's correct," she said.

"What the hell—" Miles cut himself off. He picked up his fountain pen and scribbled circles on the engraved notepad in front of him, obliterating "Miles P. Adler, Senior Adviser, Pratt Capital." His title was ridiculous, something that he and Richard had concocted on a business trip to Geneva three years ago. Side by side in Swissair's first class, neither man could sleep despite several cocktails. Richard sipped Scotch and water. Miles preferred a good Pinot Noir. They decided that Miles should have a proper title, a position, something to use in introductions and on letterhead. "Manager" seemed too bureaucratic for an organization of two men, a secretary, an accountant, and an investment portfolio of nearly $1 billion. Miles had pushed, half-jokingly, for "the Chosen One." They had settled on "Senior Adviser."

"Pro-Chem is a great investment. I've negotiated extremely favorable terms for Pratt Capital, after a lot of time and energy, I might add. I resent your calling off the deal without even consulting me."

"I've never understood consultation with you to be a prerequisite to Richard's and my decisions."

"We're partners, for God's sake!"

How ludicrous the expression sounded. Miles could no more expect to be treated as Clio's equal than a hemorrhaging human could expect respect from a shark. His partner was Richard. Clio extracted cash from his talent and energy, but to her he was hired help, another one of many on the Pratt payroll.

"I've tracked the nutritional supplements market for months," Miles said. "I've researched every comparable product out there. The line that Pro-Chem is developing is perfectly suited to capture a significant share of the market. Plus, it's working on supplements specifically targeted for aging baby boomers and more elderly exercisers. With the change of demographics, it's a gold mine."

"Are you finished?"

Miles stabbed his pen into his pad. He heard a snap, a broken nib. "Goddamn it, Clio," Miles exclaimed. "I want this deal. It's good for Pratt Capital, so it's good for you and Richard. We've got to act fast. If we let it slip by, it'll be snatched up in a minute. I need you to call Randolph and tell him you made a mistake, that of course we're still on."

"I'll do no such thing."

"What's the matter with you?" Miles rose to his feet and began to circle his desk, a horse tethered by the three-foot lead of the telephone cord. He wished he had a hands-free telephone, or at least a cordless, but such gadgets were prohibited under Richard's regime. "Focus is crucial," Richard always exclaimed. "A conversation requires your total attention. Otherwise, you're bound to miss something. So don't try to do anything else." Too bad now. Miles made a mental note to stop by Radio Shack and get a walkabout headset on his way home. He wouldn't let his telephone conduct be dictated by his wheelchair-bound boss ninety miles east. "This deal has been in the pipeline for two years."

"A sunk cost, then, isn't that what you'd call it?" Clio spoke slowly. "An investment in Pro-Chem is out of the question. Period."

"I can't believe this."

"Pro-Chem is behind the times. Look at the papers, look at the fashion magazines. People aren't obsessed with their bodies and diets like they were ten years ago. Pro-Chem's product is a high-carbohydrate supplement that only professional bodybuilders are interested in. There's no taste, no flavor, no variety. It's a mistake."

"You're wrong. Pro-Chem is well managed, small, lean. There's tremendous growth potential. The deal gives Pratt Capital nearly sixty percent equity."

"Oh, please. It's incredible to me that a company is foolhardy enough to develop health products under the name Pro-Chem. It sounds like a poison, or at least something totally artificial. What's the crack marketing department thinking? And you're telling me this company has good management?"

Miles hated to admit she was right about that. He had urged Pro-Chem's chief executive officer to change the name several times without success.

"Besides, what do Mexicans know about healthy living? They can't even keep their own air and water clean."

Miles decided to ignore her ethnic slur. "The company's headquarters are located in Mexico City for good reason. The manufacturing plant is fifty miles outside the city limits. Labor is cheaper. Pro-Chem can avoid a lot of government scrutiny and keep the FDA off its back, at least while products are in the development phase. It makes perfect sense to be there." He could feel sweat forming on his forehead and looked about his desktop for a tissue. Too late. The beads of moisture fell onto the papers in front of him.

"Look, Miles, I've said what I have to say on this subject."

"I don't suppose talking to Richard would make any difference?"

"No, it would not. You're not the first person today who has tried that tack to get me to change my mind. Richard and I are in complete agreement."

"Please, Clio . . ." Miles softened his tone. "Can I come out to Southampton and meet with you and Richard? I really think that you should reconsider. I'm not trying to railroad you, but I think if I can show you some of the numbers, the business plans, the research I've done, you may understand the value in this investment."

Clio laughed. "Oh, Miles, you know me well enough by now to know that I never go back on a decision. Not to say we wouldn't otherwise like to see you any time you feel like a day in the country. Bring Penny, too."

Typical of Clio, Miles thought. Make a business nightmare into a social occasion.

"Now, while I have you on the line," Clio continued. "I'll be in the city next Thursday. We need an office meeting. I want to discuss where we are, new ideas, proposals on the table. I want to hire an assistant. You're what? Senior adviser. This position will be an associate adviser, perhaps. Also I plan to reupholster the conference room chairs and replace the main table. Last, just to let you know, I'm giving Belle a raise, twenty percent. She's an exceptional secretary, and Richard doesn't want to lose her."

"I don't need an assistant."

"The assistant's not for you. It's for me, and Richard. It's clear that we're not being kept up-to-date. For example, and this is just one, I'm still waiting for the materials on Bi-Star you promised to send last week. This adviser that I have in mind could do research, follow up on questions I might have. I can't be coming in and out of the city just to pick up paperwork."

"Belle can get that material for you."

"In this particular case I'm sure she could. Or you could, as I asked you to." She paused, seemingly to emphasize her reprimand, then continued. "The point is that Belle can't do everything. You keep her busy. We keep her busy. What I had in mind is a college graduate, someone looking for some experience before business school. If we offered sixty or seventy thousand, we would be sure to get excellent candidates. Where else can they make that kind of money?"

With the title associate adviser, Miles thought. A kid with no experience, nothing to contribute but brute labor, gets a substantial salary and a title hardly different from his own. Was Clio grooming a lackey to replace him as insurance against his independence, or did she want to drive him out?

"Anyway, why don't you set up a meeting for five o'clock. Ask Belle to order us a light supper. We should be done by eight."

Miles resisted the urge to beat the telephone receiver against his desktop. Instead he rubbed his eyes, kneading his fist into his sockets. The pain distracted him momentarily.

"Miles, are you still there?"

He did not respond.

"Miles? . . . Miles?" He listened to her repeat his name several times until, apparently satisfied that they had been disconnected, she hung up.

Miles replaced his receiver, sat back down in his chair, and rested his forehead in the palms of his hands. Then he ran his fingers through his thinning hair, pulling out several dark brown strands as he did. He gazed at the loose hairs wound around his fingers, wondering if any would remain on his head for the celebration of his fortieth birthday, only five months away. He had always thought of bald men as old. Now he was fast becoming one of them, the unfortunate souls who had to put sunblock on their scalps.

Where had the years gone? Miles remembered so well his first day at work, parading through the marble-floored lobby, nodding to the security guard as if to say "I belong." He had stood in this very office in a Brooks Brothers suit, striped suspenders, paisley bow tie, and beige trench coat, a Burberry with the recognizable tan, black, and red tartan lining. His first-day-at-work outfit had exhausted the credit line on his Visa card, something he'd gambled he could repay when he got his paycheck. That day he had felt an uncontrollable urge to touch everything, the blinds, the thick Oriental carpet, the Le Corbusier chrome-and-leather chairs. Richard had come in with Belle several steps behind carrying Cristal Champagne at $200 a bottle to drink at nine-fifteen in the morning. "Welcome, welcome to my world," Richard had said, raising a glass to toast. Belle had toasted, too.

Although the view remained the same, life changed with money. At twenty-seven, after only a year on the job, his income astonished most of his contemporaries, and Miles quickly learned that money attracted money. Rich people ate together at the same restaurants, socialized at the same cocktail parties and charitable functions, even exercised together at the New York Health and Racquet Club. He joined in, spending his own money, and his considerable expense account, to mingle with potential investors and convince them to take part in Pratt Capital's newest deal. Then he made money to spend again. A cycle. But it worked. The overall pie increased.

Plus, Miles's income gave him an even bigger borrowing capacity. Three years later, a million-dollar mortgage bought him a four-bedroom apartment on 65th and Park, which in turn led him to his wife. She was twenty-three, seven years his junior, and still lived at home with her parents six floors above him. Penny Kraft, now Mrs. Miles Adler, had come with an impressive trust fund and a comparable dowry. His mortgage got him an asset, in addition to a place to rest his weary head. The same cycle.

In the early days, Richard urged him to gamble and rewarded him greatly for his successes. "If you think it's sound, I'm behind you," Richard always said. "Nothing about this business is guaranteed, and I'm not looking for zero risk. All I ask is that you do your homework. Give me an educated, informed basis for your recommendation. If it turns out you're wrong, so be it. There'll be other chances. You can't second-guess a decision once made, and I won't, either." Later on, Richard hardly questioned him. He knew it was all about empowerment. Putting together a deal quickly became what Miles Adler did best.

Miles noted with some pride that he had rarely been wrong. Cleavage-enhancing lingerie, a luxury home goods catalog company, an X-ray technology for detecting plastic explosives, a non-allergenic synthetic material for use in artificial limbs, all had yielded substantial returns. With each success, he and Richard shared cigars from Richard's private stash. The safe behind his desk held the humidor. Richard's praise warmed him like a Turkish bath, soothing the tense muscles and knotted intestines that he lived with every day.

Although Miles knew he viewed the period before Richard's stroke through a nostalgic lens, by comparison to his present situation, it had been a great time.

That changed May 20, a little more than a year ago, the day he learned that Richard was in the hospital. He couldn't remember which one of the Pratt daughters had called him at home early that morning, interrupting his breakfast and his *New York Times* with the dreadful news. "Clio thought I should let you know. She asked if you can be home at ten-thirty. She'll call you then." He had begged to come to the hospital to wait with the rest of them, but the daughter had made it very clear he wasn't welcome. He wasn't family.

He had been home at ten-thirty, and eleven, and

eleven-thirty, all day, in fact, waiting for Clio, and then all evening on the off chance she might still call. He should have known then to get out. He should have realized that he would be subject to her whim, her unchecked veto, if he stayed on at Pratt Capital, but instead he convinced himself that she had more pressing things to attend to. Her husband's health was deteriorating rapidly. He could understand her distraction. Or maybe in the shock of the news, he had misunderstood the message, and it was his fault.

Miles missed the writing on the wall.

Now, the noose of his lousy 43 percent equity strangled him, prevented him from leaving, but also from exercising independence. He needed a controlling interest or nothing at all. Miles sighed and rubbed the back of his neck. No one missed Richard more than he.

His office door was closed, and Miles sat in peace. He liked the deliberate quiet of this place. The walls were double insulated, improving the acoustics for the operas that Richard listened to—*La Traviata* was his favorite—as he mulled over proposals and studied business plans. He was the only person Miles had ever met who never raised his voice. "If you have to yell to get what you want, it's not worth getting," Richard always said. Richard's legacy saturated Miles's pores.

How had Clio and Richard found each other? Despite his fondness for Richard, and considerable length of time in his employ, Miles knew virtually nothing about his wife or their only child, Justin Henshaw Pratt. Miles had never met Justin, but he had seen the eight-by-ten photograph in the silver frame on Richard's desk of a smiling boy with sandy hair and red cheeks at the tiller of his sailboat, "Lake Agawan, 1988" engraved underneath, an image taken shortly before Justin's accidental death. The Adlers had sent a significant contribution to the foundation established in Justin's memory, but Penny Adler, not Miles, wrote the note of condolence. He convinced himself that she was better at social protocol, but in retrospect, he recognized that his inability to convey sympathy stemmed from an irrational hatred of Justin. Justin was the blood son. Despite Richard's interest in Miles's professional development, their relationship could never be familial.

Clio remained an enigma to Miles. Even after Justin's death eliminated the threat of a true heir, Miles never made any real effort to get to know her and paid her scant attention when she passed by the office to have lunch with Richard. The Adlers saw the Pratts at certain charitable affairs for YOUTHCORE, the American Cancer Society, the Botanical Society, underprivileged children, diseases and plants being causes to which virtually everyone who was anyone in the city donated. Less frequently, they socialized at cultural events, a Museum of Modern Art opening or the Metropolitan Opera, but most affluent New Yorkers attended these as well, and, at best, small pleasantries were exchanged as the Adlers and Pratts mingled in the crowds.

Clio Pratt had been on the board of the Guggenheim Museum, that Miles knew, and had been involved with YOUTHCORE, maybe still was. Richard had been president of that organization. Together they raised money to help sponsor activities for inner-city boys and girls, met with city officials to promote its programs in Harlem, Alphabet City, and parts of Brooklyn, Staten Island, and the Bronx. Richard had pictures of Clio with Mayors Koch, Dinkins, and Giuliani framed on the wall in his office. YOUTHCORE was the kind of group that politicians loved, and posing with the socialite wife of financial magnate Richard Pratt suited the public office holders just fine.

Miles realized that Clio had made up her mind on the Pro-Chem matter. Convincing her to change it would be difficult, perhaps impossible. Besides, Pro-Chem wasn't really the issue. No single deal was. The issue, if one could euphemistically call it that, was that Miles remained a minority shareholder, a useless position when it came to making decisions about investments. Miles needed leverage, real leverage, something that would give Richard and her no choice but to sell him an additional 8 percent in Pratt Capital, to give him back the autonomy he wanted and deserved. But money wouldn't work. He had tried that several times before, offering substantially more than any reasonable calculation of per share value. Although Richard may have been content to hand the company over, Clio was nobody's fool. She wanted control as badly as Miles did, and she wasn't going to part with it lightly.

Besides cash, cold hard American currency, what could possibly make her change her mind? This Miles contemplated as he gazed out over the lush greenness of Central Park.

Doesn't everyone have a secret, he mused, something deep in their past or their present that makes them vulnerable, an experience that is too painful to be exposed? What was it about Clio that could be exploited, not with an outright threat—he wouldn't resort to blackmail—but something that he could use in a more subtle manner, something that he could hint at, or gently suggest, that might prod her to part with enough stock to give him control? Certainly there were things in his own background that he wanted to protect, some more, some less, important, but all worthy of keeping concealed, even at a price. He had cheated on an Economics 102 exam his sophomore year at Brown University. He had insisted that his then girlfriend, a devout Catholic, abort her accidental pregnancy, although in retrospect he felt certain that she had gotten pregnant to force a marriage proposal anyway. Then there was his baby sister, Rebecca. He couldn't have known what would happen to her, but it still made him feel guilty.

Clio had to have something.

Miles pressed the intercom on his desk. "Belle, can you come in here?"

"Certainly, Mr. Adler."

After fourteen years, couldn't she call him Miles? While he respected the civility upon which Richard had insisted, the old-guard customs in the office increasingly annoyed him. Miles resisted the urge to push the button once again and explain that he didn't insist on such formalities, but the conversation was futile. She would thank him for his consideration and ignore his instructions. He didn't need to repeat that exercise.

Moments later his door opened and in stepped Annabelle Cabot, a well-preserved woman in her late fifties wearing a fitted brown tweed skirt, high-necked cream blouse with a gold daisy pinned above her left breast, matching earrings, and suede loafers. Meticulous in her appearance, Belle was a handsome woman. "What can I do for you, Mr. Adler?" Her diction was excellent.

"Belle, does Richard have any information on Clio in his office?"

She looked perplexed. "What kind of information?"

Miles coughed to collect himself. "For Clio's birthday, Penny and I thought we would throw Clio a surprise party. Lord knows she has had a tough time, especially recently. She could use a good celebration. Anyway, I realized that I don't know very much about her, her childhood, her background, information that might be helpful to the party planner in developing a theme. I could ask Richard, but as you know, it's difficult to speak to him on the telephone, and I can hardly ask Clio."

"Her birthday is not until October."

"I know," Miles lied. He should have remembered that Belle had a calendar imprinted on her brain with important dates concerning people relevant to her employers. Clio Pratt's birthday was one of these. "But we've got to get organized now. I had no idea of the preparation involved."

"I'm sure she'll be pleased."

"Well, I thought she might be more pleased if we could really make it personal, not just another affair, a stuffy black-tie dance in the ballroom at the Waldorf. So I wanted to see if Richard had any materials I could use."

Belle wrinkled her forehead, a sign Miles couldn't read. "Certainly Mr. Pratt has some personal files in his office, but nothing of the sort that might help with your party."

"I think I should be the judge of that." Miles regretted the words even as they slipped out. He knew Belle was territorial, a lion protecting her boss-cub from outside interference, but he didn't like to be second-guessed. He was her senior, in case she had forgotten. "Where are these files?"

"Sir, with all due respect, they are Mr. Pratt's personal files. I just don't see how I can give them to you without his permission."

Miles could practically see her hackles showing through her well-coiffed, professional demeanor. The last thing he meant to do was raise her suspicions. "You know, you're right. I guess I'll just have to use my imagination."

"A good idea."

Miles put his head down and appeared to study the notepaper in front of him. He hoped Belle could not make out from where she stood the circular scribbles all over it.

"Will that be all?"

"Actually, you could do me one more favor. I need to pick up a little something for Penny. It's kind of a special day today," he said, hoping that she would not ask the occasion. "I'm swamped with calls this afternoon. Could you get something for me?"

"What did you have in mind?"

"Oh, I don't know, something from Tiffany's. She always likes the blue box."

"How much would you care to spend?"

"Whatever. Just get something nice."

Belle nodded. "That's quite an open-ended instruction."

"Within reason, then."

Belle smiled. Miles felt relieved.

"I won't be needing anything for the immediate future if you care to go now."

"Are you sure?"

"Yes."

She turned to leave.

"Belle. Thank you."

Miles watched her shut the door behind her. He paced the length of his office in slow, deliberate strides as he listened for sounds of her activities. He heard nothing through the bunker-thick walls. He imagined that she was gathering her things, a purse from her desk drawer, a lightweight trench coat from the foyer closet, all the articles that she would need to venture forth on an errand. Perhaps she needed to use the rest room. He calculated the minutes, then carefully opened his office door. Belle had left.

Miles had little time to spare.

He removed the key to Richard's office from where Belle kept it in the top drawer of her desk. He fitted it into the lock, heard the bolt give, turned the heavy brass knob, and opened the eight-foot mahogany doors into an expanse of space even more magnificent than his own. Situated on the southwest corner of the turn-of-the-century building, it had a panoramic view north of Central Park, west along Central Park South, and south down Fifth Avenue. Richard's rosewood desk had to be nine feet long, the wood polished to a shiny glow. His chocolate leather chair was worn and crackled on the back, armrests, and seat, the mark of his ghost. Behind the desk was a leather-covered credenza with brass drawer pulls. Silver frames cluttered the top, the picture of Justin on Lake Agawam, a formal portrait of one daughter, it must be Blair, in what looked like a debutante dress with layers and layers of white tulle, another of Frances kneeling beside two dogs, and several of Clio, including a large wedding picture of Richard and his young bride. God, Clio really was beautiful. Her thick black hair cascaded over her smooth shoulders.

To the left of the desk, against the far wall, two club chairs with ottomans and a butler's table between them settled atop a plush Oriental carpet. The table held a silver monogrammed tray with a cut-crystal decanter partly filled with a light brown liquid and two matching glasses. This corner of the room was where the real work occurred, Richard Pratt at his best selling a deal. Men with small companies or brilliant but unfunded inventions had sat in these chairs, facing Richard, desperate for his money and willing to settle on any terms he pleased. Here was where Richard extracted what Pratt Capital needed, a controlling interest, the right to select the chief executive officer, indemnities and releases that would minimize risk. Then a celebratory drink was offered, a toast to the finalized terms, and a handshake given to the exhausted but relieved pigeon.

Miles scanned the cozy opulence. Where would Richard keep his personal files? The only obvious place was the credenza, kept locked, but Miles easily found the key tucked away behind the wedding picture of

Clio. How quaint, Miles let himself think for a moment. The wife holds the key.

The lock popped, exposing drawers filled with files on Abacore, Blast Off, CranWorks, Dectron, DxPlan, the alphabet of projects that had consumed the last year of Richard's active working life. Stuffed inside were pages of financials, handwritten edits on legal documents, brochures, notes, insurance policies, lists of key players. Miles flipped faster, snapping at each of the plastic-covered typed labels. Nothing but work, work, and more work, the evidence of Richard's detail-oriented brain lined up in alphabetical order.

Given more time, Miles might well have perused the contents of these business folders. They interested him, as did the notes and types of information that apparently Richard found relevant enough to keep. Miles could always learn more from the Pratt master, could pick up tips from watching him operate. He made a mental note to do just that at a later date, when each minute was not so precious. Right now Miles feared discovery by Annabelle Cabot.

Moments later he found what he was looking for. Three folders, each slightly more worn than the next, marked "re: Clio Henshaw." Richard apparently used his wife's maiden name. Miles noticed with some alarm that his fingers shook ever so slightly as he opened the first folder. Bank statements. Receipts. The financial file. Nothing out of the ordinary for an affluent man on his second wife. A similarly quick glance of the second folder revealed apparent medical information, doctors' names, insurance receipts. It was the most well-worn folder, the only one in the whole drawer with a handwritten label, that caught Miles's attention. He tucked it under his jacket, relocked the credenza, and replaced the key behind Clio's photograph. He pulled the doors shut behind him, returned the office key to Belle's desk, and retreated into his own sanctuary.

Miles jumped when the telephone rang, the distinct trill of his private line. Only a handful of people knew the number, and of those who did, few used it, preferring instead to leave messages with the efficient and charming Belle, who, Miles now noticed, had still not returned.

"Darling? It's Penny." He heard the soft voice of his wife. "Did I get you at a bad time?"

As if caught by a ubiquitous spy, he instinctively covered the folder in front of him with an annual report from the pile on his desk. "No, it's all right."

"I just found out about this lecture tonight up at Barnard. Sally and I want to go."

"That's fine."

"You'll have to order in. I'll leave the menu from China Garden by the kitchen phone."

"Okay."

She paused. He heard her inhale. "Are you sure you don't mind? Your voice sounds odd."

"I'm sure. Have a good time."

"Are you feeling all right?"

Her questions irritated him. "Yes," he said firmly.

Miles heard the smacking sounds of a series of kisses being transmitted through the telephone, then the click of the receiver. He replaced his.

He pushed aside the annual report and opened the

folder he had removed from Richard's office. He ran his fingers along the yellowed edge, then opened the folder. Printed prominently in block letters on the inside flap were the words *KATHERINE HENSHAW*. Trembling slightly, he began to read.

Thursday, May 28

*B*everly Winters exhaled a plume of smoke and watched it float upward, dissipating in the thick air of Dr. Fritz Prescott's office. She leaned back against the vinyl chair, uncrossed and recrossed her legs, and tipped her long ash into the ashtray by her right knee. She avoided Dr. Prescott's focused stare by surveying her drab surroundings, a nondescript armchair, an oak end table big enough to hold the ashtray, a box of Kleenex, and a clock, a natural-wool area rug with tassels, a long armless couch for those most troubled patients who spent their time flat on their backs, free associating. Every shrink must use the same bad decorator or shop at the same discount furniture outlet, she thought. The clock arrangement especially irritated her. Positioned with its back to her so that only Dr. Prescott could monitor the time, she was left to wonder about the minutes remaining or to check her own wristwatch, a gesture that could not go by unnoticed.

Along one wall, bookshelves held copies of the *Diagnostic and Statistic Manual* volumes I through IV, back issues of disease-filled periodicals, *Psychiatric Annals, Journal of American Psychiatry, New England Journal of Medicine, Psychopharmacology,* and books on every emotional trauma a person could suffer, titles filled with words of loss, loneliness, dependency, and dysfunction. Beverly wondered whether Dr. Prescott actually read all this material or if it was carefully selected to give the appearance of wisdom. Behind his chair hung his diplomas, a bachelor of science from Bowdoin College and a doctorate of medicine from Columbia University, impressive but not too intimidating.

Twice a week for the last five years, Beverly waited outside in the eight-by-ten-foot entranceway, sitting in a tan upholstered armchair and staring at the white walls and two color photographs of the Cape Cod seashore, images whose every detail she had studied. She listened to the blurring hum of the white noise machine and read outdated popular magazines. Dr. Prescott offered *People, Newsweek,* and *The New Yorker,* all from months earlier, with pages that were curled and dog-eared. Reading old information presented as current created in Beverly an odd emotional state, an unsettling feeling of being invisible, as if her life had stopped, combined with an empowering sense of security, as if she could foresee the future. It was often in the midst of experiencing just such emotions that Dr. Prescott would open the inner door and greet her with, "We're ready." These words uttered in his warm tone of voice evoked the perpetual hope that inside awaited, along with the doctor, the man of her dreams lying on the armless couch in satin boxer shorts.

Beverly participated in this ritual week after week all for the dubious pleasure of sitting uncomfortably, talking to herself, and paying a $210 fee. Highway robbery, it was. She often wondered whether her mental state would benefit more from a massage, lunch out, and a new pair of cashmere socks, roughly the equivalent in value, but somehow her answer was always no. Perhaps Dr. Prescott's subtle message that she would crumble into a million pieces without him had infiltrated her subconscious. In any event, although she couldn't articulate exactly why, she felt compelled to return Tuesdays and Thursdays of every week, eleven months out of every year.

August was the exception, her mandatory break. Dr. Prescott, like every other psychiatrist on the eastern seaboard, went to Truro, a small town near the tip of Cape Cod, Massachusetts, for the month. There must be discounts on summer rentals to shrinks there, or some such enticement, but the annual psychiatric vacation reminded her of humpbacked whales, swimming from halfway around the world to return year after year to the exact same place to spawn. She imagined what those beaches of Cape Cod must be like, a pod of pale men in bathing suits and ankle socks, asking each other over and over, "If I were to kick sand in your face, how would it make you feel?" She was glad she summered in the Hamptons. Even at $210 an hour, no psychiatrist could afford it out there.

She looked up at Dr. Prescott. He appeared the exact

same every time she saw him, clad in a plaid shirt buttoned to the top, gray vest, and pressed khaki trousers. He was actually a handsome man, although she had never told him that. That was one of those issues she was supposed to address, a latent attraction to her psychiatrist, but certain things seemed too embarrassing to admit, even to him. Time hadn't thinned his thick brown hair, which he brushed away from his prominent forehead and over the back of his scalp, or wrinkled his slightly olive complexion. His earnest face and lithe body made him ageless, or rather without a precise age; he could have been anywhere between thirty-eight and sixty.

Dr. Prescott remained perfectly still during her sessions, apparently oblivious of fanny fatigue, backache, or the host of ailments that kept her shifting constantly in her chair. His only movement came at the end of her hour, when he removed his tortoiseshell glasses and leaned forward to check his appointment book. "So, I'll see you on Tuesday." Tuesday and Thursday, Tuesday and Thursday, couldn't he remember that after five years without looking at his calendar?

Two hundred and ten dollars, more than $18,000 a year, for her hour-long meetings that were actually only fifty minutes. Only in the surreal world of psychiatry did fifty minutes constitute an hour. Promptly at ten of, she was supposed to shut off the tears, the anger, the despair, often midsentence, and save it for the next time, a bottled emotion with a resealable cap. Beverly would be sent back out into the world, and he would have his precious ten minutes to do whatever it was shrinks do with six-hundred seconds of down time.

"Does my smoking bother you?" Beverly asked. She had never before inquired whether he minded her persistent stream of cigarettes.

"Why do you ask?" Dr. Prescott's long body seemed glued to his ergonomically designed chair with head- and footrests.

"It just occurred to me you might be too polite to say it bothered you."

"And how would that make you feel?"

There it was. The typical shrink answer. Never mind, she thought. She did not intend to let an issue of manners become a focus of analysis. She sat silent, realizing how tired she was. Whatever minuscule benefit of insight she might glean into her own psyche by answering his question didn't seem worth the effort of trying to understand the varying degrees of her own emotional temperature.

"Last time, we were discussing an experience you had over Memorial Day," Dr. Prescott prompted.

We weren't discussing anything, Beverly thought, I was talking, and you were sitting there. She wondered whether, in fact, Dr. Prescott even listened to her or if he affected a pensive stare while he thought about whether his vest was too worn, whether he had consumed too many calories in his morning muffin, or whether he could afford a new Toyota Camry with leather interior. That was the thing about psychiatrists. They packaged a pretense of care in a posture of compassion. How could she ever know if it was sincere?

Beverly checked herself. Hostility, the dragon of emotion spewing fire across the landscape of her conscience, she knew all too well.

"I'm feeling irritated today." She looked at Dr. Prescott. He didn't move, only raised his eyebrows slightly, as passive a silent gesture as possible. This was the process. Under his guidance, she supposedly led herself into self-awareness. She closed her eyes. "Irritated's the wrong word. I'm angry, still angry." She took a long drag of her cigarette and felt the smoke burn in her lungs. Semantics in this therapy business seemed to make such a huge difference, but even that angered her. She didn't feel like being so precise in the classification of her emotions. Frustration, irritation, humiliation, anger, and rage could all be muddled together in a general feeling of angst and displeasure, like undigested pizza crust balled in her stomach.

"I haven't done anything to Clio Pratt. I was perfectly pleasant at the Von Fursts' cocktail party, and she went out of her way to be a bitch. Snide comments. I saw the way she looked at me, the conspiratorial smirk of disgust she shared with Jack. Does she think I'm too dumb, or too drunk, to notice?" Alcohol consumption during the cocktail party thrown by Jack and Constance Von Furst at their home in Southampton had not blurred Beverly's memory of her encounter with Clio Pratt one week earlier. That Clio could circulate the rumor that Beverly drove her husband to suicide was ludicrous, worse than ludicrous, cruel, deliberately and unequivocally cruel, the worst kind of gossip because it hurt so much. Whom had Clio told? Clio and Valerie were little more than passing acquaintances. If Clio had actually told Valerie herself, Clio was on a mission to publicize her theory to a general audience.

Beverly had tried not to let the evening get to her, but as the days passed, Clio's comments festered. None of the insults, carefully disguised as sociable conversation, alone would matter much, but collectively the innuendos and pointed remarks were designed to make Beverly look as bad as possible in front of their gracious host. Beverly suspected that they succeeded. Although she'd been invited to the Von Fursts' Memorial Day cocktail party, the engraved invitation came with no handwritten note such as she had received in the past, a *Can't wait to see you,* or *Won't it be fun?* tucked in the corner in Constance's rounded script. No, this year Beverly had been just another of their guests, probably several hundred in all, who received the formal ivory card with navy blue inscription. Constance Von Furst had not called her in months and had barely acknowledged her presence last weekend.

How did that make you feel? She could just hear Dr. Prescott's words before he even opened his mouth. "It made me so mad," she said, answering his unspoken question. "What does she know of what I've been through?" Beverly could feel tears well up in her eyes and reached for a tissue. "What does anyone really know about someone else's marriage?" Her questions were rhetorical. She knew that Dr. Prescott would not respond.

Beverly never doubted that she had once loved Dudley. She loved his slightly naughty sense of humor, his stadium-size smile, and, more than anything, his gentleness, his gentle voice, gentle manner, gentle touch. During the early years of their more than twenty-five years as man and wife, she couldn't have asked for more. He hadn't been handsome, but his lean body and long arms held her safe. He hadn't been wildly successful, but he earned a decent living, and so what if she drove a Ford Taurus instead of a Mercedes? She had never felt deprived. Dudley read the *Sunday Times*, could follow virtually any conversation, and managed to hold his own in a tough crowd by charm and a quick wit. So what if he wasn't an intellectual? Neither was she.

How that all changed, she had never figured out. His emphysema came later. The debilitation of their marriage was well under way by the time he got sick.

Beverly traced the origins of their marital difficulties to Deirdre's leaving home, but obviously something else had been going on, slowly rotting the fabric of their relationship, or their daughter's departure would never have triggered the animosity it did. Dudley insisted that Deirdre go away to boarding school and gave her the limited choice of Miss Porter's or Garrison Forest, both schools for girls and both too far away. For reasons Beverly never understood, Deirdre directed her rage at her mother, not her father, who had issued the mandate. She refused to speak to Beverly, except to chastise her for lacking maternal instinct and to accuse her of attempting to exterminate children from her household. When Deirdre returned home for school vacations, her animus was worse than ever, infecting the aura of the Winterses' home. Defiant, hostile, Deirdre disobeyed her mother and ignored her father. Beverly, in turn, began to despise the man who had ruined their family.

Of course, Dr. Prescott over the years had helped her to understand that this grossly simplified version of events was just that, a gross simplification. There had been problems. Beverly had been jealous of Dudley's affection for his daughter. A part of Beverly had wanted Deirdre to leave them alone. At the same time, Beverly grew bored by the empty household and longed for her daughter's return. Waiting for Dudley to come home each evening, study the mail as if it held the secret to the hydrogen bomb, and pour himself a Scotch on the rocks lost its appeal. The magic of folding Brooks Brothers boxer shorts, ironing linen handkerchiefs, and keeping up with their social correspondence wore thin. Even participation in the lecture series at the Metropolitan Museum of Art and weekly yoga classes weren't enough to rejuvenate her interest in their life.

"Are you present?" Dr. Prescott's voice interrupted Beverly's ruminations.

"What is that supposed to mean? Of course I'm present. I'm sitting here paying you, aren't I?" Beverly regretted the tone of her voice even before the words had left her lips. She took a hard drag on the butt of her cigarette, then squashed it down into the ashtray. "You know what it is? I'm sick and tired of struggling, struggling to make a life for myself." Beverly felt herself exhale with this realization. The articulation of her emotions provided validation to the torment she felt and encouraged her to continue. "Doesn't Clio understand how hard it is? The irony is that she'll soon be a widow, but she lacks even an ounce of empathy, or sympathy, or whatever you call it, understanding."

Beverly uncrossed her legs, reached down, and scratched her ankle. This was the process. This was what made Dr. Prescott worth his weight in gold, the flood of words, the purging of herself that she needed on a regular basis to prevent the buildup of pressure on her spirit. "I should have divorced Dudley, but I didn't. I hung in there. He got sick, and I hung in there still. I cared for him, cooked for him, looked after him. If he needed to be driven to the doctor, I took him. I kept track of his medications. I rolled him over and pounded on his back to dislodge the mucus. I rubbed his legs so he wouldn't get bed burns. I bathed him and changed his sheets. I did it. I did it. Clio Pratt hasn't had to lift a finger to help poor Richard."

Beverly slouched in her chair. "I wasn't asking for thanks from anyone. I felt loyal to Dudley. For God's sake, we were married more than twenty years. He was the father of my only child. Even though I didn't love him, didn't want to be his wife, I cared about him. I'm no saint, I know that. But I did everything I could to ease his pain. Finally, I had it. When he asked me if I still wanted a divorce, I couldn't lie to him. What was I to say? 'It's okay now, because you'll be dead soon enough. Why bother with the formalities?' Would it have been better if I had said that? But then, then—" Beverly stopped speaking as her voice cracked.

"Then what?" Dr. Prescott spoke quietly.

Beverly couldn't bring herself to tell Dr. Prescott the whole truth. Certain details of her relationship to Dudley and their negotiations were too horrible to confess. She could skip a few facts without altering the basic thrust of her story.

"Then he killed himself. Because of me, in spite of me, to spite me, I don't know. But people don't seem to realize that I suffered from his death more than anyone. I bled for him, despite what Clio Pratt may think. I wasn't liberated. I was imprisoned, and I still am. His death still pains me, keeps me up at night, the images won't leave my brain." Beverly reached for another tissue and blew her nose. Just the thought of Dudley, his wasted white corpse tethered to his wheelchair at the bottom of their in-ground swimming pool, made her want to vomit. Her stomach contracted as her mouth filled with water. She swallowed hard and reached for another cigarette.

"I wish she would be run over by a bus on Madison Avenue, or kidnapped by an Iranian cabdriver and slaughtered under the Brooklyn Bridge." Beverly laughed, delighted by the horror of her imagination. "I know it's terrible of me to say, but it's true." She sat silent, acutely aware of the seconds ticking away with no words exchanged. She shredded her tissue and then twisted the pieces into tight white wads. An arsenal of paper pellets collected in her lap.

"I see," Dr. Prescott said finally.

"You couldn't see. You can't possibly know what it is to hate." Beverly's words were slow, deliberate. Her anger made her feel strong, empowered. She didn't care what Dr. Prescott thought of her. "You're always in control. You control our schedule, our discussion, even the time of our meetings, so how could you possibly understand what it is to have unchecked rage, rage that's bubbling out of your system, an inferno of rage ready to explode?" Beverly paused and looked across the room into her psychiatrist's eyes. "Clio Pratt is trying to destroy me for reasons that even I don't understand."

Beverly stared at her doctor. He returned her gaze but didn't speak. She knew that it was up to her to continue, to perpetuate the one-sided dialogue, but she felt tired. Her neck couldn't support the weight of her head, and her arms and legs tingled. She dreaded the trip downtown from Dr. Prescott's office on 168th Street, even if she took a taxi. Yes, she needed a cab. Today was not the day to wrestle with the subway just to save twenty bucks. All she wanted was to be home in the privacy of her own bedroom, wrapped in the red bathrobe with satin trim she had bought on sale at Loehmann's, a glass of Chardonnay in her hand.

"What makes somebody actually kill another person? I think about that sometimes, how we all deal with anger and hatred and rage. What makes me any different from the kid on the street that shoots his friend over a pair of sneakers? I want Clio to disappear because I perceive that my life will be easier without her. The street kid thinks his life will be easier if he gets the Nikes. Clio, shoes, they're all the same." Beverly smiled again, amused by her philosophical discourse. She had never thought of life in these mundane terms before.

Dr. Prescott leaned forward. "Our time is up, but I think it's important for us to continue with this conversation." Then he reached for his calendar, flipped a page, and said, "So I'll see you Tuesday? You can call me before then if you want to talk."

Beverly gathered her dirty tissue pieces and stuffed them into her pocketbook. Then she stood up and smoothed her burgundy skirt. "Tuesday it is. Good-bye, Dr. Prescott." As she left, she realized that she had never before addressed her psychiatrist by name. Maybe it had been a breakthrough kind of day.

Miles Adler kept the door to his office partially open so that he wouldn't miss Clio Pratt's arrival by even a millisecond. Although he sat at his desk with an assortment of correspondence, proposals, and several quarterly reports spread out in front of him to read, he couldn't concentrate. The materials provided only the appearance of business as usual. Other than listening for the sound of the elevator, Miles had been idle since four-fifteen.

The air conditioner pumped cold air into his office. He had turned the thermostat down ten degrees to a cool fifty-five, but even the temperature couldn't shut off the flow of perspiration. His underarms were soaked in sweat while his cheeks, fingertips, and toes were numb.

Despite Clio's specific instructions that she wanted to begin at five, Miles had scheduled the Pratt Capital office meeting for half-past. He needed at least a few minutes alone with her without Belle; Stu Wassermann, the company's accountant; Bob Michaels, its lawyer; and Gail Davis, whom Clio had brought in from Long Island to redo the office interior. Even considering

Clio's notorious tardiness, he calculated that thirty minutes was plenty of time. Miles didn't intend to take long, nor did he want Clio to have the opportunity to engage him in protracted discussion.

Miles glanced at the roman numerals on his platinum desk clock, a gift from Penny for their first anniversary. Two minutes past five. He picked up his pen and tried to think of something to add to the agenda, delivered by courier that morning, a single page of points that Clio intended to cover: existing proposals, upcoming board meetings where Pratt Capital required representation, the need for director and officers liability insurance. This item was followed by a question mark, as if Clio didn't know whether insurance was something that the company had, or needed, but had heard the term dropped at a cocktail party and decided to throw it around herself. Also listed was the budget, the interior redecoration, and, last, the assistant, that amorphous human being who was soon to invade Miles's essentially solitary space. Clio's agenda was comprehensive. Miles couldn't think of anything else to include other than clarification of beneficiaries for key man insurance. He would like to know what 43 percent ownership in Pratt Capital entitled him to when Richard died.

Five-seventeen. What if the meeting had been called for five o'clock? Apparently Clio had no qualms about making others wait, even if, like Bob Michaels, they were paid by the hour. She hadn't bothered to call from the backseat of her chauffeured limousine, her preferred method of transportation to the city. The woman can't even drive herself in New York City traffic, and she's telling me what to do, Miles thought. If only Richard could be here.

Miles jumped in his seat as he heard the elevator bell ring and the door open. He took a deep breath, tried to collect his thoughts, and started to get up but was interrupted by the sound of Belle's pleasant voice. "If you could be so kind as to do the setup in here," he heard her direct. It must have been the caterer, probably Mortimer's At Home, arriving with some gourmet meal, a "light supper," as Clio had directed. This was not the paper plates crowd.

His stomach turned, and a wave of nausea ran through his system. *Get a grip, Miles.* The last thing he wanted was to be in the bathroom when Clio arrived.

Miles sat back in his chair. He had spent the better part of the last week trying to determine precisely how to phrase his demand for 8 percent of Pratt Capital. Although he had real ammunition, it was potentially volatile. He opened his desk drawer and glanced, for perhaps the twentieth time that day, at the file folder. *KATHERINE HENSHAW.* It was still there.

Hidden secrets. Everyone's got them. He smiled to himself. *Some people just care more than others that they don't get discovered.* Luckily for him, Clio apparently took great pains to keep hers carefully shrouded. But he had to tread lightly if he was to avoid an extortion charge.

Miles's thoughts drifted to his sister, Rebecca. Why his mind turned to her whenever he felt extreme pressure, he couldn't understand. To haunt him in his worst moments of insecurity and vulnerability seemed to be her legacy, memories of her death adding injury to his otherwise injured emotions. After her death, Miles's mother relayed the reality that belied Rebecca's charming face. Miles learned the details of her depression, the massive amounts of lithium she ingested every day in an unsuccessful effort to keep her mood stable. Miles heard of the various doctors, rabbis, and teachers, all of whom had tried to help her but had ended up merely providing comfort to her distraught parents, his parents. Why hadn't anyone told him earlier? Because, said his mother, there was nothing he could do. He was building his career, starting his own family. She hadn't wanted him to worry about his tormented sister. The truth was, Miles realized as he lay awake at night wondering why he hadn't noticed Rebecca's problems himself, even if he had known, he wouldn't have intervened. He had been too busy, too preoccupied, to focus on anyone besides himself.

Please, Miles, I'll do anything. I just need a place to stay. He could hear Rebecca's voice, muffled by tears, so filled with pain that the words seemed to emanate from a ragged opening in her chest instead of her vocal cords. Her landlord had thrown her, and her few meager belongings, out on the street. He hadn't asked her why she chose to call him, why she didn't turn to their parents for help. *It won't be long, I promise. You don't understand.*

It's you who don't understand. I have a wife now. We have a home. You've had twenty-eight years to pull yourself together. He remembered his harsh reply as if it were yesterday. He hadn't asked her why she had been evicted. All he knew was that he was fed up with her. She had a master's in English literature but had never held a permanent job. Her part-time work bagging vegetables at a neighborhood grocery store was, to say the least, an embarrassment.

You can put me to work. I'm sure Penny needs help.

We have a maid. We don't need two.

I could work at Pratt Capital. I type. I'd be a good messenger. Her begging was pitiful. Miles could not bear the thought of Richard Pratt seeing Rebecca Adler mop the marble floors around the reception desk.

Look, I've got to go. The answer is no.

His last words to her.

The next afternoon an NYPD patrol car responded to a call from a postal delivery man. The two officers found Rebecca Adler lying amid her belongings under a stoop on 94th Street, a few blocks from her former apartment. She had been stabbed several times in the chest. A locket she had received for her Bat Mitzvah was missing, as was a Cartier love bracelet, a gift from their father for her twenty-first birthday, Miles remembered, which she had fastened to her wrist with a tiny gold screwdriver. To get the bracelet off, the robber had cut off her hand.

After her death, Miles went home, sat shivah with his mother for several days, made arrangements for Rebecca's burial, and never said a word about what had transpired between them shortly before the police found her dead. Nor did he say anything during the weeks and months following, when his mother and father searched for answers as to why their baby girl had been out on the street, why she hadn't asked anyone for help. He tried to convince himself that nothing he could have done would have changed events, but he knew that wasn't true. He could have given her a safe place to live temporarily. He could have made sure she got proper professional help. Instead he had turned his baby sister away, a deed so horrible he couldn't bring himself to ever confess. That was his secret.

Bob Michaels and Gail Davis arrived, were greeted by Belle and ushered into the conference room. At five twenty-five Miles heard Stu Wassermann's door open, the click of Stu's heels as he crossed the marble foyer, and then his nasal voice chatting with his compatriots, asking Gail about the scope of her plans, chiding Bob on the exorbitant rates he now charged for his legal services.

"Forty bucks for a two-minute phone call," Stu said. He laughed, able to see humor in it, Miles supposed, because it was not his dime.

"Tenth of an hour, six minutes or less," he heard Bob reply. "That's the smallest increment our billing department can accommodate. I can't do any better, or you know I would. At least you're getting our regular rates. I could charge a premium." Laughter.

The minutes passed as Miles listened to idle banter of the Pratt Capital employees. At five thirty-three there was still no sign of Clio. The puddles under his arms had cooled, and he wondered for a moment whether sweat could actually freeze. Not at fifty-five degrees, he reminded himself. He knew he should go into the conference room, greet Bob, whom he hadn't actually laid eyes on in several months, meet this decorator, act as though he were in charge. After all, these people should be following his orders and instructions, even his choice of fabrics and colors for a redecorated conference room.

There was no point in hiding in his office. He wasn't going to have a chance to talk to Clio alone before the meeting, not with everyone waiting, but he sat at his desk, paralyzed, unable to work, unable to get up. What infuriated him most of all was that Clio would never see his power. She would never know that he had disregarded her and scheduled the meeting for five-thirty. She would assume they had been assembled since five, and the meeting would begin as soon as Her Highness graced them with her presence.

Miles wondered whether he would have an opportunity to speak to Clio after the meeting adjourned. Unlikely. She always had some reason to hurry out, her driver waiting to take her back to Southampton, a rendezvous with girlfriends for which she was already late, something that would prevent her from staying behind to talk to Miles. His information, his demands, would have to be communicated some other time, but it needed to be done in person. He wanted to see the look on her face.

Miles lifted the receiver of his telephone and pressed speed dial button number 3. Penny picked up on the first ring.

"Hi, sweetheart," she said, her airy voice seeming to drift over the telephone line.

"I'm about to run into my meeting, but I was just thinking. Do we have plans for the Fourth of July?"

"The Fourth? It's barely June. Since when did you think so far in advance?"

"I know what day it is. I'm asking if we have plans for the holiday weekend." He had hoped to sound casual, but his voice, harsh and flat, seemed unfamiliar.

"Are you all right?" she asked.

"Do we or do we not have plans?" he repeated.

"We talked about going to visit your parents. They're moving down to the shore later this month, or at least I think that's what your mother said. Zack, Marci, and the girls are planning to go, too."

His brother, sister-in-law, and nieces. A family reunion planned on the Jersey coast. The Sabbath supper on Friday followed by an all-American weekend, sunburns and barbecues, sure to make his parents happy.

"I want to go to Southampton," Miles said. "I want to see Richard." His plan crystallized as he spoke. "It has been a while. Quite frankly, I've been neglectful of him recently. Things have been so busy."

"What will I tell your mother?"

"I'm sure you can make her understand. Richard's been awfully good to me, to us, and he's very sick. Just let her know it's important for us to be there for him. Then can you call Clio and tell her we're coming out? If she doesn't offer to have us stay with them, see if she can put us up somewhere, the Fair Lawn Country Club, some place like that."

"Why don't I find a hotel? The Southampton Inn, maybe. I'd hate to have us add to Clio's burden."

"It's a burden her servants will have to bear."

There was silence on the other end of the telephone

for several seconds before Penny asked, "Why don't you talk to her about it tonight? Won't it be odd for me to call right after she's just seen you?"

"It's better coming from you."

Miles heard his wife mumble something about how she thought he was acting strangely lately, then she said good-bye. He continued to hold the receiver for several moments longer. The line was dead.

Just then Miles heard the click of Clio's heels on the polished floor and voices gushing forth in friendly greetings.

He smiled to himself as he rose from his desk. He may have missed his opportunity this evening, but she couldn't avoid him forever.

Friday, June 5

$\mathcal{A}$s Aurelia stood at her kitchen sink rinsing the last of her dishes, she saw the navy blue Range Rover pull into her driveway from Halsey Neck Lane. She opened the window, pressed her face closer to the screen, and called out, "Who's there?" There was no reply. The glare of the late afternoon sun on the windshield made it impossible to see inside. She wiped her hands on her apron and walked out onto the porch. The engine turned off.

Aurelia approached the car slowly until she recognized Henry Lewis seated in the driver's seat. "Henry, Henry, why, what an unexpected surprise."

He said nothing and continued to stare blankly straight ahead.

"Are you all right? Henry? . . . Henry, what's wrong?" Aurelia grew increasingly alarmed as each of her questions went unanswered. "Can I get you some water?" She reached through the open window and touched his cheek lightly. He felt flushed, but nothing out of the ordinary for a warm June day.

After several moments he turned his head slowly to look at her. "May I come in?" he asked.

"Why, of course. Please." Aurelia stepped back, giving him room to get out of his car. In silence they entered the house. She offered him a chair at the kitchen table and placed a tall glass of lemonade in front of him. Then she sat down opposite.

Henry took a sip of his drink. She looked at his full lips glistening with wet lemonade, his strong square jaw, his smooth brown skin. Even his bloodshot eyes did not detract from the majesty of his face.

"Driving over here just now . . . ," he began. His voice was dull, the words flat. "I wondered to myself about our relationship. Are we friends? The thought never would have occurred to me until the last several weeks, you know, defining what you are to whom. I guess I was naive. I thought friends were friends, colleagues were colleagues, patients were patients. That pretty much would have covered everybody I know." Aurelia was silent, not understanding but not wanting to interrupt. "In any event, I need to talk to you. Maybe it's inappropriate. Maybe I'm overstepping my boundaries, but I couldn't think of anyone else. You can tell me if you want me to leave."

"Don't be ridiculous," Aurelia said, realizing that she hadn't the faintest idea what Henry Lewis was doing in her kitchen, seemingly disoriented but also fixed on something. She settled in her chair and rested her interlaced fingers on the edge of the wide-pine table. "What is it that you want to talk about?" she prompted.

"Are you a member of the Fair Lawn Country Club?"

A chuckle emanated from her throat before she could stop it, but the look of seriousness on Henry's face stifled the louder laughter bubbling inside her. She looked at her hands as she spoke. "I was. A long time ago. When I was married to Richard. When he and I divorced, I resigned. That had to be in '66, maybe early '67."

"Why'd you resign?"

"Actually, Richard urged me not to because of the girls, tennis clinic, that sort of thing, but it was his world, not mine. I had no particular interest."

"Did you know that Clio Pratt is on the Membership Committee of Fair Lawn?"

"I didn't, although it doesn't surprise me. Richard was on it himself at some point. He's always cared terribly about that place. He urged me constantly to get involved. He must have done the same with Clio. Unlike me, apparently she does what he asks."

Aurelia fingered the pleats in her faded flowered skirt. Richard had wanted her to do many things differently. Her lack of involvement with the ladies' activities at the Fair Lawn Country Club was only one of his disappointments.

Aurelia wished she had some sense of where this conversation was headed, what Henry wanted from her, but his face was difficult to read. His gaze seemed far away. She had known Henry Lewis for nearly a decade, since he'd been the chief surgical resident at Columbia Presbyterian Hospital in Manhattan, but she realized that she knew very little about him. When they met she'd been his patient, referred to him for consultation on her cardiac arrhythmia. Although her problem had been minor, a mitral valve prolapse that was treated with certain dietary restrictions and antibiotics before she had any dental work, she and Henry remained in contact. With a common interest in art, they spent several Saturdays together at shows—Magritte at the Metropolitan Museum of Art, Calder at the Museum of Modern Art, most recently a Mark Rothko exhibit at the National Gallery in Washington, D.C., a full day's excursion including the round-trip train ride.

The odd part about their friendship, Aurelia now thought as she looked at Henry sitting across her kitchen table, was that in the time they spent together, there'd been no personal discussion. On occasion he mentioned his wife, Louise, or his daughters, but only in passing. He rarely spoke of work. Art, their shared passion, was the focus, and Henry grew increasingly animated in conversation about the detail in a background, the texture of a canvas, the innovation of a mobile, art, art, and more art, execution, style, and history. Despite the intensity of their experiences in front of paintings, their relationship was hardly intimate.

"Clio Pratt threatened to blackball me and Louise when the Membership Committee was about to vote on our application. From what I understand, she pretty much single-handedly kept us from joining."

"If you ask me, Henry, that's a blessing. That club is pernicious. You don't want to be a part of it."

"Don't tell me what I want," Henry blurted out, rising from his chair.

Aurelia's astonishment must have shown on her face, because Henry immediately took a step back, then turned away from her and walked over to the window above the sink. "I'm sorry. I don't mean to take my temper out on you," he said quietly. He turned on the faucet and watched the clear water run out. "I'm just so sick and tired of people, white people, telling me what I do and don't want for my family. If I want my family to play tennis on the grass courts of Fair Lawn, for my girls to play bingo on Wednesday nights and win gift certificates to Lily White's or some other toy store, then that's what I want. Why is that so hard for everyone to accept?"

Aurelia didn't respond. She studied the well-dressed, attractive man standing in her kitchen. This was only the second time that Henry Lewis had ever been inside her house. Henry's other visit had been on a Saturday about a year after they'd first met. He'd been out in Southampton with Louise, staying with Louise's parents to make the final arrangements for their upcoming nuptials, and had asked to see her artwork. His request had surprised and flattered her. She had quickly assembled a small display arranged on easels throughout her garden. His enthusiasm that day had been infectious, a mixture of careful commentary, praise, and curiosity. The next day he'd gone to the small, out-of-the-way gallery in Manhattan that showed her work and bought several of her landscape paintings to donate to the cardiac care unit at Columbia Presbyterian. Her gallery's director had been thrilled. Aurelia appreciated his generosity. It couldn't have come at a better time.

Aurelia still felt indebted to Henry.

"I should start at the beginning, I suppose," Henry said, lowering his voice. "If that's okay?"

Aurelia nodded.

"I just don't know where else to turn. Louise is adamant that we not involve her parents."

"It's fine. Go ahead," Aurelia said, trying to sound soothing.

"Fair Lawn, historically, has been a big part of Louise's life out here. As I'm sure you know, her family's been involved with that place for generations, and Louise became a junior member when she turned twenty-five without thinking about it."

"Yes, I know. She and my daughter Blair were friends as children. I think they played in the twelve and under tennis tournament together."

Henry didn't appear to hear her. "Obviously, though, when the time came for us to apply, we questioned whether it was what we really wanted. We knew we would be the only interracial couple, and I'd be the only African American member. But Louise's friends, the people we saw socially when we came out here, were members, and we decided that it would be nice for the girls. I had some simplistic notion that my race wouldn't matter, that I was the right kind of person, a doctor. I had money. I actually didn't see it as that big a deal. I viewed it as a nice resource to have for Louise, for the girls. God, I'm such an idiot." He held onto his head with both hands and pulled at his hair.

"When did this happen?" Aurelia asked, referring to the actions of the Membership Committee. She couldn't bring herself to say "blackball" out loud.

"The membership process took all winter, interviews, introductions, parties. Louise's parents were terrific. Made sure we met all the right people. Even gave us a dinner that Clio Pratt had the gall to attend. Makes me sick to think about it. I can see her now, working the crowd with that saccharine sweetness of hers. 'Ooohhh, it's wonderful to see you,'" he said in falsetto imitation. Then his voice dropped. "She never gave us an inkling that she had a problem, a problem with me."

"How do you know she did?"

"I know. I've heard. Trust me on this one. She threatened to blackball me, us, if the Membership Committee forced a vote on our application."

"I'm sorry." Aurelia could think of no other words to say. Henry was quiet. Hesitantly she added, "What can I do?"

Henry's large brown eyes stared at her. "I can't describe how this feels, the idea that someone would want to keep my family, my girls, out because of something we have no control over. We're a good family. We're decent people. This shouldn't have happened to my girls."

Aurelia felt tears coming, and she pushed down hard on her eyelids with the fingers of her right hand.

"You've known Clio a long time. I thought maybe you could help me to understand."

"Clio's been married to my ex-husband for a long time. I don't know her," Aurelia said matter-of-factly, although her voice quivered. While it was true that she and

Clio rarely crossed paths, through the lives of her two daughters Aurelia had seen how Clio operated, a tornado wreaking havoc on the newly planted seeds, the shingled roof, the swing set in its path. But Henry wanted to know why Clio did what she did. He wanted an answer, some neat, rational response that would take away the pain he was so obviously experiencing from Clio's decision to exclude him. That Aurelia could not provide.

Henry's face filled with the same imploring look that Aurelia had seen too many times before on the tearstained faces of her daughters, Frances and Blair, also vulnerable, also begging for explanations. Each time the girls returned home from weekends or vacations with their father, they asked why they were treated the way they were. Why did they have to share a room when Justin, their half-brother, had his own and there were six other largely unused bedrooms in the house? Why did the cook make French toast for Justin's breakfast and nothing for them? Why were they not permitted to have friends over to the house? Why, even as teenagers, were they prohibited from using the swimming pool without Clio's express permission? Why were they excluded from dinner unless they had informed Clio by noon that they would be home that evening? Why had Clio refused to let Blair get married in their home? Some trivial, some profound, the girls' questions boiled down to why Clio was the way she was.

Aurelia had no answers. As children, Frances and Blair simply assumed that they had done something wrong, that they were somehow deserving of the disparate treatment they received, even as they struggled to determine what it was they had done. They offered to help around the house, didn't they? They kept their rooms neat. They did as they were told. They were quiet. They hadn't damaged anything. Aurelia had tried, over and over, to convince them that they were not at fault. What she couldn't bear to explain was that Frances and Blair, two well-behaved, studious, adorable girls, were hers, the product of Richard's first marriage. This simple fact, though totally beyond their control, was enough to condemn them in Clio's eyes.

"You know, I've asked myself over and over again, did I do the wrong thing? Should I have subjected my family to this process, this scrutiny, this judgment? Should I have subjected myself?" Henry paused for a moment and bit at his lower lip. "I think I fooled myself. In Manhattan, in my profession, I'm treated with respect. People turn to me, they rely on me, to help them. I save lives. But out here, none of that seems to matter. It's not good enough to be educated. It's not even enough to be rich. *Everybody* is. Even though the people in this community have every benefit and privilege imaginable, they still find an excuse to hate. I must have been crazy to think attitudes could change."

"If it's any consolation, I believe that Clio Pratt is threatened by a lot of things that you and I might not understand." *Two little girls who love their father*, Aurelia stopped herself from adding. "She's created a life surrounded by barriers, deliberately insulated from those who are different. Most of the people out here have done the same thing. That, Henry, is what you don't understand about Southampton. People are rich. People are powerful.

They've found a place where other rich, powerful people just like them want to come to play."

"Then why are you here?"

The question surprised Aurelia. She paused, thought for a moment, and tried to answer as honestly as she could. "For purely selfish reasons. The landscape I love to paint. The home that I have been in now for nearly fifteen years, since Blair went off to college, a home that I created only for myself, just exactly how I wanted it. For the reminder of happy times with my girls, even with Richard. Southampton is where I've stored my memories. I guess you could say that Southampton is the only future I can envision, and as far as I can recall, it's the happiest part of my past."

They were silent. Henry pulled on his lower lip. Aurelia watched him. She had not meant to talk about herself, and her disclosures made her feel funny.

"That's what I wanted it to be for me, for my family." Henry's tone was bitter. "We're entitled to enjoy this place as much as the next person."

"What does Louise think?"

"She says she's mostly upset for me."

"And you're upset for her."

"Louise is incredibly strong, stronger than I am in many ways. I just hate myself for putting her through this. She deserves better."

"You both do."

"Clio should be in my place. She wouldn't have gotten half as far as I have. And yet she's the one to sit in judgment."

"Should you try to talk to her?" Aurelia knew this was a futile suggestion.

"What good would that do? A conversation can't change ingrained attitudes. Besides, she'd probably deny it was her doing." Henry laughed. "I should kill her, is what I should do. She deserves nothing less than to be removed from this planet." He paused for a moment, then smiled, a flash of brilliant white teeth. "You must be thinking I'm crazy. Crazy to have tried to belong, and crazier now to be surprised that I don't, or can't."

Aurelia forced a smile. "No more crazy than the rest of us."

Saturday, July 4

$\mathcal{F}$rances Pratt kneeled in the fertilized earth, pulling small weeds and stray grasses from the rose bed in front of her and aerating the topsoil with her three-pronged claw. She sprinkled handfuls of Rose-Tone plant food around each bud eye of her seven Grand Finale rosebushes. Working from the ground up, her dirt-covered fingers removed the few yellowed leaves from the thorny stalks. The dead heads of formerly creamy white blossoms she cut off at an angle, just above the closest cluster of five leaves facing away from the center of the plant. These gardening tricks, developed over the years through much trial and error, served her well. Her roses were bushier and healthier than ever.

Frances sat back on her heels, rubbed the small of her back, and pushed her hair off her face. Felonious and Miss Demeanor, her canine companions, lay on the grass nearby, half sleeping, half watching her labor. She surveyed her work. After she finished with the roses, the bed of delphinium, cosmos, and foxglove needed weeding. Then she would turn her attention to her sunflower patch, this year's experiment. Some kind of bug was eating the thick, fibrous stalks. While Frances could solve most of her gardening problems on her own, these insects had baffled her. She needed to get advice from Sam Guff, her neighbor and the best gardener she knew.

Frances heard the telephone ring inside the house. The dogs pricked their ears but didn't move from where they lay in the sun. Frances counted the rings, realizing after four that she hadn't turned on the answering machine. Eventually the caller would hang up and try another time if it was important. She didn't feel like talking to anyone. Summer Saturdays were for gardening, and the Fourth of July holiday was no exception. Frances bent over and resumed her work.

The ringing persisted. The caller was someone who knew her well enough to know that she rarely answered the telephone, either her sister, Blair, her mother, or retired Federal Bureau of Investigation agent Robert Burke, now employed like her by the Suffolk County District Attorney's Office. The only other possibility was Sam, but he rarely bothered to call. He could walk across the street if he had something to say to her.

Leaving her claw, trowel, and rake where they lay, Frances got up and went inside.

"Hello?"

"Why didn't you pick up? Goddamn you, Fanny." Frances recognized Blair's voice, although the pitch was higher than normal and her words were slightly muffled, as if she had been crying.

"What's wrong?"

"It's Clio. Oh, my God, you're not going to believe it." Frances heard sobs mixed with wheezing breaths at the other end of the line.

"What happened? Where are you?"

Several seconds passed. Frances heard Blair blow her nose and cough before she responded. "I'm at the Fair Lawn Country Club. I found her, found her in the bathroom. Dead. In a stall. It's horrible, Fanny."

"What happened?"

"I don't know. She's dead."

"Are you sure?"

"What's that supposed to mean? Of course I'm sure."

"Did something happen? Did you hear a gunshot? Is there any sign of a struggle? Is she bloody?" Frances spoke mechanically, asking the series of questions ingrained in her by her law enforcement background. Oh, my God, we're talking about Clio, she thought for a moment, then forced her mind to stay focused. She couldn't allow herself to be personally affected and felt frustrated by Blair's inability to communicate basic information.

"Oh, Frances, how can you even say such things?" Blair started to cry again.

"Who's with you?"

"Everybody. Everybody's here."

Of course, Frances thought. It's July Fourth. The summer tennis tournament was under way. The Fair Lawn Country Club would be packed with people.

"You've got to come. I can't be here without you. Please hurry," Blair pleaded.

"Where's Jake?" Frances asked.

"He's in Ohio with his family for the weekend."

The answer didn't surprise her. Frances couldn't remember Jake ever being around to help in times of crisis. When Blair's appendix burst three years earlier, Jake was meeting with some banker about extending their line of credit and didn't answer his cell phone. When Richard had his stroke, Jake actually stayed on in Hong Kong to deal with his clients rather than accompany his wife on the long journey home. He seemed to have an uncanny ability to avoid bad situations, and today was no exception.

"Does Dad know?"

"This just happened!" Blair screamed. "Just this minute!"

"Have you called the police?"

"I didn't, but somebody else did, I'm pretty sure. Everyone's running around. It's crazy here. They just stopped the tournament." Frances could hear her sister's quick, raspy breathing. "You've got to get here. You've got to tell Dad. I can't, Fanny. It's going to kill him."

Frances tried to sound calm, in control. "Blair, listen to me. Stay right where you are. When the police get there, tell them what you know, and tell them about Dad, his condition. I'm on my way."

"Hurry."

"I'm coming as fast as I can."

Frances dialed the home number for Robert Burke, the first person she'd think to call in a time of crisis. Since his mandatory retirement at age fifty-five from the Federal Bureau of Investigation, "Meaty," as he was affectionately known, worked for the state. He ran every major investigation that District Attorney Malcolm Morris chose to pursue, and he oversaw the younger, less experienced investigators assigned to the office from the local police.

While with the FBI, Meaty had worked out of the Manhattan office. He and Frances knew many of the same people, law enforcement officers from the New York Police Department, the United States Attorney's and Manhattan District Attorney's Offices, and Meaty was well aware of Frances's reputation as a serious, hard-working prosecutor before she'd ever set foot in Malcolm Morris's office. For that reason he exhibited a deference to her that he otherwise withheld from prosecutors. He listened to what she wanted and involved her in the strategic side of investigating more than a dozen cases they had worked on together over the past seven years. In return he never had to worry about the adequacy of her search warrants, the precision of her grand jury presentations, or the efficacy of her direct examinations.

Meaty had told Frances what he considered to be the basic parameters of his personal life shortly after they'd first met. "It's all you'll ever need to know about me," he'd said at the time. "Because what you see is what you get. I'm not a very complex sort of guy." He had married his wife, Carol, forty years ago, when she was sixteen and he was twenty. They had one daughter, who was, and would remain, an incurable alcoholic. He and Carol had instituted legal proceedings against her to gain custody of their baby granddaughter. Now neither liquor nor their only child was allowed in the house, and they had raised the little girl for the past nine years. Frances also knew that Meaty's passions were the New York Yankees, deep-sea fishing, and floating island meringue desserts.

In exchange, Frances disclosed that she had once been engaged and that she had family on Long Island. She left her personal life at that, and Meaty had not probed. In seven years Frances had revealed little else.

Carol Burke answered the telephone on the second ring.

"It's Frances. Is Meaty there?"

Forty years of marriage to an FBI man must have given Carol an intuitive ability to assess a situation without asking a single question. Frances was relieved that she omitted her customary chatter and good cheer and called immediately for her husband.

"Meaty," Frances said as he got on the line, "I need your help. Clio, my dad's wife, is dead."

"How?" he asked in his gruff voice.

Holding the portable receiver in place with her chin, she relayed the substance of Blair's call. "That's all I know. I haven't talked to anyone besides Blair. I need a favor. A blue light to Southampton." Frances knew that it would take her more than an hour to get from Orient Point to the Fair Lawn Country Club with the speed limit and holiday traffic. Meaty, behind the wheel of his Crown Victoria with his blue light flashing from the roof, could cut the time in half.

"I'm on my way," Meaty said.

Frances stood for a moment, trying to collect her thoughts, but she felt numb. Looking down, she saw her blackened fingernails, her soil-covered overalls. She went to the bathroom, washed her face, scrubbed her hands, and then changed her clothes. Back in the kitchen, she took several dog biscuits out of the canister, called for the dogs, and rewarded their responsiveness. "Okay, guys, I'll be back." She heard her own voice shake.

Waiting for Meaty's arrival, Frances paced the length of her porch, then leaned against the sagging railing. As she thought of her father, and what she was about to see, she rubbed her eyes to force back tears. Now is not the time to cry, she told herself, but her self-control diminished as she imagined his devastation. He would sink farther into his wheelchair and obscure his face to hide his pain. Lily, his nurse, would hover and flutter about him. The scene would be unbearable. Clio had been the center of his life, even more so in the past year since he had been unable to work. She was his reason to live.

Now this woman, who seemed the picture of health, was dead in a toilet stall. Frances couldn't recall a time that Clio had been sick. Thin, physically active, she worked to stay fit. Plus, she had spent the last year living amid nurses, health care professionals. It wasn't possible that something serious could have gone undetected, yet she was dead at fifty-one.

What happened? Frances wondered. What went wrong?

Meaty turned off First Neck Lane and pulled his Crown Victoria into the pillared entranceway of the Fair Lawn Country Club. He slowed down long enough to flash his police badge at the blond teenage boy who sat slouched in a green-and-white-striped folding chair by the gate. The guard glanced up from his bag of potato chips and waved Meaty through.

"What the hell is this place?" Meaty said as they drove slowly up the paved drive. Acres and acres of manicured green lawn divided by white lines and nets spread out before them.

"Grass tennis courts," Frances remarked absentmindedly.

"Tennis where I grew up was a couple of kids on a cement court. This grass looks like a putting green," Meaty muttered.

They drove past several tennis courts, a soccer field, and rows and rows of Mercedes, Range Rovers, BMWs, and Jaguars, parked in perfect lines. "Could feed a small country for a year off the sale of this lineup," Meaty said, chuckling. "Impressive. Quite impressive."

"Over there," Frances directed, pointing toward the gambrel roof of the main clubhouse. The sun shown down on its darkened shingles. Three police cars, a fire truck, and two ambulances were parked near the building. Meaty pulled up alongside one of the ambulances.

"Meaty," Frances said grabbing his arm before he could open the driver's-side door. "Do me one favor."

"You bet," he replied.

"Let me be anonymous today, just an assistant DA along for the ride."

"It's your stepmother."

"I want to know what's going on, to hear what the cops have to say."

"You don't need to be a professional, kiddo."

"Just let me do it my way?" Frances asked.

"You got it." He squeezed her hand, then opened his door.

Frances felt relieved that he hadn't resisted. She wanted to focus on what had transpired and wasn't prepared to deal with the panoply of police officers well schooled in the removal and consolation of grieving family members.

The porch that ran the length of the clubhouse was filled with people. Most were dressed in tennis clothes, white shorts, skirts, and dresses, and held tennis rackets emblazoned with the Wilson or Prince logo. People clutched drinks in clear plastic cups as they milled about on the grass. An elderly man in a bright green blazer packed several belongings from the umpire's chair into an athletic bag. In the distance Frances could see a group of small children chasing each other around in a circle. Beyond them a tennis game was still in progress.

Despite the crowd, the place was relatively quiet. People spoke in hushed tones. Seated in canvas director's chairs, several women slumped forward, crying. Frances kept her eyes down, not wanting to be recognized by someone from her past. It had been more than a decade since she had set foot at the Fair Lawn Country Club, but she feared her face hadn't changed enough to protect her anonymity. She watched Meaty's sneaker-shod feet taking long strides toward the main entrance.

What an odd place this must seem to him, she thought for a moment. A private tennis club, impeccably groomed, filled with suntanned families dressed in white. Timeless. In fact, little had changed that she could notice since she had spent July here as a child, participating in morning tennis clinic, running drills, practicing ground strokes. She had played her share of challenge matches on the ladder, competed in the tennis tournaments year after year, even won the best sportsmanship award when she was thirteen. Her father had the small silver-plated bowl she had won engraved with her name and date: "Frances Taylor Pratt, 1973. " Meaty could never understand a place like this. She wouldn't believe it herself if it hadn't been such an integral part of her childhood.

Frances felt disoriented. She wanted to reach out for Meaty, to feel his muscular arm, to have him support the weight of her body, which felt too much to bear, but she didn't dare touch him. If he thought she was in pain, or that her emotions might hinder her objectivity, he would protect her by keeping her out of the investigation. She quickened her step to stay in stride behind him.

The interior of the Fair Lawn Country Club clubhouse was cordoned off with yellow police tape. Meaty and Frances stood at the barrier. A lean man with a buzz-top haircut and wire-rimmed glasses stood just inside, smoking a cigarette. His ash dropped onto the rose-colored pile carpeting.

"Hank," Meaty said to the man.

"Meaty, what brings you to these parts?"

Omitting her last name, Meaty introduced Frances to Detective Hank Kelly of the Southampton Police Department. "She's with the district attorney's office," Meaty added. "What can you tell us?"

"Female. Probably late forties. Apparent heart failure." He took another drag of his cigarette. "Name's Clio Pratt. She's well-known around here."

"Where is she?" Meaty asked.

"The bathroom."

"Can we take a look?"

"Be my guest." Detective Kelly led Frances and Meaty through a door marked "Powder Room" in gilt lettering. They stepped into a small, windowless room with green-and-pink floral wallpaper, coordinated plush carpet, a large gilded mirror, and twin marbled sinks on which sat stacks of hand towels, each embroidered with a green "FL." The air smelled of freshener.

"This way," Detective Kelly said, pointing into a larger room beyond.

The floor and walls of the larger bathroom were similarly decorated. Several pink toilet stalls lined the far wall, and the bottled smell of gardenias thickened the air. Frances saw two Tretorn sneakers, red-and-white-checkered panties, and a pair of thin crumpled legs protruding from the center stall. "We need a minute here," Detective Kelly announced. Two police officers wearing rubber gloves stepped out of the stall and backed away.

Frances moved forward. Clio's body lay partially draped over the toilet bowl. Her short tennis skirt was hiked up around her waist, exposing a perfect bikini-waxed triangle of dark pubic hair. Clio's arms hung limp by her side, her manicured fingers just touching the floor. Her head tilted back on her neck, eyes wide, mouth agape. The ends of her dark hair, pulled back into a ponytail behind her head, dangled into the toilet.

Frances raised her hands to cover her mouth. She was used to the police photographs that filled the office, images of dead bodies, knife wounds, gunshots, all the gore of a crime scene captured in Technicolor, but she felt unprepared for this nonviolent death. The toilet paper had come unrolled from its gold dispenser, as if Clio had grabbed on to it for support as she slid to the floor. Otherwise, little had been disturbed. Frances stood and stared. She tried to discern what besides Clio's awkward body position made her look different. Was it the paleness of her skin, the emptiness of her corpse? Clio would have hated the humiliation, the exposure to the gawks and gasps of her fellow club members.

Frances wanted to feel sad about her father's wife, the woman he had loved for almost as long as Frances could remember, but the sight seemed too surreal to evoke emotion.

She felt Meaty touch her back.

"You okay?" he whispered.

"Yeah."

"Her stepdaughter, a Blair Devlin, found her," Detective Kelly said matter-of-factly as he checked his spiral notepad. "I spoke to her briefly, but the paramedics had to take her to Southampton Hospital for sedation. The poor woman's hysterical. As she's getting in the ambulance, she gives me her car keys. Says just leave them in the car." He shrugged, flipped the page, and continued, "We got the call at eleven oh-three. A guy named Jack Von Furst called it in. He said he was out on the porch watching a tournament—there was a men's doubles match going on—and heard a scream. Von Furst said he ran inside and found Blair screaming right here. Another guy, a George Welch, arrived about the same time. He'd been doing some paperwork in the lobby of the clubhouse when he heard the screams. Nobody else was in the bathroom at the time. Von Furst knew the deceased. Said they were close friends. 'Close' was his word."

"Did anyone try anything, CPR, anything like that?" Frances asked.

"Von Furst said they checked Pratt's wrists and neck, but there was no pulse. They knew enough not to move her. Then he left to call 911, and Welch stayed with the body. That's pretty much it. Von Furst said he would hang around in case we need him."

"Have you talked to Welch?" Frances and Meaty said in unison.

"Yeah. He didn't have much to add."

"Is Forensics going to do any work here?"

"We've secured it for now, as you can see. We're trying to reach Lieutenant Batchelder to find out what he wants us to do. He hasn't returned my page. Probably playing golf with your boss," Detective Kelly said, nodding to Frances. "If anyone asks my opinion, which they don't, I'd say we've got to let Crime Scene do their stuff. It's now or never."

"Any reason to think there's been a crime?" Meaty asked, echoing the question in Frances's mind.

"Look, I don't want to be the guy accused of botching the job if facts turn up. These are fancy people here."

Meaty raised his eyebrows.

"I dunno," Detective Kelly said. "But if you ask me, she looks pretty healthy. I'd sure want to know what got that specimen of a woman."

"Has Mr. Pratt been notified?" Frances asked.

"The husband? Not yet. We understand he's in pretty bad shape himself."

"I'd like to talk to him," Frances said.

"You?" Detective Kelly asked.

Meaty nodded.

"I should've said something earlier. I'm with the district attorney's office, as Meaty told you, but I'm also . . ." She paused to clear her throat. "This is my stepmother. My sister called me at home. That's why Meaty and I are here."

Detective Kelly took a step back from Frances. "I'm real sorry for your loss."

"Thanks. Thanks a lot." Then, remembering Detective Kelly's words, Frances added, "If you don't mind, I'll take my sister's car. I can find it in the lot. I need to go see my father."

"Sure." Detective Kelly handed her the set of car keys.

"You want me to follow you?" Meaty asked.

"No. I'm okay. Just let me know if anything happens. I'll be at home by this evening." She turned to Detective Kelly. "We'll want an autopsy. If you need authorization, I can get it."

Frances turned away from Clio's corpse and walked out of the powder room, leaving Meaty and Detective Kelly behind.

The crowd had begun to dissipate, and Frances watched as people walked to their cars. She wondered where they were going on this beautiful holiday Saturday now that their scheduled event, the tournament, was ruined by the death of a friend, an acquaintance, a fellow club member. Perhaps they'd go over to the exclusive

Bathing Corporation, informally known as the Beach Club, just a quarter of a mile away. Most Fair Lawn Country Club members also belonged there. The Beach Club served lunch, and it was almost that time.

Frances found Blair's Mazda Miata parked at an angle near a high privet that concealed a practice backboard. The door was unlocked, and Frances settled herself into the soft leather seat, adjusting it a few inches to accommodate her slightly shorter legs. In the passenger seat next to her she noticed a thick stack of papers. Instinctively she picked them up and flipped through the loose pages of what appeared to be draft legal documents and several architectural drawings. She paused to read the single-spaced text. According to the documents, the Devlin Gallery planned to lease ten thousand square feet of commercial space at an annual rent of $1 million. She looked again at this startling sum. She had no idea her sister's gallery was doing that well. Surprise, and a pang of jealousy, distracted her momentarily. Then she forced herself to remember that she had no business snooping into her sister's affairs and that she had more pressing matters to deal with. She started the engine.

Frances wished the drive from the Fair Lawn Country Club to her father's house on Ox Pasture Road was longer, but the mile and a half passed quickly behind the wheel of her sister's convertible. The sun shone on the hood of the Japanese racing green convertible and on her blue-jeaned thighs. The wind blew in her face, cooling her flushed cheeks. Frances pulled down the visor. The motor revved, then purred, as she switched into fourth gear.

She imagined her father's face, his large brown eyes, his crooked mouth. He would know as soon as she arrived that something was wrong, that there was another sorrow to add to his store. She visited on Fridays, not Saturdays, and she, like he, was a creature of habit. That's the problem, she thought. Uncompromising schedules get compromised only for bad news.

Frances hadn't been with her father when he learned that Justin, his son, had died. September 8, a date etched indelibly in her mind. How odd that she had forgotten Justin's birthday more than once, but the anniversary of his death never passed unrecognized. Justin, only fourteen, Richard's only son and Clio's only child, killed on a windy day when his sailboat capsized. The boom struck his head, knocking him unconscious, and he drowned. A tragedy that could have been prevented if someone else had been in the boat or if someone on shore had seen the boat go over. But Justin fell into the black water of Lake Agawam unnoticed. He wasn't reported missing until several hours later when he didn't come home for supper, and his body wasn't found until the next morning. A freak accident given Justin's experience as a sailor, the shallowness of Lake Agawam, and the relative calmness of the water even with the wind. "Like being struck by lightning," the medical examiner supposedly had said, but Frances had never known anyone to be struck by lightning.

Richard hadn't called Frances until the following day to tell her of Justin's death. Their conversation had been brief. His voice was flat. He explained what had happened as far as he knew, then asked her not to come, not right away, not until the memorial service at the end of the week. He and Clio mourned their son in private, and Frances would never know what passed between them in those sorrow-filled days. By the time Frances saw her father in church, he and Clio looked composed. Neither shed a tear in front of the mass of mourners in attendance.

Now Frances had to tell her father that Clio was dead.

Frances parked the Miata by the front door of the Pratt residence and sat for several moments with the engine off. The house was still. She heard birds chirping, saw a rabbit nibble at the newly cut grass, watched two large bumblebees buzz around a pink geranium in a stone planter at the edge of the drive. No one would ever know that something is terribly wrong, Frances thought.

She saw Lily, her father's nurse, standing at the top of the handicapped ramp, smoking a cigarette.

"Oh, Frances, what a surprise! I saw the car and thought it was Blair," Lily called out as Frances opened the door and stepped out onto the gravel.

"I'm using Blair's car," Frances replied. She knew Lily was disappointed. Blair and Lily were friends, or at least friendly in a way that she couldn't be.

"Your father will be delighted to see you, I'm sure, but he's asleep right now. He had a difficult night."

"I need to talk to Dad," Frances said. At that moment she wished her sister were with her. She wanted someone to help her deal with the intense emotion that was sure to come in the next several minutes.

"Is everything all right?" Lily asked. She leaned over and stubbed out the butt of her cigarette.

"Clio's dead." Frances didn't know how to say it any

other way. None of the euphemisms for death ever sounded right.

Lily gasped, then started to tremble. She wrapped her arms around her waist as if to comfort herself with an embrace. Frances could see tears in her eyes. "I'm sorry, oh, I'm so very sorry. Oh, I just don't know what to say. Your poor father," Lily rambled.

Frances walked past her and entered the house. Lily was the health care professional. This was her job. If Lily fell apart, Frances was not at all sure that she could remain in control. "Please get my father now," she instructed, forcing her voice to sound authoritative.

Lily wiped her hands on her starched white uniform, followed Frances inside, and left to awaken Richard.

As Frances waited she walked quietly around the perimeter of the living room, stopping to study the built-in bookshelves at one end. Photographs in blue-and-white-checkered frames were perched amid rows and rows of hardbound books, Richard's golf trophies, plaques that he'd received from appreciative investors, other memorabilia of glorious days at Pratt Capital, and a model of a wooden motorboat with a wide deck of varnished mahogany. There were pictures of Richard and Clio, smiling, hugging, wearing straw hats on a sailboat, holding hands on a golf course, clinking Champagne glasses in some cozy restaurant. All Clio's doing, Frances thought. She gave him a happy life, and now she's left him surrounded by happy memories.

Frances turned as she heard the sound of rubber squeaking on the wood floors. Richard sat up in his wheelchair, looking straight at her as Lily pushed him from behind. He wore a seersucker robe, and Frances could see his white pajamas with blue piping underneath. Lily had not bothered to dress him.

"Is it Blair?" he asked as soon as his wheelchair came to a halt. Lily secured the brake so he wouldn't roll. She sniffled and dabbed at her eyes with a tissue.

"No, Dad. Blair's fine." Frances stood a few feet from him. "It's Clio. She's . . . she . . . Dad, Clio's dead." Even though she spoke in a low tone, the words seemed to bellow about the big space, resonating against the walls.

Richard lowered his head. His thin torso slouched forward so that Frances could not see his facial expression, and his body started to tremble. As his forearms fell off the armrests of his wheelchair, his hands dangled toward the floor. His feet turned inward, pigeon-toed on the metallic foot stabilizers. It was precisely the posture she had imagined, but this physical reaction looked worse in real life.

"I'm so sorry," she heard herself say in a voice that seemed miles away. She reached out to touch his shoulder but realized the space between them was too far, and her feet seemed unwilling to move closer to him. Her arm dropped to her side.

Richard mumbled something that Frances couldn't understand. Then he slurped his saliva back down his throat.

"She was found at Fair Lawn. The cause of death hasn't been determined for sure, but it appears to be heart failure," Frances said, anxious to share what little information she had. "I've told the police to go ahead with an autopsy. I thought it best."

Richard said nothing.

Frances felt lost, unsure of what to do or whether she could do it even if she knew. She shifted her weight from side to side, feeling her feet sweaty in her leather loafers. She looked at Lily, who was gently rubbing Richard's back. Frances watched her hands as they moved in small circles. First Justin, then the stroke, now Clio, was all Frances could think. It was more pain than any one person should have to bear. Her throat and eyes burned. She needed to leave this house before she herself broke down, but she knew she should stay.

"Should I call Dr. Farley?" she asked. She wanted her father's physician to prescribe a sleeping pill for him, maybe one for her, too. They could both drift off into peaceful sleep, hoping this entire morning were a nightmare that would disappear when they awoke.

"I can contact him if we need him," Lily replied.

"There must be something I can do," Frances said, more to herself than her father. Neither Lily nor Richard responded. "Is there anyone you want me to call?" she asked, knowing the answer. Clio had no immediate family, and friends could be notified later. "Do you want to be left alone?"

"Maybe he should rest," Lily said softly. "I can reach you if there's anything he needs."

"I'll let you know as soon as I hear anything from the medical examiner. That is, if you want to know." She assumed her father would be anxious to hear details, but she knew that nothing she could say or do would lessen the horror of the situation. "Clio loved you so much. You have to remember that. You two made each other incredibly happy, and that's more than most people ever have."

Her offering sounded feeble, a Hallmark sentimentality, and she faulted herself for her inability to articulate the sorrow she felt for him.

Frances closed her eyes, wishing she could put this scene out of her mind. Her father's words, the only discussion she and he had ever had about death, returned to her from her distant memory. She had been eight, and her first pet, a guinea pig, had died. She remembered holding the limp, furry body in her cupped palms and crying to her father. She had wanted him to comfort her, to console her, to give her an explanation for what she perceived as a monumental unfairness. Instead Richard had rubbed his index finger along the spine of the creature and said, "There's nothing I can do to make you feel any better. That's the problem with losing what we love. No words can replace it. No tears can fill what must be a huge hole inside you. Others may tell you that time will make you feel better, that as the weeks go by your pain will lessen. I'm not going to tell you that, Fanny, because I don't think it's true. We learn to live with our pain, to tolerate it in a way that allows us to continue to go on, but nothing makes it disappear. And no one else can ever really understand what you are feeling. As much as I love you, you are ultimately alone with your sadness."

"I'll check in with you later, see if there's anything you need," Frances said. No matter how hard she tried, she couldn't lessen his burden. She walked quickly out the door to the Miata, got in the car, and fixed her gaze on the road ahead as she sped away. As the distance between her green sports car and the house on Ox Pasture

Road increased, she felt the sea of her emotions flatten and calm.

Frances pushed the accelerator and sped east along Montauk Highway. Planted fields and fresh produce stands overflowing with corn, potatoes, and tomatoes filled her vision. After six miles she turned left at a blinking light and headed toward Sag Harbor. The road twisted and turned past gabled churches, a high school with basketball courts empty for the summer recess, and lawn after lawn leading up to well-kept Colonial homes. She headed toward Peconic Bay.

It was nearly four when Frances reached the dirt road leading to Blair and Jake's house. The cottage with its pair of doghouse dormers sat perched at the top of a small hill overlooking the water. Someone had removed the shutters, and Frances could see the discolored rectangular outline on the shingles where they had hung. A variety of mosses spilled over the sides of the two Mediterranean planters that were placed on opposite sides of the black painted door.

The place was quiet. Frances parked the car and sat for a moment, looking out to sea. Wind formed whitecaps on the surface of the blue expanse. The temperature had dropped. She promised herself that she would check briefly on her sister and then head home.

Frances walked around to the back of the house. On the weather-treated deck, her sister lay on a lounge chair with a small white pillow over her eyes and a cotton blanket over her feet. She wore gray sweat pants and a striped T-shirt. Her hair was wet.

"Blair, it's me, Frances," Frances said quietly so as not to startle her.

"Fanny, I'm so glad you're here." Blair removed the pillow and placed it behind her head. "I tried to wait for you at Fair Lawn, but the paramedics insisted I get to the hospital. I must say, I think they were right. Valium is a wonderful drug." She smiled sheepishly.

"I'm glad you're feeling better," Frances said.

"Can I get you anything?" Blair asked, reaching to pick up the glass of red wine on the deck beside her. "There's white, too, if you prefer, or beer."

"No thanks." Frances sat in an Adirondack chair next to her sister.

"Did you talk to Dad?"

"Yeah. I told him."

"How did he seem?"

Frances didn't know how to answer. Sad, weak, pathetic, old, all words that described her father, but none of which captured the sadness he must have felt. "I didn't stay long. Lily was with him."

"Don't tell me you just told him his wife was dead and walked out." Blair closed her eyes in seeming disgust.

"It wasn't exactly like that, no. He was asleep when I arrived. I told him what I knew, which wasn't much, and he was quiet. There wasn't anything else for me to do."

"What do you mean? He's our father, for God's sake. You couldn't stick around to comfort him?"

Frances didn't need Blair's accusations. For the last twenty minutes she had asked herself over and over why she couldn't do a better job of sharing her father's grief at the loss of his wife. "I came to check on you, but I'm too tired to argue." Frances started to get up.

"Don't go."

"What do you want me to do? You asked me to tell Dad because you didn't want to. I did that. I did it in the only way I knew how."

"I'm sorry, Fanny," Blair apologized. "You're right." She pulled the blanket up over her waist. "I tried calling a little while ago, but Lily told me he didn't want to be disturbed. I should go over there myself, but, frankly, I feel too weak. You can't imagine what it was like just walking into the bathroom and finding her dead."

"Had you seen her earlier in the day?"

"Briefly, just to say hello. I had been on the porch of the clubhouse, like everyone else, watching the men's doubles tournament. She was there, too. I can't remember who she was with. Anyway, the next thing I knew, I went to the bathroom and found her."

"Was the stall door open?" Frances interrupted.

"Partly. Enough so that I could see that someone had collapsed inside. Then I pushed it open farther, thinking I might be able to help whoever was in trouble, and saw it was Clio."

"Then what?"

"I don't really remember. I screamed. People came running in. I called you. That's about it."

"Did you talk to anyone about what happened?"

"The police, briefly. The paramedics arrived and pretty much took me away. Why does any of this matter?"

"It doesn't. I don't know why I'm asking," Frances

replied, realizing how easily she fell into her role as lawyer, questioner, and examiner. She scratched at a mosquito bite on her ankle.

Blair took a sip of her wine. "I'll head over there tomorrow. There's probably a lot to organize, and I doubt Dad's up to much. Someone's going to have to take charge of that monstrous house, all her stuff, figure out what to do with it. There actually may be things we want."

Frances hoped Blair's words were Valium induced. She watched Blair run her finger around the rim of her glass absentmindedly. Moments like this made Frances realize how different she and her sister were despite their shared genes, shared experiences, and deeply felt affection for one another. Neither the material remnants of Clio's life nor the organization of the house on Ox Pasture Road had occurred to Frances.

"I won't miss her. I know that's a terrible thing to say about the dead, but she was a horrible woman."

"Dad loved her," Frances replied.

"Dad wanted a wife who wouldn't leave him, that's all. Look what he put up with to get it. She made our lives hell. I can't believe that was a good thing for Dad."

"Dad didn't have to let it happen." As she spoke, Frances regretted her words. She didn't want to be drawn into a conversation about growing up with Clio. Frances and Blair had gone on to live their own lives. What had happened over the course of the thirty years that Clio had been a part of the Pratt family was over, and rehashing childhood memories was not particularly productive, especially now.

"Do you remember the time she locked me out?" Blair asked.

Frances didn't respond.

"It was the summer after sixth grade, so I must've been eleven. I can't remember where Dad was, a business trip or something because it was a Saturday in July and otherwise he would've been there." She closed her eyes as she spoke. "It had been a bad week. I lost in the semi-finals of the twelve and under to Hilda McLennen. Bobby Carter broke up with me because I wouldn't let him get to second base, and Felice Finlay had a slumber party and didn't invite me. God"—Blair laughed—"it's so vivid, it feels like yesterday. Anyway, I called Mom in the city that morning and begged her to come out to see me. I actually remember whispering into the kitchen phone so Clio wouldn't hear me. I had to lie to Clio and say I was spending the day at a friend's house because I was nervous about her finding out that Mom was coming during our time with Dad. The irony being that Dad worked all the time so we hardly saw him anyway."

Blair continued. "Of course, Mom came out. We had a great time. She took me to lunch, listened to me cry and babble about the hardships of my life, how I really and truly loved Bobby and would never survive our breakup, but by the end of the meal, she convinced me that he was a loser and I was lucky to be rid of him." Blair laughed. "Something only a mother could do. Anyway, she bought me a sundress from Lily Pulitzer, you know the ones that were hot pink and chartreuse in wild patterns? Mine had shells and seahorses on it. At the end of the day, Mom had to go back to the city. She dropped me off at the end of

Dad's driveway so Clio wouldn't see her. When I got to the house, the door was locked. I knocked and rang. No one came. I walked around the house calling for help. Still no one. When have you ever known that house to be empty? I banged on windows. Nothing. I actually saw Kitty, I think that was her name, the Irish nanny we had with the mole on her nose, remember? She walked right by, as if I were invisible. It got dark and I was scared. I kept ringing the bell. I was crying and no one came. I debated breaking a window, but thought Clio would get really mad if I did that. Anyway, I ended up sleeping on the terrace. Kitty came out early the next morning to get me. I asked her why she hadn't come for me sooner, when I was begging to be let in. She told me that Clio had instructed all of the servants to leave me outside overnight. That I would never lie again."

"Did it work?" Frances asked.

Blair laughed. "What do you think?"

"Did Clio ever say anything?"

"Not a word. Neither did Dad."

"Where was I?" Frances wondered.

"Who knows. At a friend's house, if I had to guess. You slept out as much as possible."

Frances looked at her sister, reclining with her glass of wine. She sensed relief in Blair's voice, a seeming nostalgia for the bad memories now that her stepmother was dead and out of her life forever. It made Frances uneasy.

The light had changed, and the sky showed the first swatches of pink, the precursors of the sunset that was yet to come. Frances could see a flock of geese flying away in a V-shaped formation. Their wings rose and fell in perfect unison. Blair got up, disappeared through a sliding glass door, and returned a few minutes later with her wineglass refilled.

"So when's Jake getting back?"

"Too soon," Blair said sarcastically. "He called and said he'll be out here sometime tomorrow."

"What was he doing in Ohio?"

"Apparently he didn't get to Ohio. There was some rambling explanation that I didn't follow. For all I know, he never left Manhattan."

"What are you talking about?"

"Jake's spending most of his time trying to rescue the gallery from financial ruin. He had counted on Clio to help us out, but, no surprise, that backfired. I can't keep track of what strategies he's using now. He's frantic. I guess I am too in my own way, but he does his thing and I do mine. Let's just say we haven't seen eye to eye on how to deal with our solvency problems."

Despite the obvious inconsistency between Blair's remarks and the papers Frances had seen on the front seat of her Miata, Frances let her sister's remarks go without response. She had learned long ago that criticizing someone else's spouse was a no-win proposition unless divorce papers had been not only filed but finalized. "Have you spoken to Mom today?"

"Yeah. I called her from Fair Lawn after I spoke to you, and then again when I got home. She offered to come over, but I told her I'd be okay."

"How did she react to Clio?"

"Shocked, I guess. I didn't pay much attention. I doubt Mom really cares."

The two sisters sat quietly as dusk settled over the deck. Blair rubbed her feet together under the blanket and sipped her wine. Finally Frances stood up. "I should head home. I'm going to call for the jitney schedule," she said, referring to the bus that could take her back to Orient Point.

"You can take the car."

"That's okay."

"Well, just leave it at the jitney stop. I'll pick it up later, or tomorrow."

"Thanks. Will you be all right alone?" Frances asked.

"I'm fine. I don't need a thing. And if I do, a friend is staying with me," Blair responded wistfully. She looked at the small gold watch on her left wrist. "He should be back any moment." The "he" hung in the air.

Frances didn't want to ask anything more.

Except for the porch light, the house was dark when Frances returned home. She opened her door, heard the sound of padded paws alighting from the couch onto the floor, and felt the furry warmth of Felonious and Miss Demeanor as they came to greet her. "I missed you guys," she said as she felt for their velvety ears and scratched their heads.

Frances and the dogs made their way into the kitchen, where she turned on the overhead light. On the butcher-block counter was a note held down by a bunch of wild-flowers in a jelly jar. *I missed seeing your smiling face. Where were you this afternoon? I came over and saw the truck but no trace of you. I took the liberty of feeding the dynamic duo around 4:30. They have been out and done their business.* Frances recognized Sam's thick-lettered script. He never forgot her dogs, or her, for that matter.

She opened several cupboards in search of a graham cracker, or some other snack, realizing that she hadn't eaten all day, but found nothing except a can of black beans, expired vitamins, a box of oyster crackers, instant oatmeal, and several bags of assorted dog biscuits. As she opened the refrigerator the telephone rang. She resisted the urge to let it ring. Not tonight, it could be important.

She grabbed a bottle of Amstel Light, shut the fridge, and answered the telephone.

"Let me first express my condolences to you and your father." Frances recognized the voice of her boss, District Attorney Malcolm Morris, whom she had known since childhood. Malcolm had been her father's partner in the annual golf tournament at the National Golf Club in Southampton for years, and he'd been an occasional guest at Richard and Clio's larger dinner parties. After witnessing some of his rowdier moments during these evenings, his Hawaiian hula dance, his moose yodel, Frances often had difficulty treating him with the reverence that his elected office deserved. Tonight, though, his voice was stern.

"However, I want to tell you in no uncertain terms that you are to have no role, official or unofficial, in investigating Clio's death. I know you were over at the Fair Lawn Country Club with Meaty today. It doesn't surprise me that he brought you along, but that's the end."

"He didn't bring me along. I got the call. I brought him in."

"I am not talking about semantics, Frances, and you know it."

"We're not investigating anything. There's no signs of violence, a struggle, nothing. Heart failure, that's it."

"Apparent heart failure. Let's wait until we get the pathologist's report. Then you and I will talk. Until then, I don't want you involved. It's family."

"She was my father's wife. It's not the same thing."

Malcolm was silent for a moment, presumably processing the import of her last comment. "Look, I don't want to get into the middle of anything personal. All I'm asking you, all I'm telling you, is that I sure as hell do not want to see your face in front of any cameras about this one." Then his tone softened. "Again, I'm really sorry. Please tell your father that I send my regrets. I'll get in touch with him myself in the next couple of days."

Frances replaced the receiver and surveyed her kitchen, the butter yellow walls, the spice rack that hung crooked, the square table covered in a green-and-white-checkered cloth, all that was familiar. She opened her beer and took a long sip. She needed to run a tub, add bubbles, and submerse her body, but even as she thought of this comfort, Malcolm's call haunted her. His vague reference to something suspicious was unusual for a man who was normally brutally honest and straightforward.

Frances had interviewed for her job with Malcolm at one of the lowest points in her life. She'd needed something concrete to make her decision to get out of the city irrevocable, to end any vestiges of her engagement. Pietro Benedetti would never follow her to the north fork of Long Island, to the acres upon acres of potato fields and vineyards, to the quiet, rural life. Malcolm must have sensed her anxiety because he hadn't asked a lot of questions. He hadn't explored, while others might have, the reasons for Frances's sudden departure from the Manhattan District Attorney's Office, nor had he asked why a young, single, talented woman wanted to live alone in Suffolk County. He also hadn't gone behind her back to talk to her father. He'd only wanted to know of her experience, her credentials. That was enough. He had given her the break she needed.

Since that day Malcolm had treated her well, promoting her to chief of the Financial Crimes Unit, the first woman ever to hold that position in the Suffolk County District Attorney's Office. Frances appreciated all he had done for her. In return she worked hard for him. He rarely interfered in her work and, as far as she knew, had always been candid with her.

So why was he being mysterious about Clio's death? Whom had he talked to? Apparent heart failure . . . The words echoed in Frances's mind. What wasn't he telling her? She tried to dismiss the thoughts. Maybe she had been a prosecutor too long. Or maybe not.

Sunday, July 5

$\mathcal{F}$rances hadn't slept more than a few fitful minutes all night. When she did manage to doze off, her dream left her more agitated than her insomnia. She had dreamed she was diving into the murky water of Lake Agawam, searching for Justin. She called his name and saw her bubbles float away from her face and disappear into the blackness, but there was no trace of her half-brother. Each time she came up for air, she saw her father, seated erect in his wheelchair, staring at the surface of the water. He showed no signs of noticing her. She dove under again and thrashed her arms to try to feel a piece of the sailboat or the softness of her brother's arm. She awoke, sweaty and disoriented with her fists clasping her quilt, her pillows on the floor, and her dogs staring at her in bewilderment.

Frances tried to read but couldn't concentrate on the pages in front of her. Lying beside the warm bodies of Felonious and Miss Demeanor, listening to the sounds of their unsynchronized breaths, she closed her eyes and prayed for rest, only to have the darkness filled with Clio's face. Something about Clio's mouth, the white teeth and painted lips frozen open in an oval, seemed evidence of a last gasp or an attempted shout. Had she been in pain? How quickly had death come?

Frances ran her fingers through the black fur of Felonious's soft coat. Clio hadn't been dead more than twelve hours before Malcolm had called. Why had he mentioned an investigation? What could he possibly have known in such a short period of time over a holiday? She wouldn't be able to find out for at least another day. The medical examiner's office was unfamiliar territory to a financial crimes prosecutor. Besides, any public servant at work on a Sunday would do his business as quickly as possible. He couldn't be expected to answer her call to the morgue.

Frances arose with the sun, made herself a pot of strong coffee, then returned to the gardening she had abandoned so hastily the previous day. She listened to the crickets and watched the early morning worms wriggling their way back into the soil. Nothing held her attention for long. By nine, showered and dressed, she found herself nestled into the cab of her red pickup truck on the way to Southampton. She drove straight to the Fair Lawn Country Club.

The same blond boy from the day before attended the entrance gate. This morning he was busy talking to a young woman with auburn hair and sunglasses, who was just leaving the club in a burgundy Jaguar convertible. Without removing his mirrored sunglasses, the attendant leaned his elbows on the driver's-side door and chatted with considerable animation. Thus engaged, he failed to notice Frances as she paused briefly and drove through.

Frances parked her truck by the service entrance.

The grass tennis courts were filled with players, not unusual for a beautiful summer Sunday morning. Frances walked up the steps onto the porch. A man sat alone, leaning back in a chair, legs stretched in front, ankles crossed. A canvas tennis cap covered his face. At the far end, four women sat together in a circle. On the table between them were cans of Diet Coke and tennis balls. One woman in a pink headband threw back her head and laughed a loud honk of a sound that pierced the relative quiet. Otherwise the porch was empty.

Tacked to the shingled side of the clubhouse were the summer tournament draws, a careful matrix of elimination with the list of top seeds in the upper-left-hand corner. Frances remembered that her father had made that list long ago for both singles and, with his partner, Jack Von Furst, doubles. "Canceled" had been written in red letters across the draw for the men's doubles. That had to be a historical first.

Frances opened the screen door to the right of the main entrance and stepped into the bar. Commentary from a newscast piped from the television mounted on a wall bracket in the corner. No one was around. Apparently the Sunday morning Bloody Mary crowd hadn't yet arrived.

Frances walked over to the bar and climbed up on a leather stool. She ran her fingers along the edge and felt the tightly spaced row of metal tacks that held the leather onto the circular cushion. The door behind the bar swung open, and a white-haired man in a green plaid vest and starched shirt came through from the kitchen.

"What can I get for you?" he asked.

Frances ordered a ginger ale and watched as he pushed a button to dispense the bubbly golden liquid into a tall glass. The bartender set the drink on a monogrammed paper napkin in front of her. Then he removed a pad of charge slips and a pencil from his vest pocket and looked up at her expectantly.

"Pratt, Richard Pratt," she said.

The man looked at Frances intently.

"I'm his daughter Frances."

"I'm real sorry about Mrs. Pratt," he said without hesitation.

"Thank you. That's very kind." Frances felt the awkwardness of her response.

The bartender continued to stare at her. She straightened up on the stool to correct her slouched posture.

"Weren't you here yesterday with the police?" he asked.

"Yes."

"I thought so." He nodded to himself.

"I'm an assistant district attorney with the Suffolk County District Attorney's Office. We assist the police in their investigations," she said, wondering if an explanation was actually owed.

"Well, I remember you because it struck me as unusual you know, to see a lady policeman. I hope you don't mind my saying so."

Frances smiled. She didn't bother to correct him. A

lawyer or a cop, he probably had the same view of women in either law enforcement profession.

"You say an investigation, huh? People are going to be pretty curious if it turns out to be something worth investigating. We've never had anyone die right here at the club before." He put his pad back in his vest pocket. Then he cleared a partially filled wineglass and a tumbler from the end of the bar and began to wash them. "Mrs. Pratt was a fine lady. Far as I could tell, she had a lot of friends here at Fair Lawn," he remarked.

Frances watched his small hands scrub the inside of the glasses with sudsy water, then rinse them under the tap. He worked fast. "Did you see Clio Pratt yesterday?" she asked.

"Nope," he said without looking up.

Frances took a large swig of her soda. The ice cubes rattled as she replaced the glass on the counter. "Thanks." She slid off the stool.

"She bought drinks, though," the bartender said. Frances stopped. He brought out a stack of charge slips from behind the bar and flipped through it. "I was looking through my slips last night, and I noticed this. Here . . . yes. Six drinks were charged to the Pratt account yesterday morning. Time on the chit says ten forty-one. Two Southsides—that's our specialty here—a Diet Coke, a Perrier water, and two Shirley Temples."

"Clio Pratt charged all that?"

"As I said, I don't remember seeing Mrs. Pratt myself. Someone else might have gotten the drinks. A guest, maybe, another member, I couldn't tell you. It was pretty busy here with the tournament going on. People coming in and out all morning. I fill the orders. People sign their own chits. It's really an honor system."

"You mean I could charge my drinks to another member?"

"Sure. Besides, people are always buying rounds for each other. We've never had a problem. No complaints. Our members can afford their own drinks, as well as a few extras, I'd imagine."

"It was a large order. Do you remember anything at all about filling it?"

"I'm sorry, I don't. There's really nothing that sticks in my mind." He furrowed his brow, concentrating. "I suppose it's possible that Mrs. Pratt was here, and that I just don't remember, but I'd be surprised. She was a nice lady, attractive, too. I usually remember those ones."

"Were people talking about Clio yesterday, after she died?"

"Oh sure. The place was crazy, at first, anyway. I heard some remarks, compliments of Mrs. Pratt, sympathies expressed for your father, what you might expect under the circumstances. I must say, though, my focus was one girl, I guess it was your sister, come to think of it, the one that found Mrs. Pratt. She was causing quite a scene, very upset she was, wailing. I gave her a drink, tried to calm her down. Then the paramedics arrived and took her away."

"How late were you here?"

"I left around five, but the place had been pretty much deserted for hours before that. I think some members hung around for a bit to see what was going on with the police, but most were pretty upset. They wanted to get out of here."

"Did you help clean up before you left?" Frances couldn't figure out exactly what information she was searching for. It just seemed natural to keep the questions flowing.

"I clean up the pub. The porch is done by the clubhouse crew, although some members throw their own stuff away. Porch drinks need to be in plastic."

"Were the drinks charged on the Pratt account in glass or plastic?"

"I couldn't tell you. The price is the same, so there's really no way to know. I generally ask, 'Glass or plastic,' but I don't make a note of the response."

"I appreciate your help. Look, if you remember anything else, or if you hear anything, can you call me?"

The bartender nodded. "By the way, my name's Arthur."

Frances wrote her office telephone number on a paper napkin and handed it to him. "Thanks, Arthur," she said, and walked out.

Frances could see Clio's silver Mercedes sedan parked in front of her father's house as she turned off Ox Pasture Road into the driveway. Someone must have brought it back yesterday, after Clio's body had been carted off to the morgue, the Fair Lawn Country Club emptied, and an extra luxury automobile was discovered still in the parking area.

The front door was ajar, and Frances walked in. A chandelier that hung from the double-height ceiling in the entryway was illuminated in spite of the ample natural light that streamed in through the windows. A silver tray piled with mail, a bouquet of several dozen white lilies in a crystal vase, and a small shopping bag covered part of the top of the ivory-inlaid circular table. Beyond, she could see the sunroom and, through the glass walls, the garden outside. Daylilies were in bloom.

Frances listened but could hear no sounds. She walked forward until she saw the fragments of a shadow, a distorted profile and torso reflected on the floor. Richard sat in his wheelchair, staring straight ahead. As she approached she could see that dark circles edged his deep-set eyes. In his lap he held a silver picture frame with a photograph of Clio in a wide-brimmed hat smiling and holding Justin, a pudgy toddler. Her azure eyes stared out from the blanket that covered Richard's knees.

"Dad . . ." Frances spoke quietly, not wanting to alarm him. He didn't move. "How are you?" she asked, realizing as she spoke the absurdity of her question to a man who had lost his wife less than twenty-four hours earlier.

"We need to discuss something." Richard's voice was flat. He spoke slowly, but his speech was difficult to decipher. "Clio's memorial service. You could help with the flowers."

"Of course," Frances said, somewhat startled by his request. His face evidenced exhaustion, a long night spent thinking about Clio and preparing for a proper burial.

He glanced toward the wicker chair beside him, and Frances took a seat. "Maybe you'll need notes," he said.

He lifted one hand and seemed to gesture in the direction of the telephone.

"I'll remember," Frances replied. Then, thinking better of it, she got up, walked toward where her father had indicated, and opened the drawer of a small table in the corner of the room. The inside was filled with sharpened pencils and pads engraved with "Clio and Richard." Frances removed a pad and waved it toward her father. The gesture felt awkward, and she quickly sat back down.

Several minutes passed without another word between them, and Frances wondered whether her father had become disoriented and forgotten she was there. She wasn't used to seeing him in the main part of the house anymore or, for that matter, being there herself. Her weekly visits to her father over the past year had transpired in "Richard's wing," as Clio referred to it. Now that distinction was unnecessary.

The bright sunroom where they sat was filled with white wicker furniture and oversize pillows covered in a green-and-yellow lattice fabric. Orchids in painted pots of varying sizes lined the perimeter of the room. Piled high on and underneath the painted coffee table were Clio's books on gardening, flowers, and flower arranging. By the door, a basket held clippers, cloth gloves, plant markers, and a frayed straw hat. Next to it was a pair of green rubber gardening clogs, awaiting Clio's feet. Frances realized why her father had gravitated here. Clio seemed present.

"What did you have in mind?" Frances asked softly.

"Clio was so fond of Hemerocallis." He paused, and his tongue seemed to hang suspended in his mouth.

Frances tried not to exhibit her surprise at her father's use of the formal name for daylilies. "I don't suppose they do well in arrangements," he continued.

"We could use other types of lilies, if that's what you want. Tiger are pretty. They're the orange ones with darker spots. Yellow calla are beautiful. Do you have any thoughts about color? That might be a good place to start." Frances tried to be helpful.

"For Justin, Clio wanted everything to be white. Different whites. White roses. Some cream, others the color of champagne."

"I remember," Frances said. Justin's memorial service had been unforgettable in more ways than the floral palette. Frances remembered all the boys and girls, Justin's friends and his friends' siblings, who filled St. Andrew's Dune Church, a small, wooden-beamed building nestled into the beach. This Episcopal church where the sounds of the ocean rolled into the chapel and sunlight spilled through the brightly colored stained-glass windows, was the site of virtually all the Southampton society baptisms, weddings, and funerals.

Frances remembered the tears, some sniffling, some crying loudly. For many of these children, she surmised, it was the first tragedy in their lives. Justin's death had robbed Richard and Clio of their only child and had robbed a whole generation of Southampton children of their naiveté. An accidental death, a disastrous sailing excursion, such a tragedy was not supposed to befall a healthy fourteen-year-old boy. In Frances's memory the entire episode had an air of unreality.

"Clio did it all herself. The arranging. She didn't trust

anyone else to do it right. She wanted bouquets all over the church, all over our house. Did you see Justin's room? No. Nobody did, but it was covered in hundreds of flowers, the bed, Justin's desk, covered in a canopy of roses."

"It sounds beautiful."

"An altar. It was her way of showing respect." Richard spoke to himself, conjuring up the memories of Clio's labors to honor their son. "That work helped her. There's nothing like work to help forget pain." Without looking down, he caressed the picture frame in his lap with bent fingers. "She loved flowers, the color, the texture, the perfume, but most of all she spoke of the miracle that they came from the soil, just grew up to surprise her. She was pleased that you loved flowers, too."

"My garden is nothing compared to hers."

"She told me once that it was the only thing she had been able to give to you." He spoke operosely, with heavy breaths between pairs of words. "As a child, you sat and watched her arrange flowers in a vase, or work in the garden. She told me many times how she explained things to you. She said it enabled you to share something with her that you didn't with your mother. Your mother was never a gardener, but I suppose you know that."

Frances did have vague memories of watching Clio assemble a pile of newly cut stems in a vase. Sometimes she used a metal frog to hold each stem in place. Other times she was able to balance the flowers against each other. That Clio had considered this time with Frances special came as a revelation. Frances's only recollection of any discourse between them was Clio's brief instruction not to touch the flowers. "The dirt on your palms will wilt the petals," she had said.

"I suppose Clio had a difficult time feeling close to you. You and Blair are so like your mother."

Frances didn't know quite how he meant this last remark and wondered if she should respond. Was the suggestion that Clio couldn't like them because they were their mother's daughters a justification for the way they had been treated? Perhaps she would never understand, but that excuse seemed irrational. In any event, Frances didn't want to explore the subject of her relationship with her stepmother, especially now, when there was no hope that anything would change. "Do you want white flowers for Clio as well?" Frances prompted, hoping to direct the conversation back to funeral preparations.

"I don't think she would think it appropriate. She had lived through too much." Richard turned his face away from Frances. She wondered if he was crying, but she couldn't tell. "Peach, pink, yellow, pale colors would be best. No orange, no purple. We don't like purple."

Frances noticed the "we." She wondered how long it took someone who had been part of a couple for so many years to begin to think as an individual again. It had been a struggle for her after her breakup with Pietro, and they had never married.

"Roses?"

"Yes."

"What about lilies?"

"Her lilies are here. They'll always be here. Even after I'm gone." He looked down at the photograph in his lap and ran his index finger over the glass, as if to wipe away a drop of spittle, or a tear, that might have marred the surface. "Have bills sent to the house. Blair will pay them."

Frances leaned forward slightly. "You've spoken to Blair?"

"She came last night. It was late, but I wasn't asleep. She brought Clio's car back from Fair Lawn."

"Was she alone?"

"She came in by herself, but someone waited outside. Lily could tell you who it was." Richard closed his eyes and swallowed. Frances could see his Adam's apple move up and down his thin throat. "Blair will be back later today. To take care of the checkbook. She's offered to help me get organized."

Frances recalled her conversation with Blair the previous evening. She had given no indication that she planned to visit their father late that night. In fact, she had said otherwise, that she would wait until the morning. What had made her change her mind?

"When is the memorial service?" Frances asked.

"On Wednesday morning. At the Dune Church. You know, it's easier to be the one to go than the one left behind," Richard said. "We both learned that when Justin died."

Richard's words hung in the air. Frances shifted in her seat. He seemed more comfortable with their silence than she, or perhaps he was simply consumed by his own thoughts. She looked down at her hands and tried to think about floral arrangements.

A freckled-faced girl with warm green eyes and a turned-up nose appeared, carrying a tray. Her pale pink uniform stretched tight across her ample bosom. The sun-room suddenly smelled of chicken broth and toast.

"You must be Frances," the girl said. Frances thought she recognized an Irish accent. "I'm Mary. I fill in for Lily. It's her day off today, but she won't be taking it. She's just gone for a bit on some errands. We're both awful sorry about Mrs. Pratt." As she spoke, she held the tray in one hand while, with the other, she opened a small folding table in front of Richard. "Would you care for something? There's plenty."

"No, thank you," Frances said.

Mary placed the tray in front of Richard, then checked the brakes on his wheelchair. She ran her finger along his forehead, gently pushing a hair out of his eye, then leaned over him and added, "Shall I stay?"

Richard didn't respond audibly but shifted his head toward the door.

"If you change your mind about lunch, then, you give me a holler," Mary said to Frances. She turned and walked out, her rubber heels squeaking on the marble floor.

Richard ignored the food in front of him: cubes of potatoes and broccoli florets afloat in yellow broth, neatly cut and buttered rectangles of toast, thin slices of cheese. Frances watched the steam rise from the porcelain bowl.

"Why didn't you marry Pietro?" Richard asked.

The question punched Frances, and for a moment she struggled to catch her breath. After seven years she wasn't prepared to explain why she had called off her engagement to Pietro. The passage of time had dulled the intensity of her emotions, making the ostensible reason for their breakup—that Pietro wanted her to convert to Catholicism—now seem insignificant. Frances hadn't had a religious upbringing, never attended church and rarely gave religion of any kind a second thought. Pietro's benign request should have been treated as what it was: an effort to have her share something that was a crucial component of his family life; but as the months wore on and their nuptials approached, what had seemed relatively simple evolved into an insurmountable barrier. She had felt betrayed. That he made this demand to control her, that he placed conditions on their marriage, that he insisted that she become something she was not, these were the issues that had torn them apart.

"It was a long time ago," she said finally.

"You never told me why."

You never asked, she wanted to reply, but she stopped herself. "We weren't well suited." Frances hoped to dismiss the conversation with an easy answer.

"Was he upset you weren't Catholic?"

She didn't have the emotional energy to figure out how her father knew or why he had decided to wait until the day after Clio's death to ask her about it.

"Pietro alluded several times to something that made me assume religion was the reason," Richard mumbled in response to her silence. "I just hope he never hurt you. I never want you or Blair to be hurt."

That he had chosen this moment to display paternal concern struck her as ironic. How many times, over the years, had she wondered whether her father had ever given a thought to her well-being? He had never even bothered to explain why he allowed Clio's mistreatment of his daughters. Frances had been left to imagine how he felt about their familial situation. As a child in search of answers, she had invented a conversation with her father. Now she allowed herself to remember the imagined dialogue.

I want you to know, Frances, that just because I've remarried, it doesn't mean I've forgotten about my family, about you and Blair.

But it seems that way.

I know it must, but I want to change that. This is your home. You are always welcome here. I want you to feel safe.

But why does Clio hate us?

She doesn't hate you. Being a stepmother is hard. She's not your mother, but she feels constantly compared, and that can be threatening. It threatens her that I had a bond with your mother that produced you two girls.

What have we done wrong?

I'm not sure I can make you understand, but perhaps one day, if you fall in love with someone who's been married before, you'll know how Clio feels. You must realize that people aren't perfect, and if they do things that are less than considerate, it doesn't mean they're bad.

You don't see how she is.

If I haven't seen, that's my fault, and I'm sorry. I should have paid better attention. Clio and I spoke about the situation, and it won't continue. She's sorry she hasn't been nicer. Things will be different, I promise. Come here, sweet Fanny. Let me hug you. You must understand how truly sorry I am.

She never had the courage to challenge her father, and

this dialogue remained a fantasy. Unlike her sister, Blair, who was better able to demand her father's attentions, Frances had forged a relationship with him characterized by formalized respect and aloof fondness. She admired her father, but they had never been close.

"Did Clio have any health problems?" She wanted to change the subject, but her voice sounded more timid than she expected.

He shook his head.

"Was she taking any medication?"

"She was a strong woman, although nobody can be that strong."

"What do you mean?"

"She had experienced too much pain, been forced to live with too many fears. My stroke, my condition, was the last straw. She wasn't prepared to be prematurely old."

Frances stopped herself from asking anything further when she noticed that her father's body had begun to twitch spasmodically. His shoulders shook slightly. Then his elbows and hands did, too, as the impact of his emotions worked its way down his frail body. He grasped the armrests of his wheelchair, as if to steady himself. Frances wondered whether she should call for Mary but decided against it. He was entitled to his grief without professional intervention.

Frances wished she could understand her father's relationship to Clio, the intensity of their bond, the mysterious place that two people share where their identities become so intermingled that they truly can think and act as one. She wished that she could put aside the distance she felt and actually empathize with his loss. Instead she felt empty.

After what seemed an interminable time, Richard spoke again. "Marriage is a precious gift that I wish you could have."

"You needn't worry, Daddy. It's not what I want," she lied. Then she leaned toward him and, trying to sound efficient, remarked, "I'd better get in touch with the florist. We don't have much time."

"It should have been me," Richard said without looking at her.

Frances didn't respond. As usual, her father was right.

Rocking back and forth in a creaky chair, Frances watched the flames flicker in the half dozen mismatched kerosene lamps placed randomly around the porch. The afternoon had disappeared in a blur of activity: a visit to St. Andrew's Dune Church to see how many arrangements were needed, a meeting with the minister to ensure there were no pastoral restrictions on types of flowers, or size of bouquet, then several discussions with area florists to see what could be designed on relatively short notice. Throughout the day Frances felt oddly disconnected, a planner in charge of decorations with no particular attachment or investment in the event, but by the end of the afternoon her orders had been executed successfully. Then she walked the beach in an effort to make the exhaustion in her body equal to that in her mind.

Now, as the chair's gentle movement lulled her, Frances tried to recall times spent alone with Clio over the years. Such memories were few—a trip to Bloomingdale's one Saturday afternoon to find what Clio called "appropriate school shoes," leather Oxfords with tight laces; several theater matinees, *Grease, The King and I,* where Frances sat next to an empty seat because her father had an unexpected meeting or important conference call that prevented his attendance. She couldn't conjure up any of the flower arranging scenes that apparently held some significance to Clio.

"You're going to rock that chair right off its rockers," Aurelia said as she came out onto the porch. She held a plate piled high with cheese, crackers, olives, slivers of prosciutto, and roasted peppers and extended it toward Frances. "Here, have a little antipasto."

"No thanks." Frances looked up at her mother and thought she caught disappointment drift across her face.

"What about something to drink?"

"I'd love a glass of wine if you're offering."

Aurelia smiled rows of large white teeth. She set the plate on the porch, wiped her hands on the checkered apron tied over her loose denim dress, and disappeared back into the house. Frances could hear her humming, then the sound of a cork unplugged. She returned with two filled glasses.

"I suppose it's inappropriate to make a toast under the circumstances." Aurelia sat in a straight-backed chair next to Frances. "But we might raise a glass to Clio. May she rest in peace." She took a sip of her wine. "How's your father holding up?"

"I can't tell."

"Weren't you there for most of the day?"

"He's focused on preparations for the memorial service, but that's probably just a distraction. Clio's death has also brought back memories of Justin. It's all so sad for him."

"Do you know what he'll do?" Aurelia asked.

"Do?" Frances wasn't sure she understood. Her father was physically and emotionally debilitated. She doubted he had any plans to do anything at all except try to survive another day.

"Will he stay in the house, I mean?"

Frances closed her eyes and rocked several times before answering. "I'm sure. His memories are there. It's his home."

"I have memories of that house, too."

Frances stared at her mother. She had forgotten that the house on Ox Pasture Road had originally been theirs, a home that Aurelia and Richard had picked out together early in their marriage before she or her sister was born. No amount of renovation or redecoration could change the simple fact that Aurelia had been there first.

Frances tried to read the thoughts passing through her mother's mind, but Aurelia's expression provided no clues. She had been a handsome woman, but her bronzed face was wrinkled by the sun and age. Her graying hair had thinned, and her eyes seemed smaller and deeper set in her face than Frances remembered. Her ample hips spilled over the sides of the small chair, and her ankles looked thick in her thin-soled red sneakers. Frances noted with some sadness that she had inherited this same body, destined to pass ungracefully into middle age.

"Do they know why she died?" Aurelia asked.

"Apparent heart failure. The coroner hasn't issued a report, though."

"Do you believe it?"

Frances twisted in her seat. Her mother appeared to be focused on the meniscus of Pinot Grigio in her glass. "Why shouldn't I?"

"I wouldn't know. I just was wondering whether you believed it was a natural death, that's all." Aurelia smiled. "I bet you have a hunch one way or the other."

"Dad says Clio was in excellent health. Her death is certainly surprising."

"Would he know how healthy she really was?"

"I assume so."

"Be careful about what assumptions you make in life," Aurelia said matter-of-factly.

Frances felt unnerved. First Malcolm, now her mother. It seemed that she was surrounded by people with suspicions about Clio's death. She rubbed her eyes, realizing how exhausted she was.

"Did Dad ever talk to you about Clio?" Frances asked.

Aurelia chuckled. "Not in years." She took a large sip of wine and swirled it in her mouth before swallowing. "When they first met, he mentioned it. He never said much about her specifically, only that she was relatively young, that he respected her, and that he thought he might like to see a bit more of her. She was a friend of Jack Von Furst's, if my memory serves me. He didn't mention her again until he decided he wanted to marry her. He called to find out how I felt."

"He did?"

"He certainly didn't have to. We had been divorced for

quite a while. He was free to do as he pleased, but, at the time, he seemed genuinely concerned with my feelings."

"What did you say?"

"What you might expect. I was happy that he had found someone to make him happy. I certainly couldn't."

"So that was it? You gave him your blessing."

"I wanted him to make a life for himself. Our marriage hadn't worked, but that wasn't to say he couldn't make a good husband."

"Did you ever talk about her again?"

"Your father and I had a lot less interaction after he re-married. Occasionally, issues arose with you and your sister, whether to send you to sleep-away camp, whether you should stay in New York for high school, that sort of thing, but we seldom disagreed. Besides, both of us were inclined to give huge deference to what you girls wanted to do, so you might say there was little parental interference. Several times I tried to tell him how you and Blair felt about Clio, to talk about how she treated the two of you, but he wouldn't discuss it."

"You did? Why?"

"How could I not? I saw how upset she made you. Remember the time she insisted that you change your clothes before some dance? She was embarrassed that you wore stripes with checks, or stripes and flowers, I can't remember the details, but you called me, upset. She humiliated you. Frankly, it was none of Clio's business what you wore, and I told your father so. You were de-veloping your own style."

Frances remembered the episode well, how she had stood in front of the mirror studying her carefully chosen outfit, a navy-and-white-striped T-shirt and pale blue corduroys with red flowers on them. She had been as anxious about the dance, and her appearance, as any slightly chubby thirteen-year-old with budding breasts could possibly be, and she had changed her clothes a dozen times before settling on something that pleased her. Then, without knocking, Clio had come into her room. "You may not leave this house dressed like that. Don't you see you clash? You look ridiculous," she'd said. Frances had held back her tears only long enough for Clio to leave the room. She hadn't changed, but she hadn't gone to the dance, either.

"Of course, my information came from you and Blair, the stories you told me, the complaints you had," Aurelia continued. "Richard told me everything was fine."

"I never had the courage to say anything." Frances felt her chest constrict. How many times over the years had she waged an internal battle over whether to stand up to her stepmother and risk the consequent wrath or swallow her own desires and remain the obedient daughter? It seemed like the dilemma that defined her childhood. Perhaps, Frances thought, that's why she ended up at law school. She couldn't defend herself, but she could make a career out of standing up for others.

"It was a lot harder for you to speak up than it was for me. I had nothing at stake in the relationship with your father by the time Clio came along. You did. I should have been more insistent with him, but he didn't want to hear. I gave up pretty quickly."

Frances didn't respond. She never expected anyone to

come to her rescue and was touched that her mother had tried, even if her efforts had been unsuccessful.

Aurelia reached over and held on to Frances's arm. "I'm sorry for your father's loss. Being old and infirm is not a particularly nice way to spend your golden years, but I'm more sorry for what that witch of a woman did to my girls." She leaned over and kissed Frances on the cheek. "I'll fix us some dinner," she said, standing up.

"Do you need help?" Frances asked.

Aurelia shook her head and moved toward the screen door. Just before entering, she turned back to look at Frances. "I'm awful to speak poorly of the dead. Perhaps I shouldn't judge someone else's relationship," she said with just a hint of sarcasm.

*S*cott Bendleton, known to most members of the criminal bar as "Bender," a small, thin man in a navy blue double-breasted suit with oversize brass buttons, was just finishing his plea for leniency on behalf of the defendant, William Howard Avery III. Frances, stuck in her chair only ten feet away from his booming voice, resented his long-windedness, typical of lawyers who were paid by the hour. As far as she could discern, Bender's pitch was unoriginal: despite the jury's finding that his client was guilty of larceny, Avery wasn't a bad guy. He had meant to invest the victims' money wisely and provide them with a substantial return. He hadn't meant to use it to purchase a new Range Rover, a condominium in Boca Raton, or a twenty-five-foot Grady White motorboat with twin 150-horsepower engines. The Suffolk County prosecutor had been overzealous in coming after this quiet, well-liked man, a vestry member of the Saint Francis Episcopal Church, the dutiful husband of Sissy Avery, who volunteered at the local chapter of the Red Cross twice a week, and the father of two adopted boys and a little girl with special educational needs. Bender seemed to think that because his client was such an upstanding citizen, the court should excuse his embezzlement of nearly half a million dollars.

"My friend here . . ." Bender paused for dramatic effect and touched his client's right shoulder as he looked up at the judge. "Bill Avery has suffered more than you'll ever know, Your Honor, more than any punishment our fine system of jurisprudence could ever mete out. He's received more punishment than any period of incarceration could ever signify. He's suffered the shame of his family, of his community, of his colleagues at Mitchell and Avery Investment Advisors, and of his fellow parishioners at Saint Francis. He'll have to explain to his sons what has happened. He'll have to live with this, this . . ." Bender cast his eyes upward, as if searching the heavens for assistance. "I implore you, Your Honor, to let him return to his family and begin to put this horrible episode behind him."

Bender's gaze hung for a moment on Judge Frank Cohen, who wrote something on the pad in front of him and then turned to Frances. "I'll hear from the assistant district attorney. Ms. Pratt," he prompted her.

Frances rose and buttoned the front of her dark green gabardine jacket. She felt the pull of the fabric in back and, for a moment, considered undoing the front button. No, she decided. Too much fidgeting with her attire might make the judge think she was nervous, which she was, but she wouldn't give Judge Cohen, or Bender, for that matter, the satisfaction of seeing into her soul.

Frances looked down at the notes in front of her, the sum total of her labors from the night before. Pushing images of Clio's body from her mind, she had forced herself to concentrate. The Avery prosecution was important, too. The criminal process marched on despite a death in the Pratt family.

Even without the distractions, though, Frances's argument was difficult to fashion because she knew almost nothing about the middle-aged man in the black robe who now stared down from his perch in the front of the courtroom. Judge Cohen was relatively new to the bench and hadn't come from the criminal bar. A politically connected New York corporate lawyer with a substantial home on the beach in Westhampton, he apparently had decided to spend his remaining work years presiding over a courtroom in Suffolk County. Rumor had it that Judge Cohen was liberal, even though he had run on a Republican ticket. If so, Frances could only hope that, while he may be lenient toward defendants convicted of crimes of poverty—drugs, robbery, domestic abuse, crimes that arose out of addictions and lack of opportunities—he would have little sympathy with a relatively affluent defendant who had simply gotten greedy.

The problem Frances perceived was that Avery could have been one of Judge Cohen's own corporate clients. He looked the part. Avery's black hair was parted on the right side and held in place by a slick of goo that emanated a spicy, clean odor. He wore a khaki suit and striped shirt and tie, held his collar in place with a gold tie pin, and kept his hands clasped together in front of him as though he still wore handcuffs, which the bailiff had removed more than an hour ago. Avery's brown eyes were rimmed in red and seemed shrunken in his round, blotched face. Frances had to admit that he did look genuinely sad.

Appearances aside, jail time for defendants of so-called white-collar crimes, a phrase Frances had never really understood, was hard to come by. The defendant had no criminal record; the amount of money stolen was small by financial crimes standards, and what Bender said was true: Avery had the trappings of being a good guy. But jail time was warranted, Frances had no doubt. She just had to remind the court of the victims, an elderly couple from Avery's own congregation who had entrusted him with their life savings. How was this any different from sticking his hand in the offering plate and making off with cash? Mary Lou and Roger Horton, who had spent every day of the trial in the front row of the courtroom, were completely wiped out. These people would not be able to put the "horrible episode" behind them. They had to live with the consequences immediately and forever. At seventy-eight years old Mary Lou was going back to work, scooping cookie dough ice cream for $6 an hour at the Candy Kitchen because William Howard Avery III had absconded with her retirement fund.

Frances began. "I'm not going to waste the court's time. Your Honor presided over a lengthy jury trial and heard all the facts, including the defendant's own self-serving testimony, which, I might point out, the jurors obviously disbelieved. Mr. Bendleton argues that his client's been punished enough. I ask you, how much is enough? Mr. Avery had a prosperous investment business. He didn't need money. He used his contacts in his community and his church to lure Mary Lou and Roger Horton into his carefully planned scheme. These people had worked and saved for more than forty years so that they could enjoy a peaceful, comfortable retirement. Then he stole their money. They trusted him to act on their behalf, and he betrayed that trust for personal profit. He spent their life savings on luxuries for himself. It is the coldest, most calculating type of greed imaginable. Any shame he has suffered is nothing compared to the hardship and suffering he has inflicted on the victims in this case." Frances turned toward the back of the courtroom. She wanted the judge to focus on the two wrinkled faces huddled together, the human dimension of her prosecution.

"For this reason, Your Honor, the people request that the defendant be sentenced to a two-year period of incarceration and ordered to make restitution in the amount of $517,386."

Bender was on his feet. "Your Honor, my client—"

Judge Cohen cut him off. "Sit down, Mr. Bendleton. You've had your turn."

Then he turned to Frances. "How are you contemplating restitution if the defendant is in jail?"

"The defendant has substantial assets, including the boat that was purchased with money stolen from the Hortons, the house in Riverhead where he and his family live, and, I believe, he still owns the condominium in Florida."

"The bank owns it. There were foreclosure proceedings several weeks ago." This time Bender spoke without rising.

"The point is," Frances continued, "this defendant is not without means. I'm sure he's been able to pay significant sums for the first-rate representation he's received." Frances smiled at Bender, pleased with her own attempt at sarcastic humor. "He should be ordered to make restitution. If he liquidates his assets and still has a shortfall, he can serve an additional six months on a suspended sentence to make up the remainder, but the restitution order should be entered as a condition of his probation. These people deserve to get their money back."

Judge Cohen sat silent for a moment. Frances was unsure whether to continue or to give him time to think. As she debated how to proceed, he spoke. "Ms. Pratt, while I understand your concern, and I, too, am sorry for what the victims have been through, this court is not in the collections business. The Hortons are entitled to bring a civil suit, obtain a judgment, attach assets, and use any other legitimate means at their disposal to get their money back. In fact, I would strongly urge them to do so. But, I repeat, that is not the business of the criminal courts."

"Recouping the money they are owed will be small recompense for the hardship these people have suffered. Your Honor, please don't make them go to the additional expense and agony of a civil suit. It's within your power to order restitution along with any sentence you may impose."

"There is a limit to what I'm willing to do. Mr. Avery has a family. Besides, if Mr. Bendleton's account of his client's finances is accurate, you can't get blood from a stone."

"Your Honor—"

"I am making my ruling. The defendant is sentenced to one year suspended for two and ordered to pay a fine of ten thousand dollars. Mr. Bendleton, I expect payment by Mr. Avery no later than close of business tomorrow. You may make arrangements with the probation department."

Before Frances could interject a further word, the court officer announced, "All rise." Judge Cohen stepped down from the bench and disappeared into his private chambers through a door at the back of the courtroom.

A year suspended. Frances stood perfectly still. Not a day in jail. Not even the money he stole returned. Avery would be on probation for two years, free to do as he pleased. That was it. Basically, his $500,000 theft cost him only $10,000, plus Bender's fee. Easy money. The investigation and prosecution had cost the state of New York significantly more than that between overtime for the investigators, grand jury fees, and time spent by Frances, plus the court expenses incurred from a two-week jury trial. This was the system.

Frances couldn't bear to move. She couldn't face the Hortons' inquisitive expressions as they looked to her to explain what kind of justice they had received.

Frances listened to the shuffling of feet and the low murmur of voices as the spectators filed out of the courtroom. She heard Avery thanking Bender, and Bender offering to buy his client lunch. Sissy Avery squealed something in delight, presumably, as she threw her arms around her husband's neck. She would be able to keep the diamond pendant purchased with the Hortons' hard-earned cash. The little Averys were probably there, too, hugging Dad and praising Bender for saving their father. They could all go home together and ride around in their fancy motorboat without a care in the world. It made Frances sick.

"Miss Pratt?" She heard the unmistakable voice of Roger Horton close behind her. She turned to see him and his wife standing a few feet from her, their eyes desperate for an explanation. They were dressed impeccably. It was ironic that the victims seemed to respect the majesty of the legal system. Mary Lou's white hair was enclosed in a net so that it didn't stir, although her head trembled slightly. She dabbed at her eyes with a pale blue handkerchief held between gloved hands. Roger had one arm around his wife's waist and supported himself with the other by resting it on the bar that separated the counsel tables from the public seats.

"What happened?" he asked.

"Will he pay us back?" Mary Lou's voice was high-pitched but soft.

Frances shook her head.

"Why not? The jury found him guilty."

Frances took a deep breath and exhaled slowly. "Yes." The words felt like rubber cement on the roof of her mouth. "The jury did find that Mr. Avery stole your money. Unfortunately, though, the judge didn't want to send the defendant to jail. He didn't even order Avery to give you back your money."

Both Mary Lou and Roger had expressions on their faces that Frances couldn't read. Did they not understand or, like her, were they shocked by the unfairness of what had just transpired?

"Judges in state court have discretion over how to punish defendants. We talked about that before the trial ever began. Judge Cohen apparently felt that a fine and a period of probation was sufficient punishment. I can't lie to you. It's a terrible outcome. I thought, given how well the trial went, that we would get a better result. I don't know why this happened."

"What did the judge mean by a year suspended?" Mr. Horton had been listening closely to the precise words of Judge Cohen.

"With a suspended sentence, if Avery does anything to violate the conditions of his probation, his sentence, in effect, becomes 'unsuspended' and he goes to jail for a year. But since there are no special conditions of probation, he simply has to report to his probation officer and stay out of trouble—not socialize with known felons, not commit a felony himself, all things that will be pretty easy for Avery to do." Frances looked at the Hortons, realizing that her explanation was futile. The Hortons wanted their money back, and they wanted Avery punished. They had gotten neither, and there was nothing more that Frances could do. "Judge Cohen recommended that you file a civil lawsuit. That's something you may want to consider."

"But we haven't any money to pay for a lawyer. As it is, we're just managing on our Social Security and the bit that I earn at the Candy Kitchen. If Roger's arthritis were better, perhaps—"

"You might be able to find someone who'd be willing to represent you on a contingent fee, meaning that you'd only have to pay your lawyer when you had a recovery. The criminal conviction will make the civil suit very easy. I can get you some recommendations for good civil lawyers." Nausea washed over Frances as she spoke. Assuming a contingent fee lawyer could recover most of the money from Avery, it would still end up costing the Hortons one-third, more than $150,000, fifteen times what Avery's theft cost him.

"How long will that take?" Roger Horton said.

"I don't know." Frances couldn't bring herself to tell them that it could be years before they saw any money. The civil docket was jammed. Even if the Hortons got a quick judgment against Avery, they would still have to attach assets, force a sale. They could lose additional time if they got bogged down in an appeal. The morass was too hard to explain. "I'm sorry. I truly am. I wish the outcome had been different." Frances turned away, not wanting the Hortons to see the tears that welled in her eyes. They had counted on her to help them and she had failed. Blaming it on the system was a feeble justification for her inability to deliver a favorable result.

Frances cleared her throat. "Let me see what I can find out for you about contingent fee lawyers. There's also the possibility that I can get you some money from the Victims Assistance Program. It's an organization that generally compensates only victims of violent crime, but maybe there can be an accommodation in your case. Why don't we talk tomorrow." To steady her nerves, she focused on gathering up her papers.

"What time tomorrow will you know?" Roger Horton asked.

"As early as possible. I'll call you at home. I promise." Frances stuffed her file back into her briefcase and walked quickly out of the courtroom.

Frances wished there were a back entrance to her office, a way to avoid the crowd of colleagues eager to express condolences, inquire about details, and otherwise involve themselves in the death of her stepmother. An early arrival at the office of District Attorney Malcolm Morris would have provided the opportunity to slip in unnoticed, but by ten o'clock the rumor mill had worked its wonders. Now the litany of sympathetic phrases showered forth.

"Thank you. I appreciate your support," she mumbled to a group of assistant district attorneys gathered in the hall as she walked briskly past. She rounded the corner, leaving the group behind, and turned into the office of Special Agent Robert Burke.

"Hey, Meaty," Frances said as she entered the small, windowless room.

Meaty sat at a metal desk, the newspaper spread out in front of him. A jelly doughnut, as well as a partially eaten cream one covered in powdered sugar, lay within arm's reach on a piece of waxed paper. In one hand Meaty held a paper cup of coffee. He took a sip and looked up. Frances could hear him swallow.

"Have you seen the ME's report?" she asked.

"Only a preliminary."

"And?"

"Have a seat." Meaty indicated a vinyl armchair across from him.

Frances cleared a stack of papers off the cushion, added it to similar piles on the floor, and settled herself facing Meaty.

"Want some?" Meaty gestured toward the jelly doughnut.

"No thanks."

Meaty licked the ends of his thick fingers, then picked up a pair of half-glasses and positioned them on his nose. From the top drawer of his desk he removed a single sheet of paper and scanned the page, mumbling aloud. "Caucasian female, age fifty-one, height five feet nine inches, weight one hundred nineteen pounds. No lacerations or abrasions. No signs of any injury or trauma. Probable cause of death is acute cardiac arrhythmia. Here we go . . ." He paused, then continued in a loud, clear voice. "Toxicology screen evidenced approximately eight hundred milligrams of Dexedrine and traces of phenelzine. That's what got me thinking."

Frances knew that Meaty had considerable medical expertise in part from years on the job, in part because his wife had been an emergency room nurse for three decades. She waited for him to translate.

"Dexedrine is an amphetamine. It's most common

nonprescription use is as an appetite suppressant. It's the key ingredient in a lot of diet pills."

Clio always had been thin. She appeared to have tremendous control over what she ate and discipline in the regularity of her exercise. "Clio had nothing to lose," Frances thought out loud.

"The amount in her system was about ten times the recommended dosage for weight loss."

"What was the other drug you mentioned?" Frances asked.

"Nardil's the brand name for phenelzine. It's what's called a monoamine oxidase inhibitor, a class of drugs prescribed for certain kinds of mental illness, serious anxiety or panic disorders, social phobias, especially hypochondria."

"What kind of anxiety disorders?"

"Well, there's all kinds. Agoraphobia, where a person is afraid of crowds, obsessive-compulsive disorder, where a person does things over and over, checking the locks on doors, that sort of thing, to ward off perceived dangers. Phenelzine's also used to treat post-traumatic stress disorder and, as I said, hypochondria, a debilitating fear of serious disease. There's dozens of these anxiety disorder classifications. The shrinks are all over human behavior, labeling and prescribing."

"I had no idea," Frances said. She suspected there was a lot about Clio that she didn't know.

"As the ME tells it," Meaty continued, "monoamine oxidase inhibitors like phenelzine are dangerous, really dangerous. You can't mix them with anything. No narcotics or alcohol, especially red wine. There's also a lot of dietary restrictions—no cheese, no pickled herring, no marmot, not that anyone eats that anyway. Presumably a shrink of some sort prescribed it, given the small level, which is consistent with a range for therapeutic use. We'll find out. She must have used a pharmacy in Southampton. There can't be that many, and it's a pretty unusual drug." Meaty paused for a moment and rubbed his neck. "I have to think that Clio would have been told over and over again about the prohibitions, the things she could and couldn't do if she was taking phenelzine. The manufacturer's warning labels are serious, too. Any doctor, any pharmacist, would have made sure she understood exactly what she was getting into."

"But she might not have asked her doctor about interaction with diet pills. Looking at her, you would have no reason to think she took them. Her doctor might not have thought to mention it."

"Perhaps," he said, although Frances could tell by the look on his face that he found such a scenario implausible. "The amphetamines alone could have killed her, made her heart race so fast and so irregularly that it gave out. In combination with phenelzine, death was certain, probably very fast." Meaty removed his glasses and ran his fingers through his thick, graying hair. Frances knew what was coming next. "The medical examiner's report isn't final, I understand that, but I think we're looking at a homicide. The ME does, too, given the mix. The combination of drugs was too potent, too lethal, to have been ingested by accident. It's either a homicide . . ." He paused and looked at Frances. "Or a suicide."

"Clio doesn't strike me as the type."

"You would know almost as well as anyone." Meaty rested his elbows on his desk and leaned toward her. "I happen to agree. The scene doesn't fit a suicide. A healthy woman finishes a tennis game at roughly ten-thirty, then kills herself in a toilet stall shortly thereafter. No note, no nothing."

Frances nodded in agreement. Clio had been far too private a person to have wanted such a spectacle for her death.

"I've advised Malcolm to treat this as a homicide."

"Is he going to?"

"Yeah. He's having a press conference at eleven."

Frances glanced at her watch. Malcolm's public announcement, designed to make the noontime news, was less than half an hour away.

"Has he assigned the case yet?"

"I'll be heading up the investigative end. Perry Cogswell is the ADA."

Frances sat back in her chair, folded her hands in her lap, and sighed. Of the more than thirty assistant district attorneys in Malcolm's office, Perry Cogswell was the one Frances most despised. He had been hired less than three years earlier, but his ambition and sycophancy had propelled a meteoric rise to chief of the Violent Crimes Unit. He never tired of boasting to her that violent crime—homicides, rapes, assaults—was the stuff of real prosecutors, not the paper trails she pursued. "Where's the excitement in reviewing canceled checks and bank statements?" he had said on more than one occasion.

"I'm sorry," Meaty said. "I wish it were otherwise. I truly do."

"I know," Frances replied, even as she felt a pang of betrayal.

"You know I'll fill you in on everything I can."

"Yeah." She tried to force a smile.

Frances looked intently at his round face, sunken eyes, and dimpled cheeks. His retirement from state government was only a year away. With a second pension to supplement his federal one, he could look forward to a comfortable old age with his wife and their granddaughter. Meaty was pragmatic. Frances knew he wasn't about to jeopardize his plans for her. Any information he gave her would have to be done quietly.

"Is any Crime Scene information back yet?" Frances asked.

Meaty had consumed his jelly doughnut in the brief interlude of silence. He wiped his hands on the waxed paper. "Some stuff was gathered, but I doubt any tests have been run. Saturday this didn't look like a murder, and isn't Sunday the day of rest?" Meaty smiled. "I was surprised the ME's preliminary report was back this morning." He looked up expectantly, opened his mouth again as if to speak, but said nothing.

"What does Malcolm know?"

"He called me on Saturday night, and I gave him a brief overview, although there wasn't much to report. The ME sent him a copy of this report yesterday. Last night I advised him to open a homicide case. Otherwise, I don't know who he's talked to."

Frances's own conversation with Malcolm the evening of Clio's death was still fresh in her mind, but she decided not to discuss it. Not now. The thought unsettled her. Although she didn't keep secrets from Meaty, their relationship was no doubt headed for change. "Can I get copies of all the witness statements?"

"I knew you'd ask." Meaty removed a yellow envelope sealed with a metal clasp from his desk drawer and handed it to her. "Here's everything we've got. Copies of all the statements and information taken by Detective Kelly and his team, the paramedics' report, even my notes from July Fourth."

"Thanks," she said, knowing that they both knew he shouldn't be giving her the information.

Meaty smiled again. "Hang in there, kiddo."

Frances returned to her office quickly, shut the door behind her, and leaned back against the wall for balance. She scanned the familiar sight: a metal desk with two folders that she had left out on Friday; a leather pencil holder stuffed with pens, scissors, pencils, and a curled Crazy Straw that Meaty had given her for her birthday the year before; a stack of legal pads; a single photograph of Felonious and Miss Demeanor in a maple frame; and a mahogany placard she had received for her work on the federal-state joint task force on public corruption. Against one wall, a metal bookcase overflowed with legal treatises on various components of criminal law, several versions of the *Prosecutor's Handbook,* notebooks on sentencing, and a directory of resource agencies for victims of crime. Her files were stacked against the opposite wall. The file cabinet she had requisitioned nearly five years ago had yet to arrive.

Although her office was exactly as she had left it Friday, and virtually every other night before that, it felt different today, as if she had stumbled upon a largely forgotten scene from her past with which she needed to become reacquainted. The partial disarray, the papers that evidenced hours of investigation, research, and trial preparation, seemed foreign. Frances walked around her desk, fingering the papers, the wrinkled files, the drawer pulls. Then she dropped Meaty's envelope on her desk, collapsed into her chair, and hugged her knees to her chest.

She remembered the last time she'd seen Clio alive: an opening at the Devlin Gallery. Clio had come alone. In front of a charcoal drawing of a dead bird, they'd spoken briefly, exchanging praise for all that Blair and Jake had done to build their business. It had been an awkward conversation filled with pregnant pauses and forced smiles. Eager to escape the second-rate art crowd, Clio had finally excused herself. Frances had followed her out and watched her climb into a black limousine. The capped chauffeur had shut the door behind her.

That had been nearly three months earlier, a literal lifetime ago. Now Frances was left to wonder who in the world hated Clio enough to actually kill her.

The pungent smell of bottled air freshener filled the press room for the Suffolk County District Attorney's Office. As Frances moved through the crowd, trying to find free space, her eyes burned with aerosol fragrance. She could feel a bead of sweat run between her breasts and down her belly. Her gabardine skirt clung with moisture to her thighs. She settled in a corner by the window and crossed her arms in front of her to prevent them from touching any of the people standing just inches away.

Malcolm Morris's media staff certainly had done their advance work. The room was packed with reporters, television and radio crews, and area law enforcement, many in uniform. Malcolm stood at a wooden podium, reviewing his prepared remarks as the crowd settled. He looked handsome in a double-breasted suit, a crisp white shirt, and a red tie anchored with a gold clip that caught the light. Frances watched his lips purse and his forehead wrinkle, then relax. He appeared to be practicing appropriate looks of gravity. Then he raised his head, focused his eyes directly into a camera for the ABC affiliate station, and began to speak.

"As you already know, Clio Henshaw Pratt, a fifty-one-year-old resident of Southampton and the wife of financier Richard Pratt, was found dead at a private tennis club over the weekend. Based on evidence gathered by this office in coordination with local police, it is now apparent that Mrs. Pratt's death was, in fact, a homicide. I cannot discuss details of this investigation, but I can say that everything possible is being done, and will be done, to apprehend and prosecute this vicious killer. My personal condolences are extended to the Pratt family."

Cameras flashed. Frances heard a blur of "Mr. Morris!" as reporters jockeyed to be recognized.

"I will do my best to answer questions." He flashed a smile.

Malcolm was in his element. He loved the publicity, the excitement of feeling in control of information. This time, though, it was her family, her father's loss, that was providing Malcolm's momentum. Frances hoped that her father wouldn't watch the noontime news.

"Who's in charge of the investigation?" asked an attractive woman in a bright blue suit.

"Special Agent Robert Burke and Assistant District Attorney Perry Cogswell."

Frances looked around for Meaty and noticed him standing off to Malcolm's left. Perry stood beside him. At the mention of his name, Perry stepped forward and raised his hand over his head. This case was Perry's dream, a chance to probe the details of her father's life and business, of her stepmother's friends and social world, amid the spectacle of media attention. How many times had Perry chastised Frances for being born rich, given her his unsolicited opinion that she could never be a great prosecutor because she was alien to the run-of-the-mill Suffolk County jury? "Private schools, summers in Southampton, who are you trying to fool with your rustic existence on Orient Point?" Perry had said with a sarcastic laugh at the Saint Patrick's Day office party last year. She had wanted to hit him.

As Perry stepped back next to Meaty, Malcolm seemed to scowl. He apparently didn't like the competition.

"Is it true that a family member of the deceased works in your office?" another reporter asked.

"Frances Pratt is the victim's stepdaughter. She is also the chief of our Financial Crimes Unit. She is a first-rate prosecutor with an impeccable record, and an invaluable member of this office. Our entire office expresses its condolences to her and her family on this terrible tragedy."

"Will she be involved in the investigation?"

"As in any case, we will certainly keep the victim's family apprised of major developments. However, we want to give Ms. Pratt the time and space to grieve her terrible loss. As I said, Mr. Cogswell, who heads up Violent Crimes, will conduct the investigation."

Frances squeezed her sides. There it was. The public pronouncement that she was shut out. She suspected that Meaty was trying to catch her eye, perhaps to send some signal that it wasn't his fault, but she couldn't look at him.

"How was Mrs. Pratt killed?"

Malcolm frowned. "This is an ongoing investigation, and we'll have to keep many details to ourselves. I assure you, at the appropriate time you'll get all the relevant information."

I'm sure they will, Frances thought. She had no doubt that Malcolm would extract every possible ounce of attention. Wealthy socialite murdered. A rare occurrence, and one that attracted both the regular media and the society pages. Just what Malcolm needed to get his third term in office off to a dramatic start, dramatic enough, perhaps, to launch him into the congressional race just two years away. That it was a quest for justice on behalf of an old friend and financial supporter didn't hurt, either.

Frances felt dizzy. She wiped her forehead, darkening the cuff of her blouse with a stain of perspiration. Slowly she began to make her way through the crowd to the exit. As she was leaving she heard another question posed. "Will this case receive top priority?" A softball.

Frances didn't need to wait to hear the answer.

Back in the solitude of her own office, she turned on her electric fan and watched the head swivel slowly from left to right, circulating warm air. The building's outdated air-conditioning system had been shut off for the three-day holiday weekend, and by Monday at noon the offices still hadn't cooled down. She scanned her illegible messages and returned several calls. The lawyer for a fourteen-year-old girl indicted for grand larceny after she stole more than $100,000 worth of sterling silver, china, and jewelry from the homes where she babysat requested the results of the state's psychiatric evaluation. The office's trial court coordinator wanted to review upcoming trial dates for line assistants in Frances's unit. Frances signed several vacation request forms, authorized an overtime voucher, then drafted a memorandum to the Victims Assistance Program, urging it to bend its criteria for the Hortons' sake.

Frances cleared space in front of her to make room for the materials that Meaty had given her and began to read.

The telephone ring made her jump in her seat. Frances glanced at her watch. More than an hour had passed, and she had missed the news coverage of Malcolm's announcement. She lifted the receiver.

"Fanny, I just saw what's his name, your boss, on the news about Clio. Murder, my God. How awful. This whole situation is just awful." Blair's voice sounded breathless. "I was just stunned, you know, shocked and stunned. Poor Dad."

"Have you spoken to him?" Fanny asked.

"Not yet. I don't know whether he would've heard from anyone else. Maybe you should call him."

Blair's act, Frances thought. Get me to do the dirty work. The dynamic of their sibling relationship never changed.

"But, you know, the oddest thing happened to me as I was watching the story," Blair continued. "I remembered this conversation I had." She stopped. Frances heard the sound of a match lighting and then Blair's exhale, presumably from a cigarette. "Have you spoken to Beverly Winters?"

"Who?"

"Beverly Winters. She goes by Bev. Bev Winters. I'm sure you've met her at some point. Bev and Dudley Winters have been coming to Southampton for years. He was a CPA, worked for one of the big New York accounting firms. Arthur Andersen, maybe? Oh, I can't remember. Anyway, he died two or three years ago. Suicide. He drowned himself in their swimming pool. He was sick anyway. He had terrible emphysema, years of smoking, I guess, and was confined to a wheelchair. He pushed himself right into the pool. At night," she added, as though that made it worse. "Apparently he and Bev slept in separate rooms. It was okay to leave him alone, I guess. Anyway, when Bev awoke the next morning, he was in the pool. Dead."

"What does this have to do with Clio?"

"I'm getting there." Blair sounded exasperated.

Frances heard her take another drag of a cigarette.

"Bev and Clio were friends, friendly, we should say. They ran in the same set, anyway. For many years they had a standing tennis game, a ladies' doubles. I'm trying to think who the other players were. At one time I think I knew." Blair's voice trailed off. "In any event, apparently Clio was ruthless to Bev after her husband's death. Dad and Dudley were great friends. Oh, I forgot to say that Bev asked Dudley for a divorce. Dad suspected another man. Anyway, he and Clio blamed Bev for Dudley's unhappiness. They shunned her, cut her off, socially, I mean. Bev wasn't invited to their summer party. Clio made a big deal of ending the tennis match and spread all kinds of nasty rumors about her."

"How do you know all this?"

"Deirdre Granger, the Winterses' daughter. You remember her, don't you? She went to Nightingale-Bamford, then Garrison Forest. We saw her in the summers. Anyway, she and her husband, Frank, are good clients of the gallery, and they know everybody. Jake and I have seen quite a bit of them socially."

"And she told you what exactly about Bev's relationship with Clio?" Frances asked, trying to draw some connection between Blair's ramblings and Malcolm's news conference. Despite the social intrigue, that Bev Winters no longer made the A-list hardly made her a murderer.

"A month or so ago, just after Memorial Day, I think it was, Deirdre talked to me about what happened, and how miserable Clio made her mother's life. She and I were out to dinner, and I think she had too much to drink, but she told me all about how much her mother hated Clio. Deirdre isn't that close to her mother, but still it was hard for her to see her mother so upset. Bev had supposedly said some horrible things about Clio, although, from what I heard, I agreed with most of them. Saturday, I was at Fair Lawn as Deirdre's guest. I didn't see her after I found Clio, but she called me Sunday to say how guilty she felt."

"Why would Deirdre feel guilty?"

"Just because. Because she repeated all these bad things about a dead person. Because Bev hated Clio."

"What are you wanting me to do?" Frances asked.

"I'm not the prosecutor. I only mentioned it because I thought you'd want to know."

"Okay. Thanks." Then before she hung up Frances added, "Did you go over to Dad's after I left you on Saturday?"

"Oh, didn't I tell you? I did. It was late, but I just couldn't bear the thought of him in that house all alone. Besides, Clio's car had to be returned. I'm heading back over there now after I run a couple of errands. There's a ton of stuff to organize. Poor Dad."

"Tell him I'm thinking of him."

"And you'll call him now, right? To tell him about the murder investigation."

"I'll let him know."

Frances placed the receiver in its cradle. Chewing on the end of a plastic pen, she replayed the conversation with her sister. Nothing that had transpired during the last forty-eight hours seemed right, and Blair's call only added to her sense of uncertainty. She felt claustrophobic and needed to get outside. She had to call her father, but not from the office, where anyone might walk in and interrupt.

Frances grabbed her briefcase and the yellow envelope of materials Meaty had given her and headed out the door. "I can be reached at home if anyone needs me," she said to the receptionist, although it hardly mattered. She had no intention of answering the telephone.

Frances sat at the kitchen table. Her dogs lay on the floor nearby, panting. The saccharine in three glasses of diet iced tea had given her cramps, and she rubbed her stomach, then reached her arms overhead to stretch. She had read and reread the police interviews of various Fair Lawn Country Club members. All said they knew Clio, liked her, and felt very sorry for what had happened, but no one claimed to have seen or heard anything out of the ordinary. Everyone's attention was focused on the tennis tournament.

The answering machine picked up after the second ring. She heard Meaty's voice, "I'm sorry to bother you, kiddo, but I need—"

She picked up.

"What do you know about Miles Adler?" Meaty asked.

"He's my father's business partner. Why?"

"How well do you know him?"

"I've known him and his wife for a while, but not well. I saw them over the years at Dad and Clio's parties. Dad speaks highly of him. His wife's nice enough, nondescript. I think she worked at a bridal salon once, but I doubt she's still there. They don't have kids."

"How long has Adler been your dad's partner?"

"They've only been partners since Dad's stroke, but Miles started working for Pratt Capital right after business school. He graduated from Columbia and, I imagine, came in as a salaried employee. I assume Dad made him a partner recently to encourage him to stay on after Dad was basically unable to work. What's up?" Frances didn't like the one-way nature of the questions and wondered whether she was being interviewed as part of Meaty's official business.

"I've just been looking at an undated copy of the partnership agreement that your father and Miles Adler executed. Your dad and Clio jointly owned fifty-seven percent of the company, and Miles has forty-three, but you probably know that."

"I know very little of the details of my father's business arrangements."

"Under the terms of the agreement, if Clio dies, Miles has the right to purchase their share of the business. The money goes to something called YOUTH-CORE."

"It's a charitable organization that provides jobs and opportunities, summer camp, that type of thing, for inner-city kids. Dad and Clio were both very involved with YOUTHCORE," Frances explained. "Dad was the president not too long ago."

"Well, it's a good deal for Miles. The price per share seems low. It's a complicated formula, but as far as I can tell, Miles can get fifty-seven percent for slightly more than twenty million. I've looked at audited financial statements of Pratt Capital for the last several years. It's had annual net profits of somewhere around fifteen million. Based on historical performance, then, Adler's shares pay for themselves in less than two years."

"You think Miles killed her?"

"I'm not saying that. All I'm looking for is who might have reason to kill a wealthy socialite. Money's certainly a motivator."

"Miles has a right to purchase the rest of the business now that Clio's dead?"

"That's right."

"Even though Dad's still alive?"

"Yeah. I found that a bit unusual myself," Meaty added, placing particular emphasis on the word *unusual*.

"How did you get the partnership agreement?"

"I went to your father's house, right after the press conference. Your sister was there. She showed me a whole file cabinet of Pratt Capital business records. Mostly duplicates of stuff, but it's a start."

"Why didn't you call me?" Frances knew that her voice sounded defensive.

"I heard you left for the day. I figured after Malcolm's performance this morning, you might need some time to yourself. I didn't even want to bother you now, but you're my best information source."

"It's no bother."

"What can you tell me about Miles's relationship with Clio?"

"I'm not sure they had much of one."

"Was she involved in the business?"

"I don't know."

"Who else works at Pratt Capital?"

"It's small. There's Annabelle Cabot, Dad's secretary. She's worked for him forever. She's one of those old-fashioned secretaries like you see in the movies. You know, attractive, smart, eager to please, basically the opposite of what we've got. She keeps track of everything for him, although she's way too discreet to ever let on."

"Is she married?" Frances could hear Meaty's pencil scratches on the other end of the line as he took notes.

"Yes. Still is, as far as I know. No children. She adored Dad, and he did her. I haven't seen her since Dad was hospitalized, but she visited every day when he was."

"Who else is there?"

"There's an accountant. Stuart something, I can't remember his name. And Miles Adler. That's it. Dad uses outside counsel, so there's no lawyer on staff."

"Who's his lawyer?"

"A guy named Bob Michaels. Pratt Capital's been his principal client for years, although he's switched firms a couple of times. I don't know who he's with now."

"Would you talk to the secretary for me?"

Although Frances couldn't imagine Annabelle Cabot answering probes about Clio or her father, she dreaded the thought of learning something she might not want to share with the district attorney's office. If anyone knew family secrets, Belle did. She had been Richard's loyal confidante and aide since Frances was an infant.

"Look, Frances, I told Malcolm to put you on this

case, that it would be good for you and good for the investigation. You know the people. We need your help. But he wouldn't listen. He's concerned for you, for your family. He seemed almost protective, like he didn't want you to be hurt any more than you have been. He's the boss, after all. It's his call. I did everything I could. You've got to know that. You know how much I hate working with Cogswell." Meaty chuckled, an easy joke.

"Does Perry know we're talking now?"

"Nobody knows but me and you. And I'd like to keep it that way. If you find out anything, I'll relay it to those in command, but while we're exploring, I thought we could keep it to ourselves."

"Sure." Frances and Meaty hung on the line for a moment. They had nothing to say, but both seemed reluctant to end the conversation. Finally Frances said, "Belle's not likely to talk even to me, but I'll see what I can do."

"Thanks. I owe you one, kiddo."

Frances got up from the table, fixed herself several slices of heavily buttered cinnamon toast, and fed the dogs. Then she dialed her father's office. Despite the hour, past the close of business, Annabelle Cabot's sweet voice answered promptly. Frances deliberately kept the conversation short and arranged a lunch meeting for the next day. Then she sat back down and picked at her crusts. The habitual motions of feeding herself, tending the animals, the tasks she normally performed without thinking, now seemed overwhelming. Her arms barely had the energy to hold the bread knife or the bowl of kibble. Her legs seemed unable to support the weight of her body. Odd, she thought. She hadn't expected to feel such emptiness over Clio's death.

She replayed Meaty's questions in her mind. Would Miles Adler really have a motive to kill Clio over ownership of Pratt Capital? She couldn't imagine that his 43 percent interest wasn't sufficient to give him everything he needed. Frances tried to remember when last she'd spoken to Miles. She couldn't think of a time since she had called to tell him of her father's stroke. She remembered the panic in his voice that Sunday morning fourteen months ago. He had spoken as though Richard were his father. He'd wanted to come to the hospital immediately, and she'd had an awkward time explaining that he should stay home, that the Pratts preferred to be alone. She could tell he was hurt.

Was it possible that Miles's relationship with Clio was tense? Perhaps Clio resented Richard's affection for his prodigy, their paternal bond. Clio wouldn't have wanted a professional relationship to evolve into a replacement of their son in Richard's eyes. Without thinking, Frances looked up Miles's home telephone number. Her directory contained few names, and his was the only listing under "A." She dialed. After several rings a woman's voice answered.

"Hello?"

"Penny?" Frances asked. "It's Frances Pratt."

"Fanny, I just don't know what to say. I'm so sorry, sorry for Richard, sorry for all of you. Miles and I are devastated." Penny Adler's concern sounded genuine. "We were devastated when we heard, and now even more shocked to hear it's a murder. It's just awful, beyond awful, unthinkable. I do hope they catch whoever did this."

"Me too."

"I was in the hosiery department of Saks of all places, when I ran into a friend who had just seen the news. She told me. I couldn't believe it was true," Penny rambled. "We were actually at the Fair Lawn Country Club, staying as guests of Clio and Richard's. We were supposed to have drinks with them that night. Of all nights to have a cocktail invitation."

"You were?" Frances felt her pulse quicken.

"Miles had wanted to stay with them, you know, to have a little more time to see Richard. He so loves Richard, but Clio said it wasn't a good weekend for houseguests. We understood, of course. They don't need guests on top of all they have to deal with. They put us up at the club. It was very nice." Penny started to cry. "Oh, I feel so terrible. I wish there was something I could do to help."

Frances hadn't seen either of them at the Fair Lawn Country Club on Saturday and wondered where they had been that morning. "Were you at Fair Lawn when they found her?"

"No. Actually, Miles was, but I wasn't. We had both gone to the beach early, before it got too crowded, but Miles forgot his sunscreen, and you know how easily he burns. He has to wear SPF thirty, at least. He went back to our room. When he returned, he told me what had happened, that Clio was dead, that she had died right there in the clubhouse bathroom and that everyone was frantic. He collected our things, packed our bags on the spot. He seemed out of his mind, distraught like I'd never seen him before. I thought he was going to have a heart attack. He could hardly breathe. He wanted to go back to the city immediately, so I drove us."

Frances listened, amazed at Penny's candor. "Did Miles talk about Clio's death on the drive back?"

"No. He didn't say a word. He seemed almost in shock."

"Are you familiar with the terms of Miles and Dad's partnership agreement?"

"No. Miles doesn't involve me in any of his business deals."

"Does Miles have his own lawyer?"

"Yes. Excuse me." Frances heard Penny put down the receiver and blow her nose. When she returned, her voice was clearer. "Ian Feldman is Miles's lawyer. He handles everything."

"Do you know where he works?"

"He's a corporate lawyer at Stockton and Purvis. On Wall Street. I seem to remember Miles mentioning he specializes in partnerships, business arrangements of some kind, but I'm not sure. I only met him once, myself, when Miles wanted me to sign some papers."

"I see." Frances knew of Stockton and Purvis by reputation. Small by New York standards, it had made a name for itself in the eighties representing several parties in high-profile hostile takeovers. It was known for aggressive tactics, although that described most lawyers Frances knew.

"Did you want to speak to Miles?" Penny asked after

several moments. "Because unfortunately he's out of town."

"Where did he go?"

"Mexico City."

"When did he leave?"

"On Sunday. It was rather unexpected, but some business deal came up at the last minute."

"Before or after you went to Southampton?"

"When we got back home on Saturday, he was on the telephone late into the evening. He told me he was leaving the next morning. That he had to go for important business. That's the way Miles is. He copes with grief by being efficient. I think his primary concern is keeping Pratt Capital going, you know, so that Richard won't have to worry about that on top of everything else."

"When do you expect him to return?"

"I'm not sure. I know he wants to be back for the memorial service, but he's not certain he'll make it. I sent some flowers to the house. You don't know if they've arrived, do you?"

Frances wasn't listening. Miles had left town twenty-four hours after his partner's wife died. What possibly could have been so important? "If you could let him know I called, I'd appreciate it."

"I'll give him the message. I'll see you on Wednesday. If there's anything at all I can do, please let me know."

"Yeah. Thanks." Frances hung up.

Frances quickly called Stockton and Purvis. Ian Feldman's secretary informed Frances that Mr. Feldman was out of the office. She promised to relay Frances's name and number when he called in for his messages.

Frances led the dogs outside and settled herself on the porch step. The air had cooled, and the slight breeze soothed her flushed cheeks. The two canines sniffed at smells perceptible only to their astute olfaction as she watched the changing light of dusk and listened to the sound of crickets.

Crossing the street, Sam approached, carrying a basket of potatoes.

"Harvested today," he said, extending the basket toward her. "You look like you could use some comfort food."

"My mood is that transparent?"

"How about if I mash you some? It won't take more than a few minutes. They're mighty good. Yukon gold. Nothing like a mashed potato to calm the spirits."

"Thanks, Sam." Frances smiled. "But I'm not hungry. How about a drink instead?"

"Sure, Miss Fanny. Coming right up." Sam disappeared inside Frances's house and returned moments later with two plastic tumblers of dark rum on ice. He hiked up the legs of his khaki trousers and settled himself on the step beside her. They clinked their glasses and sat in silence, sipping their drinks. The strong alcohol burned in Frances's throat.

"I saw the news. Do you want to talk?" Sam asked after a while.

Frances looked directly into his hazel eyes. His wavy hair fell in all directions, and wisps covered the lines in his forehead that she knew were there. He had sun-browned skin and thin, cracked lips. "I trust you, Sam. I trust you more than anyone I know." Her voice quivered. She glanced down at his bony ankles, bare feet, and long thin toes with recently clipped nails. "Help me. I can think of a lot of people who disliked Clio, myself included, I suppose, but I can't think of anyone who would actually kill her, anyone who would risk getting caught."

"Why do you think it's someone you know?"

"It had to be someone from her world. I mean, given how quickly they think she died, it had to be someone with access to the Fair Lawn Country Club. No one saw anything unusual. The killer must have literally been one of them." Her sentence hung in the air. Frances raised her glass, inhaled the scent of rum, and took a sip.

"Did she have a lover?" Sam asked.

"You mean besides my father?"

"Well, since your father's stroke." He looked away modestly.

"Not that I know of. Although I'm realizing that I know very little about their life."

"You know your father loved her. That's something."

"It's odd, though. There are moments, like when I was talking to Meaty about the medical examiner's report, when I feel like I'm investigating the death of a total stranger. And then someone will say something or make a reference, and I'm reminded that this person was a part of my family, that my dad is devastated, that none of us will ever be the same."

"You know as well as I do that you shouldn't be on this case."

"You sound like my boss. Malcolm's doing everything possible to keep me away."

"Can you blame him?"

"No. But whether I'm on this case formally or not makes no difference. All I have to do is close my eyes and see Dad's face, his eyes, to know that I've got to find her killer."

"Finding out who killed her is not going to change that sadness."

"I know, but at least I'll give him an answer."

"Give him or yourself?"

"Both of us, I guess."

"Why does that matter to you so much?"

Over the past two days Frances had wanted to be in control, but she was slipping. At that moment she felt like a lost child, scared, vulnerable, and desperate to get home. Was it possible to explain to Sam that if she solved the crime, if she did something special for her father, it might make up for their years of relative estrangement? Could he understand that her drive to find Clio's murderer might be a mission to lead her back into the warmth of her father's embrace? Such thoughts were irrational, she knew, and she felt ashamed to speak them aloud.

Tears filled her eyes, and she looked up at the sky, hoping to keep them from spilling out. Sam put his arm around her, and she could feel the firmness of his muscles against the top of her back. She turned her head away from him and stared at his hand resting on her shoulder, the two scarred stumps of flesh. He had lost his fingers in a tractor accident, working corporate fields in Washington State.

"Can I ask you something?" she said.

"You can ask me anything."

Frances felt his grip tighten slightly on her shoulder. "Do you ever miss your fingers?"

"Not much anymore. I'm not surprised like I used to be when I look down and see that they're gone. Although I do miss wearing my wedding ring. Rose wouldn't like that one bit."

Frances laughed quietly at his humor. Sam had been a widower since before Frances had met him, and he rarely spoke of his late wife, who died after a brief illness at the age of thirty-eight. My age, Frances thought. Sam had come east after her death. With the money that workers' compensation paid for his lost digits, he'd bought himself the small potato farm where he now lived.

"Rose insisted that men should wear rings, too. 'Why should married men waltz around with nothing to show their status? Only gets 'em into trouble,' she used to say."

For the second time in as many days, Frances recalled her own engagement. On the carousel in Central Park, Pietro had proposed. He had climbed up on the bobbing painted horse that Frances rode, put his arms around her, and showed her the ring in his hand, too garish for her taste, a huge emerald-cut diamond that cost more than she now earned in a year. She'd never put it on, just watched him hold it as it reflected the colored lights. They had whirled around in circles with circus music playing.

"You know, maybe I could use those mashed potatoes after all," Frances said, turning to face Sam.

Sam smiled again. Together they went inside. The many questions surrounding Clio's death could wait until tomorrow.

"$\mathcal{M}$alcolm wants to see you," Sue muttered as Frances walked past the secretarial station toward her office at the end of the hall. Frances didn't stop. Sue won the prize for worst secretary in the world. She couldn't spell, couldn't type, couldn't articulate, and rarely transmitted a telephone message or number accurately. Given that Sue snacked without interruption, the few documents Frances did ask her to prepare were returned covered with fingerprints, food stains, or grease. Sue used her limited mental power to calculate and recalculate the number of vacation days she had accumulated.

Frances set her briefcase on her desk and picked up the telephone to dial his extension.

Malcolm Morris answered on the third ring. "I'll be right down," he informed her before she even said hello. Apparently caller identification had eliminated the need for introductions or pleasantries.

True to his word, Malcolm appeared on the threshold of Frances's office moments later. His dramatic figure nearly filled the threshold where he stopped and leaned against the door frame. A college quarterback who still ran six miles every morning, he kept thirty-pound dumbbells under his desk so that he could lift weights in his office. His deep brown eyes shone out from his tanned forehead and wide cheekbones. Underneath the flourescent overhead lighting, his silver hair looked almost blue.

"What's the story with the Bryant case?" he asked.

Bryant. It took Frances a moment to remember the name. So preoccupied had she been the last seventy-two hours that her investigations had been forgotten. Andrew Bryant, whose palatial home across the street could be viewed from several of the dirt-encrusted windows of the Suffolk County District Attorney's Office, was chairman of the local Democratic committee and had backed Malcolm's opponent in the last election, John Wetherbee. With high hopes of attracting the attention of people in the national Democratic machine, Bryant had done what so many wealthy political contributors do: funneled money in excess of legal limits to his candidate through his children, relatives, and household servants. The New York State Ethics Commission had referred the case for criminal prosecution while it simultaneously pursued its own investigation and sanctions. Malcolm had been particularly vehement that Bryant be indicted since the file first arrived in the office.

"You know, Malcolm, I'll be perfectly honest with you," she said, pleased that even under the circumstances the details returned to her. "Bryant was stupid, but he didn't do anything that thousands of others haven't done, including some of your own contributors, I'm sure."

"Don't start that, Frances. You know damn well that my people spend a lot of time reviewing my list of contributors, checking names, addresses. This doesn't happen in my campaign. We would have caught so many people with the same street address. We would have checked on the ages of the Bryant kids."

"I didn't mean to offend you. My only point is that I think we should let Ethics deal with it."

Malcolm took a step into Frances's office and closed the door behind him. He appeared taller than before as he stood directly across the desk from her, looking down. When he spoke, his voice was low and firm. "I thought I made it perfectly clear that I wanted an indictment in this case. Have you or have you not presented the evidence to a grand jury?"

Frances paused for a moment before responding as she recalled the status of the case. "I've done most of the presentation. They've seen back records. We subpoenaed the Bryant kids, one of whom is eight years old, whose testimony, by the way, was that his allowance was fifty dollars a week, and that he saved up to make a political contribution. It was cute."

"Are you telling me there's no case?"

"No. That's not what I'm saying. Detective Marsha Kendrick told the grand jury about her interviews with the cook, the maid, and the Bryants' driver, all of whom said that Bryant gave them cash as a gift, and that they made contributions to Wetherbee's campaign shortly thereafter because they wanted to. Kendrick asked one of the servants what they knew about Wetherbee. Basically, she didn't even know what office he was running for. That's where we are. Disgusting conduct, but I don't really know that a prosecution makes sense given that Ethics will sanction him anyway."

"That's not a decision you're in a position to make."

"Why not?"

"I'm the district attorney. I'm charged with enforcing the laws, including the campaign finance laws. There has been a violation, an egregious one at that. I want an indictment."

Frances tried to give him a bemused look, a look that would break the mounting tension. She wanted them both to laugh about the eight-year-old campaign contributor, the lying servants, the shared humor of prosecutors brought on by witnesses with incredible stories, but Malcolm's face showed no sign of amusement. He put one foot up on the edge of her desk and leaned forward as if he might leap across it. The muscles of his legs strained the seams of his pinstriped pants.

"Let me be perfectly clear. There's no discussion about whether to bring this case. The decision's been made. By me. Let me know when the grand jury returns the indictment." He took his foot down. "I'm sorry about Clio, I really am, but if you're going to stay in this office, I need you to concentrate on your work." He turned and walked out.

Stunned, Frances watched his long stride down the hall and listened to the click of his hard soles on the linoleum floor. Never once in her seven years as a prosecutor in Malcolm's office had he questioned her decisions, her judgment, or the exercise of her prosecutorial discretion. His concern was always the scoreboard, and his chief financial crimes prosecutor had a fourteen-to-three track record in this fiscal year. So why now?

Malcolm's reputation as a crime fighter above politics, as a district attorney who made decisions based only on the facts and the law, was too good to risk tarnishing by his appearing to use the criminal process to exact vengeance on his enemies. He didn't need this case. The ethics commission would do it.

Frances sat back and picked at a slowly spreading hole in the well-worn upholstery of her chair. It was barely one o'clock and she was exhausted. She rifled through a pile of message slips. The Victims Assistance Program coordinator had called to say that the Hortons weren't entitled to compensation because Avery's crime wasn't violent. Bureaucracy at its finest, Frances thought. Had he broken into their home, beaten them, and locked them in a closet while he stole their money, the state would help them out, but where they were merely emotionally ravaged and financially wiped out by a slick con man, they got nothing.

Frances rarely allowed herself to question why she did what she did. She enjoyed the criminal law, the intellectual intricacies of putting together a case, her work as a prosecutor since she had first started twelve years ago in the Manhattan District Attorney's Office fresh out of law school. The work fit her disposition. Prosecutors and the state troopers they worked with were a jovial lot, unpretentious, content to share stories over beers or doughnuts, depending on the time of day. Assistant district attorneys, by and large, did not spend their professional lives in emotional quandaries about what they were doing. They had Right on their side. They protected victims. They put away criminals.

Then, every so often, or increasingly more often, Frances now thought, something like the Avery case came along. A simple case: Bad guy befriends innocent elderly couple and steals their money. Avery should have sold his assets, paid the Hortons $517,000, and gone off to a minimum-security facility to pay his debt to society. But instead the Hortons lost and Avery won. Were the Hortons guilty because they had been stupid enough to trust a fellow church member? Frances shook her head as if to rid her brain of this thought.

Dreading the telephone call she had to make, she dialed the Hortons' number. Roger picked up on the fifth ring.

"It's Frances from the DA's office."

"Oh," he said expectantly.

"Unfortunately, I'm calling with only bad news. I wish it were otherwise." Frances paused and tried to think of how to explain what she dreaded relaying. "Do you remember the Victims Assistance Program, the one I told you about?"

"Yes."

"Well, I tried to get that organization to bend its rules a little bit so that you and Mary Lou could be compensated for your losses like other victims of crime. But the problem is that, by statute, the money available to the Victims Assistance Program isn't intended for restitution.

It's limited to victims of violent crime, to pay for medical expenses, funeral expenses, that type of thing."

There was a long pause. "Well, I suppose, then, we're lucky. Apparently things could have been worse."

Frances was silent. Why was Roger Horton stoic when he had been treated so badly? "I'm sure it doesn't seem that way. I know how badly this case has gone for you. I wish it could have been different. I wish I could have done something more to help."

"We thank you for all you've done, and all you've tried to do, for us. We know it hasn't been easy."

"It has been my privilege," she managed to say. His graciousness in the face of such unfairness astounded her, and she felt at a loss for words. "I'll still keep trying to find you a good contingent fee lawyer if you want."

"If it's no trouble."

"No. No. Of course not. It's the least I can do."

"Well then, we'll wait to hear your recommendation. Have a good afternoon, Miss Pratt."

Frances replaced the receiver, swiveled her chair around to her left, and stared out through the smudged glass panes. As she pushed open the window, sounds of cars, kids laughing, a skateboard hitting the curb, floated in on the warm July breeze. Across the street, the sun beamed down on the gravel of Andrew Bryant's driveway, making it sparkle. A red BMW convertible pulled up to the front door of the house, and Bryant got out. Poor bastard, Frances thought as she watched him disappear through his front door. A criminal prosecution is coming your way.

Frances picked at the sugar-crusted crown of her blueberry muffin. She dreaded stepping outside the confines of her small office. The buzz of Clio's murder seemed to be everywhere, the subject of virtually every conversation, the source of endless speculation. She couldn't listen and wondered what had happened to all the other homicides, robberies, rapes, and home invasions that the office was supposedly trying to prosecute. Clio seemed to be the only crime that mattered.

Frances heard a knock on the door. "I'm not here," she called out.

The door opened, and Meaty peered inside. "Can I bother you for a moment?" he asked tentatively.

"Yeah."

Meaty stepped through the threshold and shut the door behind him. His collar was open, and he loosened the knot of his tie.

"You look tired," Frances said.

"You would be too if you had Cogswell breathing down your neck every two fucking seconds."

Frances's eyes fell on several sheets of paper in his hand. "What's that?"

Meaty shook the pages. "The ME's final report. Clio's cause of death is listed as toxicosis. Heart failure induced by lethal interaction of phenelzine and Dexedrine. No surprise. No different from the preliminary."

"Any idea how the drugs got in her?"

"She probably ingested Dexedrine in a drink. It's water soluble. The lab's running tests on every used plastic cup at the Fair Lawn Country Club to check for traces. So far, we've found nothing. We can't test glassware because it was run through a dishwasher before we started on this needle-in-a-haystack search. Frankly, I think it's a waste of time. It's a pretty efficient cleanup operation over there, and we started too late."

"Anything else?"

"Yeah. Forensics turned up several black hairs. One was at the table where Clio had sat shortly before she went to the ladies' room, and two were found on her body."

Frances looked puzzled.

"I mean black as in belonging to a black person, an African American, as you politically correct people say." Meaty's tone was sarcastic. He cocked his head to one side, trying to catch her eye. "Don't be naive, Fanny. What black person do you know with access to Fair Lawn?"

"I have no idea." Frances understood his insinuations. It wouldn't have taken a doctorate degree in sociology to figure out that the Fair Lawn Country Club was racially and ethnically exclusive. "Meaty, you're not suggesting that because there were a few hairs, a black person killed Clio." She tried to reflect her disapproval of such reasoning.

"All I'm saying is we need to explore options. If someone, anyone, was out of place, I want to know why. And you should, too."

"Who are you looking at?"

"We've collected lists of clubhouse staff and grounds crew. There's one guy, part of kitchen cleanup. He's black. But as far as we can tell, he wasn't working July Fourth, although we haven't talked to him yet."

"Perhaps Forensics made a mistake about the hair."

"Look, kiddo, I don't purport to defend the quality of the forensic work that this department performs. They make mistakes. But apparently the characteristics of Negro and Caucasian hair are such that not even a beginner would confuse them."

"Have you considered the membership?"

Meaty looked skeptical.

"I thought private clubs had to allow minorities," Frances said. "Although I have to tell you, your theory, if you can even call it that, is disgusting. If you had found a platinum blond hair, we wouldn't be having this discussion."

"It's not a theory. It's just a hunch."

"Go to Cogswell with it, then."

"I already have," Meaty said reluctantly. "He says it's too much of a political firecracker to explore without more evidence. He's more interested in looking good in the media than looking for suspects. I keep reminding him that we don't have much to go on here. The bathroom had a million prints, makeup smears, used tissues, and, I admit, platinum blond hairs, most with dark roots, I might add. But none of it adds up to a lead."

"What about Miles?" Frances said, reminding him of their conversation the night before.

"At best, we've got a motive. We haven't found one shred of physical evidence linking him to the scene."

"He was at the club. His wife told me they were staying there as guests of my father and Clio." Frances proceeded to relay her conversation with Penny Adler from the night before. "So you've got motive, and I've given you opportunity," she said.

Meaty cracked a smile, amused at her detective work. "Did the Adlers see your father last weekend?"

"No. They were supposed to see him and Clio for drinks on the Fourth, but they hurried back to Manhattan instead, and Miles spent the night on the telephone arranging his business trip to Mexico City."

"Interesting," Meaty remarked. "We weren't able to locate him. All I got from his secretary was that he was out of town. You're right. She's discreet."

Annabelle Cabot gets paid to be, Frances thought. She broke off a piece of her muffin and ate it. "I'm about to leave. I've got an appointment in the city." She checked her watch.

"Who's in charge of the club's membership?" Meaty asked, ignoring her.

"There's a committee, unless things have changed recently. A friend of Dad's, a woman named Gail Davis, used to be on it. She might still be."

"Could you check now? I'd appreciate it," Meaty said. Before she could respond, he settled himself in the chair opposite Frances, apparently intending to wait. He bit at a fingernail.

Frances called directory assistance and had the number patched in.

"Davis Design," answered a female voice.

"Gail?"

"Yes."

"It's Frances Pratt."

For the next minute or so Frances felt Meaty's eyes staring at her as she listened to Gail's expressions of sympathy and sorrow. "Clio was absolutely adored by everyone," Gail said in an airy tone like an exhale. "Just a lovely person, so gracious. I can't understand who would do this."

"I need to ask you a favor," Frances interrupted.

"What can I possibly do to help?" Gail asked in a way that made clear she had nothing of import to contribute.

"Are you still on the Membership Committee of the Fair Lawn Country Club?"

"Yes. I'm the secretary."

"I'm trying to find out what information you might have about African American members."

There was silence on the other end of the line. Then Gail said stiffly, "That's a rather odd request. Might I ask why you're interested in this information?"

"I need to know if Fair Lawn has any black members." Frances had no intention of disclosing Meaty's hunch to Gail Davis.

"We don't," she said matter-of-factly. "It's not that they're not welcome, mind you, but we've never gotten any qualified applicants. The financial burdens of membership are quite considerable, you know that," she added by way of explanation.

"Could you at least check your records?"

"I will if you want."

"I'd appreciate it. Members and applicants to membership as well."

"You're interested in applicants, too?"

Frances thought she detected a hesitancy in Gail's voice but didn't know how to interpret it. "Yes. Thank you." Frances gave Gail her office and home numbers before saying good-bye.

"Well?" Meaty asked as soon as she hung up.

"She'll check, although there aren't any black members."

"We'll see," Meaty mumbled as he walked out.

A uniformed bellman met Frances at the curb as she pulled up to the Plaza hotel. He opened the driver's-side door of her pickup truck and held out an oversize umbrella for her to step under. "Will you be staying?" he asked.

"Just for lunch," she replied. "At the Palm Court."

"You can let the maître d' know when you'll be needing your—" He stopped, unsure of how to refer to her truck. "Vehicle," he announced, obviously pleased, as the word came to him. A pickup was undoubtedly a rare commodity for the Plaza's valet service.

"Thank you."

He walked Frances to the expansive awning and nodded for her to proceed up the carpeted stairs. "Through the revolving doors and straight ahead. You can't miss it."

Frances didn't need directions. The Palm Court had been one of her favorite haunts as a child growing up in Manhattan. The small, marble-topped bistro tables, wire chairs, and potted palms were separated from the rest of the opulent hotel lobby by a series of polished brass posts connected by velvet rope. A tuxedoed violinist and his piano accompanist played popular melodies and familiar show tunes. But the music and decor served merely as background to the central attraction, the multishelved display rack of desserts. Linzer torte, cheesecake with strawberries, white chocolate mousse, German chocolate cake, lemon meringue pie . . . each sweet temptation decorated in flowers and flourishes of frosting or whipped cream sat on its own doily-lined silver platter. It was overwhelming. Although the Palm Court served lunch, dessert was the highlight, the reason to be there.

Frances spotted Annabelle Cabot already seated at a table in the corner. Her hair was pulled back in a bun. She wore a pale pink sweater underneath a beige fitted jacket with a gold cat pin attached to her left lapel and a matching pleated skirt. As Frances approached she looked up from the red leather day planner she was reviewing.

"It's so good to see you," Belle exclaimed, rising to her feet.

"You too. You look great, elegant as usual."

Belle smiled and tilted her head modestly. "For a moment, I was wondering if I had the wrong time. But here you are," she said.

"I'm late. Sorry."

"Shall we?" she said, indicating the seats. They sat down and a waiter appeared to fill their glasses with lemon water.

"I haven't been here in years," Frances said, looking around. "But nothing's changed. It still looks like a set from *The Nutcracker,* a home for the Sugar Plum Fairy."

Belle laughed.

"Dad used to take Blair and me here. He never made us order lunch. Just let us get right down to it and have dessert. He ordered only iced coffee and a bowl of raspberries. No cream." How vividly the memory returned, Frances thought as she spoke. She remembered the excitement of going over to the shelves of displayed desserts, examining each one, imagining the sweetness, and comparing relative quantities of frosting before making her selection. Occasionally, unable to choose, she would ask to order two. She, Blair, and her father would eat slowly, savoring their treats and discussing recent events at school, projects at home, progress on lessons. Blair did most of the talking. Even as a young child she had an uncanny ability to sustain her audience.

"How's your father doing?" Belle asked.

"You would know better than me."

"Not really, no. I called the house several times, but Mr. Pratt apparently didn't feel up to talking, understandably, of course. Monday I did speak briefly with Blair."

"I guess he's hanging in there as best he can. It's a shock, a shock to all of us."

"I'm sure."

The waiter returned to take their order, a smoked-salmon-and-watercress sandwich for Belle, a mocha almond tart for Frances. After he had departed Frances continued, "I suspect things will be easier for him after tomorrow. He seems quite anxious about Clio's memorial service. I hope when that's behind him, he can begin to grieve."

"Your sister told me he was concerned about preparations. He's always been meticulous about plans, but how can one plan for this? He's a great man, your father, a real gentleman with a heart of gold." She dabbed at the corner of her eye with a handkerchief. "Is there anything at all I can do to help?"

"I don't think so, thank you. We're all set." Frances sat

for a moment, collecting her thoughts. "There are a few things I'd like to ask you about work, if that's okay."

Belle nodded.

Frances cleared her throat. "Did Clio spend much time in the office?"

"Mrs. Pratt? Not really, no."

"So she wasn't much involved in Pratt Capital?"

"I wouldn't say that." Belle sighed and seemed to search for words. "Since your father's stroke, she's been quite involved in the business, helping him out, you know. She reviews all the projects, or at least I think she does because I send her all the materials. I believe she speaks directly with clients and investors. She just doesn't come into the office very often." Belle seemed momentarily to have forgotten that Clio's activities were now part of the past.

"How did she get along with Miles?"

"Oh, I wouldn't know."

"Did they have a lot of interaction?"

"About a month ago, Mrs. Pratt hired an assistant, a nice young man, just graduated from Harvard Business School. He was scheduled to start work at the end of the summer. I don't know what will happen to him now, but I believe Mrs. Pratt's intention was to have this young man report to, and assist, her and Mr. Pratt, but work in the office here with Mr. Adler." Belle was too smart to unintentionally evade the question.

"What did Miles think of that?"

"Well, I really couldn't say. I'm not sure Mr. Adler even interviewed the young man. Perhaps he didn't feel there was a need to take on somebody else." Belle stopped talking as the waiter brought their food.

"Bon appétit," he said as he set the gold-rimmed plates in front of them. Belle picked up a crustless triangular sandwich and took a bite.

"Look, Belle, we've known each other a long time, and you know that verbal delicacy is not my strong suit," Frances said, leaning forward. "So I'll be blunt, and I hope you can be honest with me because it's important. I'm trying to find out who murdered Clio. I need to know everything I can about her life in order to determine who might have had a motive to kill her. You might think I would have places to start myself, but, quite frankly, there's a lot I don't know about her life. I haven't wanted to bombard Dad with questions, not yet, anyway, although I'm sure the time will come for that. So what I'm asking you is whether you can think of anything at all about Clio, her involvement in Pratt Capital, her relationship with Miles, or anybody else, for that matter, anything at all that might help me. Was there anyone you can think of who was angry at her, owed her money, anything?"

Belle shifted in her seat and fingered a loose strand of hair from the nape of her neck. Then, seeming to catch her own nervous tic, she folded her hands in her lap. She said nothing.

"You've known Dad a long time. Probably better than most of us. Please, Belle, for him, if you have any information, you've got to share it."

"I don't want to add to his sorrow," she said flatly.

"You won't. I don't intend to trouble Dad with details

of this investigation until everything is over and we have a suspect."

"I don't know—" Her voice cracked, and she momentarily covered her mouth with her hands. Her fingers trembled. She clenched her fists and rested them on the edge of the table. "I don't know whether it means anything or not, but, well, things at the office have been rather strained since Mr. Pratt's stroke. Mr. Adler and Mrs. Pratt didn't interact much, but when they did, it was hardly what I would call civil. At an office meeting about a month ago, the one where Mrs. Pratt announced that she was hiring an assistant, that was the worst. Mr. Adler got so incensed he left the meeting, just banged his notepad on the table and walked right out. He was carrying on in quite a way about all he had done for Pratt Capital and how this assistant was the final insult. He accused Mrs. Pratt of hiring a spy. I believe that's what he said, or something along those lines."

"Did anything else happen at the meeting?"

"There really wasn't much to it. Mrs. Pratt wanted to institute a review procedure to ensure that she received all information on all projects under consideration at Pratt Capital. The discussion was logistical. We talked about getting materials forwarded to her at the Southampton house in a timely manner. Mrs. Pratt was planning to redecorate the offices. She had hired a firm called Davis Design, and its principal, Gail Davis, made a brief presentation. Mr. Wasserman spoke about certain changes in the accounting system, and Mr. Michaels summarized the settlement of a shareholder lawsuit where Pratt Capital was one of the defendants. We were voluntarily dismissed by the plaintiffs, so that was a bit of good news."

Frances listened to Belle's perfect recall of the meeting more than a month ago. It was a testament to her steadfast attention to detail, one of the many qualities that made her a perfect secretary.

"Was Miles still around when the meeting ended?"

"Oh yes."

"Did Clio speak with him?"

Belle seemed to contemplate her sandwich as she thought of how to answer. After several moments she looked up and focused intently on Frances. "They did speak. I'm sorry to say. I left the office right after the meeting, but when I got to the lobby, I realized I'd forgotten my taxi voucher. I went back upstairs. Mrs. Pratt was in Mr. Adler's office, and they hadn't shut the door. They were both very angry."

"What did they say?"

"I didn't stay long."

"Did you hear any of what their argument was about?"

"Yes, but you know there've been several police officers that have come to the office wanting to ask me questions. I've said nothing. I don't think it's appropriate for me to be sharing information about my employers, especially information that I may have understood out of context. Your father and Mrs. Pratt, and Mr. Adler as well, have been very good to me."

"Please, Belle, what did you hear?"

"All right." She leaned forward and lowered her voice so that Frances could barely make out what she was saying. "Mr. Adler apparently wanted Mr. and Mrs. Pratt to sell him a controlling interest in the company. He thought he was entitled to it, you know, because he had kept the firm going so well since Mr. Pratt's illness, or at least that's what he said. Mrs. Pratt refused. She said, I remember this much, 'Richard made you what you are. It's you who owe him.' Mr. Adler then got very angry. He called her names. I had to leave. It was too upsetting. Poor Mr. Pratt." Belle's voice was shaking.

"This is very helpful," Frances said, trying to sound consoling.

"There's more, unfortunately." Belle reached down to her handbag on the floor beside her, opened it, and removed an envelope. She placed it on the table next to Frances. Then she took a sip of water. "That's a copy of a letter that Mrs. Pratt gave to me. She asked me to keep it in a safe place. I have the original at home."

Frances tore the envelope and removed a single sheet of folded paper. The letter to Clio was dated May 30.

> *Since I first walked through the doors of Pratt Capital, I've worked tirelessly. I knew when I came on board that Richard had built the company and took great pride in what he'd accomplished. He treated me well—like a son—compensated me fairly, and encouraged me with the knowledge that one day I would be his partner. In exchange, I helped the company grow. In the several years before Richard's stroke, two of our most profitable deals came through me.*
>
> *As we discussed last night, none of us expected Richard's health to fail so suddenly and so com-*

pletely. Nobody was as devastated as I. I assumed that he would retire and thought that he would offer me the opportunity to buy his company from him. To my surprise, you and he decided to keep Pratt Capital operating with you at the helm. You asked me to stay in exchange for 43 percent ownership interest. I agreed. At the time, I should have foreseen the problems inherent in having the only person with the institutional knowledge and skill to effectively run Pratt Capital be the minority shareholder. I somehow thought that it would work, that we could all just get along. I was wrong.

You have made our arrangement impossible. You have done everything in your power to undermine me. You have questioned my judgment, threatened my reputation in the financial community, and ruined the Pro-Chem deal. I warn you once and for all: Stay out of my business.

You and I both know that with the profits I have generated over the last year, I am entitled to a majority stake in Pratt Capital. I have earned that much. I urge you to reconsider your refusal to sell me an additional 8 percent of the firm. In case you didn't hear me, I mean what I say. If you do not honor my request, you will not like the consequences.

The letter was signed *Miles Adler.*

"I can't believe Mr. Adler would do anything to harm Mrs. Pratt. He so adores your father. He couldn't possibly want to hurt him," Belle said.

"When did Clio give you this letter?"

"Several weeks ago. She stopped by the office briefly, unannounced, and handed it to me. As I said, she asked me to keep it in a safe place."

"Did you read it at the time?"

"No. I put it in an envelope and did as she instructed. Only after I heard of her murder did I open it. I had to make a decision about what to do with it. Then I also remembered something that happened about the same time."

"What was that?"

"Well, one afternoon, rather unexpectedly, Mr. Adler wanted the key to your father's office. He had a story about why he needed it. He said that he wanted to throw a party for Mrs. Pratt and wanted personal information about her to help the party planner, information that he somehow thought might be in your father's office. I could tell something was odd."

"Did you give him the key?"

"No. But I'm quite sure he took it. He sent me on an errand to buy a present for his wife. There was no occasion for a gift, at least not that I knew, and Mr. Adler's hardly what you would call the compulsive romantic. He wanted me out of the office. When I returned, Mr. Pratt's office was still locked, but the key had been moved. I keep it on the right side of my desk drawer. It was in the center."

Frances was impressed. With her own disorganization, she would have no way of knowing whether something had been rearranged or removed altogether.

"I should've taken the key with me, but, you know, at

the time, I really didn't think much of the conversation. I thought his request was peculiar, but I had no reason to be suspicious. It's only been because of recent events that I've rethought that afternoon."

"When was this?"

"I don't recall the exact day. The end of May, shortly before the office meeting I mentioned."

"What kind of information might Miles have wanted?"

"Your father kept meticulous files on everything. I filed materials relating to projects for him, but I know he has one cabinet with personal files as well. He took care of those himself, and no one's touched them in the last year."

"What's in them?"

"I don't know. I assume personal records, probably financial information, although what Mr. Adler would have wanted with any of that, I couldn't begin to imagine."

"Did Clio ever use his office?"

"No. I don't think Mrs. Pratt could even bear to go inside it. I certainly never saw her go in. In fact, one of the reasons to redesign the office space was so that she could put in an office for herself. But Mr. Pratt's office was to stay just as it was. It was not to be touched."

"Have the police gone in?"

Belle took a sip of her lemon water, wiped her mouth, and replaced her napkin in her lap. "Yes. They came first thing this morning with a search warrant and removed several boxes of files. As far as I could tell, the police took information on current and past employees and projects, as well as some materials from Richard's personal files. I was told I would receive an itemized inventory once the material had been logged at the station."

"Did they give you a copy of the warrant?"

"Yes." Again Belle reached into her handbag and removed a thin piece of paper, a sheet from a triplicate. She handed it to Frances.

Frances skimmed the search warrant. Perry Cogswell had signed it. The paper indicated that the affidavit in support of the warrant came from Special Agent Robert Burke. It had been submitted to the court. Blair's cooperation, the partnership documents, undoubtedly provided the information Meaty needed to establish probable cause.

"What's Miles doing in Mexico City?" Frances said, folding the search warrant and stuffing it into her pocket.

"I didn't know he was there until he called the office yesterday morning."

"Is there any project that you know of in Mexico City?"

"The Pro-Chem deal, the one referenced in his letter. The manufacturing plant is just outside the city limits. That's the only one I can think of."

"What was the deal?"

"From what I understand—which, I remind you, is only what a secretary learns in the course of correspondence and such—it's a nutritional supplements company. It's quite small, run by only a handful of gentlemen, but Mr. Adler thought it had tremendous potential. He was very interested in investing in it."

"Clio didn't approve?"

"All I know is that Mr. Adler's communications with

the company, phone calls, letters, faxes, stopped in late May. Since then we haven't received anything from them, or sent anything to them, or at least nothing of which I'm aware."

"When do you expect Miles back?"

"I don't know. He didn't say." Belle interlaced her fingers, rested them on the edge of the table, and leaned forward. She lowered her voice. "He's become increasingly private over the last months. He keeps his office door shut, and doesn't tell me where he's going or when he'll be back when he leaves the office. It can be quite awkward, really, if clients call wanting to know when they can expect to reach him. He hired his own attorney after your father's stroke. He won't use Mr. Michaels anymore. He even talked about getting himself a personal secretary. It wasn't my place to tell him that wasn't necessary, that I'm perfectly capable of handling his workload, always have been, and certainly am now. As you might expect, things are considerably quieter without your father around." Belle's voice cracked. Again she covered her mouth with her hands.

"You've been a huge help."

Belle didn't reply. She removed a handkerchief from the pocket of her jacket and blotted again at the corners of her eyes.

Frances signaled to the waiter for their check and insisted on paying. She stuffed Miles's letter and the carbon copy of the search warrant into her already crowded bag. Meaty would want Belle's off-the-record information, but these disclosures, given at considerable emotional cost, would stay with Frances, at least for now.

*   *   *

Traffic leaving the city had been brutal, with cars bumper to bumper along the FDR Drive, over the Triborough Bridge, and out past Kennedy Airport. It was after four when Frances turned onto Montauk Highway. She drove straight home, not wanting to return to the office to face Meaty's interrogation. If her prolonged absence from work was objectionable, so be it. Malcolm had told the press that she needed time to grieve. Let them think she was doing just that.

The message light on her answering machine blinked. She pressed the button and listened to the miniature tape rewind. The first call was Gail Davis, shortly after two. "I have the information you requested," was all she said. The second was from Malcolm Morris, whose brusque voice seemed to jump from the machine to fill the silence of her empty kitchen. "Fanny, it's me. Your boss. Remember that I am the boss. I do not want you involved in this investigation. Period. Cogswell is in charge, and Cogswell will remain in charge. Call me." The third was Sam, who didn't need to identify himself. "Miss Fanny, I fed the dogs at three. There's some turkey hash in your refrigerator, because I have the sneaking suspicion that you made no provision for supper. Also, I took the liberty of throwing away your milk. Check the expiration dates, will you? Call if you need me. Any time. I'm here." She smiled to herself as she opened the refrigerator door to see a new quart of milk, a basket of strawberries, and a Tupperware container filled with Sam's home cooking.

Frances turned on the kettle and, while waiting for the water to boil, leafed through the stack of mail that had accumulated on the kitchen table over the past several days. Catalogs, bills, an invitation to a fund-raiser at Guild Hall, no doubt her name placed on the mailing list by her mother, notice of a retirement party for a state trooper she hardly knew. She longed for something new.

The life she'd once shared with Pietro in a one-bedroom apartment just off Central Park West seemed worlds away from the quiet homogeneity of Orient Point, a community of farmers, contractors, a few heavy equipment suppliers, and the host of people employed by the ferry service to New London. It was a town where children bicycled in the street with various mutt dogs running behind them, Town Hall closed for the annual Strawberry Festival, and churches still played a major role in people's lives. Frances liked the solitude, the fact that nobody bothered her or cared much what she did. Because she blended into the community and drew no attention to herself, she was allowed to mind her own business. Sometimes, though, she had to admit, she missed the excitement of Manhattan.

She and Pietro had spent countless Saturdays at sidewalk restaurants, watching the crowds wander along Columbus Avenue, a couple pushing a baby stroller beside homosexual lovers in leather vests with their hands in each other's back pockets, followed by an Asian student covered head to toe in designer clothing. Pietro puffed on unfiltered Camel cigarettes and commented on the amazing variety of New Yorkers. "You could be anything here. Nobody cares." Frances watched his chest expand with each deep inhale, then watched the thick ribbon of smoke escape his lips.

There were evenings, especially when they had both had a glass of wine too many, that their conversations were heated. Pietro's ideology and hers clashed in animated discussion of the necessity of rent control in a city where soon only the rich could afford to live, of the censorship effect created by the National Endowment for the Arts' distribution of funds. Andres Serrano, the famous piss Christ image, had been the topic of many late night debates between them. She'd thought then that the difference in worldviews of a New York University Law School graduate turned public servant and a financial analyst at Citibank could coexist.

More than the lively New York life or intellectual banter, though, Frances missed the intimacy, the comfort of their silence. Snuggled together on their down-filled sofa, Pietro would pull her toward him and blow softly in her ear, sending a shiver down her spine. Absentmindedly he fiddled with the ends of her hair, running the long strands over his face, using them to tickle his ear. It was this connection that she cherished more than anything.

The kettle's whistle brought her back from her reverie. She opened a package of instant hot chocolate and watched the miniature marshmallows melt under the stream of hot water. Then she picked up the telephone and dialed Gail Davis.

"I don't know whether this is important," Gail began in an official-sounding voice. "But, given your request, I thought it only appropriate to call. I certainly would want to do anything possible to help find Clio's murderer."

"What is it?"

"Louise Bancroft, you know her, don't you? Her family has belonged to Fair Lawn for years. She married, and she and her husband recently applied to join as a family. They have two little girls, too."

"I knew her growing up. She's my sister's age."

"Her husband is Henry Lewis. He's a cardiac surgeon in Manhattan. Apparently quite successful. He's at Columbia Presbyterian Hospital. Anyway, that's not what's important. The reason I called you, and am telling you all this, is that he's black. Their children are mulatto," she said, making "mulatto" sound like a bad word.

"Is he a member now?" Frances asked.

"No."

"What happened?"

"When a member marries, the spouse becomes what's called a provisional member while the application of the newly constituted family is under review. Louise had been a junior member since she turned twenty-five. Henry Lewis became a provisional member last year, when they decided to pursue membership as a family. As a provisional member, he could come as a guest of Louise's, but without restrictions on the number of times that he could use the club. It's rather complicated, but normally the same guest cannot come more than twice a month or three times in a season. As a provisional member, these limitations don't apply."

"What changed?"

"Well," Gail stalled. "The Lewises weren't accepted."

"Why not?"

"Now, dear, you must understand that the actions of the Membership Committee are secret. All I can tell you is that the committee abstained from voting on their application."

"What does that mean?"

"It means that the Lewises can reapply in future years, but for this season, they were not voted into membership."

"Can Henry remain a provisional member?"

"No. He's now subject to the regular rules governing guests."

"So Henry Lewis can only use the club as his wife's guest three times a summer?"

"That's right. I mean, he could come as anyone's guest, but for all intents and purposes, he'll be Louise's. The same thing applies to their children."

"What about Louise?"

"She can remain a junior member until she's thirty-five, another six months or so, if my recollection serves me. Then she has to either join with her family, or resign. You can't be a junior forever." Gail laughed nervously.

"When did this happen?"

"Shortly before Memorial Day. The Membership Committee met for its final vote of the season."

"Why were the Lewises turned down?"

Gail paused for a moment. "It was a difficult year. Let me put it that way. The club is getting crowded. It's simply becoming a lot harder to join."

"But most junior members get accepted as a family, don't they?"

"Most do. Yes."

"Who's on the Membership Committee?"

"Let's see. Jack Von Furst, he's the president. George Welch was on the committee, but he resigned."

"When?"

"The beginning of June, I believe. I can check the exact date if you need it."

Frances looked around for a notepad. She settled for the utility company's bill and began to scribble notes. "Was he there when the Lewis application came up for review?"

"Oh yes. Certainly he was."

"How did he vote?"

"I can't tell you that. As I said, these things are confidential."

"Why did he resign?"

"I . . . I don't know exactly how to answer that. He is fond of Henry and Louise. I do think the outcome of their application upset him. I'm sure he had reasons."

"Who else is on the committee?" Frances prompted.

"Well, there's myself. I'm secretary. Wallace Lovejoy, Peter Parker, they've both been on for years, and Clio Pratt. Clio, of course, was exercising your father's proxy. He remained the named member of the committee."

"Did Clio approve of the Lewis application?"

There was a long pause. Gail did not respond.

"It's important," Frances encouraged.

"I'm sorry I can't be more helpful," Gail said, speaking slowly. "It's just that all of this is supposed to stay confidential. You might speak to your father about Henry Lewis. I suspect that he can help you more than I."

"What did you think of Dr. Lewis?"

"From what I know, Henry and Louise are wonderful people."

"Does that mean you wanted them to be members?"

"As I said, it never came to a vote. The committee abstained."

"But how would you have voted?" Frances persisted.

"I'm fond of Louise."

"What about her husband?"

"I accept that there were issues with their application. We don't have any African American members. It would have been difficult for Henry to have been the first, although, I suppose, that was his choice."

"Do you happen to have an address for the Lewises?"

"They live in the city, 1010 Park Avenue. Their house out here is on the beach, Gin Lane, about a mile past the Beach Club."

"Thank you."

With that, Gail hastily said good-bye and hung up.

As she drank her tepid cocoa, Frances thought about what Meaty had said. He had a hunch. Was it possible that something so attenuated as the existence of black hairs could link Henry Lewis to Clio's murder? Could anyone possibly have cared so much about membership at the Fair Lawn Country Club that they would kill for it?

"What is the world coming to?" Frances mused out loud. From where they lay on the floor, Felonious and Miss Demeanor looked up at the sound of her voice. Frances stood up, waited for the dogs to ease themselves up as well, and went into her bedroom. It was hardly dark yet, but she was too exhausted to worry about whether bedtime had arrived.

Frances awoke to the telephone ringing. She glanced at the clock. It was past midnight, and she had been in a deep sleep for hours. She fumbled for the receiver on her bedside table.

"How dare you try to badger my wife for information!" a voice screamed at her through a crackling line.

"Who is this?" Frances said.

"I also know you tried to reach my lawyer. Don't think I don't know what you're up to. Who do you think you are, prying into my business? Besides, Miss DA, you should know he can't talk to you. Attorney-client privilege, remember? And you'd better believe I'll see him disbarred if he violates it."

Miles Adler, calling from Mexico City, Frances presumed, judging from the bad connection. "I'll discuss it with you in the morning. Call me then. I was asleep."

"I don't care whether you were screwing the maharajah. You listen to me. You've got some nerve waltzing around with your innuendos. I love your father, and God knows I'd do anything for him. In fact, if you want to know the truth, I've supported him and his wife for the past fifteen months. I've given them everything. Do you actually think I would kill Clio? You're insane." Miles slurred his words. Several stiff drinks must have fueled his call.

Frances sat up and turned on the light. Seeing her surroundings made her feel more in control. "What are you doing in Mexico City?"

"It's none of your goddamn business. Leave me and my wife alone."

Frances said nothing.

"First that stepmother of yours. Now you. I've had about enough of you Pratts meddling in my affairs." Frances heard a crack as he slammed down the telephone. The line was dead.

$\mathcal{F}$rances knew as she stood on the clubhouse porch overlooking the acres of grass tennis courts that she shouldn't have come. She should have been the good daughter, gone to her father's house, and tended to whatever needs he might have in the moments before Clio's memorial service. But she couldn't bring herself to watch him, his painstakingly slow movements, his efforts to conceal his agony behind his half-paralyzed face. Besides, Blair would be with him. She had stayed over from the night before, just in case.

The sole source of activity at the Fair Lawn Country Club seemed to be the children's morning tennis clinic. Bicycles in every color, brand, and size were stuffed into an inadequately small bike rack to the left of the porch steps or abandoned on the grass. Through the clear morning air Frances could hear shrieks and giggles coming from the four clay courts behind the clubhouse. She imagined twenty or more boys and girls swinging rackets bigger than themselves at balls thrown to them from the other side of the net. She had been one of them once.

The clubhouse porch was empty. Most members, Frances assumed, were home preparing to attend Clio's memorial service in less than an hour. Some friends, others who felt compelled to attend, the crowd was sure to be large, but dressing for a summer funeral took time. It was difficult to set hair or smooth nylon stockings in the July heat.

Frances had tried to pay attention to her appearance, but she realized how out of practice she was. She smeared mascara under her eyes several times before washing it off all together. The lipstick she found in a basket under the sink smelled funny, so she had to settle for Chap Stick. The navy-blue-and-white-plaid jacket and navy skirt was her most solemn lightweight summer suit. It would have to do.

She had the perfect funeral dress, simple without any frills, lace, or buttons, but the zipper no longer closed and the fabric pulled over her thighs. It was the dress she had bought for Justin's funeral, a dress that Pietro had picked out for her, a dress that she'd never worn again. Still in its dry-cleaning plastic bag, it hung at the back of her closet.

The night Frances had learned of Justin's accident, she'd sat in a corner of the living room of the apartment she shared with Pietro, her knees tucked under her. She had wanted desperately to be numb, devoid of feeling. Each time she closed her eyes, she saw her half-brother struggling with no one there to help. The image was intolerable. Despite their age difference, despite the fact that Justin was Clio's son, she had loved him, felt protective of his sweet innocence. But she also knew that her own emotions had to pale in comparison with her father's grief. She couldn't bear the thought of his pain, couldn't imagine the desperation he had to be experiencing from the death of his only son.

Pietro offered her a drink, food, implored her to conserve her strength because her father needed her. Then, defeated, he pleaded with her to come to bed. His cajoling hadn't worked, and she stayed immobile for eighteen hours, long past the point where the muscles in her back and legs had knotted in pain. The next morning Pietro managed to dress her and get her out on the street in search of something to wear to the funeral. "You'll want to look nice," he said as he took her hand and led her into the subway. They emerged from underground to find street cafés brimming with life. Frances remembered girls wearing tight black pants that rested on their hips, navels exposed, and platform shoes. They sat in clusters, smoking and drinking bottled water. A table of tourists, laden with shopping bags, watched the passersby. Young bored men in mirrored dark glasses slouched in their seats, nursing hangovers, their arms dangling on the enclosure rail. To these people, musing over whether to continue drinking or to saunter to an air-conditioned movie theater, it was another carefree day.

Frances wanted to scream.

She and Pietro entered Barney's through the huge double-glass doors and walked up the internal winding stairs to the women's department.

"Can I help you?" A blond woman with lips outlined in purple pencil stepped forward to greet them.

"Yes," said Pietro. "We need a black dress for her. Something simple."

She walked over to a rack and pulled out a sleeveless dress with a layered skirt.

"I want sleeves," Frances said.

"Is this for a particular occasion?" she asked.

"Uh. Yes. A funeral," Pietro mumbled.

"For my brother," Frances added. "He drowned."

"Oh, I'm so sorry," she said awkwardly.

The saleswoman and Pietro selected several dresses. Then she showed Frances into the dressing room and gently pushed her inside, as if she were uncertain whether Frances could move from the place where she stood.

"I'll wait right here," Pietro said.

"Let me know if there is anything I can assist you with," the saleswoman added.

Alone inside the plush, mirrored dressing room, Frances felt her knees begin to buckle. She tried to take off her clothes, but the zipper to her pants stuck, her shoelaces were inextricably knotted, and her head was unable to fit through the neck hole of her T-shirt. Overcome by emotions she didn't fully understand, she sat on the carpeted floor and began to cry.

"Are you all right?" the saleswoman asked.

"No."

She heard a key turn in the lock of the dressing room and felt Pietro's arms around her. He hugged her and kissed the back of her head. She appreciated his silence. He didn't condescend to tell her that everything would be all right, to soothe her with platitudes about how time would heal her pain. She knew that he would sit with her on the floor of the fitting room, surrounded by black dresses, soft light, and flattering mirrors, all day and night if that was what she wanted. In their many years together, it was the one moment when she had no doubts.

"I can't do this," she'd said after several minutes. "You pick something, anything, I don't care."

Pietro had looked at the dresses hanging on the hook for a moment, selected one, and handed it to the saleswoman, who hovered in the doorway. Then he'd reached into his pocket and handed her his credit card. "If you could ring it up, we'll be out in a minute."

Ten years later Frances faced a second Pratt funeral. Two sizes bigger, navy blue and white was the best she could do from her existing wardrobe.

Frances took a deep breath and smelled the salt air on the mild westerly breeze.

"May I help you?"

She turned to see a stocky, muscular man with tanned skin and blond hair. He wore tight white shorts and a white polo shirt with green trim on the collar.

"Yes."

"Are you a member here?"

"My father, Richard Pratt, is. I'm Frances."

"I'm sorry about Mrs. Pratt." He stood looking uncomfortable for several moments, then bent over to retie his shoelace.

When he straightened up again Frances asked, "Were you here on July Fourth?"

"Virtually everyone was. I had lessons scheduled all morning."

"Are you a tennis teacher?"

"We like to say 'coach.' It sounds more professional, but yes, I give lessons." He extended a hand. "I'm Paul."

She shook his hand. "Did you ever coach Clio?"

"Not one-on-one. Occasionally, she did the ladies' clinic on Thursday mornings. It's more of a social thing, but we do drills, set up matches, work on specific strokes. She wasn't a regular."

"Did you see her here last Saturday?"

"I may have passed her on the porch, but I can't be sure. The place was pretty crowded, weekends usually are, plus there were spectators for the tournament. Once my lessons start, I don't have much down time. Of course, after we got the news, after they found her, at that point everything pretty much came to a halt."

"I understand she played tennis earlier in the morning."

Paul shrugged.

"Is there any way I could find out whom she played with?"

"If she played, sure. We keep track for billing purposes. The ladies who play regularly tend to split the fees. Men rotate. One guy pays the whole thing one Saturday, the next week someone else does. I don't know why it tends to fall into that pattern."

"Another one of the many mysterious gender differences," Frances said facetiously.

The tennis coach nodded in agreement. Then he consulted a board covered in sheets of white paper diagrammed with numbered rectangles. Each rectangle had times and lines inside it. The lines were filled with penciled scrawl. Frances must have looked confused, because the man explained, "Each rectangle corresponds to a tennis court. People sign up for a particular court. Even though we like to think all the courts are equal, some people have pretty strong preferences about where they play." He flipped back four pages to expose Saturday's sign-up. "Let's see. Yeah, here it is. Nine o'clock. Pratt, Helmut, Carver, and Winters."

"Would that be Beverly Winters?"

"Sure. Ann Helmut, Susan Carver, and Bev Winters."

Frances glanced over his shoulder at the tennis court diagram. "Lewis plus guest" was written in the adjacent rectangle on the nine o'clock line. "Who's that?"

"Lewis must be Louise Bancroft Lewis. She's supposed to go by Bancroft. That's the way she's billed, but we all know Louise's married name so it doesn't matter."

"Are you sure it's her?"

"Yeah. The only other Lewis members we have are Reginald and Monica, but they're elderly. They don't play anymore. Mostly they come for a cocktail, or to watch some of a match. Social members, we call them."

"Can you tell me who Louise Lewis's guest was on Saturday?"

"Certainly." Paul consulted a green leather book embossed with a gold "Guest Register" on the front. Overhead, on the bulletin board, Frances focused on the sign that read "Members Must Register Their Guests."

"Here it is. Saturday. A Ms. Aurelia Watson."

Frances stood on the terrace with her back to the house and her face turned up to the sun. A random birdcall and the distant laughter of the neighbor's child mixed with the sounds of purring motors. A fair-haired, shirtless boy gave a last-minute trim to the boxwood hedges, while another cut stray grasses growing up through the brick with an electric edger. Not a single bug or stray leaf marred the serene surface of the swimming pool's turquoise water. Through the kitchen windows, open to the faint breeze, she heard the rattle of preparations, a symphony of kitchen sounds. Lids clanged on pots. Boiling water burbled. A steel knife chopped rhythmically against a cutting board. China plates clattered. "We'll start with the cold hors d'oeuvres. Let's have four servers passing. Check for toothpicks and shrimp tails. I don't want to see platters covered in refuse. Remember, we're expecting a crowd of two hundred, maybe more. We need to keep the food moving. After the crowd thins, we'll start the buffet. They're expecting only about half to stay for lunch." Frances could hear the strange voice of the coordinator Blair had hired to oversee the funeral reception as she delivered instructions.

Frances looked out across the green lawn that stretched for more than an acre away from her father's house. This field had been the site of many "capture the flag" games where Frances had ended up the prisoner waiting to be rescued from jail. Her father, the quickest, most agile player of the troops she and Blair were able to round up on a Sunday afternoon, never let her down.

Looking at the lawn, Frances thought of a Christmas long ago, the year she turned ten. By then her and Blair's holiday routine had been established: Christmas Eve and morning with Aurelia in Manhattan, then a driver transported them to Southampton for the afternoon and night with their father. The emotional disruption had been explained as good fortune. "You get two Christmases," was the parental line, the assumption being that two was better than one.

"Your present is outside," her father had said that Christmas afternoon. Frances and seven-year-old Blair had put on parkas over their party dresses and started out across the brown winter lawn, the frozen grass crunching underneath their red Mary Jane patent-leather shoes. Frances remembered holding her father's hand as she skipped alongside him to keep pace with his lengthy stride. He chatted about how much he loved Christmas and was glad that they were all together, conversation she later realized was meant to distract her, to keep her attention focused on him, to keep his gift a surprise as long as possible. Partially sheltered by a large maple tree was a trampoline with a painted aluminum base and a large black surface.

"Merry Christmas!" Richard Pratt's enormous brown eyes registered delight at the excitement of his two daughters.

He lifted Blair up over the high railing and set her down on the jumping mat. Frances scrambled up herself, catching her dress on the metal coiled springs. Together they shot up into the air at odd angles like water streams from a swirling hose. Frances's legs tingled as she pushed off and leapt up. Then, as gravity reversed her, her long hair stayed up over her head to linger one brief moment before following her body back down. Watching, her father beamed.

* * *

"We were wondering when you would arrive."

Frances's reverie was interrupted. She turned to see Jake. He looked thinner than she remembered, and his pinstriped suit fell loosely from his shoulders. He embraced her stiffly.

"When did you get here?" Frances asked.

"This morning, why?"

"No reason. I'm sorry to hear your visit to your family was canceled."

Jake retracted his chin and wrinkled his nose, obviously puzzled. "That's right. I had some work to attend to in the city."

"Over the holiday?"

"Those of us who aren't government employees don't get every holiday. Look, Blair and Lily are loading your father into the limo. We're ready to go."

Frances, Blair, Jake, Richard, and his nurse sat in silence as the black-capped chauffeur drove slowly toward the beach. As they rounded the bend from the Fair Lawn Country Club, Frances could see the small brown church up ahead. The parking space directly in front was empty, waiting for them. People milled about on the strip of lawn between St. Andrew's and the street. Next door to the church, the flag at the Bathing Corporation flew at half-mast. Otherwise life continued seemingly unaffected by the ceremony twenty yards away. Barefoot children with peeling noses and ice-cream cones loitered by the club's front steps. An elderly woman in a wide-brimmed hat stood supporting herself on her metal walker, waiting for her driver to arrive.

Several of Richard and Clio's closest friends lined up

in a row by the front of the church to usher in the guests. Frances recognized a few familiar faces peppered in the crowd: Jack Von Furst at the front of the line, his hands crossed in front of him, his head down; Aurelia in a dramatic black hat with a lace veil that partially covered her face; Malcolm Morris working the crowd, shaking hands. Standing next to Annabelle Cabot, Penny Adler clutched a small quilted bag. Her chin quivered.

Lily pushed Richard Pratt's wheelchair. Jake held Blair around the waist, supporting her as she walked behind. Frances, alone, brought up the rear of their small procession as they made their way to the handicapped-accessible entrance at the back of the church. Frances couldn't look up as the crowd of mourners parted to let them through. She couldn't bear to see the sympathetic stares. She knew what people thought: The poor Pratts, the pitiful shattered family beset by tragedy once again.

Lily negotiated Richard into the church and found him a place in front. His wheelchair filled the narrow aisle. Blair, Jake, and Frances slipped into the adjacent pew. Frances listened to the organ music and the rustle and murmur of guests as they settled in their seats. She noticed that Lily stood by the back wall in attendance.

Blair, sitting on the aisle, leaned over and closed a button that had come undone on her father's shirt. Then she took his hand in both of hers and proceeded to rub his fingers gently.

The air was filled with the sweet smell of the many bouquets that the Pratts had received. These arrangements covered every inch of the floor around the altar and pulpit and effectively masked the two rose-filled urns that

Frances had selected. That her only contribution to the occasion was superfluous made her sad. Her father needn't have asked for help.

Frances felt dazed, unable to concentrate fully on Jack Von Furst's eulogy, the stream of prayers and hymns. She lifted her eyes and searched the crowd. Could Clio's murderer actually be among these mourners? It was hard to imagine any of the well-coiffed, hymn-singing participants as a cold-blooded killer. As she sat, Frances tried to figure out what she actually knew about Clio's murder, but the bits and pieces of information she had gathered seemed no more than fragments of a broken kaleidoscope. What had the police been doing? Testing paper cups and interviewing all the dozens of people who happened to gather at the Fair Lawn Country Club last Saturday. Why did she have the feeling that they were off in the wrong direction? And why did she feel a compulsion to find the killer first? She had no experience with homicide investigations and had been told specifically not to get involved. *If someone, anyone, was out of place, I want to know why, and you should, too.* Meaty's words haunted her.

Frances leaned back against the wooden pew and felt the hard seat underneath her. She wanted to forget about motives and suspects and to concentrate instead on the loss of her stepmother, but if she blocked out the investigation, she felt nothing at all.

Afterward the mourners gathered on the lawn outside the church, intentionally loitering to give Richard time to get home and settled before the reception began. But their wait was longer than expected. Richard remained alone in the church after the service ended to say his private good-bye.

"Fanny . . ." She recognized him from the way he said her name with the emphasis on the second syllable and a slight inflection. Pietro Benedetti came up behind her. As she turned to face him, he stepped forward, arms outstretched, and embraced her. Her face went into his chest. She felt his warm body and tight grip.

"Fanny, I can't tell you how sorry I am," he whispered, then added knowingly, "For your father." His arms released and she stepped back, stumbling slightly.

Pietro looked as regal and elegant as the last time she had seen him. He had large walnut eyes, an angular nose, broad brow, and high cheekbones. The auburn highlights in his brown hair glistened in the sun. The double-breasted jacket of his gray linen suit accentuated his long, thin torso and small hips. She recognized his tie, black with gold specks, the last present she had given him. He had remembered.

"You're nice to come," she managed to say. She felt beads of perspiration forming on her forehead. "Did you see Mom? I'm sure she will want to say hello."

"We spoke briefly before the service. She looks well."

"She pulled off quite an outfit for this morning's ceremony. The hat's really something."

Pietro smiled. "She always was dramatic."

"And you always were her biggest fan," Frances replied. She felt disoriented. The rest of the people, the steepled church, the parked cars, and the sandy dunes whirled around her. She had the urge to move closer to Pietro and wrap his arms around her a second time.

"You look good," Pietro said.

"I appreciate the lie," Frances said, trying to sound lighthearted. She felt self-conscious and folded her arms in front of her chest as if to cover herself. What did he see as he stood staring at her? She imagined he viewed her as a thirty-eight-year-old matron, the spinster Pratt sister. He had once told her in a moment of candor that she was attractive but not beautiful, then had attempted to ameliorate the insult by telling her repeatedly that she was so special, looks didn't matter. She had never known exactly what he meant, and the thought had plagued her throughout their relationship.

"How's work?" he asked.

"Obviously Clio's murder is the top priority. My work's the same. Plenty of financial crime to keep me busy."

"And life?"

Why was he asking questions that she didn't want to answer? She resisted the urge to tell him there were still times that she missed him, but her stepmother's funeral seemed neither the time nor the place for that conversation. "Good. Life's good." She laughed nervously. "How about you?"

"Emanuella and I are expecting another baby. A boy this time." His eyes twinkled. "Cristina is almost three. She's not at all pleased about the prospect of a brother."

"Congratulations." Frances's voice was flat. A marriage and two kids. Pietro hadn't lost any time.

"We're leaving soon, returning to Italy. Citibank's finally decided to send me home. They're transferring me to Milan. We haven't found an apartment yet, but I'll let you know when we get settled. You should come visit. I'd love for you to meet the kids. I honestly think you and Emanuella would hit it off. She's a great girl."

"You better check with her first."

"I know what she'll say." He smiled. "I'm sorry I can't come back to the house. I've got to get back to the city." He rested his hand on her shoulder, leaned forward, and kissed her lightly on the cheek. Frances didn't move. "Take care."

He turned and walked toward the curb. She watched his broad shoulders outlined against the sun as he left once and for all.

"Come on, Fanny. Dad's in the car," Blair said. Then, following her sister's gaze, she added, "It was sweet of him to come."

Frances's eyes burned as she fought back tears. She put on her dark glasses and walked with her sister to the awaiting limousine.

Frances couldn't think of anything to say to the friends and acquaintances who filled her father's house following the memorial service. Standing around while others reminisced about Clio made her uneasy, yet the idle, unrelated chatter that took over after a few moments seemed inappropriate. Frances tried to keep track of who wasn't there, as if absence from their victim's funeral could shed insight on who the killer might be. There was no sign of Henry or Louise Lewis, although Louise's parents mingled in the crowd. Miles Adler hadn't made it back. "He's so sorry," Penny apologized for him. Blair confirmed that Beverly Winters hadn't appeared, either, although her daughter, Deirdre, had sent an overly extravagant bouquet.

As Frances moved to the makeshift bar set up in the sunroom, she noticed a familiar face she hadn't seen at the church. Sam stood in a corner, holding a glass of beer. He looked different to her in a starched white shirt, striped tie, and blue blazer, but the formality suited him. His gentle eyes fell on her as she made her way toward him.

"What are you doing over here all alone?"

"Well . . ." He paused. "I didn't want to barge through all those people to find you. I don't know anyone else here. I never met Clio, so it's a little hard to make conversation under the circumstances, and I figured I'd wait until I ran into you. This is a nice enough spot, and I've got a very good beer." Typical Sam. He could make the best out of any situation.

She smiled. "I hadn't expected you to come."

"That's what friends are for."

Frances took a step closer, wishing for a brief moment he had chosen different words. The waves in his thick clean hair shone in the light. Standing so close to him, she could smell his oatmeal soap. She felt her eyes well with tears for the second time in as many hours. "I wish you could take me home," she murmured. Then, embarrassed by her own directness, she felt her cheeks flush.

"I can."

The image of Pietro leaving the church flashed in her mind. It was the same silhouette she had seen walking away from her seven years earlier, when she had broken off their engagement. A final lunch with few words exchanged confirmed the decision she had already made. Outside the restaurant, Pietro had kissed her quickly and turned into Central Park. She hadn't intended to end up alone, but here she was, trying to avoid acknowledging her own loneliness while craving someone to hold her, to keep her safe. Frances wondered for a moment whether that person could ever be Sam. She tried to imagine resting her head on his chest as he ran his palm over her hair or patted her back. Maybe he could whisper a fairy tale about two semi-recluses who found each other living in Orient Point, or he could talk to her about a new garden design as she listened, enjoying the sound of his voice. Temporarily these thoughts soothed her.

"Do you want to leave?" His voice interrupted her daydream.

She sighed audibly, collecting her thoughts. "I better stay. This is one reception I don't think I can escape."

"I take it you'll want to pass on bingo tonight."

"Yeah. I doubt I'll be home in time. You go, though. Win for both of us."

"It wouldn't be the same without competition from you."

Frances forced a chuckle.

"Will you call me if you need anything?" Sam asked.

"Yes."

He extended his hand and covered her knuckles with his wide palm.

"Thanks, Sam."

"By the way, in case no one else said anything, you look really stunning . . . beautiful."

Frances laughed.

"I mean it." He smiled again and headed toward the door.

As guests started to leave and the caterer set up a lunch buffet for the more intimate group, Frances slipped up the back stairs to her old bedroom overlooking the entrance to the house. The room was neat but unchanged: two white cast-iron beds with polished knobs, comforters with pink flowers and matching sheets and shams, a painted dresser, and two small armchairs upholstered in a coordinating sage green. She opened the bureau drawers, ones that had been filled with T-shirts, bathing suits, and tennis shorts. Now they were empty except for crisp lavender-scented drawer liners and several silk sachets.

Frances pulled an armchair over to the window and sat, watching the endless line of cars snake in and out of the driveway below. She saw her mother leave, talking animatedly to Malcolm Morris, her black hat bobbing as she held on to his arm and tried to balance walking in high heels on gravel. Frances watched Malcolm help her into her car. Now he's met the other half of my family, she thought.

Frances wandered into her father and Clio's room, where Clio had slept alone for the last fifteen months of her life. A large four-poster wooden bed with pineapple finials faced a marble mantel. An arrangement of dried flowers filled the unused fireplace, and a pale Aubusson rug covered most of the floor in front. On either side of the bed were round tables skirted in a gold toile with vignettes of a milkmaid and a lute player on the hills of France. The right bedside table held a gilt-framed portrait of Clio as a bride. On the left was a similar frame with a formal portrait of Richard, as well as a stack of books and a portable telephone. She stayed on her side even without him there, Frances thought.

She found what she was looking for in the adjacent marbled bathroom. The orange plastic bottle labeled Nardil, the brand name for phenelzine, Clio's prescription for 15 milligrams three times a day, sat on the bottom shelf of the medicine cabinet. The prescribing physician was a Dr. Prescott. The prescription had been filled at Columbia Presbyterian Pharmacy, 168th and Broadway. There would be no trace of it at any Southampton drugstore.

Frances returned to their bedroom and sat at Clio's bird's-eye maple desk. One drawer held engraved stationery, stamps, and a letter opener. The other contained several invitations, a newspaper clipping from *Town & Country* on a small town outside of Paris, France, and a leather desk diary. Frances removed the worn diary and flipped through the pages, scanning notations for cocktail parties, charity events, meetings, reminders to buy gifts or send notes. Two entries were repeated. Every Wednesday was marked *3:00—FP at CP*, each Friday noted *10:00—RC*. Clio's code. Apparently Blair hadn't thought to give this to Meaty on Monday, along with the business documents, or else, perhaps, she hadn't discovered it herself.

Frances replaced the diary and closed the drawer.

Moving back toward the bed, she felt reluctant to sit down, to disturb the sanctity of the perfectly folded sheets and smooth cover, so she leaned against one of the four posts. She dialed information and got the number for Henry Lewis.

A woman's voice answered.

"Louise? It's Frances Pratt. I don't know if you remember me. It's been a while."

"I do," she said. Her tone was decidedly unfriendly.

"I was wondering if I could talk to you and your husband about my stepmother, Clio. I promise to keep it brief."

"I don't know what we have to say."

"Look, I know what happened with your Fair Lawn membership application. You must be very angry with my father."

"I am," Louise said bluntly. "I wish I could excuse his bigotry, but I can't. I don't have much patience for it, and neither does my husband."

"I can appreciate that."

"Can you?" Louise's polite tone was unnerving.

"I just need a few moments of your time."

Frances heard a muffling sound as Louise covered the telephone. There were voices in the background, but Frances couldn't make out what was said. Finally Louise returned to the line. "Isn't your stepmother's service today?"

"Yes. That's why I'm in Southampton."

"When did you want to talk?"

"This afternoon? In an hour or so."

"All right. We're on Gin Lane, the right-hand side, seven-tenths of a mile past the Beach Club. There's a sign by the driveway. Says Lewis."

The living room had emptied by the time Frances descended. Penny Adler lingered at the front door, and Frances watched Blair say good-bye. She thanked her for coming and added, "You must stop by our gallery this fall. We're expanding, thanks to Dad. Our new showroom will be open by October. It's a terrific space for a sculptor who's just signed with us. You really must come," Blair said.

Thanks to Dad, Frances thought, remembering the legal documents and architectural sketches that she had seen in her sister's Miata. She wondered when Richard had become part of that deal.

"I've got to head back to the city," Jake Devlin said, rolling up his shirtsleeves as he came toward Frances. He had already loosened his tie. "Wish I could stay, really I do, but the gallery beckons." He leaned forward and lightly kissed his sister-in-law's cheek.

"When will you be back?" Frances asked.

"Saturday morning."

"Oh." Frances paused for a moment, then added, "I understand you've got an expansion under way. That must be thrilling."

"Yeah." Jake nodded and looked at the floor. "Wish I could say it was my own success, but, once again, I'm thanking your father."

"So I hear."

Jake lifted his tired eyes and glanced at her curiously. "Richard's been extremely generous to us. Always. Don't think we take it for granted."

Always? Frances wondered. Or recently? She wanted to ask Jake about the specifics of the gallery's development and Richard's involvement, but the end of a long funeral reception seemed hardly the appropriate forum. Her inquiries would have to wait. "I'll see you this weekend, I'm sure," she said.

"Great. We'll look forward to it." His words sounded forced.

As Blair saw the remaining guests to the door, Frances wandered into the sunroom and found her father gazing out at the lawn.

"How are you holding up?" she asked.

"I can't imagine life without her," he said softly. "I expected her to bury me."

Blair appeared and sat on the floor by her father's feet. "Everyone's finally gone." She rubbed his legs, as if increasing his circulation could mend his broken heart. "Quite a tribute, Daddy. There must've been two hundred people here at one point or another. Clio would've been pleased."

Richard smiled faintly in a crooked twist of his lips. "My girls," he murmured. "I appreciate all you've done."

"Don't be silly." Blair looked up at him. "We love you. I just wish there was something more we could do."

Frances watched Blair's nimble fingers massage his frail limbs. Why did her sister have such an easy time displaying affection? Her touch seemed to reassure him, and Frances noticed her father's hunched shoulders drop slightly.

"Fanny, I've been thinking," Blair said in a matter-of-fact tone. "Maybe you should part with your ramshackle residence and move in here."

Stunned, Frances glared at her sister.

"Just think about it." Blair flipped her wrist in

Frances's direction. "It makes a lot of sense, doesn't it, Dad?"

"I don't know that Dad wants his privacy invaded by me and two dogs," Frances said, trying to dismiss her sister's idea. Richard Pratt didn't respond.

"Well, I think it would benefit both of you."

The thought of Sam flashed in Frances's mind. She had no interest in giving up her own home and her life in Orient Point to move in with her father. She stood up, feeling suddenly more awkward than usual.

"Where are you going?" Blair sounded irritated.

"You'll have to excuse me, Dad," Frances said, ignoring her sister. "There's something I have to do. It's important." She left quickly to avoid any further questions.

Frances drove through town, down South Main Street, and headed toward Gin Lane. More than ten years had passed since she had seen Louise Lewis. She remembered her as tall and thin, with bony knees that knocked together and a thick French braid that slapped against her back as she ran. Louise had spent a considerable amount of time at the Pratt household visiting Blair. They had built a clubhouse in one corner of the attic with an old carpet remnant, two twin mattresses, and a badly damaged Chinese screen to separate themselves from the rest of the clutter-filled space. They'd paid dues; that Frances remembered because Blair constantly reported on the sums in their treasury. Boys and Frances, as the older sister, were strictly excluded from the club, but the giggles and gossip of Blair and Louise often floated down the stairs to where Frances perched, listening.

When had Louise married? Frances had heard nothing

about her engagement or wedding. Blair, Frances's most reliable source of gossip and goings-on, had never said a word.

Louise opened the front door before Frances could knock. Hanging on either leg were two daughters, their molasses skin prominent against her white linen skirt. Each girl was dressed in a flowered sundress, ankle socks with ruffles, and red leather sandals. Frances's eyes wandered past Louise, up the staircase curving around to her right. A kilim runner partially covered the painted wood stairs. Nine oversize drawings of blackbirds ran along the wall. The decor seemed unusual for Southampton, where floral prints with coordinated stripes and oil paintings of golf courses seemed to fill every home. This interior felt exotic.

Louise motioned for Frances to come inside.

Frances followed Louise through an elegant living room with spectacular views of the Atlantic Ocean through a pair of doors to a deck off the side. Henry Lewis sat in an Adirondack chair, reading. A tray with plastic tumblers and a pitcher of iced tea rested on a table beside him. As Louise approached, he put down his copy of the *New England Journal of Medicine*, stood up, and shook Frances's hand.

"You're with the Suffolk DA?" Henry asked.

"Yes."

"Malcolm's office. It's a good one," Henry said, seemingly to Louise. The two girls extricated themselves from their mother and retreated to a corner of the deck, where several Malibu Barbies with platinum hair, suntanned plastic flesh, and neon orange bikinis lay amid an array of pink plastic accessories, a Barbie dune buggy, and several miniature beach chairs.

"Barbie's changed quite a bit since my day, I see," Frances said awkwardly.

Louise ignored her comment. "I heard you were in New York City."

"I was after law school."

"When did you leave?" Louise asked.

"I moved out to Orient Point in '92."

"Why?"

"I'd had enough, I guess." Frances paused. "I needed a change." She wasn't about to disclose the real reason. Again the image of Pietro's elegant form flashed in her mind, along with the sensation of his earlier embrace. He had been kind to attend the memorial service; Blair was right.

"What's it like here year-round?" Louise asked.

"Orient Point, the north fork, is different from the Hamptons. It's less a summer community. Beautiful landscape. A pretty slow pace." She smiled. Louise didn't return the gesture.

"I can't pretend that I am unhappy about Clio's death," said Henry, interrupting the social preliminaries.

"Henry, please." Louise looked frightened.

"It amazes me that we're going into the twenty-first century with people just as close-minded about race as they've always been. People will trust me to open their hearts up, to hold their lives in my hands, literally, but they don't want me to play on their tennis courts."

Frances was silent, not knowing what comment might be appropriate under the circumstances.

"My stupidity. I just wanted my kids to have the same experiences that Louise had loved as a child, including the Fair Lawn Country Club, but your father is a formidable opponent. I guess I'll have to build my own court." Henry laughed, breaking the tension.

Frances relaxed her shoulders, realizing as she did how tense they were.

"What is it you wanted to talk to us about?" Louise asked, handing her a filled glass of iced tea. The liquid smelled of lemon and sugar.

"I'm interested in what happened at the Membership Committee meeting on your application. I was wondering if you knew anything."

"We weren't privy to the details. You should talk to the committee members. Those that are around, anyway," Henry replied.

"Can you tell me anything?"

Henry and Louise glanced at each other, as if silently deciding who would speak. Henry began. "When Louise turned twenty-five and could no longer use the club on her parents' membership, she joined as a junior. For the first several years of our marriage, it never occurred to us to join as a family. On the rare occasions when we were out here, I used the club as her guest. Exorbitant initiation fees were something we wanted to avoid. Then last year we bought this house. Our older daughter had started playing tennis indoors in the city and really loved it. The younger one's just about ready to take it up, too. Louise planned to spend most of the summer out here with them, so membership made sense. We indicated our intent to apply at the end of last summer, sometime shortly after

Labor Day. At that point, I became what's called a provisional member based on the overwhelming presumption that the family of a junior member will be accepted. As I understood it, my provisional membership was a formality. But in our case, the expected didn't happen."

"Why not?"

"The party line? Something about crowds and parking. But the truth? I'm black." Henry snorted in disgust. "You probably noticed that. As I understand it, Clio, exercising your father's proxy vote, threatened to blackball me. The few supporters I had managed to work an abstention so that I could try to join again, which I won't."

"How can you be sure race was the dispositive factor?" Frances asked. While she didn't mean to suggest there was any valid reason to exclude the Lewises, she wondered if a heightened, though understandable, sensitivity had made Henry jump to conclusions.

"I don't know how much you know about membership, but Louise and I have every possible credential, including that her parents and grandparents have been influential members. The only thing that separates us is race, mine and our children's," Henry added, glancing at Madeleine and Eliza. The two girls were absorbed in their dolls and seemed oblivious of the conversation.

"Did you know Clio well?"

"I met her a couple of times at most. She's been to our house. She and your father were at our wedding, but so were five hundred or more Southamptonites."

"It was a rather large wedding," Louise said as if to explain her husband's sarcasm. "My parents are quite close to your father, and to Clio, too. Dad thinks the world of your father."

"Even after what happened with you?" Frances asked.

"I haven't had the heart to tell Dad that Clio was responsible for our not getting in. I think he assumes that she was a supporter, and that someone else caused the holdup. In any event, it doesn't matter now." Frances wondered about Louise's reference. As if reading her mind, she continued, "That is, since we have no interest in joining Fair Lawn after all. In all honesty, I'm not sure what got into us. It's not the life we want our girls to grow up in."

"It was a mistake," Henry agreed. "We assumed we lived in a different world."

"Were you at Fair Lawn last Saturday?" Frances asked.

"Yes. Actually, I played tennis with your mother," Louise offered.

Frances feigned surprise.

"I've known Aurelia for a long time," Henry explained. "Louise played tennis earlier in the summer with her. Then, when we saw her several days ago at a Guild Hall opening, she suggested a rematch."

"I've had a very hard time returning to the club given the circumstances. My only two visits have been to play with your mother," Louise said somewhat apologetically. "I agreed to play the second time because, well . . ." She paused. "My parents had been asking me why I never came to the club. They know how much I love tennis. I didn't want them to think there was anything wrong. It's hard enough for us. They didn't need to suffer, too."

So she had compromised her principles to keep up appearances, Frances thought. "After your tennis game, did you stay to watch the tournament?"

"Yes. Although it hadn't been my plan. You see, Henry had the girls with him, but then he got paged by his office. There was some problem with a patient."

"That's right," Henry agreed. "I thought I had to get back to New York right away. I had no choice but to bring the girls to the club to try to find Louise. When I got there, I saw Beth, Louise's mother, up on the porch. She offered to watch the girls until Louise was finished."

"My game ended at ten, maybe a little after. As I was leaving, I saw Mum, Madeleine, and Eliza. Mum explained Henry's change of plans."

"So how long were you there?" Frances asked, turning to Henry.

"Believe me, if I could have avoided the place, I would have. I stayed only long enough to drop the girls off and tell Beth what I was doing so Louise would know. That was it."

A clatter distracted Frances. Louise had dropped her glass. Ice cubes flew across the deck. "How stupid," Louise mumbled as she knelt and blotted the liquid with a handful of paper napkins. She got up, wiped off her skirt, and took her seat. Frances noticed that her hand was trembling.

"Did you see Clio?" Frances asked.

Neither Henry nor Louise responded. Frances repeated the question. "Yes," Louise replied.

"I saw her briefly as well," Henry added.

"How was that?"

"As unpleasant as you might expect," Louise said. "I tried to be civil, but quite frankly, it was difficult."

"Do you remember any of the conversation with Clio that morning?"

"She and I didn't have a conversation," Louise corrected. "She and my mother were talking about some fund-raising event, an auction, I think it was, to benefit YOUTHCORE. They're both involved with that organization. I wasn't paying too much attention."

"And you?" Frances directed her question to Henry.

"As I've already told you, I just dropped my kids off. I didn't even see right away that Clio was at the table with Beth. I didn't speak to her. I had no interest in pretending we were friendly. I left."

"Where did you go?"

"I went home briefly to collect a few things I needed. Then I called the hospital to see how my patient was doing, and to tell them I was on my way. The cardiac resident told me he'd gotten everything stabilized. He didn't think I needed to come. That's the life of a doctor, I guess. One moment, it's an emergency. The next, everything's fine."

"So what did you do?"

"Well, I certainly wasn't going back to Fair Lawn. I went into town. I tried to go to Silver's to get a paper and a couple of cigars, but it was closed for the holiday. I went home."

"Did you see anyone you knew?"

"What are you getting at?" Henry asked loudly.

"You didn't run into anyone in town?"

"No. And there was nobody here, either, because my family was at Fair Lawn."

So Henry had been near Clio shortly before her death. Frances shook her head slightly, wanting to dislodge Meaty's theory from her mind. "And Clio was already at the table when you arrived?" She turned to Louise.

"Yes." Louise glanced at her husband, then continued. "Aurelia and I came up on the porch after our match. I don't know how much detail you care to hear, but what I remember is that my parents were there with Madeleine, Eliza, and Clio. I never saw my husband. When Aurelia saw Clio, she excused herself. My mother explained why Henry had brought the girls. After I had been at the table briefly, my family wanted drinks. I offered to go to the bar. It was packed. I didn't feel like waiting, so I left the order with the bartender and asked him to send a waitress out to the porch to deliver them. Aurelia found me in the bar to tell me she was leaving. I returned to my daughters. A short while later, Clio got up from the table, and that's the last I saw of her. The rest you know."

"When did you know Clio died?"

"Oh. We heard a scream. It was really loud, chilling. I grabbed the girls. My father, and several other people, hurried inside the clubhouse. It was chaotic."

"Did you see anyone coming out of the clubhouse?"

"I can't tell you. The club was packed with people anyway, and after the scream, people were moving in all directions. I do remember seeing your sister, Blair. She was yelling that Clio was dead. I felt so sorry for her. She was trembling and shaking. Then she just collapsed in a heap on the floor."

"What did you do?"

"To be perfectly honest, I didn't do anything. I couldn't figure out what was happening for several minutes. I just stayed with the girls. They were scared by all the commotion. The police arrived pretty fast. I left as soon as I could and haven't been back since."

"Did you talk to the police?"

"An officer was taking names and telephone numbers from everyone. I gave ours. But that was all. I wanted to get out of there."

"Has anyone spoken to you about all of this since then?"

"Yes. A Detective, Detective Kelly, called. He said he was following up with everyone who was there that day. I told him what I knew, what I've told you. That's all."

"Thank you. Thank you both." Frances nodded to Henry. "I appreciate your time. Please don't get up. I can let myself out."

Back in the enclosed cabin of her pickup, Frances sat for a moment, rolling her head in circles to loosen the muscles in her neck. She rubbed her eyes. She wanted Dr. Lewis to have an ironclad alibi to instantly dismiss Meaty's suspicions. Instead he was at the exact location where Clio had been killed less than an hour before she died. Worse still, he was a cardiologist. He more than anyone would understand how lethal a combination of phenelzine and Dexedrine would be.

Frances couldn't bear to return to her father's house despite her promise to do so. There didn't seem to be any point with Blair there trying to rearrange everyone's lives. Nothing she said or did would take away the horrible emptiness her father had to be experiencing. She was too poor an actress to pretend she understood his grief.

As she drove toward Halsey Neck Lane, the image of Blair at the door of her father's house with Penny Adler filled her mind. Petite and well groomed, Blair looked as though she had stepped from the pages of *Vogue* in a slate blue cropped jacket and short pencil-pleated skirt. Was her sister as self-assured as she appeared? Underneath her confident air, what was really going on? What had Jake been doing over the Fourth of July? *Let's just say we haven't seen eye to eye on how to deal with our solvency problems.* She remembered Blair's words. How frantic had they been about their gallery's expansion?

No. Frances shrugged. The very thought was absurd.

As she pulled into her mother's driveway, she could see her mother in paint-splattered overalls and a large straw hat, standing at an easel on the grass. Frances honked.

"I thought I'd impose on you for some dinner," she said.

"Isn't it your bingo night?"

"I'm not up for the drive home just yet."

Aurelia put down her brush and came over to her daughter. She gave her a hug, squeezing her tightly. Then she kissed Frances's forehead. "Come on in. I'll see what I can concoct."

Frances sat at her mother's kitchen table while Aurelia scrubbed her fingernails with a stiff brush. "This paint never comes off. I've almost given up being clean," she said with a smile.

"You looked good at Clio's memorial service," Frances remarked. "I was surprised to see you there."

"I didn't go to honor Clio, don't misunderstand the gesture, but Richard was my husband, and he's your father. I went because of that. As for my outfit, well, if you're going to the funeral of your ex-husband's wife, you sure as hell better look good." Aurelia threw her a smile, wiped her hands, then opened the refrigerator to look inside. "Ah, we're in luck. There's actually something to eat." She pulled out lettuce, tomatoes, beets, and a wedge of parmesan cheese wrapped in a damp towel. "I want you to just sit and relax. It's been quite a day."

Frances sipped a glass of Chianti as she watched Aurelia prepare dinner.

"How do you know Henry and Louise Lewis?" Frances asked.

Aurelia paused in midpeel of a beet. "Let's see. I met Henry years ago. He purchased several of my paintings from the Durham Gallery, one of my first shows. The place doesn't exist anymore, but it used to be downtown, just off Greene Street in the Village. He said my landscapes were so inspirational that he was buying them for the cardiac ward at his hospital, as a donation. I was surprised he had the money, but I wasn't about to look a gift horse in the mouth. Anyway, since then he's followed my work. We speak from time to time. I was thrilled when he met Louise. Of course, we've all known her and her parents for years. A small world. They seem very happy together. Last summer, they invited me to their housewarming party when they bought the place on Gin Lane. Clio was there, too, I remember. It was only a few months after your father's stroke. I've been there several times since."

"How come you never mentioned him?"

"Henry?" she asked as if uncertain of the reference. "Well, it's not like we're close friends. Colleagues is a better word. He admires my work. We share an appreciation of art. He's wonderful company."

"You played tennis with Louise last weekend, the day Clio died."

"Oh yes. Louise is such a graceful player, and a patient one, too."

"I didn't know you were playing tennis again."

Aurelia laughed. "I need some sort of exercise. This body of mine is fading fast."

"Did you see Clio?"

"For a fleeting moment. I couldn't believe the gall of that woman to sit with Marshall and Beth Bancroft after what she did to their daughter. But what do I know? This country club crowd has the most hypocritical set of values. I can't begin to figure it out. Anyway, I left almost immediately after our game. All that socializing wasn't for me, especially with her."

"So you knew about what happened with their application?"

"Everyone in town did." Aurelia wiped a wisp of hair off her brow. "Who was it who said 'Malicious gossip runs faster than a triple crown winner'?"

"Is there any other kind of gossip?" Frances asked rhetorically.

Aurelia smiled. "I see I raised quite a cynic." She placed the plates, salad bowl, and cheese on the table and sat down. "I thought you weren't supposed to be a part of this investigation," she said, unfolding a napkin and placing it in her lap.

"How did you know that?" Frances asked.

Her mother cut hard into the wedge of parmesan. A chunk of cheese separated, and the knife clattered against the plate's surface.

"There was something in the paper. Right after the initial news that Clio's death was a murder. I can't tell you exactly where I saw it. Here, have some salad." She handed Frances the bowl.

"Well, you're right, anyway." Frances helped herself. "Perry Cogswell is the ADA assigned. I probably agree with Malcolm's decision from an investigative standpoint, but it's hard to stay out."

"Are there any suspects?"

"Plenty of people had reasons to dislike Clio. But that doesn't make them murderers. The forensic evidence may help, but so far it doesn't pinpoint anyone."

"What kind of evidence?" Aurelia asked.

"Just some hairs collected at the scene. It's too early to determine whether they're significant."

"When will you know?"

"I'm not sure."

"I see. How frustrating."

They ate in silence for several moments.

"What happens if the murderer isn't caught?" Aurelia asked.

"After some period of time, the file will be closed, at least for internal purposes, meaning that the office won't expend any resources pursuing it. Then, our only hope is that sometime down the road, someone comes forward with information, or something, that leads us to the killer."

"Does that happen?"

"Occasionally. It's been known to, anyway. Years later, someone with knowledge of a crime gets arrested, a drug bust, something serious, and sings for his supper. It's unlikely here. The odds of someone from the Southampton crowd ending up in a situation where they could trade information about Clio's murder for a free ride in the criminal justice system seems small." Frances took a bite of her food. "No, this one's got to be solved now, or it won't be solved at all."

"Perhaps you should raid Wall Street and see if any insider traders can help you out." Aurelia laughed.

"Maybe."

"Well, I'm sorry that you have to be in the middle of this."

"I've done it to myself."

"As usual."

Aurelia reached over and touched Frances's hand. Her fingers felt warm. "I worry about you," she said.

Frances pulled her hand away. "I saw you and Malcolm chatting it up."

"He's charming."

"The consummate politician. He's even working a donor's funeral," Frances said.

Aurelia sat back in her chair and took a sip of wine. "Are you happy in that office?" she asked.

"What do you mean?"

Aurelia furrowed her brow. "Is it possible that my own

daughter doesn't understand what 'happy' means? I'm asking if you like your job, if your work is satisfying."

Frances hadn't thought about the issue so directly. As she tried to formulate an answer, she realized how saturated she was by her frustrations with the legal system, with its inability to help the victims of crime, and by her mounting sense of the futility of what she had done, day in and day out, for the last thirteen years. The sweet Hortons, whose life savings were wiped out by a crook who wouldn't serve a day in jail, the Andrew Bryants of the world who would be prosecuted for political revenge . . . Frances felt little pride in what she had done recently. Although her focus on Clio's murder had distracted her in recent days, it didn't change her basic feelings.

She watched her mother chew. What did Aurelia want her to say? Did she really want to explore the complexity of Frances's attitudes? Was she just making conversation? If so, perhaps all that was required was a dismissive answer.

Aurelia always had put her own happiness before that of anyone else. Her work, her art, her identity as an artist, these things had seemed in Frances's mind to take precedence over her children or her husband. Frances and Blair had spent months in Southampton under the critical eye of Clio Pratt while their mother had searched for some notion of happiness and self-satisfaction in various art programs, summer colonies, and European retreats. How many times had Frances begged her mother to come back and rescue them? Her pleas to Aurelia, like her pleas to the judges before whom she appeared in her role as a prosecutor, had fallen on deaf ears.

Frances wanted to think she and her mother were very different, but looking at Aurelia across the table, she wondered if that were true. Frances's stomach turned as she thought of her father, alone. Unlike Blair, who was able to demonstrate tenderness on what had to be the worst day of his life, Frances stood behind her emotional wall. She had focused on the flowers in the church, as if somehow an elegant arrangement would lessen her father's pain. Instead the quantity and diversity of arrangements sent by others to fill the altar made her efforts seem wasted. Would her ability to find Clio's killer turn out to be similarly futile? It seemed as if she could do nothing right in terms of helping her father.

"Work's great," Frances said. "Dinner's great. What more could I possibly want?"

Thursday, July 9

$\mathcal{T}$oo tired to drive home,
Frances had spent the night on Aurelia's large worn
couch. Her mother had insisted. Hadn't she been driving
the forty-five miles between Orient Point and Southampton back and forth for days now? Aurelia had offered her
own bed, but Frances's willingness to stay was contingent upon not displacing her mother. The compromise
was struck. Aurelia fixed a makeshift bed, puffed a pillow, and made chamomile tea as Frances took a hot bath.
A call to Sam insured that Felonious and Miss Demeanor
would be fed and let out.

Frances awoke, disoriented. She couldn't remember
the last time she had spent the night in a room not her
own. The interlocking ring patterned quilt that had covered her when she'd fallen asleep lay in a heap on the
floor. Her back ached from the sagging springs, and her
sinuses felt clogged. Summer allergies. She heard sounds
in the kitchen.

"I'm making blueberry muffins," her mother called into the living room when Frances started to stir. The domesticity was unfamiliar but appreciated.

The Blue Book of the Hamptons on the coffee table caught her eye as she headed for the shower. A combination social register and telephone book, it listed residents of the Hamptons, Water Mill, Sag Harbor, and Quogue who were willing to pay $60 to advertise their summer and winter addresses, children, and children's schools. Frances flipped through her mother's copy of the distinctive directory. Aurelia Penelope Watson, home on Halsey Neck Lane, *Miss Frances Taylor Pratt, Brown University '84, New York University Law School '87; Mr. and Mrs. Jacob Robert Devlin (Blair Pratt), Trinity College '87*. She found Beverly Winters, with her maiden name of Blodgett indicated in parenthesis, located on Meadowmere Lane. She had one daughter: *George Washington University '87*.

Did the Blue Book of the Hamptons list Clio's killer?

Frances stuffed the directory into her backpack.

After breakfast she stepped outside into another cloudless day, got into her truck, and headed in the direction of Meadowmere Lane. She decided not to call first. The distance from her mother's house to the home of Beverly Winters, a five-minute drive, would give her a moment to think what it was she wanted to ask.

Beverly Winters lived in a Tudor-style stucco home with a slate roof and midnight blue shutters. The landscaping of boxwoods, azalea, and rhododendron, though unoriginal, was well maintained. A slate patio off the left side of the house overlooked a swimming pool. As

Frances stood at the front door, she could glimpse the water through the slats of weathered fence surrounding it. The image of Dudley Winters wheeling to the edge in the middle of the night and toppling himself to his drowning death, the scene that Blair had described in their initial conversation about Beverly, flashed in Frances's mind. She shivered despite the warm temperature.

Frances rang the doorbell and heard the timbre echo inside. After a few moments a woman appeared. Her streaked hair was wet, accentuating the difference between the blond highlights and darker roots. She wore a pink terry bathrobe belted loosely at the waist and smoked a cigarette. Frances diverted her eyes from the woman's partially exposed breast.

"May I help you?" She spoke in a raspy voice.

Frances introduced herself to Beverly Winters.

"I'd offer you a condolence or something, but you didn't come over here uninvited just to hear me say I'm sorry for your loss, now, did you." Beverly's eyes seemed focused behind Frances on a spot out by the road. She tightened the belt around her waist and leaned against the door frame, rubbing one foot on top of the other. The ash of her cigarette dropped to the floor, and she brushed it away with a burgundy-painted toe.

After several moments it became apparent that Frances would not be invited in. Beverly seemed in no mood to play hostess.

"I wanted to ask you a couple of questions." Frances tried to sound official. As Beverly leaned toward her, she could smell the stale cigarettes that saturated the woman's pores. "You were one of the last people to be with Clio before she died. I understand you played tennis together that morning."

Beverly gave her a suspicious look.

"What time was it that you played again?"

"Nine." She stretched out the word. *Ny-anne*.

"For an hour?"

"A little longer."

Frances took a step back away from the door and Beverly's nicotine perfume. "Who else played?"

"Ann Helmut, Susan Carver, Clio, and I. Why are you asking me these questions?" Beverly sounded bored. She slouched her shoulders.

"I'm trying to reconstruct Clio's last moments. Did she talk to you at all, I mean, during the game?"

"Other than to keep score or make a call? Not really, no."

"What happened after you finished?"

"I can't remember. Listen to me, early onset of Alzheimer's. Either that, or too much sun." She took a drag of her cigarette and blew the smoke in Frances's direction. Frances coughed but didn't move. "Ann left. She was meeting her personal trainer. It exhausts me just thinking about her schedule." Beverly twirled her cigarette around in her fingers.

"And the other women?"

"Susan and I went up to get a drink. We saw Clio again a few minutes later on the clubhouse porch. I figured she hadn't wanted to be seen socializing with us." She took a long drag. Frances prepared herself for another nicotine onslaught, but it didn't come. Instead Beverly tilted her head back and exhaled up to the sky.

"I understand you two had your differences." Frances tried to sound diplomatic.

Beverly raised her eyebrows. "I'd just as soon let bygones be bygones, under the circumstances. I've put her out of my mind."

"Why did you play tennis?"

"It wasn't Clio's idea, I can tell you that much. Clio, Ann, and Susan have a regular match. I was filling in for Constance Von Furst, their usual fourth. I assume they tried everyone who can hit the ball over the net before they called me. But Saturdays it's hard, and July Fourth is especially tough. Women out here have their matches booked long in advance. Susan asked me to play."

"Did you talk to Clio on the porch?"

"I might have made a reference to our match in passing. Just to let her little group know." Beverly laughed again.

"Do you remember who was with her?"

"Marshall and Beth Bancroft. I don't remember anyone else."

"Louise's parents," Frances confirmed.

"A nice girl. She's not much for the club anymore. Not since it turned down her husband." This first piece of unsolicited information from Beverly made Frances wonder why the Membership Committee's proceedings weren't simply open to the public. The pretense of confidentiality seemed to last no longer than the meeting itself.

"What do you know about that?"

Beverly squinted at Frances. "Not much."

"Please, it could be very important."

"I've heard what I assume everyone's heard."

"Which is?" Frances prompted.

"Henry's black. Clio objected on account of his race. Jack Von Furst, he's the president of the Membership Committee, certainly agreed. Gail Davis, the secretary, kind of straddled the fence, as did Peter Parker, although he never has an opinion about anyone, just votes the way the momentum is going. Only George Welch—he was vice president—put up a fight. He flew off the handle. Wallace Lovejoy was with him in principle, wanted Henry Lewis to be admitted, but not to the same extent. Wally wasn't adamant like George. George resigned from the committee in protest." Beverly spoke as if she were reading from a grocery list.

"Who did you hear that from?"

"A good reporter never reveals her sources." Beverly flicked her butt past Frances into the driveway. "That's all I can tell you."

"Were you at the club when Clio's body was found?"

"I certainly was. Now if you'll excuse me, I have to dry my hair." Beverly stepped inside and started to shut the door.

"Just one more thing." Frances put up her hand to block the door from closing.

Beverly Winters released her hold on the door frame. "What?" she barked.

"I have to ask you about your husband, your late husband."

"What about him?"

"Uh . . ." Frances fumbled for words, not knowing precisely how to lead into what she wanted to ask but wanting to keep Beverly engaged in conversation. "When did he die?"

"August twenty-third. Three years ago."

"I'm really sorry."

"I bet you are," Beverly snorted.

"Before his death, you and he were friends with my father and Clio."

"I guess you'd call us that. Richard and Dudley played golf occasionally at Shinecock. We weren't members of the National."

Shinecock Hills Golf Club, the site of several major PGA tournaments, was considered the more challenging of the two private golf courses in Southampton, but nothing compared with the beauty and luxury of the National Golf Club's well-kept greens, expansive vistas, and first-class clubhouse. It was a golfer's Mecca. Richard belonged to both clubs.

"We saw them socially out here, but not much in the city," Beverly said.

"Any reason?"

"I didn't have the time or the money for the ladies' charity circuit."

"The what?"

"You know, women who aren't employed, and who hire domestic help so that they don't have to raise their own kids. They've got to have rich husbands. The money buys them control of charities to keep them busy. It gives them an excuse to get dressed up and do lunch, plan some fund-raiser. Dudley never had that kind of cash. I wasn't part of that scene."

Frances sensed the bitterness in her voice. Apparently she had wanted to be.

"What does this have to do with anything?" Beverly removed a pack of Marlboro filters from her bathrobe pocket and lit another cigarette.

"Did you have any conversations with my father about Dudley's death?"

"We talked. He called me periodically, at least in the beginning." Frances could sense that Beverly had lost patience.

"Then what happened?"

"What always happens. Life goes on. We went our separate ways. Look, I don't know what this is all about. Dudley has been dead for three years. I thought you were interested in Clio's death. That has nothing to do with my personal life. Now, I have to go. I have an appointment in the city." Beverly stepped inside and quickly pushed the door shut in Frances's face.

Frances rang the bell again. She heard footsteps and a loud cough, but Beverly did not come back to the door. The interview, and the extent of Beverly's cooperation, was over.

As she climbed back into her truck, Frances realized how mentally exhausted she was. For the past four days she had done nothing but probe and ponder who might have had reason to kill her stepmother. All she'd found was bitterness and discontent behind a veneer of affluence. What had she been thinking? Grasping at straws. Various hunches and theories seemed to be leading nowhere, so she had seized on some ill-conceived notion of her sister's to question a bitter widow about her late husband's tragic demise. It had been a while since she'd stooped that low.

Frances felt as useless as her navy blue funeral suit curled in a ball on the floor of her cab. Maybe the police had come up with something. They couldn't be doing worse than she. She settled herself in the driver's seat and undid the waist button of the rayon skirt she had borrowed from her mother. The button had dug into her skin, and she had a red welt just below her navel. She looked down at her roll of white flesh. She hadn't even had kids. What was her excuse?

Besides Beverly, a tragic widow, who else was there? Frances hadn't heard from Belle, which meant that Miles Adler had not returned from Mexico City. Neither had she heard from Meaty, so apparently Cogswell and company were unwilling to share the results of the search warrant they had executed at the offices of Pratt Capital. Meaty's speculation based on a few flimsy hairs led to Henry Lewis, who couldn't be ruled out, although it was hard to imagine someone would actually kill for membership at the Fair Lawn Country Club. But was it possible that Clio's conduct on the Membership Committee offended others as well? Frances ran through the list of names that Gail Davis had given her: Jack Von Furst, Wallace Lovejoy, Peter Parker, George Welch. Both Henry and Beverly had mentioned Welch as the one who was the most outraged by what Clio had done. She might as well see what he had to say. She removed the Blue Book of the Hamptons from her backpack and looked him up.

George Welch's home on South Main Street was easy

to miss, and Frances drove by the entrance several times before locating the drive. The high, thick privet camouflaged the house from view of the road, and the small driveway had no sign or mailbox to mark its entrance. An enormous U-Haul truck was parked in front. The door was ajar.

Frances stood in the doorway, staring into the foyer. "Hello," she called. Packed boxes and several rolled rugs were stacked against the walls. A bucket of cleaning supplies sat in the middle of the floor. Shoes, books, tennis balls, and what looked to be the miscellaneous contents of a hall closet formed a loose pile next to it. "Is anyone home?" she called again.

"Who is it?" She heard a male voice upstairs.

"It's Frances Pratt. I'm from the Suffolk County District Attorney's Office. I'm looking for Mr. Welch."

A round, flushed face leaned over the top of the banister. "I'll be right down."

A few moments later a balding man with a boxy frame appeared. He wore khaki Bermuda shorts, a baggy polo shirt with a tear at the bottom, and Docksiders. There was perspiration on his broad forehead. He wiped his hands on a rag as he descended the stairs.

"I'm George Welch," he said.

"I'm sorry to interrupt you."

"Depending on why you're here, I may or may not be glad for the break. I'm in the process of moving," he explained in response to Frances's wandering gaze. "The house is on the market, if you know anyone who might be interested."

"I'll keep that in mind."

"What can I do for you?" he prompted.

"I'm looking into the murder of Clio Pratt. I just wanted to ask you a few questions, if you don't mind," Frances said. "Clio was married to my father."

"So you're Richard's daughter." George Welch eyed her suspiciously. "I can see the resemblance. Richard and I have known each other for years. We're both Andover graduates, although he's quite a few years ahead of me."

Phillips Academy, the preparatory school in Andover, Massachusetts, was her father's alma mater. Frances hadn't wanted to go to boarding school, despite her parents' strong encouragement, but Blair had gone and thrived, much to her father's delight. It was simply one more in the long list of attributes that linked Blair and Richard.

"Small world," Frances remarked absentmindedly.

"In this community, people try their damnedest to keep it as small as possible."

"I need to ask you about your role on the Membership Committee of the Fair Lawn Country Club."

George looked at her intently, as if he hoped to read her mind by staring at a point on the bridge of her nose. "Do I need a lawyer?" he asked.

The question startled Frances. She reminded herself that she had come because he, of all the members, had been the most upset by Clio's decision on the Lewis application. Should she be advising him of his rights? Was it possible that his anger had overwhelmed him? Frances allowed herself to imagine the scenario. George Welch, a prep school graduate turned Southampton businessman, murdered the bigot socialite because he wanted to create a kinder, gentler Fair Lawn Country Club, one that would embrace all creeds and colors. The middle-aged man in front of her didn't look the part of a calculating killer, although she wasn't exactly sure what the proper look would be.

"It's your choice, of course, but I'll only take a moment of your time."

George shifted his weight, hesitating, then shrugged. "All right. Come in. I think we can find a seat in the other room." He led her into a small study through a maze of boxes, books, and furniture wrapped in brown paper. Two striped armchairs were pushed into one corner. "Sorry about the mess." He gestured for her to have a seat.

"It's neat compared to my place, and I'm not going anywhere," Frances said.

George chuckled politely.

Through the row of windows, Frances could see a gunite swimming pool. Scattered leaves floated on the surface. "You've got a nice place here. Why are you moving?"

"Let's just say things haven't worked out exactly as I planned." He sighed. "I'd offer you something to drink, but I'm not sure I could find you a glass in this chaos."

"I'm fine, thanks."

"Well, what can I tell you?"

"When did you resign from the Membership Committee of Fair Lawn?"

George raised his eyebrows. She noticed his shoulders pull back. "From the committee? June first of this year. My resignation from the club is effective September first, although I don't plan to set foot in that place between now and then anyway. But my wife, or rather my soon-to-be-ex-wife, wanted to stay there for August."

"Stay at the club?"

"Yes. It's convenient, and there weren't many options this late in the summer. Hotels are booked."

"How long have you been a member?"

"Probably twenty years. We bought this place in '75 or '76. We must've joined the club shortly thereafter."

"Did you resign because of what happened with Henry Lewis's application?"

George leaned forward and rested his elbows on his slightly spread knees. "I wasn't aware that the Suffolk County District Attorney's Office took a particular interest in the workings of a private country club."

"We don't, but I understand Henry Lewis raised quite a stir with the committee. Clio Pratt didn't want him to be accepted, and others, including yourself, did."

"That's true."

"And I also know that you were pretty mad about that. Henry's your friend, isn't he?"

"I like and respect Henry Lewis, though if we were friendly at one time, we're not any longer."

"Why is that?"

"Because he blames me. He blames me for the way this society operates, for its inability to change. I'm not his enemy, but he thinks I am. He thinks I'm no different from anyone else out here."

"Even after you resigned?"

"In his view, too little too late. Principles, however good or noble they are, don't matter much in the end.

Don't you agree? What matters ultimately is the way people act."

"Why do you think there was such opposition to him?"

"I think if you asked anyone, they'd come up with a reason that has nothing to do with the color of his skin. Except for Clio. I got to hand it to that woman, she was candid. Others use euphemisms. 'He and his wife seem like loners' or 'We haven't had an opportunity to get to know him' or 'He might bring in the wrong kind of guests.' Sometimes people use the word *tradition*. You know, 'We don't want to change tradition.' Anyway, it's all just double talk. Henry's black. They're white. They don't want him on their tennis courts. As much as it infuriated me, Clio was the only honest person in the group."

"Why the paranoia?"

"I'm no sociologist. But what I see is a very affluent, very insecure group of people that want to keep the rest of the world out. They're under the misguided notion that their society can be protected from all the evil that infects the rest of the world if they can keep themselves entertained at expensive catered dinner parties making small talk about who's marrying whom, and who's buying which house. The problem is, they can try for a while, but they're doomed to failure. All the money in the world won't keep you free from disease, divorce, sadness. Just look at the young generation out here. The kids drink too much, spend their parents' cash on recreational drugs, and then get themselves killed driving the Porsches that their parents buy them when they turn sixteen. Nobody achieves. Nobody cares about anything except having a good time. And if they're not partying, then they don't know what to do with themselves. Two kids I know out here killed themselves last year. What do you think the odds of that are?" George paused, reached into his back pocket, and removed a handkerchief. He wiped his forehead. "Nobody wants to examine what's going on, the social deterioration that comes from too much money. So instead they worry about infiltration, penetration by blacks or Hispanics or Jews or whoever, those who are more successful, enlightened, attractive, or cultured than the has-beens out here. Southampton's created its own society and proclaimed its social leaders. Nobody else is welcome." Then, as if remembering why the conversation had arisen in the first place, George added, "Clio Pratt was exactly what I'm talking about."

Frances remembered seeing a needlepoint pillow in Clio's dressing room. *You can never be too thin or too rich.* The Southampton motto.

"You can't be a lone dissident in a place like this. It's too hard. These people are comforted by the fact that they're all alike. They think their friends reflect on them and they want the reflection to be lily white. I can't effect change. I can't impose my views. I'm a pretty mainstream guy myself and I'm not out to lead a social revolution. But I can't be a hypocrite, either. If I don't approve of what's going on, I shouldn't enjoy the place myself." George slumped back in his chair, seemingly exhausted.

Frances waited a moment before speaking. His explanation needed silent punctuation. Then she asked, "Were you at Fair Lawn last Saturday?"

"Yes. I'd gone to clean out my locker. I haven't been there since."

"Did you see Clio that morning?"

"No. But I was in the clubhouse when I heard the scream."

"What were you doing?"

"I was filling out some paperwork at the front desk. It's in the entranceway, just around the corner from the ladies' powder room. As I said, I'd resigned from the Membership Committee and terminated my membership effective Labor Day. It's pretty threatening to that place if you actually want to leave voluntarily, and the paperwork's voluminous. I'd hoped to finish before the tournament crowd arrived. I knew it was going to be the last time I was there."

"Did someone assist you with the paperwork?"

"There was a young girl behind the desk. She was answering the telephone. The manager had left the documents for me with her. The forms were self-explanatory. It was time-consuming, but I didn't need assistance."

"What did you do when you heard the scream?"

"What anyone else would, I suppose. I ran toward it. There was a woman screaming in the bathroom, and then I saw Clio on the floor in the stall. I tried to revive her, you know, I patted her face, but she didn't move. I checked her pulse. Nothing. Jack Von Furst showed up right behind me. He left to call 911. I stayed with her, although I didn't want to move her. When the police came, I gave them a statement. That's about it."

"Have you spoken to anyone about what happened?"

"Only the police, like I said. In all honesty, I've been

pretty involved with my own problems recently and haven't seen many people."

"What about Henry Lewis?"

"I spoke to him after his application was turned down. It wasn't a pleasant conversation to have, and it didn't end well. I've gone over to his place several times to try to talk to him again, but his wife answers the door and says he's not there, or he's too busy. I've given up trying to understand. It's time for me to leave."

"Where are you going?"

"My current plan is to head south, the outer banks of North Carolina, I think. I'll either find a house or get myself a sailboat that I can stay on for a while. I love to fish. For now, that's as far as I've gotten. My wife's keeping our place in Manhattan."

"Giving it all up?" Frances said, smiling.

"That assumes the 'it' is something worth having to begin with. I'm not sure I'd agree with that characterization of the life out here."

Frances stood up and extended her hand. He held it for just a moment longer than was customary between strangers. "Thank you for your time," she said.

He smiled. "Good luck with your investigation."

Just outside George Welch's drive, Frances pulled her truck over to the curb. For no apparent reason her breath came fast and furious. She tried to collect herself. Had the conversation hit a nerve? She knew the desperate, frantic sensation of needing to escape. She had been there. George Welch would run away and reinvent himself, because at the end of the day he was disgusted with himself, with what he had done with his life.

Maybe Malcolm was right. Maybe she should have stayed out of this investigation instead of delving into the personal lives of various people whose paths had crossed Clio's, however tangentially. Perhaps the world in which her father and his wife lived, battered souls all scrambling for acceptance, was better left uncovered. The underbelly was too raw, too vulnerable, to be exposed.

It appeared that Richard hadn't moved from the sunroom in twenty-four hours. He still wore the same dark suit, white shirt, and gray tie that Blair had dressed him in for Clio's memorial service. He had dark circles under his red-rimmed eyes. In the afternoon light his skin looked bluish gray. Lily was perched on the couch nearby, a tray of tea sandwiches, cheese, and crackers on her lap. The cheese glistened with moisture. Apparently she had given up trying to coax him to eat but was reluctant to return his dinner tray to the kitchen.

"I'm sorry I didn't come back yesterday," Frances said. She spoke softly as she approached so as not to startle him. Richard made no physical sign that he heard her or even recognized that she was in the room. She looked at Lily, who pursed her lips and shrugged. Lily looked equally exhausted. "I wanted to, but there are a lot of people to talk to, a lot to do in this investigation." Her father still didn't move. "Blair stayed with you, right?" Silence.

"She was here until quite late," Lily said.

"I talked to Henry and Louise Lewis." Frances walked around in front of her father. He remained still, staring blankly ahead. She pulled a straight-backed chair over from the far wall and sat beside him with one leg curled under her. "Louise Bancroft, and her husband. As a child, she used to play with Blair."

Slowly her father turned his head toward her. "They had a clubhouse in the attic." He paused between each word.

"I remember. The walls were taxi yellow," she added, hoping he might smile. There was no reaction. "I need to ask you something." She felt her pulse rise. "I hate to ask this, but I need to know why Clio didn't want the Lewises in the Fair Lawn Country Club."

Richard said nothing. Lily rose and excused herself, taking the supper tray with her. She would be in the kitchen if either of them needed anything.

"Can we talk about it?" Frances asked. "Please."

Richard seemed to stare past her. When he spoke, his voice sounded more strained than usual. It was a forced sound, as if the words pained him.

"Fair Lawn isn't ready for a black member," he said. "We admitted the first Catholic . . . 1979. Southampton had changed by then. We knew that, but it was still a big step. A few years ago, the first Jew joined. There was a lot of opposition to that. We don't want Hollywood here. We don't want to become East Hampton."

Frances needed to move. She jiggled her foot.

"The membership needs time to assimilate change."

Frances felt her stomach turn. She didn't want the conversation to continue, yet she knew she needed to hear what her father had to say. Whether it ultimately helped in solving Clio's homicide, whether Clio's thinking had played any role in her murder, were less important than for her to listen to her father's views. She didn't have to agree, but she needed to hear what he had to say.

"It was for Henry's own good. He would be ostracized." Richard paused and looked directly at her. "You can't know what that's like. Nobody can, until they've been there themselves."

It was the first time Frances had ever heard her father make even an opaque reference to his own handicap, the exclusion he felt.

"But wasn't that Henry Lewis's choice to make? He wanted to join."

"He wants to belong. There's a difference." Richard ran his tongue over his dry lips. "I don't expect you to understand. You've lived your life without social institutions, but they matter to some of us."

His accusation was unfair. Frances didn't belong to country clubs, church congregations, or even professional organizations, but that didn't mean she didn't venerate institutions. Take the Supreme Court of the United States. She believed in the nobility of that as an institution, didn't she? She believed in marriage, certainly, despite what had happened with Pietro, but she couldn't speak in her own defense. Her father's "us" symbolized the inclusion of some within his carefully guarded universe and the exclusion of others. She was the disappointing child. Despite her efforts, nothing would change that.

"Did you or Clio know Henry Lewis? Did you know anything about him?" Frances realized that she had an easier time confronting her father's unacceptable bigotry than she did understanding why he felt the way he did.

She looked at her father, old and infirm beyond his physical years.

He nodded, then bit his lip. She could see his nose twitching.

"Your opinions, Clio's. How she treated people. It's all important for me to understand," she said. "Although I wish it weren't the case, it seems possible that you, or Clio, may have made someone extremely angry by taking the positions you've taken. Don't you see that?"

Richard didn't look at her when he asked, "Do you ever experience shame?"

"Shame?" *What does that have to do with anything?* she wondered.

"You won't understand what I'm about to tell you if you don't understand the term."

"Embarrassment? Guilt? Self-loathing?" Frances searched for words, hoping to find one that would satisfy her father and allow him to continue. He didn't acknowledge the adequacy of her synonyms.

They sat in silence for what seemed an interminable period before Richard began to speak. "Clio was a more complex person than you or your sister gave her credit for being. I know what you thought of her. I know you weren't fond of her, but you didn't know her. Clio lived with a lot of demons."

"I was—" Frances stopped, as her father's knowing look prevented what was sure to be a disingenuous rejoinder.

"What I'm going to tell you may not make sense to you. You'll have to step outside your own sense of morality and try for once to empathize." Frances felt the painful jab of his words, but she didn't stir. "Clio developed a condition, a medical condition, something serious and debilitating although, unfortunately, not the type of condition that generates much sympathy. Cancer would've been easier in many ways. People feel sorry for cancer victims. They show compassion." He closed his eyes momentarily, then continued. "It started shortly after Justin's death. She believed Henry knew about it. She felt ashamed, and that made her vulnerable. She didn't trust him."

What was he talking about? There was nothing wrong with Clio. The medical examiner would've found any sign of disease.

"It became significantly more serious after my stroke. Clio had a very difficult time, as anyone would. She was convinced that something awful would happen to her. First Justin, then me. In her mind, she had lost us both. She developed fears. At first they were minor, passing nightmares, that didn't interfere with her day-to-day life, but they escalated until she became certain that the slightest headache was a brain tumor. Back pain was bone cancer. Someone who was late for a visit had been killed on the highway. She seemed to look for disaster, to expect the worst. It was irrational. I didn't pay much attention at first."

Richard lifted his hand to the corner of his mouth and wiped away spittle with his palm. As his fingers dragged across his face, they pulled on his lips. He swallowed hard, and when he spoke again, his words were clearer. "I had my work. I was busy. Later, when Clio got much sicker, I had my own physical problems to distract me.

Still do. I thought Clio needed attention, but I couldn't give it to her. As time went on, though, I realized something was horribly wrong. She wept constantly, came in to show me every lump, bump, and freckle that she claimed had just appeared. Each mole was a melanoma, each bruise a sign of a fatal blood condition. She wasn't sleeping. She lost weight. I was unable to help. It was difficult to watch." Richard gazed straight ahead at the glass in front of him. "Finally, I spoke to Marshall Bancroft. He's been a dear friend, a constant visitor. From where I am, it's hard to get help, but I figured Marshall might be able to give me some advice. He did. He spoke to Henry Lewis, his son-in-law. Henry recommended a psychiatrist. Clio was very reluctant to see anyone, any mental health professional. She was suspicious. She's a very private person. She never liked to talk about her emotions. Not like your mother." He paused. His reference to Aurelia hung in the air, and Frances wondered why he thought of his first wife at this particular moment. "I was suspicious, too, but I had seen the transformation come over her, and I was worried. Marshall assured me that this doctor was a first-rate professional, not a quack. He helped Beverly Winters when Dudley died. He also explained that the doctor used medication to manage a lot of anxieties."

"Did Clio ever talk to Marshall Bancroft herself?"

"No. In fact, when I first told her about Marshall's suggestion, she was furious that I confided in him. She viewed my disclosure as a huge betrayal, but I knew it would be all right. Marshall is discreet. He's also a very dear friend. I finally convinced her to go see this psychiatrist. The office was out of the way. She wouldn't run into someone she knew on 168th Street. Not like the risk of a midtown doctor."

"Was the doctor's name Prescott?" Frances asked, remembering the prescribing physician listed on Clio's bottle of Nardil.

"Yes. Prescott. . . ." Richard rolled the name around in his mouth. "Clio started seeing him once a week, sometimes more. He put her on medication. She was more herself. She went out, saw friends. She got involved in Pratt Capital. She almost seemed happy at times. Again. She looked more radiant than ever."

What did all this have to do with shame? Frances wondered, recalling the origin of this conversation.

"Even though the doctor was a positive experience, Clio remained extremely nervous about anyone finding out. She was convinced that Henry Lewis knew about her situation. That was why she didn't want Henry anywhere near her, or anywhere near her friends. She was afraid he would gossip."

"Did Henry know how she felt?" Frances asked, disoriented by the slow pace and difficult cadence of his speech, plus the candor of their conversation. She had never before heard her father talk so openly about his wife.

"I'm not sure Henry even knew the referral was for Clio. I never talked to him myself, and Marshall never said a word to me again. It's quite possible he asked Henry for advice without ever identifying Clio."

"Why do you think it mattered to her, all the secrecy?"

"You didn't know Clio well, but you had something

very much in common. You're both very private people. She didn't want anyone to get too close to her, to become too intimate. It scared her. Her past scared her, and the future scared her, for different reasons. Emotional distance was her protection. Just as it is for you."

His sudden turn of the conversation startled Frances. She searched his sad eyes, but they seemed blank.

"Clio and I were married for thirty years. She never did a single thing to hurt me. I hope if asked, she would've said the same for me. I was never happier."

Frances couldn't discern whether he was comparing Clio with Aurelia or simply proclaiming his love. Ultimately, she supposed, it didn't matter.

"Even though Clio knew at a rational level that this doctor was good for her, she was filled with fear, worry about what she perceived to be a terrible weakness, a failure, an inability to solve her own problems. A part of her hated herself for losing control of her emotions. Even as her irrational fears subsided, she started exerting her power, controlling situations for the simple sake of empowering herself. Like Pratt Capital. She spent hours trying to master everything that was going on with the company, challenging Miles, making decisions for herself. And the addition she built for me. She worked day and night on that, on every detail. She wanted me in a bubble, a self-contained space with round-the-clock nurses to keep me safe because she couldn't face that I was going to die."

Frances thought she saw tears forming in her father's eyes. She looked away. He sniffled.

"I don't understand what this has to do with shame." Frances spoke softly.

"Shame is a debilitating quality. It means you can't accept who you are. Clio couldn't accept who she had become, the emotions she developed because of the way her life transpired. It's hard to imagine, I know. She always seemed so pulled together, so beautiful, so poised, but underneath she had so much ambivalence about herself."

"And this happened since Justin's death?"

"Dramatically, yes. But the seeds of her emotional turmoil were there long before. Look at the relationship she had with you girls. She wanted to love you, but, well, you know better than anyone the nature of your relationship."

Was this passing comment her father's justification for years of Clio's behavior? Although Frances knew her opportunity had arrived to have the conversation with her father that she had envisioned since her childhood, she didn't know how to respond. The questions that had ruminated in her mind for so many years seemed to evaporate. *Come on, Frances,* she urged. *Ask him why Clio didn't show an iota of genuine affection. Ask him why she hated two little girls who hadn't done anything wrong.*

Before she could muster her courage, Richard announced unexpectedly, "I'm tired."

As she stood up, Frances felt dizzy. Her leg was numb. "I should go. But thank you, thank you for telling me what you have. I'm sorry if I've—"

"Think about what I said," he interrupted.

She nodded, though his remark was unnecessary. His words would haunt her for many nights to come.

*   *   *

The ship's lantern on the front door of Blair's cottage in Sag Harbor was lit. It looked welcoming as Frances drove up, exhausted. "Oh, come for dinner. Jake's not here, but there's someone I want you to meet," Blair had said on the telephone. Her cheerful voice and enthusiasm promised a pleasant atmosphere. Frances actually looked forward to the evening, a possible reprieve from the many questions that buzzed in her mind.

Blair came out onto the front step as Frances approached and waved. She wore a loose linen dress. The light shining behind her illuminated her silhouette, her trim figure. Behind her stood a tall man with long dark hair, a tanned complexion, and a turquoise shirt opened almost to his silver belt buckle.

"Fanny, Fanny, we're so glad you're here!" Blair turned. "This is Marco. He's the fabulous sculptor I was telling you about. Marco, meet my sister, Frances. Everyone calls her Fanny."

Frances stepped forward and shook his hand. His fingers were warm and long, and he gripped her hand tightly. "It's nice to meet you," she said. His enormous eyes were magnetic, and she forced herself to look away.

"The pleasure is mine."

"Blair says you're from Argentina."

"That's right. But now I'm from Brooklyn. I'm not sure whether that's considered an upward move or not." Frances noticed he spoke with hardly any accent. Blair giggled.

"Come inside," Blair said, pushing Frances forward. "Marco will get you a glass of wine. We're sampling various Spanish reds tonight."

They went into the kitchen, an open area with an island in the middle. Several bottles of uncorked wine were on the counter, along with a dish of olives, a wedge of hard cheese, and slices of crusty bread. Frances reached for an olive.

Marco had turned his back to them and stood stirring the contents of several skillets with a wooden spoon. The kitchen smelled of garlic and tomatoes.

"Marco's making a Portuguese recipe," Blair said, smiling flirtatiously.

"It's swordfish. I hope you'll like it," he added.

"I'm sure I will," Frances said.

"I'm going to take my darling sister out to the deck. Holler if you need anything," Blair said, kissing Marco's shoulder. She filled her glass from one of the wine bottles and led Frances outside.

"What do you think?" Blair whispered as soon as she and Frances settled on two lounge chairs.

The evening was cool, and Frances felt a slight chill, surprising for July. She pulled her knees to her chest.

"He's a fantastic cook, too. You'll see." Blair looked truly radiant, her white teeth shining behind her gloss-glistened lips. Was this happiness a result of Marco or newfound wealth? Frances wondered. She tried not to think about it. She didn't feel like being jealous of her younger sister, but it was hard not to envy her apparent joy.

"And Jake?"

"Not my favorite subject," Blair replied.

"I hadn't understood things between you weren't working."

"I guess you could say that." Blair laughed. "I know I shouldn't be doing this, but, well, it's just that Marco's everything Jake's not. Charismatic, sexy, talented."

"Is this because of your financial problems?" Frances asked.

"Oh, Fanny. You're so unromantic," Blair said, smiling. "Although I admit that the disaster with the gallery was the straw that broke the camel's back. Jake's too dependent, too needy. I feel like I always have to be the one in charge, the one that solves our problems. Sometimes I just want a man to take care of me."

Frances nodded. The thought was appealing. "Does he know about Marco?"

"No. I tell him we're out here marketing. Actually, it's the truth, or part of the truth. I'm introducing Marco to potential clients. If they fall in love with him, which everyone has, they'll want to buy his art when we give him a show in October. Jake actually seems to think it's a great idea. We also have millions of decisions to make for the new showroom. Since the space is for Marco's work, he should be involved in the build-out, design, lighting. He knows better than anyone what works with his art."

"I heard you mention the new gallery to Penny Adler. You must be excited."

"Long-term, if Jake doesn't dig us out of our financial mess, the gallery will be forced to close, but at least for now our expansion plans are possible. Daddy's paying the lease, and all the work to get the new space up and running. It's bigger and better than our current one."

"When did Dad agree to this?"

Blair eyed her sister over the rim of her wineglass. "Why does that matter?"

"I'm just curious."

Blair pursed her lips, thinking. "Jake insisted that I talk to Clio about it a month or so ago. She claimed to have discussed it with Dad. They said no back then, or at least that's what she said, although I shouldn't be surprised. Anyway, we had a terrible lunch. She made me beg for the money, knowing full well that she had no intention of giving me any. I don't know why I bothered to ask her in the first place. I actually amaze myself. I continued to give her the benefit of the doubt until the day she died, and all I got was disappointment, insult, and sometimes downright cruelty. If it had been up to her, our gallery, and everything we've tried to build, would have gone right down the drain. She didn't care."

Frances lay back in her chair and took a sip of wine. She wanted to turn off her brain. "So how did it come about now?" she asked automatically.

"What?"

"Dad's infusion of cash. The change of heart."

"I guess Jake and I are lucky Clio disappeared from the scene when she did." Blair smiled again. "Actually, I made up my mind to go ahead with the project with or without the help of Pratt Capital. I hired an architect to draw up plans and did a business proposal to try to get financing. Several banks were considering it, although I had no commitment. Then, when Clio fortuitously dropped dead, I thought there was nothing to be lost by asking Daddy again. I talked to him last Sunday, when I was over at the house all day helping him with things for the memorial service. He apologized for not giving us the money sooner. If Clio hadn't been such a roadblock, it all would have been done in June, and we'd be ready to open in September. As it is now, unless our contracting crew does an incredibly fast job, which I don't see happening in August in New York, the space won't be ready until October. But that's okay. At least we've got it." She sighed. "Jake seemed to be stuck wringing his hands."

"Where was he over the Fourth, anyway?"

Blair furrowed her brow, then waved a hand at her sister dismissively. "You don't honestly think that Jake had anything to do with Clio's murder, do you? Please. Jake doesn't have the balls to have bumped her off." Blair laughed. "Believe me, I wish he had. At least I could be proud of him for accomplishing something." She took a sip of her wine. "No, Jake wasn't doing anything so dramatic. He canceled his trip to Ohio because Pearl and Bartlett Brenner, this couple in Scarsdale we've sold to before, were interested in two lithographs. Shows how desperate he was. Calls off a trip to his family for what would be, at most, a ten grand sale." Frances must have looked skeptical because Blair added sarcastically, "I can give you the Brenners' number if you want to check."

"That's okay," Frances said in an effort to dispel her suspicions. Blair was her sister after all, and they were talking about her brother-in-law. Didn't she know him better than that?

"Fair Lawn must have been a nightmare on the Fourth," Frances mumbled aloud.

Blair glared at her. "Do we have to talk about that? I've tried very hard to put it out of my head."

"Not if you don't want to."

The two sisters were silent for a moment.

"I shouldn't even have gone," Blair said finally. "But every muckety-muck attends the tournament. I thought it would be good to go and mingle. I'd gone as Deirdre Granger's guest. I was going to ask Clio to let me come on Dad's account, but I couldn't bring myself to do it. I didn't want to give her the pleasure of coming up with some reason to say no."

"Did you see Clio?"

"I saw her out on the tennis court, but not to talk to."

"Did you see Mom?"

"Briefly. I think I saw her leaving. I can't remember. We didn't talk long. Just long enough for her to chastise me for not coming to visit. I promised to bring Marco over, which I haven't. But it's not like it's been exactly quiet around here."

"Did you know she started playing tennis again?"

"She wore whites and carried a racket, Mrs. Sherlock Holmes. I deduced as much. Now, could we change the subject to something more exciting, like your love life?" Blair reached over and poked her sister's arm.

Frances grimaced. An interrogation on her least favorite topic was not what she had in mind for the evening. Fortunately, at that moment Marco appeared in the doorway. Dinner was ready.

It was after midnight when Frances returned home. As she entered her darkened house, she felt a huge sense of relief wash over her tired body. She hadn't been home in over twenty-four hours, and she longed for solitude. She flopped down on her sofa. The dogs, particularly attentive after her prolonged absence, curled up next to her and licked her hands. Then they rolled over to let her scratch their velvety bellies.

The telephone ring pierced the silence. She didn't move, letting the answering machine pick up. "What the hell, Fanny? I've been calling you all day. I know you're there, so just listen up. I've tried to indulge you, given the unusual situation, but you've gone too far. Henry Lewis is a major contributor to my campaign, and I do not appreciate your unauthorized inquiry of him. Call me back as—"

Frances picked up the receiver.

"I knew you were there, goddamn it!" Malcolm shouted. "Are you trying to destroy me?"

"I don't know what you mean."

"You were out of line. You *are* out of line. How could you question Henry Lewis? How could you raise even the tiniest suspicions about him or his wife without talking to me? Did you think he wouldn't realize what you were doing? I don't know what kind of a half-assed investigation you're trying to pull on the side, but you've gone too far, even for you."

"I called Louise Lewis, his wife, whom I've known for years. She agreed to answer some basic questions. All I was doing was following up on some theory Meaty thought was worth exploring." Frances regretted mentioning Meaty's name, but it was too late.

"I know about the hair samples. Perry already told Meaty not to pursue that. For that matter, Meaty's also been told several times not to pursue anything through you."

"But you couldn't ignore something that was right in front of you?"

"It was a baseless, racist hypothesis that had no place in my office."

"If more black men commit more drug-related crimes, is it racist or logical to suspect a black man first?"

"I'm not going to have this discussion with you."

"Well, all I did was follow up on Meaty's suggestion. It led to Henry Lewis. I didn't realize that he was so important to you."

"You should have. That's the point. If you gave a rat's ass about the political office that you're involved in, you would've known."

"Why is he interested in Suffolk County politics?"

"Because some people care what happens in their local government. But that's not the point. The point is that he is involved. He hosts fund-raisers. He gives money, lots of it. He gets me exposure where I don't have much. The support of an affluent, prominent African American is extremely important to me."

"Malcolm, I was just doing my job."

"Don't give me that shit. Your job was to stay as far away from this investigation as possible. You're supposed to be indicting Andrew Bryant. Instead, everywhere I turn, I find out you're right in the thick of Clio's murder. And this latest jaunt of yours is going to cost me."

"Why have you cut me out of this investigation?"

"Because you're family. Whether you perceive yourself as that or not, to the rest of the world you and Clio were family, and you're now supposed to be coping with her death."

"Well, maybe the best way I know how to cope is to find her killer."

"The sentiment is admirable but unacceptable. You know damn well, and Meaty does, too, that your involvement raises serious questions about the objectivity of the investigation. I won't have you threatening the prosecution."

"Let me ask you one thing. Statistically, most people are murdered by someone they know. Family members are often the first suspects. Are you keeping me away because you're suspicious of me?"

"That's absurd. Despite your apparent attitudes about your stepmother, I don't think you'd stoop that low."

What a vote of confidence, Frances thought. But how did Malcolm know so much about her feelings toward her family? She couldn't recall ever mentioning a word. A lucky guess, she surmised.

"Look, either you follow directions from your superiors or—"

"Or what?"

"Or, or," Malcolm stammered, "you're fired."

"Well, guess what?" Frances lowered her voice. "I quit."

There was silence on the other end of the line. She hung up.

Friday, July 10

$\mathcal{T}$he sky was overcast and a cool wind blew. Frances focused on the thorny branches in front of her. The black spots on her roses evidenced a week of neglect. As she worked to remove the speckled leaves, she felt adrenaline run through her system, a renewal of energy that she hadn't felt in days. She pulled her dirtied sleeves back up over her elbow, wiped a loose wisp of hair from her forehead, and continued to work.

She tried not to think of what she had done the night before, her split-second decision to quit her job. She had abandoned the one compelling thing that shaped her self-perception. An assistant district attorney, that had been her identity for nearly thirteen years, an identity that survived even after she was no longer Pietro Benedetti's betrothed. She had worked hard to build a Financial Crimes Unit and was proud of what she had accomplished. She couldn't fathom a future without a secure occupation. Gardening was the one task that could distract her.

Frances didn't notice Sam approach.

"Looking good," he said.

She turned and saw him standing beside her with two stacked plastic cups dangling out of one pocket of his misshapen cotton sweater. He held a pitcher of fresh-squeezed orange juice. Pulp floated on the surface of the bright orange liquid.

"I quit my job," Frances said.

He didn't react visibly. "Can I offer you some juice?"

She nodded. Sam poured her a glass as they both settled onto the grass. Felonious and Miss Demeanor came over to sniff the citrus liquid. Felonious dug a hole beside Frances and curled up in the moist earth. Miss Demeanor lay down and rested her head on Frances's foot. For the first time in a week, Frances felt peaceful.

She relayed her telephone conversation of the previous night with Malcolm. "Last night was the worst, but we've had several not very pleasant conversations since this whole thing began. I don't know who he's been talking to, but he's following the details pretty closely. He saw my involvement as a potential media nightmare. It's a high-profile case. He's known my dad a long time. But I get the sense that something else is going on. Something more than Clio's murder, or something about Clio's murder that's triggering something else."

"What do you mean?"

"He's talking to someone, but I don't know who. Someone other than Meaty. Malcolm doesn't get involved in details. He never has. He wants results. 'Make it happen,' that's what he says. He doesn't care how the case gets made. There's this one guy he wants indicted.

It's a bogus case, one the office would call a 'barker.' No offense." Frances scratched Miss Demeanor's ear. "It's a campaign fund violation. The defendant's an idiot, someone with extra money who wanted to buy his way into becoming somebody among the Democratic bigwigs, but he's not a criminal. Anyway, Malcolm's obsessed. He won't listen to any argument why the prosecution is a mistake. Even though the race is over, he wants an indictment to embarrass his opponent. The media buzz usually wears off by the time a case gets to trial, so whether the guy gets convicted or not never really matters. That's how Malcolm operates." The puzzled expression on Sam's face made Frances realize how far off track she had wandered. "My point is that something's up. Malcolm's behavior is too strange."

"Maybe the police, the investigators, know something you don't. Maybe Malcolm has information on suspects."

"Maybe." Frances leaned back on her elbows and felt the grass tickle her forearms. She wondered silently who that might be, then dismissed the thought from her mind. Meaty would have told her if there was any hard information. "My departure's probably long overdue. I've been there a long time, longer than most line assistants." She looked at Sam's face, his furrowed brow, his worried eyes. "Anyway, these guys need a lot more attention than I've given them recently. My garden, too." She paused, looking around. "And there's Dad to think of."

"Are you all right? For money, I mean."

"For a while. There must've been a part of me that was subconsciously heading in this direction, because I've actually got money saved." She smiled. "That's a first. It should be enough to last through year end, I think. Beyond that, who knows." She forced her tone of voice to sound enthusiastic. "Time to move on."

"Do you think you'll leave here?" Sam asked. Frances thought she noted concern in his voice.

She looked behind him at her house. The wooden porch sagged, and several posts in the railing were missing. The shingles on the roof were beginning to come loose, falling off in bits and pieces, with only the underlying black tar paper to protect her from the elements; but otherwise the place looked sturdy. She had replaced most of the windows over the last two years with Thermopane, and the cheery yellow exterior paint masked some of the flaws in the woodwork. Most important, though, it was her home, the only place she belonged, the only place she felt she ever belonged. She wasn't about to give it up.

"I'm a lawyer after all. I could hang out a shingle. Go into the dreaded defense business. Who knows, enough people I prosecuted are bound to get into trouble again. They might realize my brilliance and come to me." She winked.

"Wouldn't it be hard to defend people after prosecuting them for so long?"

"Not really. It's all a big game, or should I say a crapshoot. Look at O. J. Simpson. The guy gets away with murder, literally, and the prosecutors become millionaires off books and television appearances. Or look at that nanny case up in Boston. The au pair who murders the baby, actually gets convicted, and then walks away with no punishment. She had a fan club in England to return to. Whether I'm prosecuting or defending, either one pays the bills."

"Aren't we cynical."

"You're the second person who's told me that recently." She took a sip of orange juice. "Maybe I'll take in boarders instead. Run a bed-and-breakfast in beautiful Orient Point," she mused.

"I don't see you in the hospitality business," Sam teased.

"You could do the hospitality part." Suddenly feeling awkward, Frances looked down and pulled at a blade of grass.

"Anything to help," Sam said softly. He reached out one hand and laid it on top of hers. She flinched—imperceptibly, she hoped— at his touch but didn't pull away. His coarse skin felt warm.

The telephone rang. Frances looked toward the house, wondering whether she should answer. Sam squeezed and then released her hand. "It must be Meaty," she said. "He's the only person who'd call at this hour. Excuse me." She hesitated a moment, then got up and climbed the porch steps two at a time.

"Are you temporarily insane or totally nuts?" Meaty said.

"News travels fast," she muttered.

"Call Malcolm. Tell him you've made a mistake. Tell him you're under stress. Don't be an idiot."

"No." Frances's voice was firm. "I'm done." She was in no mood to be chastised for impulsiveness.

"Stop that. You're being a brat."

"You're entitled to your opinion, but the only thing

I'm much interested in is what you found in my father's office. Or did you think I wouldn't learn about the warrant you served?"

"Frances, stop. I was going to tell you about that."

"Save your breath. I'll see you around." She hung up. The district attorney's office could find someone else to pry into her father's affairs. She would get to the bottom of Clio's murder, not because Malcolm deserved another feather in his cap, but because her father deserved to know.

Frances leaned against the kitchen counter and looked out the window. On his hands and knees, Sam was weeding around a patch of Shasta daisies to the right of the porch stairs. She watched him work, pulling out the errant shoots between his thumb and pinkie with a dexterity that made the lost fingers in between incidental. She thought of his touch and his arm around her shoulder. Had that been Monday night? So much had happened, she'd lost track of the days. But minutes earlier he had touched her again, more deliberately this second time. Despite Sam's gentle nature, he wasn't timid. She liked that.

"A man on his knees. What more could a woman want?" she called out the window.

"How about a man to cook you dinner tonight?" Sam replied without looking up from his work.

"What are you making?"

"Whatever your heart desires."

Frances smiled. Before she could answer the telephone rang again, and without thinking she reached to pick it up. It was Blair.

"Fanny, are you okay?"

"Yeah. Why?"

"Well, it's just you never answer the phone. I'm used to leaving messages."

"Well, you never call this early."

"I didn't wake you, did I?"

"No."

"Are you all right? Your voice sounds odd."

Frances didn't know what to say. She couldn't bring herself to tell her sister that she had quit. She didn't feel like dealing with the reaction, the questions, and the fact that Blair was certain to tell Aurelia. That, in turn, would trigger a panoply of frantic calls. The thought of listening to Aurelia's despair, her dashed hopes to have a daughter who might be a judge, was too much for her first day of official unemployment. Even Blair, who never understood why anyone would want to be a lawyer, was sure to criticize her decision to give up a steady income. "I'm fine," was all she could muster.

"Well, I'm calling to invite you over tonight. Slightly different company this time. Jake had a business dinner scheduled last night with a client who's a potential Marco collector. It got postponed and moved out here. This client wants to meet Marco, so they're coming out together on the four o'clock Jitney. He's single," Blair said.

"Marco or the client?"

"Very funny. The client was the one I was offering."

"No thanks."

"Why do you say no before I've told you anything about him? He's in his mid-forties, divorced with a ten-year-old daughter who lives with her mother in Arizona, so he only sees her a couple of times a year. He's successful, has his own company, something to do with computers. He's trim. He mountain climbs or rock climbs or climbs something or other, I can't remember, but he has a sweet face."

"I'm not interested."

"Come on, Fanny. Live a little. What are you doing tonight that's so compelling?"

Frances looked out the window again at Sam. His face had turned red from exertion, but his weeding pace hadn't slackened. "I'm having dinner with a friend," she replied.

"A friend? Bring her, too," Blair persisted.

"It's not a her," Frances said, pleased to sound mysterious.

Frances piled the few personal belongings that she kept in her office into an empty milk crate. She had been deliberately spare in what she'd brought in over the years. That way, she always told herself, she could just walk out the door at any time. Despite the paucity of personal effects, though, Frances had collected papers, telephone messages, notes, research, and other miscellaneous junk to fill every desk drawer and file in her office. These materials now had to be sorted on the off chance that there was anything of import. Her wastebasket overflowed.

The door opened, and Perry Cogswell's head appeared. Without waiting for an invitation, he stepped inside and stood with his legs slightly spread, his hands deep in his pockets. "We're all so sad to see you go. Couldn't take the pressure?"

Frances pretended to ignore him. She shuffled through a stack of papers.

"Hard feelings about the investigation? Homicide's awfully hard-core. Doesn't mix too well with your background. Plus there's the family issue in this one."

Frances resisted the urge to leap over her desk and knee him in the groin.

"Well, I'm glad you've finally listened to what I've been telling you all along. Your heart's not in this work."

Frances looked up. "If you've come to say good-bye, great. Good-bye. Now it's been said. Shut the door behind you."

"I just hope you'll think of me if you need any professional recommendations for a Wall Street firm. I'd be more than happy to oblige."

Frances flashed a fake smile and returned to the organizational tasks in front of her.

Moments later she was interrupted again. "I heard you were in the building," Malcolm Morris said.

"You have good intelligence at work," Frances replied.

"Fanny, you're making a huge mistake. Don't do this to yourself, to your career. Let's just forget the whole thing." He seemed irritated.

"All I need to know is who's replacing me. If you don't appoint someone fast, I'll leave my files in a pile."

"Come on, Fanny." Malcolm's tone softened. "I've talked to Meaty. Maybe I made a mistake setting up the investigation the way I did. I shouldn't have cut you out. I thought I was being considerate, giving you and your family room, but I understand now that the best thing for you is to stay engaged, involved. Cogswell and you can work it out, I'm sure. You're both professionals. Meaty wants your help." He looked at Frances, but she diverted her eyes, continuing to sort through the stacks of memos in front of her. "Don't you think we both were a little strong-headed?"

"Actually, I don't." Frances turned her pictures face-down in the milk crate.

"Look, even if you're mad at me, you can't just walk out on your unit. Your line assistants are hysterical. They look up to you. They rely on you. Kimberly has been in my office this morning nearly in tears because her first trial is coming up. You're her supervisor. She doesn't know what to do. And Mark mentioned he's got some big evidentiary problem that you'd agreed to help him with. You can't leave these people stranded."

Frances met Malcolm's stare. "Don't make me feel guilty for leaving. There are plenty of people, senior people, around here who can lend a hand."

Malcolm took a deep breath and sighed. His tone changed. "Fanny, if you need time off, to be with your father, whatever, it's yours. But you don't want to quit. What will you do tomorrow when you wake up and have nowhere to go?" He hadn't anticipated opposition to his proposal. She had never seen this mixture of worry and agitation on the face of the sleek politician.

Frances glanced at her watch. It was not yet ten. "I guess I've got the rest of the day to figure that out."

"Frances." Henry Lewis sounded startled as he opened his front door to find Frances standing on the threshold. "What can I do for you?"

"May I come in?" she asked.

He stepped back hesitantly, and she entered the house. He looked more rumpled than the last time she had seen him. The tail of his denim shirt hung out of his khaki slacks. The back pocket of his pants was torn. He was barefoot. She noticed that one toenail was completely purple. He beckoned her toward the living room, and she followed in silence. After they were seated, Henry volunteered that Louise had taken the girls down to the beach for a swim before lunch. "I wasn't in the mood," he added as if his presence in his own house needed to be explained.

"It's not the best of days for a swim," Frances remarked.

"How's your investigation going?" Henry asked coolly.

"I no longer work at the district attorney's office," Frances said.

Henry leaned back and crossed his arms in front of his chest. He had an odd expression on his face. Assuming his complaint to Malcolm had precipitated her sudden departure, Frances couldn't tell whether he felt smug or guilty for criticizing her to her boss.

"Your discussion with Malcolm about our earlier meeting had nothing to do with it," she said. She looked for a reaction. Henry showed none.

"What can I do for you?" He seemed to ignore her remark. His voice was flat.

"I wasn't aware that you were involved in Long Island politics." Frances tried to sound casual.

"No reason you should be."

"I understand you're a big supporter of Malcolm's."

"I don't know about 'big.' I think he's done a good job so far." Henry stared at her intently, then lowered his voice. "My political views are none of your business. Why don't you tell me what you want?"

Frances felt her pulse rise. She should have been prepared for hostility, and she silently reprimanded herself for making herself vulnerable. "Do you remember about eight months or so ago that your father-in-law asked for a recommendation of a psychiatrist?"

Henry nodded.

"Whom did you recommend?"

"Dr. Fritz Prescott."

"How did you know of him?"

"I don't know of him. I know him."

"How?"

"He's on staff at Columbia Presbyterian Hospital. He and I were roommates in medical school. He's a very competent and caring man."

"Did you know at the time that the referral was for Clio Pratt?"

"I assumed as much. Marshall Bancroft said he had a friend in trouble who needed a professional in grief counseling, preferably a specialty in 'spousal loss or incapacitation.' I believe those were his words. Clio was the obvious mystery patient."

"Were you aware that Clio began to see Dr. Prescott?"

"I was." Apparently Henry was prepared to make her work for her information.

"How did you know?"

"I ran into her at Columbia Presbyterian. In the lobby."

"And she told you about it?" That didn't sound like Clio.

"The first time, no. She tried to pretend she hadn't seen me. I wasn't surprised. It's a sad commentary on our society, but people are still embarrassed to seek psychiatric help. We haven't gotten to a place where we recognize it for what it is—another form of medical care."

"If she didn't tell you, how did you know about her relationship with Dr. Prescott?" Frances prompted.

"The second time we saw each other at the hospital, she was very polite, bordering on friendly. She thanked me. She said she liked Dr. Prescott."

"Did she say anything else?"

"Not that I recall. It was a short conversation."

"Did she tell you whether Dr. Prescott had put her on any medication?"

"No she didn't."

"Did he?"

"My only conversation with Fritz on the subject was when I called him to make sure that he had availability to take on new patients. I wasn't about to recommend anyone to Marshall who wasn't in a position to help. It would've been a waste of everyone's time. At that point, I told him what I knew, which was very little."

"So you never asked Dr. Prescott anything about Clio after you knew she was a patient?"

Henry's disapproval was obvious. "That is between them. I would never interfere like that. It would be highly unethical for me to inquire, or for him to disclose."

"Well, when Clio said the guy was helping her, did you ask her anything about it?"

"She said she liked him. I was pleased it had worked out. That's all. Besides, it was quite clear to me later on that Clio regretted having said anything."

"Why do you say that?"

"I can't tell you exactly. All I know is that after our one conversation—which, by the way, was only in passing—Clio did an about-face. She hardly said a word to either me or Louise. When we were doing all the ridiculous stuff to try to get into Fair Lawn, all the parties and meetings with members, Clio actually let people introduce me to her without giving any indication that she already knew who I was. She couldn't do the same to Louise, given the history of Richard's friendship with Marshall, but she was very formal."

"What do you know about Dr. Prescott?"

"I've known Fritz for years. He's a very decent man and a good doctor, as I said. Both his parents were psychiatrists. He's a bachelor and lives in Riverdale. I'm downtown from the hospital, so our paths rarely cross, socially, I mean. He and Louise get along, but he's not particularly fond of children. He calls from time to time, primarily to discuss various drugs. He's extremely interested in psychopharmacology."

"Which is?"

"Managing mental illness through medication."

"Why does he call you?"

"Many of the drugs in use today for psychiatric purposes are prescribed 'off-label,' meaning that they were developed and tested for a specific disease or condition but have been shown to be effective for other, often unrelated problems, including emotional illness. Many of these drugs have side effects, some significant. It's a constant struggle to balance the potential psychiatric benefits and quality of life that may be gained against the physical ramifications. Fritz calls me because I'm a cardiologist. Many of the medications he considers have some effect on the heart, even if it's simply an elevated heart rate."

"So you give him advice about drugs?"

"I wouldn't call it advice. We discuss certain risks. Knowing Fritz as I do, he talks to lots of specialists. He's meticulous in his research."

Frances leaned forward. "May I ask you something in confidence?"

"You may ask me whatever you like. I don't promise to maintain your confidentiality, but I expect that my answers may not remain confidential, either."

"That's fair." Frances took a deep breath, trying to maintain her composure. Henry Lewis had done nothing to make her feel the least bit comfortable. In fact, he seemed to go out of his way to keep the conversation tense. "Clio's body had significant levels of amphetamines in it, as well as trace levels of phenelzine. The coroner believes the amphetamines could have come from over-the-counter diet pills, although there were no actual capsules in her stomach. She had been given a prescription for Nardil by Dr. Prescott. Whether our killer knew that or not, we can't say. The amphetamine level was high enough to have killed her on its own. Can you think of anyone, anyone at all, with access to Fair Lawn who might have known this information?"

"That phenelzine and amphetamines don't mix, or that

amphetamines can kill?" Henry's tone made it clear that he thought Frances's question was pedestrian. "Virtually every woman, or any man, for that matter, I don't want to make sexist assumptions, anyone who's ever taken a diet pill would know about the dangers of amphetamines. The precautions, especially dosage levels, would be right on the warning information. And the warnings have intensified since the onslaught of litigation over diet drugs."

Frances remembered a recent newspaper article about a combination of drugs prescribed for seriously overweight individuals that had resulted in several deaths, a gold mine for the plaintiffs' bar.

"As for phenelzine, it's uncommon. It's used for severe hypochondria and paranoia. You have to look for someone with particular experience with it, or someone with exposure to pretty arcane medical information. Not even your run-of-the-mill doctor would necessarily know about it."

Their mutual thought hung unspoken in the air. Frances had wanted to disprove Meaty's theory. Instead the evidence pointed to a killer with particular coronary expertise who had been close enough to poison Clio within a small window of time before her death. Those characteristics pointed to Henry even without the hair analysis.

"I see. And there's no one you can think of with such knowledge who has access to Fair Lawn?"

"No."

"May I ask you one more thing?"

"What?"

"How did you and my mother meet?"

"Is that part of your investigation?" he asked.

"Just part of my curiosity."

"I met her several years ago. I was brought in for a consult on her heart condition. Since then, we've become acquainted socially. I enjoy her painting. Louise is very fond of her as well."

"Her heart condition?" This was the first Frances had heard of cardiac trouble in her family.

"Her mitral valve prolapse? I assumed you knew."

"I did," Frances lied. "But that was quite some time ago. I'd almost forgotten. I guess she just seems so well." She forced a smile.

"Although mitral valve prolapse can be serious, hers isn't. One of the valves in the heart doesn't function exactly as it should, so she has a slightly irregular heartbeat. Nothing to worry about. Avoiding certain things like caffeine that tend to elevate her heart rate, taking antibiotics before she has any dental work, there aren't many restrictions. She has led, and will continue to lead, a normal life."

Frances stood up and extended her hand, but Henry did not return the gesture. "Thank you for your time," she said softly as she walked to the door.

As Frances drove to her father's house, she used her cell phone to get the telephone number for Dr. Fritz Prescott in Manhattan. The operator patched her through, but Dr. Prescott's voice mail picked up before her call rang even once. She left a message identifying herself as the stepdaughter of his recently murdered patient and gave her number. Dr. Prescott returned her call less than a mile later.

"I was waiting for someone to find me," he said without identifying himself by name. His voice was soft and melodic, soothing, Frances thought. "I read about Clio's death in the paper."

"You haven't spoken to anyone from the police?"

"No. I actually thought Mr. Pratt might give the police my name, but so far I haven't been contacted. You're the first."

"Could you spare any time today?" Frances looked at her watch. She still needed to see her father, but the visit would be brief. "I could be in the city by three."

"I have patients until five o'clock. Why don't we say five-thirty. There's a coffee shop on 168th and Broadway, just across from the hospital entrance, with a red awning and a neon sign advertising waffles in the window. I'll see you there."

"How will I know you?" Frances asked.

"I'll know you," he said. "I've seen your picture."

Each time she slowed down in front of the formal gates and turned off Ox Pasture Road into her father's driveway, Frances felt the same sick feeling in her stomach, tasted the same acidic saliva in her throat. What kind of a life was this for him without Clio? Being wheeled from room to empty room, parked facing out a window, only to be turned periodically for a change of scenery. No one to talk to but Lily or an occasional visitor who passed by for a polite, brief visit, no more than an hour at most. Why go on? She wondered what would happen to him.

Frances parked but sat with the motor idling, staring at the black front door with its oversize brass knocker. The sky had darkened to an eerie gray. Rain was sure to come soon, so ominous was the cloud cover. It felt later than noon.

Frances and Pietro had been visiting Southampton during Hurricane Bob, the hurricane of 1991 that had pounded Long Island and much of the northeastern coastline. With her father they watched the interminable news coverage, reporters in slickers standing in front of pounding surf or toppled trees. Frances had a distinct memory of watching rain on the camera lens. Had some television producer somewhere determined that the storm would feel more real if the reporters were blurred by actual water drops, or had someone simply forgotten to bring an umbrella? Richard had puffed on a cigar. Pietro had smoked and intermittently jumped up from his over-stuffed chair to get a better look out the window. They'd sipped cognac, seemingly content to pass the dismal afternoon in conversational banter, discussions of investment potential in Latin America and manufacturing in Thailand, mixed with sports statistics, the fate of the Yankees, and the U.S. Open. Pietro had been so comfortable with her father, more relaxed than she had ever been in Richard and Clio's house.

Lily's knock on the driver's-side window startled Frances. She rolled down the glass. There were heavy crescents of bluish purple under Lily's eyes, and her skin seemed paler than usual. Frances could see several veins in her forehead.

"Your father's finally asleep," Lily said softly, as if her

voice might actually carry inside. "I didn't want you to ring the doorbell. He's gotten so little rest. He's very weak." She stepped back from the truck, allowing Frances to get out.

Frances looked at her father's nurse, wondering whether to ask how weak, how frail, her father really was, but she couldn't bring herself to utter the question. She never wanted to hear the truth about Richard's declining condition. She understood at some level that his health was beyond repair, but hearing the words from Lily's lips would make it too real. "Is it all right if I have a look inside?" she asked.

"You don't need to ask me," Lily replied. "Hannah's gone into town for groceries, so there's nobody here but us."

"I won't disturb anything," Frances promised. She followed Lily back inside, and they both stood in the entranceway, staring at the enormous arrangement of delphinium in a cobalt vase on the hall table. Apparently nobody had bothered to cancel Clio's standing delivery order with the florist.

"Has anyone been through Clio's things?" Frances asked in a hushed tone.

"The police were here on Monday. They wanted to go through Mrs. Pratt's personal effects, her correspondence, her checkbook, if that's what you mean. Blair showed them some business papers, I know that, but your father refused to give them anything else." Frances listened, recalling the subsequent search of the Pratt Capital offices. "Then," Lily added, "they came back yesterday with a warrant for the house."

"Did they take anything?"

"Yes. They left an inventory with your father, but he threw it away. 'Meaningless documentation,' he called it. He was displeased by their invasiveness." She paused as if waiting to see if Frances had any more questions, then dismissed herself. "I'll be in the kitchen if you need anything."

The police would've taken Clio's diary this time. They would see the regular notations *3:00—FP at CP*, and *10:00—RC*, Clio's code. It was clear now that the first referenced her visits to Dr. Fritz Prescott at Columbia Presbyterian Hospital on Wednesday afternoons. The second reference remained indecipherable, something perhaps only Richard could explain.

Frances wandered through the entrance hall, listening to her sandals flap against the marble floor. Despite all the time spent in this house, she still felt like a trespasser, tiptoeing around Clio, who seemed just as omnipotent in death as she had in life. Apprehensive, Frances felt an ingrained sensation that she was doing something wrong, even though there would be no one to accuse her of tracking dirt through the house, sitting down in a wet bathing suit, dropping crumbs that belonged in the kitchen.

She opened the porch doors and stepped outside. Despite the gray sky and the cool temperature, Frances found herself slipping out of her clothes. She dove in. After thirty-eight years she was finally able to skinny-dip in her father's pool. The water made her heart race, and she swam rapidly back and forth lengthwise. She was a strong swimmer, and her strokes were steady; the water fell away from her bare skin as her arms pulled her forward. After several laps she paused for breath in the deep end. She held on to the side and felt the tile against her breast. Then she noticed a pair of stockinged ankles and white shoes. Lily stood above her. "Your father's awake." She placed a towel on the ledge by Frances's face.

Lily turned her back while Frances pulled herself out of the pool and wrapped the towel around her. "He's in his bedroom. Why don't you come in when you're ready."

Frances's damp bare feet squeaked against the wood floors as she ventured into the bedroom where her father had slept since his stroke. He couldn't have made it up the stairs to the room he once shared with Clio.

Richard was propped up in a large brass bed. Several wedged pillows under his arms appeared to be holding him in place. The navy blue damask comforter had been pulled back, and Frances could see the outline of his thin legs through the cotton blanket that covered him. There was little natural light through the partially opened drapes, but a porcelain bedside lamp cast a warm glow. The room was cozier, more personal, than Frances had expected, with shelves along one wall filled with books. The bedside table was covered by a stack of books, an army of medicine bottles, and several photographs, all angled so that he could see them from his bed—Clio laughing, her head tilted slightly back, Justin building a sand castle on the beach, Blair and Jake at their wedding, and Frances at what looked to be her law school graduation. She had never seen the picture before. Her own image startled her. She wouldn't have expected to be included in this collection.

Richard didn't acknowledge her when she entered the room.

"Dad," she said softly as she approached the bed. He looked up. His eyes were glassy. "How are you feeling?"

He said nothing.

"I need to ask you one question. It's about Clio."

Still nothing. Frances looked back toward the door, where Lily hovered. From her expressionless face, Frances couldn't tell whether it was all right to continue or whether she should leave. She cleared her throat and took a step closer to her father.

"What does 'RC' stand for?" she asked.

Richard's jaw shifted. She watched as a word formed on his lips. "Where?"

"Clio's diary contains a notation. Every Friday at ten. 'RC,' it says. Do you know what that means?"

"Where . . . was . . . the . . . diary?" Richard's sentence seemed to take a minute.

"It was in the drawer of her desk. I found it the day of her memorial service, although I assume the police have it now. Lily told me they came back with a warrant."

Richard nodded.

"There are references in the book to her appointment with Dr. Prescott, the psychiatrist you told me about, on Wednesday afternoons. Then there's this entry every Friday morning."

"You . . . shouldn't . . . have . . . gone . . . through . . . her . . . things."

"Dad, I'm only trying to figure out what happened," Frances said, feeling defensive. Maybe she had trespassed over Clio's clearly erected barriers, but, she reminded herself, she had done nothing wrong in trying to uncover what happened.

"Privacy—" He coughed. Frances heard mucus rattle in his throat. "She . . . wants . . . her . . . privacy." He tried to push his hands into the wedged pillows to prop himself farther up in bed. He moved his torso back and forth, but his arms slipped out from under him. Lily stepped forward to assist, but he stopped her. "No," he said loudly. Then, turning back to Frances he continued, "You . . . should . . . not . . . have . . . gone . . . through . . . her . . . things." He collapsed back.

Frances looked at her father, trying to read from his distorted face what secret he was hiding. He appeared desperate to shelter something about Clio or their marriage or their life together, something that was so sacred, it might be worth letting her killer go free. Frances recalled their discussion of shame, of Clio's emotional troubles, and wondered if her father was too proud to reveal anything that might be perceived as instability or character imbalance. It astounded her that even in death, societal ostracism could be his overriding consideration. He was obviously protecting Clio's memory, but from what, she couldn't begin to imagine.

"I'm sorry. I don't mean to upset you. I really don't."

Richard said nothing. His breathing was loud. The air crackled in his lungs. He closed his eyes. "Let her memory be dignified." His words ran together. One foot had slipped off the mattress and dangled awkwardly over the side of the bed. Lily cradled it in her hand and gently repositioned it back under the covers.

"Why are you doing this?" he asked.

"I . . . I," Frances stammered, surprised by his question. She took a step backward to keep from losing her balance. Had she been wrong to think he would want an answer about his wife's death? Was she actually making his pain worse? She couldn't bear to see him so upset. She had never imagined that this investigation would uncover such personal secrets about her stepmother. "I'm sorry . . ." She searched for words but was unsure of what else to say. "I've only wanted to help for you. For Clio." Her voice sounded strange, high-pitched and timid.

"It won't bring her back. Nothing will."

A string of sleigh bells rang as Frances pulled open the door to the small coffee shop. The air smelled of stale cigarettes and grease. Several people sat at the stained Formica counter with their backs to the door. No one turned around despite the ringing. A line of banquettes ran along the wall by the windows facing out to the street. Several doctors, still in their green scrubs, filled the booth closest to the door. Despite the evening hour, they appeared to be eating breakfast. Their plates were piled high with eggs, hash browns, and muffins.

Frances looked past them. In the corner, an attractive man in his early forties stood up. He must have seen her approach.

"Dr. Prescott?" she asked, although she was quite sure she knew the answer to her own question. He nodded. They shook hands briefly, and she slid into the banquette across from him.

"Can I get anything for you?" he asked. "I've just ordered myself a cup of coffee."

"Coffee would be great."

Dr. Prescott signaled something to the waitress. Frances picked at a strip of duct tape that covered a rip in the vinyl seat. She stared at a lump of what looked like hardened mayonnaise on the table.

"This isn't the most hygienic place in Manhattan, but the coffee's drinkable and it's open twenty-four hours, so they do a good business with the hospital staff."

"Thank you for meeting me," Frances said. She felt disoriented, having traveled to 168th and Broadway to try to find out details of her stepmother's life that only a psychiatrist could know. She didn't know where to begin and, for the second time that day, felt like an interloper.

"I understand you and Henry Lewis are friends," she said, fumbling for some pleasantry to ease into a conversation.

"We were medical school roommates," Dr. Prescott explained.

"And you consult with him still?"

Dr. Prescott gave her a quizzical look. "I wouldn't say that. We discuss medical issues from time to time. Our discussions are more informal, not exactly what I would call a consultation. Why do you ask?"

"Henry Lewis recommended you to Clio Pratt," Frances declared.

"That's right," Dr. Prescott replied, as if her comment required verification.

"When did you start seeing Clio?"

"Last December."

"Did she say why she wanted to see you?"

"Ms. Pratt, you must understand. I would like to be

helpful, but I can't reveal anything that she and I discussed. She was my patient. For her sake, for the sake of my other patients, I am prepared to challenge the validity of any subpoena."

"Dr. Prescott—"

"Please, call me Fritz," he interrupted.

"Okay, Fritz." The name stuck in her throat. "You and I both know that the psychiatrist-patient privilege keeping your communications private is recognized under New York State statute, rule 501 of the Federal Rules of Evidence, and the Supreme Court's 1996 decision *Jaffee* versus *Redmond*."

"I see you've done your homework, Ms. Pratt." His tone was flat.

He was right. En route to this meeting, she had stopped at the Suffolk County Bar Association library in Riverhead for last-minute legal research. The detour had almost made her late, and she had violated every speed limit between Long Island and Manhattan to make Dr. Prescott's appointment. She needed to use the little she had learned to make her case.

She continued. "Although communications between a patient and psychiatrist appear protected from disclosure and inadmissible at any kind of trial, whether that privilege survives the death of the patient is unclear." That the law didn't necessarily protect such communications once the patient died, a possible loophole, was her only hope. "We have a murder, a high-profile murder that the Suffolk County district attorney is very anxious to solve. There's a compelling public interest, from the court's point of view, in disclosing what you may know about

Clio. In fact, based on my reading of existing case law, I'd wager good money that a court would compel you to talk," she bluffed, surprised by the calmness and certainty in her voice. She seemed to speak with an authority she didn't have. "As of now, nobody but me, my father, and Henry Lewis knows of your relationship to Clio. My father is unlikely to speak up. Dr. Lewis seems to feel quite an ethical duty to keep his mouth shut. However, if I disclose that information, you will undoubtedly be subpoenaed, and you may well be forced to abandon any pretense of maintaining your patient's privacy." She had rehearsed this response over and over as she'd driven into the city, in order to sound convincing. She hadn't meant to threaten.

"What exactly are you saying?"

"I'm saying you should tell me what I want to know because, ultimately, it may serve your patients better. You won't have to challenge a subpoena, and risk losing. I'm not part of the district attorney's office, or any law enforcement office. I was, but I'm not any longer. I have no obligations to the court or anyone else to disclose what I learn."

Dr. Prescott was quiet, mulling over the implications of what she said.

"I'm not asking for details of Clio's troubles. I know from my father that she had them, that she turned to you for help, and that you were helping her when she got murdered. Her personal demons are her own, and frankly, I'd rather not know. But there are some things I do need you to tell me."

"Such as?" He fixed his walnut eyes on her.

"Was Clio afraid of anyone?"

He sighed. "She didn't give me any information that, in retrospect, would provide you with a suspect."

Dr. Prescott paused as the waitress arrived with coffee and a bowl filled with individual creamers and packaged sugar. He ripped the end off a packet of artificial sweetener and stirred the contents into his coffee.

"Your specialty is spousal incapacitation?" Frances asked.

" 'Specialty' is not a word I would use. I do a lot of work with people who need to come to terms with a sudden change in a relationship through death, disability, or, in some cases, abandonment. I try to help them to assimilate what has happened, to grieve, and to figure out a way to reconstitute their life."

"You saw Clio once a week?" He didn't reply. "I've gone through her appointment book. She indicated that she saw you on Wednesdays, here at the hospital," Frances said.

"Twice a week, at first. More recently, once a week," he offered, slightly defeated.

"Why did she reduce her visits?"

"Patients cut down on their therapy for a number of reasons. Sometimes it's because they feel they're making progress, sometimes the reasons are financial, or there can be other commitments." Dr. Prescott was obviously more comfortable answering her questions in generalities.

"Did you think that Clio was making progress?"

"I'm not going to answer that."

"Well, she had no financial constraints."

He said nothing.

"Do you use drugs in your therapy?"

"I believe that judicious use of psychotropic medicine is extremely beneficial. However, it must be part of intensive therapy. I do not prescribe any medication alone."

"Therapy meaning discussions with you?"

"I don't know that I would characterize them as discussions. How much do you know about analysis?"

"Was Clio in psychoanalysis?"

"No. That is very intensive."

"What are you saying? That Clio's sessions weren't intense? What were you doing, then?"

"You're misunderstanding me," he said, his voice suddenly paternalistic. "Psychoanalysis cannot be done in weekly meetings, or even biweekly. It requires daily sessions so that the patient stays emotionally open, able to explore herself and her subconscious thought. Too much time passes, and a person's defensive mechanisms take over. Clio's and my work was simple therapy."

Frances thought for a moment. She reached into her pocket and produced the plastic prescription bottle that she had taken from Clio's medicine cabinet. She looked at the label. "You prescribed phenelzine for Clio," she said, handing it across the table to him.

"I did."

"Why?"

"Nardil, or phenelzine, can be efficacious in certain limited circumstances."

"What would those be?"

"Severe hypochondria is the most common application."

"Did Clio suffer from hypochondria?"

"Ms. Pratt, I don't mean to put you off, but that question is simply not appropriate for me to answer." He took a sip of his coffee. "Why don't we try this. You tell me what you know, and I will do my best to confirm or deny the accuracy of your knowledge based on my own experience with Clio."

Frances eyed him intently. Was this his way of acquiescing to her threat? Was he prepared to tell her information if he could never be credited as the source? She was willing to play along with his game if it got her the information she sought. "My father told me that Clio had irrational fears about her own health. That she became obsessed with the idea that she would die. Would you call that hypochondria?"

"Concern for one's own well-being is a common manifestation of extreme anxiety."

"My father claims that Clio was healthy, physically, I mean."

"I was not aware of any physical illness or health problem, either."

"Phenelzine has a variety of contraindications."

"That's correct. Alcohol and many foods can't be taken with the drug. Of course, we always need to be concerned about interaction with other medications."

"Was Clio aware of the contraindications?"

Dr. Prescott paused. Frances couldn't tell whether he considered this question inappropriate as well or if he was focused on his own self-interest. He had to know that he wouldn't fare well before a medical malpractice tribunal if he prescribed such a potentially lethal medication without proper explanation. "I believe that Clio understood that her diet was restricted. She didn't drink any alcohol. We reviewed the particulars at length. I had no reason to think that she wasn't following them."

"Did she ever discuss with you that she was taking diet pills?"

"As far as I was aware, Clio was not taking any other medication, either prescribed or over-the-counter."

"Clio's body had five hundred milligrams of Dexedrine in it at the time of her death."

Dr. Prescott's shock was visible on his face. As he reached for his coffee cup, Frances could see his hand shake slightly. Apparently the details of his patient's death were difficult to hear, even for a trained professional. "With or without phenelzine, that quantity of an amphetamine would have killed her," he said almost to himself.

"That's what I understand." Frances took a sip of her coffee, which had grown tepid. The liquid left a bitter taste in her mouth after she swallowed. "In your opinion, was Clio suicidal?"

"Absolutely not," he replied without a moment's hesitation. "I never saw anything that would lead me to believe that she wanted to harm herself. She was extremely sad, and nervous for her own future, but she wanted to have that future, and was making plans accordingly."

"Such as?"

"I can't give you particulars. Suffice it to say that she seemed quite optimistic about starting a new life. Don't misunderstand me. She loved your father very much. She was doing everything possible, to the best of her abilities, to make his life more comfortable and pleasant. But she wasn't unrealistic. She spoke to his doctors. She knew his prognosis, as well as his life expectancy."

Now it was Frances's turn to be silent. Although she understood that Dr. Prescott's loyalty was to Clio, his patient, it was hard for her to listen to the reference to her father's impending death in such an objective manner. Living in Orient Point, visiting her father once a week, she had been able to distance herself from the reality of his rapid decline, of his inevitable death. She thought of her earlier visit with Richard, how frail he looked in bed, how feeble he was. Clio had been forced to face something that she herself had done everything in her power to avoid.

"I take it Clio had plans, then, for after my father passed away."

"Yes. She wanted to move to Europe."

Frances was startled. She hadn't imagined that Clio would leave Southampton, the life she had, Richard's business, her social milieu.

When Frances and Pietro had ended their engagement, she hadn't been able to stay in New York City. She'd felt as if there were nothing left for her there, nothing that would be separate from memories of their life together. She had moved to Orient Point to start over. Apparently Clio had been prepared to do the same thing. She recalled her father's words, that she and Clio were alike in their need for privacy. They were also alike in their need to flee from painful memories.

"When was she planning to leave?"

"Not before your father passed away," he said defensively.

Frances sat back against the banquette. She wished she had ordered a Danish, something sweet to give her a jolt of energy. She steepled her fingers and rested them on the edge of the table. Her torso felt heavy, and she struggled to stay erect. She felt lost, disoriented by this doctor who seemed to be getting her no closer to a suspect.

"I'm sorry. I don't know how I can help," Dr. Prescott said as if reading her mind.

Frances thought for a moment. "Is Beverly Winters a patient of yours?"

He lowered his eyes. "I can't comment."

"You can't even confirm or deny?"

"No."

"Aren't you the slightest bit curious about who killed Clio?" Frances asked.

"Morbid curiosity is not something I indulge in," Dr. Prescott replied.

She got up to leave. For reasons she couldn't precisely identify, she didn't like Dr. Prescott. She knew from years of experience how easy it was to hide behind legal privileges, to withhold the truth under the guise of principle. She just hadn't expected him to be so tight-lipped about his murdered patient.

As she slid out of the banquette, she turned and left a dollar bill on the table. "By the way," she added, "when did you see my picture?"

He didn't respond.

"You said on the telephone that you'd know me because you'd seen my picture."

"Clio. The last time I saw her, she showed me a photograph of you and your sister."

It had never occurred to her that Clio would bother to mention her, the stepdaughter, not to her therapist. Frances couldn't imagine that she and Blair even passed through Clio's mind now that they were grown and out of the way. If they did, it could only have been as irritants, not something worth analyzing. What had they discussed? What had Frances and Blair done to warrant Clio's attention? Or had it been wrath? She looked at Dr. Prescott, who sat expectantly. Did he know what was racing through her mind? It was his job to know, wasn't it?

Frances turned away. Whatever Clio had shared, she didn't want to know. It was too late for reconciliation.

As she sped east on Route 495, the wind whipped around the cabin of Frances's pickup, making the truck weave ever so slightly within its marked lane. She looked at the odometer. She had driven hundreds of miles in the last week, back and forth from the north and south forks of Long Island, forty-five miles each way, plus two trips to Manhattan in less than a week, more than she remembered making in the last year. Despite her sore back, stiff legs, and the late hour, she felt compelled to add a detour to her journey, to stop in Southampton, to speak to the woman who shared her stepmother's psychiatrist. Beverly Winters was hiding something. She wanted to know what.

There were several lights on downstairs. Frances rang the doorbell and waited.

Beverly's obvious displeasure registered as soon as

she opened the door. She clutched a tumbler in her right hand and a cigarette in her left. As she pitched forward slightly, the ice cubes rattled in the glass. Frances surmised that whatever she was drinking, it was not her first of the evening.

"What can I do for you?" She seemed to strain to open her bloodshot eyes wider.

"I want to talk to you about Dr. Fritz Prescott."

If the name was familiar, Beverly gave no indication. "I don't know what the hell you're talking about, and I don't appreciate the interruption. I'm busy." Her lips tripped over her words.

"I know for a fact you do. You're a patient of Dr. Prescott's. Clio Pratt was, too, before she died," Frances added. "I need to know whether you and Clio ever acknowledged that to each other."

Beverly took a sip of her drink but said nothing.

"Did Clio know you were a patient of Dr. Prescott's?"

"What difference does it make?" she mumbled into her glass.

Frances didn't want to answer. The significance was in how Clio apparently reacted to those who she perceived had vulnerable information about her. The permutations of Clio's psyche that Frances was in the process of discovering could not be easily explained. "Were you aware that Clio went to see him?"

Beverly looked up. Her eyelids drooped. Her mascara had smeared. "Not until you appeared out of the blue."

"Neither of you knew about the other one." Frances's words came out more as a comment than a question.

Beverly leaned against the door frame. She flicked her

cigarette butt past Frances, then ran the fingers of her free hand through her hair. "Why are you here? Do you think I had something to do with Clio's death, is that what you're getting at?"

"Could I come in?" Frances asked. "I won't take more than a moment of your time."

Beverly looked again at her tumbler, rattled the ice, and nodded. "I could use a refreshment anyway," she said. "If we're going to be standing around chatting." She forced a smile.

Frances followed her down a hall dimly lit by only one of two shell-shaped sconces. The other light bulb had blown. The hall opened into a large rectangular room. Pale pink drapes were drawn in front of every window. Frances counted six couches, each covered in faded blue chintz, clustered in three different seating areas. Beverly stopped at a butler's tray table. "Can I get you something?" she asked. She lifted up a bottle and turned it toward her to read the label. "There's plenty of gin," she said, adding a healthy dose to her glass.

"If you have vodka, I'd have a sip," Frances said.

As Beverly focused on the other bottles, she rocked slightly. "Doesn't look like there is. Anything else?"

"I'm all set, then." Frances reminded herself that she still had nearly an hour to drive before she could collapse in her own bed.

"It's a shame to drink alone." Beverly wandered toward her, then half fell, half sprawled, onto one of the couches.

Frances sat across from her. She found herself playing with a loose thread in the well-worn fabric of the upholstered arm. She wanted to put her feet up but thought better of it. One edge of the glass coffee table between them already had a pronounced chip.

"So, what do you want to know about me?" Beverly asked. Her eyes closed briefly as a smile passed over her lips.

"What happened between you and Clio?"

"Hmm . . . that's a question I wasn't expecting. How shall I answer it? In the Southampton style, short and superficial, or are you interested in the real version, the ugly truth?"

Frances surmised that the question was rhetorical and sat silent.

"Let's see . . ." Beverly shifted against the cushions and stared up at the ceiling. "Dudley and your father were good friends. They trusted each other. You may not know this, but Dudley was your father's accountant up until he got too sick to work. The accountant for Pratt Capital, too. So they had known each other a long time, and there's something about being friends for many years, sharing the same basic experiences. A loyalty develops. A camaraderie and comfort that comes from having the same frame of reference. Maybe you're too young to realize that yet."

Frances thought for a moment about her own friendships, what few she had. Aside from Meaty and Sam, neither of whom she had known all that long, there was nobody. When she'd left Manhattan, she had left everything, and everyone, behind.

"Your father never said a word about his divorce. He never even officially told us. It was just that one day your mother wasn't there, neither were you two girls, except on weekends and school vacations. It wasn't hard to figure out, but your father was very private about it." Beverly kicked off her shoes. They thumped as they fell to the carpeted floor. "When Dudley and I first came to Southampton, it wasn't at all like it is now. Nobody had a forty-five-thousand-square-foot house, or armed guards. It was a very conservative, stable summer community. Everyone stayed married. Only relatively recently did the second and even third wives show up. Babies whose mothers were thirty and whose fathers were sixty. Your parents' divorce was unusual at the time."

Frances nodded. Throughout elementary school she had been the only child whose parents weren't married. Every time she went to the refrigerator, where her class list hung by an alligator-shaped magnet, she was reminded of that distinction. Ms. Aurelia Watson, designated as her parent. No Mr. and Mrs. Richard Pratt with Aurelia noted in parentheses like everyone else.

"When your father married Clio," Beverly continued, "we were thrilled for him. But the crowd out here can be tough. People knew your mother. Clio was a newcomer and, at first, wasn't treated very well. I was one of the few women who accepted her. Dudley and I saw how happy your father was, how happy she made him. Early on in their marriage, the four of us did stuff regularly. We even went to Bermuda for a golf tournament once." She looked down into her drink. "Stayed at the Reefs. I remember one night, your father and Clio were late to meet us for dinner. They arrived out of breath. Clio was wearing the most beautiful pale pink silk dress—I still think about that dress. It was exquisite. It had a square neckline, and as she breathed, her tanned chest rose and fell. There was sand on her kneecaps, and she was carrying her sandals. They'd been out walking on the beach, she said, and lost track of time. But we knew. The way they smiled at each other, a tender complicity. I could see Dudley was jealous. I was, too. It was hard not to be." Beverly's voice cracked. "Clio and Richard had themselves one helluva love affair. Even years later, after the rest of us had grown pretty tired of our spouses, they were still enamored of one another, happiest in their own company." Beverly paused, took a sip of her drink, and smacked her lips.

Discussion of the intimacies of her father's second marriage made Frances uncomfortable. She wanted to get the conversation back on track. "When did you and Clio have a falling-out?"

"Ah, yes. I was getting there, I suppose, in a rather long-winded way, now, wasn't I?" A laugh rattled in Beverly's throat. "Dudley and I began to have marital problems, I guess that's what you could call them, about the time that our daughter, Deirdre, left home for boarding school. I couldn't tell you exactly why, but things seemed to deteriorate. We were having a pretty rocky time of it when Dudley got emphysema. That brought us together, kind of a bunker mentality. I think I appreciated him more when I realized I was going to lose him. Typical, isn't it?"

Yes, thought Frances, despite her abhorrence for

clichés. She too had realized the importance of a relationship when it was too late to rescue.

"For a while, we were consumed by his illness, seeing doctors, getting second and third opinions, exploring treatment options. But ultimately, it was just a distraction. The foundation of our relationship had cracked years earlier, and no amount of crisis could rebuild it. Besides, Dudley got to the point where he needed a nurse, not a wife. I wasn't particularly good as either. It made sense for us to separate."

"Did you?"

Beverly twirled a lock of hair around her finger and chewed on her lower lip. "I told Dudley I wanted a divorce. He acted surprised, as if he hadn't even acknowledged our growing estrangement. He begged me not to go. It was quite pitiful." She shut her eyes. "He was in his wheelchair in the library of our house. By that time, he was weak and quite thin. He sat with his hands folded in his lap, as if he were praying, and he cried. He told me he'd be dead soon enough. Why did I have to leave now? He said he couldn't bear for the last major event of his life to be a divorce. I wanted to be convinced, but despite how pathetic he was, I needed to get away. I couldn't sacrifice my life to him any longer. That's what I told him." She paused, opened her eyes, and looked over at Frances. "I shouldn't be telling you this. It's late. We're both tired. And I've probably drunk too much."

Frances said nothing. Neither did she make any motion to leave. The two women sat in silence.

"Ah, what the hell," Beverly said. "I don't know you,

and you don't know me. So what's telling you gonna hurt me?" She laughed again, but it sounded forced. "Dudley had a life insurance policy. A substantial one. When nothing else worked, he told me he would change the beneficiary, give it to Deirdre, if I left him. I hadn't counted on that, on Dudley's shrewdness, but it was a lot of money. In retrospect, I probably could've gotten most of it in a divorce settlement. We were married a long time, but the thought of poverty during a protracted legal battle terrified me. I agreed to stay. He slept in the guest room, not that it made much difference, but we stayed married, kept up appearances. I wasn't proud of myself." She stuck a finger in her glass and stirred the ice cubes. "Nine days later, he strapped himself into his wheelchair, wheeled himself into our swimming pool, and drowned."

Frances closed her eyes, horrified by the image. "I'm sorry," she said, although the words felt superfluous.

"I found him the next morning. His determination astounded me more than anything else. He had been so sick, could hardly eat, and yet he managed to secure himself with leather safety straps. The weight of the chair made him sink."

"When was this?" Frances asked.

Beverly hummed for a moment before responding. "Two years, eleven months, and twelve days ago. I could probably tell you the hours if I thought about it for a moment. What time is it, anyway?"

Frances ignored her question. "Did you talk to Richard and Clio about his death?"

Beverly wiped at her eye with a red-enameled fingernail. "Most of the world was sympathetic, sweet to me. I was the poor wife who had struggled to care for her dying husband, then lost him to a horrible suicide. But Clio and Richard knew what had happened. Dudley apparently told Richard of our discussion, of my wanting to leave, and of our agreement that I would stay for the insurance. At least that's what he told me in his good-bye note, if that's what you call it. The fucker . . ." She shook her head. "His suicide meant the policy wasn't effective anyway. I would have gotten several million dollars when he died of emphysema, but I got zilch because of his preemptive strike. I guess he got the last laugh."

Beverly swung her feet to the floor and pushed herself up, wobbling slightly as she stood. Then she moved to a breakfront cabinet against the wall. Bending over, she opened the bottom drawer. "Here, this was what I meant. Dudley's good-bye. It's short. You can read it if you want." She came over to Frances, dropped the single sheet of stationery in her lap, then went back to the butler's tray to refill her drink.

To my wife, it began.

> *To say I wish things could have worked out differently seems trite. I have no intention of minimizing the magnitude of my suffering or the magnitude of my disappointment. We didn't talk because you couldn't talk, and eventually neither could I. I hope the shock of finding me will stay with you forever. The hurt you caused me would*

have stayed with me forever. No one knows of what transpired between us except Richard, who has promised to keep my confidence, not out of respect for you, but out of respect for me. I am proud of our daughter and hope that you and she can help one another in the future. She is a remarkable woman. Tell her I love her. I wish I could say the same to you. I wish our good years together didn't seem so distant.

Frances reread Dudley's suicide note several times. She didn't know what to say. She had never seen such a document and wondered why Beverly would keep it to haunt her. Finally she spoke. "Did you ever talk to my dad, or Clio, about this?"

Beverly shook her head. "What was there to say? They knew my darkest secret. They hated me for it. I couldn't blame them. I hated myself, too." She settled herself back on the couch. "I was never going to be able to explain to them that the initial problems, the intractable problems, were created by both of us. That's something most people don't understand. I guess it's easier to pick a side, cast blame, aspersions, whatever, than it is to appreciate the complexity of a marriage, to understand that people are a mixture of good and bad. Clio and Richard saw Dudley as the saintly victim and me as the materialistic bitch anxious to abandon her husband in his hour of need."

"How did you know they disapproved if you never spoke to them about it?"

"I knew. At first, I got the cold shoulder. I'd hear of

their parties, ones that a year earlier I'd have been invited to without question even if Dudley was too sick to accompany me. Before he died, they would've found an extra man to sit next to me, but I didn't get shit afterward. Clio stopped returning my calls. If I invited them to something, she'd tell me they were busy, had plans. It was always polite, but formal. She'd send a note with their regrets, as if we hardly knew each other. After Richard's stroke, it got worse. Clio started talking, telling people I killed Dudley, even if not literally, that I was responsible for his death, that I'd made the last months of his life miserable. I don't know whether she relayed the whole business with the insurance, but I assume she did. That's when virtually all the invitations started drying up. Here I was, alone, and friends that I'd seen for years didn't call, didn't include me. The only parties I ever went to were the huge ones, the ones where you invite virtually everyone you know. Those don't mean anything. It's not like the hosts care whether you're there. They just fulfill all their social obligations at once." She gulped her drink, swilling the liquid in her mouth before swallowing.

"One time, last summer, I planned a dinner. Forty people seated. Engraved invitations, custom tablecloths, the works. I figured I'd splurge and really do things right. You know, have a party that people talk about for at least a few days afterward. One person, or rather, one couple, accepted the invitation. Everyone else said no. And I'd mailed the invitations six weeks in advance. That nearly killed me." Beverly stared down at her newly filled glass and spoke into it. Her voice seemed magnified. "I wasn't going to go through that again this year. I decided that after a cocktail party that the Von Fursts threw. I heard Clio had been on a new gossip spree about me. I couldn't believe there wasn't room for two of us in this community, and I thought I should try to stand up for myself, establish some boundaries. I knew she wouldn't return a call, so one day in early June I followed her home from the Fair Lawn Country Club and confronted her in her driveway. Was she surprised to see me! The look on her face, eyes bugged. I actually think she was scared for a moment. But she kept her composure. Invited me in to talk. Clio was honest, I'll give her that. She told me she thought I was selfish. She loved Dudley and couldn't accept what I'd done, which seemed even worse to her now that she was dealing with her own husband's illness. It was an unpleasant conversation. We were both awkward. I was probably defensive and angry. She was smug and self-righteous, you know how she can be. Could be," Beverly corrected herself. "Like she was the perfect wife. But I felt better about the situation afterward. We sort of agreed to a truce, a moratorium. Our tennis game on the Fourth was the first time we'd spoken to each other since that afternoon. We played tennis. We passed briefly on the porch. And that was the last I saw of her."

Frances listened to Beverly's words with a mixture of disbelief and sorrow. What kind of society was this where alienation, or even the perception of alienation, could cause such misery, where the viciousness of rumors could destroy someone? The sick feeling that briefly washed over Frances when, in her sister's kitchen, she saw invitations to clambakes, baby showers, brunches, lunches, and dinners, all activities in which she wasn't included, returned to her now. Magnify a thousandfold that sense of isolation from the festivities, and she knew what Beverly had experienced. Frances had been able to rationalize her own exclusion: She lived in Orient Point. She chose to be separate. Beverly had not.

Lying prostrate on the couch, her stockinged feet askew, Beverly looked battered. Her wrinkled fingers with their polished nails clutched the glass of gin.

Frances glanced around the room. There were no pictures of Dudley and only one formal portrait of a girl who must be Deirdre, a tall, elegant girl in a debutante's dress. Above the mantel hung an oil painting of a younger Beverly seated on a blue chintz couch, one of the six that still filled this room. The painting revealed none of the agony that had transpired behind these pink drapes.

Frances realized from Beverly's labored breathing that she had fallen asleep, her tumbler perched precariously on her chest. Frances got up, pried the glass loose, and set it on the coffee table. Beverly hardly stirred. Frances thought for a moment to leave a note, then decided against it. She could let herself out.

She pulled into the driveway of her house and shut off the engine of her truck. Too tired to move, she debated putting her head against the vinyl seat and sleeping right where she was but realized that would only be worse in the morning. She opened her side door, heaved her legs onto the grass, and, with every ounce of energy she could muster, got herself up the porch.

The enormous bouquet of pale pink sweet pea, white lisianthus, and peach roses made her gasp. It was a loose, whimsical arrangement, as if someone had swept up an English garden in their arms and left it to fill her house with its delicate fragrance. Sam. She had completely forgotten their dinner together, his promise of grilled salmon and homemade strawberry rhubarb pie, an invitation made, and accepted, over orange juice in her front yard. She was more obsessed with following stray threads of her stepmother's life than in beginning to weave a fabric of her own. She didn't deserve Sam's kindness. He didn't deserve indifference.

Fully dressed, Frances lay on top of her covers, exhausted but unable to sleep. Despite the distances she had covered and the information she had gathered, the day had left her more confused and despairing than any since Clio's death. All she appeared to be learning was that the wealth, glamour, and etiquette of her father's Southampton society only thinly disguised a tormented, troubled reality. How it all was connected to Clio's murder remained a mystery.

Frances's weary mind wandered, and she remembered Sam's touch. Involuntarily she shivered at the thought. His disfigured hand had been anything but repulsive. His caress had simultaneously soothed and excited her. But after her conduct this evening, he would be wise to keep his distance.

Frances started to cry. She tried so hard to build up defenses, to protect herself from her own emotions, yet she felt more vulnerable than ever. She thought of her sister's proposal that she move in with her father. Blair's suggestion seemed practical, a solution to their predicaments. He needed a caretaker, and she, the unemployed, soon-to-be-destitute daughter, would need a roof over her head; but the idea of resurrecting intimacy from the vestiges of their formality seemed impossible. Their relationship had evolved over thirty-eight years and was unlikely to undergo a fundamental alteration. *Because you refuse to try*, a voice inside her admonished. *And look where that's gotten you.*

$\mathcal{F}$rances stepped out of the shower and reached for the terry towel draped over the corner of the door. The bathroom had filled with steam and the scent of gardenia soap. Her eyes were puffy from too little sleep, and her back ached, but she felt relieved to be clean. She dried her smooth skin and let herself imagine the breakfast of French toast and sautéed bananas that she was about to fix. Perhaps Sam would accept an invitation to join her, a peace offering.

She heard a loud knock on the front door, then the turn of the lock. The dogs barked.

She grabbed her robe, hurried to the top of the stairs, and leaned over the banister.

"It's me." Meaty stood in the entrance, looking up at her. He smiled, although Frances thought it looked forced. She cinched the belt tight around her waist and descended. Felonious and Miss Demeanor surrounded Meaty, their tails wagging. "Good guard dogs you've got for yourself," he remarked, reaching to pat Felonious's head.

"They can tell you're harmless," Frances said. "Do you want coffee? I need some for myself."

"That'd be great." Meaty followed her into the kitchen. The percolator had finished brewing. The aroma of strong coffee wafted out of the pot.

"What do you want?" Frances asked as she poured them each a mug. She hadn't forgotten her last conversation with Meaty and was in no mood to be overly friendly.

Meaty sat at the table. He rubbed his eyes. "Allergies. They're killing me," he remarked more to himself than Frances. Then he took a sip of his coffee and grimaced. "That's gasoline. Do you have any milk?"

Frances got up and opened the refrigerator. She removed the milk and, remembering Sam's message, checked the expiration date. It still had several days.

"I'll cut to the chase," Meaty said, pouring a generous amount of milk into his mug. "I know Malcolm offered you an official position on the investigation and that you turned him down. I also know you've been keeping yourself busy trying to solve this murder on your own."

Frances smiled. Apparently someone had been reporting on her whereabouts.

"As I'm sure you know, we've been working round the clock and, quite frankly, getting nowhere. Now that's between you and me. Malcolm's pretty anxious to string the press along, make them think we're about to make an arrest."

"You don't have any leads?"

"Nothing to speak of. That's why I'm here. I thought we might help each other out."

Meaty's code for "Tell me what you know," Frances thought. "Does Malcolm know you're here?" She needed to know whether this visit was sanctioned.

"Yes. He asked me to talk to you."

"And what if I don't want to talk?"

"Then you can just listen for a minute." Meaty sounded slightly exasperated.

Frances settled back in her chair. "Sounds fair."

"Detective Kelly, the one you met the day of the murder, he and I've interviewed everyone on staff at the Fair Lawn Country Club. The black dishwasher, the guy I told you about, he's got a firm alibi. He had the holiday off. He and his girlfriend had gone to Shea Stadium for a baseball game. Left around eight A.M. and didn't return until past midnight. Did a little partying, barhopping, on the way back." He opened a spiral notepad and flipped through several pages. "We don't have anything linking any of the other staff. Can't establish anyone who even had a connection to Clio. Nobody saw anything suspicious."

"You still think there's something to those hair samples?"

"I know your feeling. You've made that perfectly clear, as has Cogswell. Only time I've known you two to think alike."

"Did the lab run any DNA tests?"

"They tried. The techs ran a polymerase chain reaction test. The answer I got was that the testing was inconclusive, possibly because melanin in hair inhibits the PCR process, possibly because the samples were old, or possibly because of external contamination. How's that for covering your ass? The long and the short of it is we got nothing." He flipped through several more pages.

"So, here's what we know. On July Fourth, Clio played tennis with three other women. We interviewed all three, separately. Quite a group, I might add." His attempt at humor fell on an unreceptive audience. He glanced back at his pad and continued. "Clio seemed fine during the match. The group dispersed immediately afterward. Clio went up to the porch and had a drink sitting with a couple named Marshall and Beth Bancroft, old friends, I understand. They were with their two granddaughters, mulatto girls. They were dropped off by their father, Dr. Henry Lewis, around ten. A lot of people remember seeing him. Given his race, he stands out in the crowd, but no one remembers him with Clio at any time. By his own account, he left by ten-fifteen, a little before Clio joined the Bancrofts at their table."

He studied his notes. "Louise Lewis, the mother of the girls, went to the bar to buy drinks for her family and Clio. Apparently Clio insisted on picking up the tab, so Louise charged them to her."

Frances remembered her own conversation with the bartender the morning after Clio's death. *Two Southsides, a Diet Coke, a Perrier water, and two Shirley Temples.* He hadn't been able to confirm that Clio ordered them, but he knew they had been charged to the Pratt account.

"According to the Bancrofts and Louise, a waitress delivered the drinks to their table. Louise said the bar was packed, and she hadn't wanted to wait. We think the waitress was a girl named Melanie Fox, but nobody can say for sure. There are three waitresses who work the porch. One of them, a kid called Daisy, had recently started and didn't even know who Clio Pratt was. We talked to all the girls several times. None of them kept track of who they served because there's no tipping. They noticed nothing unusual. No surprise, nobody asked them to put anything in a drink." Meaty looked up from his notes. "We know Clio ordered the Perrier. We think there might have been as much as ten minutes between the time Louise's order was filled and the waitress, whoever it was, served them. The waitresses all say things were crazy and they were going as fast as they could, but there was a definite back-log on orders. It's possible that someone in the bar could have slipped the Dexedrine into the water. Forensics says ten minutes would be more than enough time for the drug to dissolve."

He returned to his notepad. "That much we know for sure. After that, things get a little hazy. The Bancrofts remember lots of people coming and going, stopping by the table to say hello, but they can't say for certain who they saw before Clio died, and who they saw after, when virtually everyone was hovered together on the porch awaiting the police. Around ten fifty-five, based on the time the call went into 911, Clio must have excused herself to go to the powder room, although, again, the Bancrofts don't actually remember that. We haven't found anyone who saw her in the bathroom until Blair found her body."

"I've read the witness statements you gave me, Jack Von Furst, George Welch, people the police interviewed that day. I know there isn't much."

Meaty nodded. Details of discovering the body, calling an ambulance, canceling the tennis tournament, and attempting to calm the crowd had brought the police no closer to finding a killer.

"What else have you done?" Frances asked.

"We've tested every glass we could find, plastic, paper, Styrofoam, you name it. We couldn't find anything with either Clio's fingerprints or traces of Dexedrine. We still can't confirm how she ingested the drugs. We've assumed it was her drink, given the solubility factor, but we could be wrong."

"The Bancrofts' table had been cleared?"

"Yeah." Meaty looked disgusted. "I hope before anyone knew anything, or the police had arrived, although at this point it doesn't help us anyway. By the time we got around to isolating material for the lab, what we wanted was probably either in an industrial dishwasher or the trash." He paused and cupped his hands around his mug. "We did find one thing, though."

Frances raised her eyebrows.

"In a trash container on the porch, one of those metal baskets. We found nine empty red-and-yellow capsules wrapped in a paper napkin. No prints. They were crushed, but contained traces of Dexedrine. Capsules have been identified as a diet pill called Thinline."

Frances had been tempted in years past to use over-the-counter appetite suppressants herself, until her common sense got the better of her. It was a high price to pay for vanity.

"Which trash container were they in?"

"The one closest to the front stairs. If I had to guess,

our murderer dropped them there on his way out. They were wrapped in a Fair Lawn Country Club paper cocktail napkin."

"Were the capsules cut or torn?"

"I believe the two ends could be pulled apart." Meaty checked his notes. "Yeah, as far as we know, the capsules could be opened."

"Which would take a lot less time," Frances added.

"Right."

"Could the killer have known in advance what Clio would be drinking and made preparations?"

"Well, you know, I thought of that. Except why, if you're doing this ahead of time, would you dump the empty pills at the club? Why wouldn't you leave them at home, or in your car, or wherever?"

Frances had no answer.

"We were able to track down Clio's prescription for Nardil through a credit card receipt from the Columbia Presbyterian Pharmacy on 168th and Broadway. She had been seeing a psychiatrist at the hospital, a guy named Prescott, but he's not saying a word. Psychiatrist-patient privilege or some other crap. That's what he told me last night, anyway."

Before or after our meeting? Frances wondered.

Meaty continued, "Malcolm's not at all sure he wants to take on a legal battle with the shrink. Some people can be pretty sensitive about what they perceive as invasions of privacy, and he can't predict which way his constituency would go. That's about it." He paused for a moment and scratched his ear. "We've gone through all the financial records of Pratt Capital. Nothing unusual. There were several deals in the works, and we've interviewed the participants. If they had complaints, they didn't share them. Mostly we heard a lot of compliments of Miles Adler, sympathy for your father, and respect for Clio, although most thought she was in over her head. One guy whose deal fell apart at the last minute was pretty pissed at Pratt Capital, but his alibi is rock solid. He was in Hong Kong at the time of the murder, putting together new venture capital. Besides, his beef was with Miles. He never even met Clio. The only other recently terminated deal was with a company called Pro-Chem based in Mexico City. We assume that's where Miles has been. From the paperwork, it looks like Miles was pretty psyched about this company. It makes health care products, performance enhancers, the kind of stuff bodybuilders are into. The files contain a letter from the principal of the company expressing regret at the deal falling through, but when I spoke to the guy on the phone, he told me that there were renewed negotiations and he had 'nothing but the utmost respect for Pratt Capital.' Those were his words."

"Has anyone spoken to Miles?"

"I know he returned from Mexico City last night. I left several messages at his office with that secretary—"

"Belle," Frances interrupted.

"Right. Belle. But Miles has not returned my calls."

"He's probably digging himself out from under a week away," Frances said sarcastically.

"Whatever."

"So you think Miles went down to renegotiate the Pro-Chem deal after Clio died?"

"That'd be my guess. But the corpse wasn't even cold when he got on that plane."

Frances remembered her conversation with Penny Adler. Miles had abruptly decided to leave Southampton, to run out on Richard, his mentor, at probably the worst moment in Richard's life, all to salvage a deal. So much for partnership.

And so much for family, too, Frances thought, recalling her own suspicions of her brother-in-law. Despite the dismissive remarks she had made to her sister, she had tracked down Pearl and Bartlett Brenner to confirm that Jake had gone to their home for a morning appointment on the Fourth of July. According to Pearl, even after she and her husband had decided not to purchase the lithographs, they couldn't get Jake to leave. Pleading with them, he had offered to reduce the price, to have them pay over time, practically given them the images rather than take no for an answer. He hadn't left Scarsdale until long after the Brenners' family and friends had arrived for a holiday luncheon. "Did you find anything else in the office?" Frances asked.

"What do you mean?"

"I don't know, exactly. Anything unusual?"

"Do I hear the protective daughter coming through?" Meaty said with a smile.

"I was just wondering," Frances said. Miles had been looking for something, according to Belle, something important enough that he lied to Belle to get access to Richard's office. "Have you come across any reference to 'RC'?"

Meaty flipped pages in his notepad. "Here. Yeah. Renaissance Commons."

"What's that?"

"A quasi assisted living facility, quasi private hospital in Quogue."

Frances was startled. Had Clio planned to move Richard out of their home? That made no sense. Clio's diary showed visits to "RC" at ten every Friday morning. She wouldn't have gone with such regularity if it were only to decide whether the facility was an appropriate resting place for her husband. "What's Clio's connection to Renaissance Commons?" Frances asked.

"She wrote checks to the place every month."

"Do you know what was she paying for?"

"Apparently the room, board, and care of Katherine Henshaw."

Frances was confused. Her face must have shown that because Meaty added, "Henshaw's her mother. I just assumed you knew."

Clio Henshaw, of course. Her maiden name. "But Clio's mother is dead," Frances said. She tried to recall when she had been told that Clio was an orphan. Hadn't her father said something? She had a vague memory of Richard explaining once that it was hard for Clio to be a mother, let alone a stepmother, since she had no role model. Clio certainly never mentioned any parents. She had no relatives at Christmas or other holidays.

"Maybe that's what she said, but I assure you, Mrs. Henshaw is alive. She's a seventy-four-year-old woman who has been at Renaissance Commons for twenty years.

Before that, she was in a state mental hospital near Syracuse."

"How do you know?"

After finding the series of checks, Meaty explained, he went to Renaissance Commons and made some inquiries. He brought along a photograph of Clio. "Everyone there, from the nurses to the cleaning staff to the administrators, knew Clio, although they knew her by the name Clio Henshaw. Apparently she sent regular gifts, fruit baskets, that kind of thing, to the nursing staff, so they were pretty fond of her. As it turns out, your father's nurse, Lily, had worked at Renaissance Commons and met Clio there."

"But nobody knew she was Clio Pratt?"

"The director did. An old-guard doctor by the name of Pierce W. Hamilton the Third. He's obviously a big fan. Said Clio was quite the dutiful daughter, weekly visits, flowers, care packages. She also did a lot for the other residents, sponsored the Thanksgiving dinner, arranged for a chamber music group to play at Christmastime. Quite the benefactress."

For an instant the image of her own mother flashed in Frances's mind. Would she be such a devoted daughter? "What's wrong with Katherine Henshaw?" she asked.

"Physically, she's in pretty good shape. Her problems are mental. She suffers from major depression and some kind of obsessive-compulsive disorder. I've got the official name down here somewhere." He flipped more pages, then turned his notebook upside down to try to decipher some scribbles on the side. "Here. Trichotillomania. Compulsive hair pulling."

"That sounds awful."

"Actually, from what I gather, the depression's much more serious. She's kind of a zombie. Most of the time she can't even get herself dressed. She hasn't been outside in fifteen years."

"And they can't do anything for her?"

"Dr. Hamilton wouldn't get into the details of her treatment."

"Did you meet her?"

"No. The place is very private, obviously designed for sick family members to be quietly squirreled away. I never even got into the area where the patients are kept."

"I'm surprised he told you as much as he did."

Meaty shrugged. "My guess? He's pretty concerned about where the next check for Henshaw's care is coming from. The place can't be cheap."

"Did Mrs. Henshaw get any visitors?"

"I didn't see the logs myself, but Hamilton's assistant reviewed them on his instruction. Over the course of twenty years, she saw her daughter and, occasionally, your father. The only other person that even tried to visit was Miles Adler. On May thirtieth, a Saturday. This year. She refused to see him. Since he wasn't family, he couldn't insist."

Frances felt tense, as if she could feel the blood pulsing through her body. What was going on? Clio had a mother with serious mental illness who had been institutionalized for decades, and she, Frances, knew nothing about it. Why had her father affirmatively misled his daughters as to the familial history of his wife and denied the existence of this woman who lived only a few miles down the Long Island Expressway? Then there was Miles

Adler, who had discovered the existence of Mrs. Henshaw. What had he done with that information? Or rather, what had his knowledge done for him?

"That's about where we are." Meaty's voice interrupted the thoughts racing in Frances's mind. "Frankly, this has me thinking that maybe this wasn't a murder at all. We could be wrong."

"What?" Frances asked.

"I don't know how to say this delicately, so I won't try." He scratched the side of his cheek. "Clio had a host of problems. She's seeing a shrink. She's on pretty potent antipsychotic medication. Her mother's certifiable. Her only child died, and her husband is—" He glanced at the floor. "The way I see it, it's possible Clio decided there wasn't much worth living for. I'm wondering if we jumped the gun in calling it a homicide."

Frances was silent. Clio commit suicide? It seemed impossible, incomprehensible. She didn't seem like the suicidal type, whatever that might be, yet Meaty's logic was compelling. Loss of the two people in the world she most loved might have put her over the edge. But, Frances remembered, Dr. Prescott had said she had been planning to move to Europe. Besides, having cared for her mother her whole life, was Clio likely to abandon her now?

"Any ideas?" Meaty asked.

Frances shrugged. "But I'd like to see Renaissance Commons. If you wait here, I'll be ready to go in five minutes." She got up from the table. Her breakfast, and her apology to Sam, would have to wait.

A few minutes later, hair still wet, Frances was back

downstairs. As she opened the door to leave, she gasped. Miles Adler stood on the threshold. The sleeves of his wrinkled trench coat covered his hands. Underneath, a well-worn T-shirt hung loose on his thin torso. She could see bluish veins through the pale skin of his face. His lips were cracked, and he had dark circles under his eyes.

"Miles!" Frances exclaimed.

Meaty, who stood behind her, stepped in front. "Miles Adler?" he said, picking up on the name.

Miles nodded.

"I'm Detective Burke. You've done quite a job avoiding me the last week."

"Yes. I mean, no. I was out of the country," Miles stammered. "I wasn't aware that you were here."

"I bet you weren't," Meaty muttered.

"Please, I need to talk to Frances. If I could just have a few minutes." He looked at Frances.

"Take all the time you want," Meaty said. "I'll just sit and listen. I won't be any bother." His sarcastic tone offered Miles no choice.

"Fine," Miles said softly. "I assume you'll need to know what I have to say anyway, so you might as well hear it directly."

Frances, still stunned, directed Miles into the kitchen. They all took seats. Frances offered coffee, but both men declined. Miles looked scared. He was thinner than she remembered, and sitting with his shoulders slouched, he looked smaller, too.

"Miles," Frances said, trying to keep the quiver in her voice under control, "you should know before you say anything that you're a suspect in the murder of Clio Pratt."

"But this is not a custodial interrogation," Meaty corrected.

"If it's about my rights, I know what they are." Miles looked directly at Frances. "I didn't have anything to do with Clio's death." His eyes welled with tears.

"Why don't you just tell us why you're here," Meaty said.

Miles picked at a cuticle on his left index finger. His foot tapped the floor robotically. "I'm sorry to have missed the memorial service," he said. "I know I should've been there. It was a terrible lapse of judgment on my part."

"Where were you?" Meaty asked. Frances glared at him, wishing for once he would keep his mouth shut.

"Mexico. Mexico City. I was closing a deal."

"With Pro-Chem?" Meaty said.

Miles looked surprised. "How did you know?"

Meaty didn't reply.

"Um, yes. Pro-Chem. It was a deal that I'd worked on for a long time. One I think is going to be extremely profitable. Clio called it off several weeks ago. I won't deny that it made me upset. Very upset. She and your father are the controlling shareholders of Pratt Capital, so there was nothing I could do at the time, but when I learned last Saturday that she was dead, I wanted to try to revive the deal."

Frances caught herself biting her lip in concentration. Meaty uttered a peculiar guttural sound but did not interrupt.

"I'm not proud of what I did." Frances could see Miles's chest rising and falling with his quick, shallow breaths. "But I didn't kill her. I know that you and the police are suspicious of me, but you needn't be. I had no reason to want Clio dead."

"Why were you and Penny in Southampton over the Fourth?" Frances asked.

"That's what I've come to explain." Miles put his hands on his knees, seemingly to stop his body from moving. "As you probably know, or you've figured out"—he glanced at Meaty—"I wanted a controlling interest in Pratt Capital. I made no bones about it. I've worked hard for your father, and I've continued to work hard for Clio over the past year. But it was very difficult for me. She doesn't, she didn't, know the business. It's that simple, and it was virtually impossible for us to continue in the manner that we were operating. It wasn't fair to me." His voice dropped almost to a whisper, and Frances had to lean toward him to hear. "I tried on several occasions to buy her out, to make some deal with her. She refused. Finally . . . I . . . I was desperate, you have to believe me."

Frances looked at Meaty. He was scowling, but Miles seemed too upset to notice.

"Have you ever wanted something so badly that it clouds your common sense, your reason? It's like you'll do anything to get it, and you don't care who you hurt or mistreat along the way. That's what happened to me. I got frantic, obsessed with owning this business, with finally being in charge. Each time she turned me down just made me more crazed to see my plan through." He looked at

Frances, seemingly seeking reassurance that his tenacity was understandable.

"And under the terms of your partnership agreement, you had a right to buy out Richard's share of the company if Clio died," Meaty interjected.

"That's right." He looked back and forth between Frances and Meaty. "But it's not what you think. I had a better plan. I found out some information that she and Richard had both tried very hard to conceal. I thought I could use it to negotiate a deal."

"Was the information you intended to use about Katherine Henshaw?" Meaty asked.

Miles seemed to choke on his saliva. He coughed without covering his mouth and eyed Meaty, then Frances. "Well . . . yes. Mrs. Henshaw. She's a very ill woman. Clio took great pains to hide her existence from the world. I figured I could use that to my advantage."

"That's extortion," Meaty said bluntly.

"I didn't think of it that way at the time." He sighed. "Although it doesn't matter now. Before I ever confronted Clio with the information, she told me that she had been rethinking things anyway. She wanted to sell the business."

"Just out of the blue?" Meaty sounded skeptical.

"In early June, we had several extremely unpleasant encounters. She was as unhappy as I was with the current situation."

Frances remembered the letter dated June 4 that Annabelle Cabot had given her when they'd met at the Plaza. Miles's threat. *Stay out of my business. . . . If you do not honor my request, you will not like the conse-*

quences. Had that been part of what Miles now characterized as "unpleasant"?

"She called me in mid-June, said she changed her mind. She didn't want the headache, the tension, the stress. She and Richard didn't need the income anyway. She wanted to be with Richard all the time. She didn't want to have to come to the city. She said in the last year, as she'd gotten more and more involved in business deals, it just didn't seem right. It wasn't the way she wanted to spend her remaining months, or years, whatever it would be, with Richard. Anyway, that was the plan. She was perfectly willing to let Pratt Capital be mine, mine alone."

Miles slumped even farther in his chair, as if his chest would collapse onto his thighs. Neither Frances nor Meaty said a word.

"My lawyer, Ian Feldman, he'll send you copies of the documents. Our buyout agreement. Transfer of shares was set for July thirty-first. The agreement we negotiated is much more favorable to me than a buyout under the partnership formula. She got half the money up front. The rest she would receive over five years payable in French francs. She had bought a place on the Riviera, Vence, Cannes, I'm not sure where, but she planned to live abroad when Richard passed away." He looked up, as if to gauge Frances's reaction to the reference to her father's death. "The details probably aren't of particular interest to either of you. Suffice it to say, her death is going to cost me money."

"Why?"

"Ian tells me that since Clio died before our deal

closed, Richard can legally demand payment under the partnership terms. If he insists, I'll have to pay the higher dollar amount to YOUTHCORE."

"Somehow, I doubt that's foremost in his mind right now," Frances mumbled, more to herself than the others. Then she asked, "Why were you in Southampton last weekend?"

"I went with Penny to make amends, I guess. We planned to go for quite some time, before this agreement with Clio had transpired. In all honesty, my original intent hadn't been benevolent. When we invited ourselves out, I wanted to try to convince Richard to sell out. If that failed, I planned to use the information I knew about Mrs. Henshaw to force Clio to sell."

"Why did you try to visit Katherine Henshaw in May?" Meaty asked.

"After I found out about her, I wanted to see it for myself, see how bad she was, to confirm the situation, but that hospital, or whatever it is, wouldn't let me in."

"Renaissance Commons," Frances said.

"Yeah." Miles fixed his gaze on Frances. "You've got to believe me, I didn't kill her. I was as shocked as anyone else to hear she'd died."

Shocked enough to get directly to the airport, Frances thought. "Why wasn't Clio willing to let you do the Pro-Chem deal, then? If it was going to be your company anyway."

Miles looked at the floor. He seemed to trace an outline of something on his thigh. When he spoke, his words came slowly. "The president of Pro-Chem was furious about the way Clio had treated him. We were very close to a deal before, and Clio had just decided, without even consulting me, to call it off. She was critical of him and his company, his products. He wasn't going to have anything to do with Pratt Capital whether she controlled it or not. But when she died, I thought I might have a chance to rescue the situation. You know, I actually thought he might take some delight in her untimely death. Like it was a sign that our deal was supposed to happen."

"But I'm asking you about Clio. Why would she have blown your deal if she was going to sell you the company anyway?"

"At the time Clio called off negotiations with Pro-Chem, she and I hadn't come to our mutual understanding. I don't think she had even decided to sell out. If I were to guess, she didn't make up her mind to sell until after things eroded in June." Miles seemed exhausted, as if the slightest push would send him toppling over. "I was hardly the gentleman, but I actually thought that my buying the company would be the best thing for everyone, including Richard and Clio."

Frances felt a queasiness in her stomach at the thought of the sordid legacy of her father's company, at the devious tactics of his prodigy. She hoped he would never find out all that had actually transpired.

"I've told Ian to answer any further questions you, or the police, might have."

"You were at the Fair Lawn Country Club when Clio died," Frances said.

"Yes. Well, sort of. Penny and I left the club early that morning, around nine, I'd say, but went back. I told her I needed sunblock. I'm really susceptible to burning.

That's why I like to go to the beach early. But actually, I had a conference call. She gets pretty sick and tired of my working on vacation, so I didn't tell her. I dialed out, so I expect telephone logs from the club can confirm I was on the telephone from about ten A.M. until close to eleven-fifteen. By the time I came downstairs, Clio was dead and the police were already there."

"How did you know?"

"I overheard someone mention Clio's name as I was coming down from my room. I saw the cops. So I asked some guy I saw on the porch what had happened. He told me. Nobody knew I had any connection to Clio or Richard."

"You made a business call on a Saturday?" Meaty asked skeptically.

"It was a call to London. I think the Brits like to schedule business with Americans on the Fourth of July. Spoil the holiday." He laughed awkwardly. "I can give you the names and numbers of the two guys I spoke to if you want to check it out."

"We will," Meaty remarked.

Miles nodded. "Anyway, that's everything. As I said, I'm not particularly proud of myself, but I'd never do anything to harm Richard. He's been a father to me."

And this was what he got in return, Frances thought.

Miles scanned their faces. He appeared to be searching for something, some consolation that he wasn't as self-interested and malevolent as his conduct made him seem; but Frances was unwilling to provide the assurances. After several minutes of silence, Miles stood up. He reached into his back pocket, removed his wallet, and dropped Ian Feldman's business card on the table. "As I said, I've authorized him to answer any questions you might have. And you know where to find me. I'm sorry I took so long to clarify this situation. I wasn't particularly proud." He looked down at the floor, then turned on his heels and walked out. Frances heard the screen door slam behind him, the purr of his Porsche as he started the engine, and the screech of his tires as he sped away.

The stucco structures of Renaissance Commons with their red asphalt roofs loomed up out of the landscape as Meaty and Frances made their way along the winding blacktop drive. Set back from the road, the facility seemed serene, surrounded by cut lawns and oak trees, with clusters of weathered cedar benches and chairs. However, in the distance Frances could make out what appeared to be an electric fence running along the perimeter of the property, partially concealed by rhododendrons, boxwoods, and Scotch broom, but there nonetheless, a reminder that the place was designed to keep its residents contained.

They followed signs to the main administration building. An attendant under the carport directed them to an appropriate parking space to the left of the entrance.

The reception area was a large, circular room with butter-colored walls, thick carpeting of green and gold, and overstuffed chairs arranged in squares. In the center of the room, a uniformed nurse sat at a small leather-topped secretary. An armed guard stood behind her.

"May I help you?" the nurse asked as Meaty and Frances walked toward her.

"We're here to see Dr. Hamilton. Detective Robert Burke and Ms. Frances Pratt." Meaty flashed his badge.

She pushed some buttons on an elaborate panel, then announced Dr. Hamilton's visitors to what Frances assumed was the director's assistant. "He'll be right there," a woman's voice replied through the speaker.

The nurse-receptionist looked up at her audience and smiled. "He'll be right with you if you would care to take a seat," she said as if they hadn't heard.

Frances and Meaty settled themselves, and Frances picked up a glossy brochure. The distinctive architecture covered the front page. *Renaissance Commons. A place you can trust with your loved ones*, it said in gold lettering. Inside there was a picture of Dr. Pierce W. Hamilton III, a graduate of Yale College and Harvard Medical School, a prize-winning psychiatrist. The list of his credentials, medical affiliations, and publications filled nearly the entire page.

Frances continued to read. Dr. Hamilton had built the facility in 1979 in response to the massive deinstitutionalization of mentally ill patients from state hospitals. *The professional caregivers at Renaissance Commons are committed to providing a therapeutic and comfortable environment and quality, individualized care, while allowing our residents to maintain their personal dignity.* The brochure continued with glossy photographs, attractive nurses administering medication and meals, group therapy, arts and crafts, an exercise class in an indoor swimming pool, and several pictures of the different types of accommodations, from a private room to a small apartment complete with kitchenette.

"Detective Burke. Nice to see you again." Dr. Hamilton, a tall man with square shoulders and graying temples, extended his hand. "Ms. Pratt, I presume. Please accept my condolences on your mother's passing."

Frances stood up and shook hands. She inadvertently dropped the brochure, which Dr. Hamilton stooped to retrieve. He handed it back to her with a smile.

"Frances here was Clio Pratt's stepdaughter, actually," Meaty corrected him.

Dr. Hamilton pursed his lips and nodded. "My apologies on the error," he said. "But my condolences nonetheless." His voice was deep and soothing. Frances wondered if he did hypnosis.

"Please," he said, indicating with a gesture of his hand. "Follow me."

Dr. Hamilton led them into a spacious office and beckoned toward two leather armchairs. His walls were covered with diplomas and certificates, most of which Frances couldn't read from where she sat. Behind the doctor's desk, floor-to-ceiling mahogany bookshelves were filled with tomes, medical periodicals, and an eight-by-ten studio portrait of a handsome blond woman and three dark-haired teenagers. To her left, through the picture window, Frances could see a young man being led across the lawn by a woman in a white uniform.

"I didn't know this place was here," she said.

"Few do. We like it that way." Dr. Hamilton smiled. He rested his interlaced fingers on his desk and leaned forward. "What can I do for you today?" His tone made clear he hadn't been thrilled by Meaty's earlier visit.

"We need to ask you a couple more questions about Mrs. Henshaw's daughter, Clio Pratt."

Dr. Hamilton sighed and glanced out the window. "Without Clio, this place might never have been built," he said, more to the glass than to the two people across his desk. "Clio recognized early on the need for top-quality psychiatric care in a private setting. There isn't a great deal of it in this country, largely because insurers won't pay, but there are wealthy individuals whose principal concern is not money, but the care of their seriously ill loved ones."

"How did you meet her?"

"We met in Manhattan, just after she and your father married. I was giving a lecture at New York University Medical Center on the impact of mental illness on families. People suffering with serious mental illness simply cannot survive in the outside world. They may have moments of relative normalcy, but nothing sustainable. That's what people don't appreciate. It isn't within their control. Coming to understand that, and cope with that, can be extremely difficult on the people who love them, or must care for them. But I'm rambling," he remarked, turning his attention to Frances.

"Clio came to your lecture?"

"Yes. She seemed very interested in my work. Came up afterward to introduce herself. She asked lots of questions. Several days later she sent me a very kind, complimentary note and invited me to lunch with Richard. She and I continued to correspond intermittently over the years, and to see each other socially every so often. Then, when I decided to try to put this place together, she was enormously helpful. Pratt Capital provided the money I needed. But the odd part was that all during those initial years, and then during the discussions and negotiations over Renaissance Commons, she never let on that she intended to place her mother here. I appreciated her tremendous support, but I had no idea that her mother was ill."

"When did you learn about Mrs. Henshaw?" Frances asked. She looked over at Meaty, who seemed uncharacteristically quiet.

"About two or three months after the main facility was completed, Clio called me and said she wanted to move her mother here. I believe Mrs. Henshaw had been in Syracuse somewhere, but I can't recall the specifics. In any event, the place probably doesn't exist any longer. We made the transfer arrangements, and Mrs. Henshaw moved in. She's been with us ever since."

"Why did you think Clio didn't tell you earlier?"

Dr. Hamilton sat back against his leather chair and folded his hands in his lap. "Ms. Pratt, mental illness is still a strange thing to most people. They don't understand it. Clio loved her mother very much, but family members often suffer feelings of shame. It's very difficult to admit."

Shame, the emotion her father mentioned.

"Did Clio ever ask you to keep her identity secret?" Frances asked.

"Not in so many words, but Clio was a very private person. She knew confidentiality is taken very seriously here. I understood that she might be concerned about what impact her mother's situation might have on her husband's business, on her reputation in the social community. Such feelings are normal. We try our best to respect that."

"Were you aware that Clio was seeing a psychiatrist herself?"

Dr. Hamilton was silent. Frances watched his Adam's apple move along his throat as he swallowed hard. "I had no idea."

"She saw a Dr. Fritz Prescott at Columbia Presbyterian."

"I know of him. He has quite a reputation as an expert in grief counseling."

"She had been taking Nardil for approximately six months before she died," Frances continued.

"She never mentioned any of that to me."

"Is there any reason to think that Mrs. Henshaw's mental illness has a genetic component, that it could have been passed on to Clio?"

"It's possible. There is certainly ample support in the medical literature for the notion that depression and other types of mood disorders are genetically linked. It's not uncommon for mental illness to run in families, especially in women. Nardil isn't prescribed much anymore, but it is given for certain types of severe anxiety disorders, including hypochondria. There could be a connection, but, as I said, I was not privy to any of Clio's medical information, and I really can't comment responsibly." Dr. Hamilton rotated his watch on his wrist.

"Would you consider Clio suicidal?" Frances asked.

"Again, I can't begin to answer that. All I can tell you is that suicide is extremely difficult to predict. We see people who threaten suicide all the time, who are obsessed with death, who exhibit the classic symptoms, but who, I firmly believe, would never do it even if no one reacted to their threats. Others, who appear to respond to therapy or medication, then quietly and efficiently kill themselves and you wonder why."

"Does Katherine Henshaw know that Clio is dead?"

"Yes. I told her myself."

"How did she take the news?" Frances asked.

"I wasn't able to get her to discuss it with me. According to the nurses, she didn't say a word for hours. Although she doesn't communicate well, she often makes noises, guttural sounds, or she hums to herself. Apparently, she just rocked back and forth in a special chair that she loves. It's one that Clio gave her several years ago."

Even though she had never met this woman, Frances felt a strange sadness wash over her. She pictured a small, hairless woman rocking in agony, unable to express the extent of her pain. It was hard enough to articulate emotions without debilitating mental illness to stand in the way.

"Can we see her?" Meaty asked.

"I'll allow you to visit, if you'll promise to be brief. She doesn't like strangers, and I don't want her pushed."

Meaty and Frances walked several paces behind Dr. Hamilton. Frances watched his long arms swing and the double vent of his tweed blazer flap in back. His strides seemed to cascade him swiftly down the corridor to where a large arrangement of silk flowers set on a marble pedestal marked the entrance to a common room. The double doors were open, and Frances could see wicker furniture and pillows in bold colors. Floor-to-ceiling windows along two walls and bird chirps wafting in through the open screens gave the sense of the outdoors. A stone fireplace at the far end held two shiny bronze decorative logs. The space felt decidedly unlike a hospital.

Dr. Hamilton directed them to the far corner, where a woman sat in a rocking chair with a yellow cotton blanket draped over her thin shoulders. She stared blankly ahead of her.

As they approached, Frances could see that Katherine Henshaw's head was shaved. Her scalp was covered with scars, as well as several crimson scabs. Despite the hospital's efforts to eliminate any hair to pull, she apparently still pried at the follicles. Nonetheless, her facial resemblance to Clio was striking, the same smooth skin, azure eyes, and chiseled features.

"Katherine," Dr. Hamilton said softly as they approached. "Katherine," he repeated. He introduced Frances and Meaty. Katherine Henshaw made no indication that she heard anything or realized he stood beside her.

"Clio told you about Frances, didn't she? Richard's daughter," Dr. Hamilton coaxed. Katherine rolled her eyes.

"Mrs. Henshaw . . ." Frances stepped forward. "I know this must be a very difficult time for you. It is for my father as well. He loved her very much." She knelt down to try to catch Katherine's gaze. Katherine began to hum and rocked slightly.

"Would it be all right if I asked you a couple of questions about your daughter? We're trying to figure out why she died."

Katherine Henshaw began to rock faster.

"Did Clio ever tell you she was afraid of anyone? Did she ever say that she felt threatened?" Even as she asked them, Frances realized the absurdity of her questions. That Clio would share any of her own troubles, no matter how serious, with this frail, disturbed woman was improbable, if not impossible. She wouldn't have burdened her mother any further. Out of necessity, Clio had been the parent, not the other way around.

Katherine's humming grew louder. She closed her eyes.

"I don't think this is possible," Dr. Hamilton said in a quiet, firm tone.

Frances kept her eyes on Katherine, watching her lips start to form around amorphous words. "We're going, we're going," Katherine repeated.

"You and Clio?" Frances asked.

"I'm not sure what you're getting at." Dr. Hamilton stepped between Frances and Katherine.

"It's nothing," Frances said, realizing that whatever plans Clio might have had for her mother were useless now. Presumably Katherine Henshaw would reside at Renaissance Commons until the day she died. Richard would see to that.

As Frances stood up, she could see tears rolling down Katherine's pale cheeks. "I'm so sorry," Frances heard herself say, although her voice felt strangely disconnected from her body.

Katherine covered her ears with her bony hands and

started to scream, a raspy gasp of noise. Dr. Hamilton indicated they should leave. As they did, he bent over Katherine and surrounded her frail frame with a tight embrace, forming a human barricade between her and the rest of the world.

Frances and Meaty sat in silence as Meaty steered the Crown Victoria through the gates of Renaissance Commons. Just outside the entrance, he pulled over and idled the engine. "I'm not the kind of person who's particularly self-analytical," Meaty began, "but that woman really makes you wonder. What happens to people?"

"Who knows." Frances sighed.

"Must've been awful watching a mother like that. What would you do?"

"What she did, I guess. Get her set up somewhere comfortable and safe. Then visit regularly." Frances thought of her own weekly visits to her father over the course of the last year.

"Sure makes you wonder about suicide."

"You wouldn't have done it."

"I can't say. It's one thing to put yourself in someone else's shoes and say you'd do things differently. It's another to actually be in those shoes. I don't know what I would've done under those circumstances."

They sat in silence until Meaty cleared his throat. "Where to?" he said. His voice sounded animated.

"Can you drop me at my mother's house?" Frances asked.

Meaty gave her a quizzical look but said nothing. He

flipped the Crown Victoria into gear and headed in the direction of Southampton.

As they approached Aurelia's residence on Halsey Neck Lane, a navy blue four-door Audi sedan turned left out of her driveway and sped past Frances and Meaty. Despite the tinted window and the large aviator sunglasses that covered his eyes, the driver's square jaw was unmistakable. Frances turned to look at Meaty, wondering whether he had noticed. Without turning his gaze from the road, Meaty smiled. "Wonder what brought Malcolm Morris out to these parts on a Saturday," he mused.

Frances asked Meaty to pull over. She assured him that she wanted to be alone and that she could get herself home. He seemed reluctant to leave, most likely intrigued by the prospect of a discussion of Malcolm's visit, but Frances deprived him of the opportunity. She shut the door quickly behind her.

As she walked up the driveway, her feet crunching the pinkish gravel, she could see her mother on the porch, holding on to the balustrade at the top of the steps. Aurelia wore a wide-brimmed straw hat with a pale blue scarf tied around it, a peach sundress that hugged the rounded curves of her full figure, and a white cardigan. Her hands were buried in its large pockets. She rubbed one of her bare feet along the calf of the other leg.

"Mum?" Frances called out, reluctant to interrupt her mother's obvious reverie.

Aurelia smiled, a flash of white teeth under her hat. She took one step down the stairs toward her daughter and extended her arms. "What a pleasant surprise on an already perfect day." Her voice was high and airy.

"Are you all right?" Frances asked.

"Of course, why?" she said, laughing slightly. "Don't I seem all right?" She tilted her head coyly and tucked her chin down toward her chest.

"Did I interrupt something?"

Aurelia paused for a moment. "No. Come in."

Frances followed her mother through the front door and entrance foyer into the kitchen. Ordinarily filled with papers, cut flowers, oil paints, canvas, and brushes, the room now was a culinary shambles, with an omelet pan, an orange squeezer, a mixing bowl and pieces of a Cuisinart piled high in the sink, dishes stacked on the sideboard, and an empty Champagne bottle on the table along with two soiled napkins.

"How was your brunch?" Frances asked.

Aurelia's face showed her surprise. Then, realizing the evidence was apparent from the state of her kitchen, she laughed again. "My daughter the detective."

"Prosecutor," Frances corrected her. "But it doesn't matter anyway. I left."

Aurelia said nothing. She opened the cupboard, removed two tall glasses, and filled them from a pitcher wet with condensation. She handed Frances a glass. "It's lemonade."

"We passed Malcolm on the way in."

"We?" Aurelia asked.

"A friend drove me over. No one you know. Or should I say no one I think you know. I've underestimated your ability to get around."

Frances had meant to tease her mother with a playful reference to her apparent relationship with Malcolm, but Aurelia ignored the remark. She sat at the table and indicated for Frances to do the same.

"I hope it's what you wanted," she said. "Quitting, I mean."

Quitting. Aurelia's emphasis made the word resonate. That hadn't been Frances's characterization. In her own mind, she had spared herself the judgmental overtones of leaving the district attorney's office, but now she felt her mother's disappointment.

"I'm not exactly sure what I want these days. . . ." She paused.

Aurelia seemed to stare at the lemon pulp floating on the surface of her glass.

"So what's going on between you and Malcolm?"

Aurelia took a sip of her lemonade and licked her lips. "You needn't worry about your old mother."

The image of Malcolm helping Aurelia to her car after Clio's memorial service flashed into Frances's mind. At the time, watching them from the upstairs window of her father's house, she had assumed that her mother and Malcolm had just met at the reception and that he had been polite enough to see the first wife off. Perhaps she had been wrong. Her view then had been too distant to notice a hint of affection or the suggestion of a mutual attraction. "How long has it been going on?"

Aurelia didn't respond.

"What? You can't tell me? He's no longer my boss, so what does it matter?"

Aurelia looked up. "That isn't it. If I'm reticent, it's

because I'm not used to having my own daughter grill me on my romantic life."

Frances realized that she and her mother had never discussed boyfriends in any detail. Aurelia hadn't even asked why her relationship with Pietro had ended. Instead of the intimacy and friendship that could have developed between them as she grew up, they had become increasingly distant. They shared little of their emotional lives.

"Let's see," Aurelia began, as if to embark on a recitation she had rehearsed several times before. "Henry and Louise Lewis invited me to a fund-raiser for Malcolm about a month ago. It was at their house here. I think they called it 'an effort to retire his campaign debt.' Henry thought I might be interested in meeting him, especially because of you. Taking an interest in my daughter's career. So I gave my fifty dollars. I was hardly one of the big donors, but it got me in the door."

Money well spent, Frances thought, judging from her mother's upturned mouth and twinkling eye.

"He's a charming man." She blushed and suppressed a smile. The color in her skin made her look years younger.

"Are you sleeping with him?"

She laughed. "Oh, Fanny!"

Frances slumped in her chair. Her mother and her boss, or ex-boss . . . that was about the last thing she would've expected. She thought of her conversations with her mother over the last week, discussions of Clio's murder and the investigation, of leads and dead ends. Now she understood how Malcolm knew what she had been up to. Aurelia had been reporting on her whereabouts, keeping the district attorney apprised of actions that Frances wished he knew nothing about. Perhaps she was also the source for information on Frances's relationship with Clio.

"Did your decision to quit have anything to do with Clio's murder?" Aurelia asked.

"Have you and Malcolm discussed the investigation?" Frances threw back.

"Not much." Aurelia had never been particularly good at bluffing, and today was no exception. Frances knew she was lying. "I know they don't have a suspect, but that's about all. I also know that Malcolm wants that to stay out of the press."

"I'm surprised the press isn't on to the two of you," Frances said.

"We're discreet. Besides, who really cares what two middle-aged divorced adults do in their spare time."

"Malcolm's not divorced."

Aurelia snorted in disgust. "He's been separated from that . . . *woman*"—she said the word as if it were a fungus stuck to the roof of her mouth—"since the election. It's only a matter of weeks until things become final. But I don't appreciate the insinuation. I'm not a marriage breaker."

"The expression is home wrecker."

"Whatever. You know what I mean."

"Are you two serious?"

"I'm surprised by your curiosity." She smiled. "Let's just say we're getting to know one another. Now, I would like to change the subject. What have you decided to do instead? For employment, I mean?"

"I don't have any immediate plans."

"I don't understand you. You were doing well there. Malcolm is quite disappointed."

"I'd rather not talk about it under the circumstances," Frances replied.

"Fine. I can respect that," Aurelia said. "But I'll just say one thing. Whatever you want to think about the situation with Malcolm, I'm still your mother. I know how much you've invested in that career of yours, and I'm concerned. It also upsets me that Clio's murder is the thing that precipitated your departure. As if that woman didn't do enough damage while she was alive."

"It's not this investigation. It's not any one case in particular. It's just the whole thing, the whole profession, the system."

Aurelia furrowed her brow.

"You don't want to hear all this," Frances said by way of cutting the conversation short.

"That's not true. You may think I don't. But what matters to you, what motivates you, matters to me."

Frances's and Aurelia's eyes met. Frances felt her heartbeat quicken as her mother extended a hand and rested it on top of her own. She shivered slightly, startled by the physical contact.

"Talk to me, Frances. I know you think you've got everything under control, and you probably do. But just tell me what's on your mind."

"It's hard to explain, really," she began, searching for words. "It's not something that happened overnight. It's just been a gradual realization that I shouldn't be in this business." She drank from her glass and felt the cold juice soothe her throat. This was not the conversation she had anticipated when she'd asked Meaty to drop her off. After her discovery of Katherine Henshaw, she'd simply wanted to see her mother, spend time making small talk, just visiting. She needed some semblance of a maternal bond, but she hadn't intended to delve into her current occupational decisions.

Frances looked at her mother and wondered for a moment what to say, then decided on the truth. "Most everyone there has an agenda of some sort or another. Malcolm wants the publicity, the attention that comes with being a politician. He'll run for higher office one of these days. People like Perry Cogswell, the assistant in charge of Clio's murder, he wants power, underlings, the feeling that he can control the day-to-day life of others. I don't want that. I don't share those ambitions. Since I don't want whatever this job may have led to, that left me with just a job. All I've done for the last thirteen years is process cases. Investigate them, indict them, try them, or plead them and try to get the court to impose a substantial sentence. My responsibility ends when the bailiff takes the defendants away, even if only metaphorically. For what? You know, I'm happiest in my garden with Felonious and Miss Demeanor." Frances stopped talking. Her mouth felt dry.

"But it's important work, keeping the streets safe and all that," Aurelia said.

"Even the Fair Lawn Country Club isn't safe. People talk a lot about justice being served. If a defendant gets convicted and sent away, then 'justice is served,' like some special item on a menu. I've seen the families of some victims where vengeance becomes their reason to live. All the rage and energy they can muster is poured into some perceived punitive goal. If they attain it, they lose the reason to live. Then there are others for whom the process—whether the killer is found, tried, even executed—is virtually irrelevant. What victim is ever really made whole? Look at Dad."

Frances thought of Richard in his wheelchair, staring out across the lawn of his exquisite, empty home.

"You know, I remember the first time that a guy I prosecuted was sentenced to prison. It wasn't even my case. Just after I got to the Manhattan DA's Office, before I'd even been admitted to the New York Bar, I second-chaired a trial, you know, helping the prosecutor out, preparing witnesses, handing him documents. The defendant was the principal of one of the public elementary schools on the Lower East Side. He embezzled funds, including state money allocated for students with special needs. It was truly heinous. The guy spent the cash that was supposed to go to build the handicapped ramp for two kids with cerebral palsy on an apartment for his girlfriend. The kids' lunch money went to pay for a trip to the Bahamas. The judge sentenced him to three years while his loyal wife and two kids were in the front row of the courtroom crying hysterically and calling out that they loved him. The special needs kids were there, too, confused by the proceeding, not really understanding why their principal was being manhandled by a couple of court officers. It was all I could do to get out to the street, before I burst into tears. Who was the winner in that situation?"

"Why now? Why did Clio's investigation make you quit?" Aurelia asked.

"I think I've had these questions simmering in the back of my mind all along, but I never paid much attention to them. Another day. Another defendant. Now I see Dad, and it finally hit me. Nothing, not finding the killer, not tearing his eyes out, not sentencing him to death, will make Dad feel any better. For him, Clio's death is no different from Justin's. Whether by murder or by accident, he's left with an unfillable void." Frances looked up at her mother. She suddenly felt exhausted, overwhelmed by articulating the thoughts that had spun in her mind. She couldn't hold back her tears. Eyes burning, she rested her head in her forearms and let the sound of her own sobs envelope her.

She felt her mother's hand rubbing her hair in slow circles. It was a familiar sensation, something that Aurelia had done over and over for Frances as a child, a soothing contact that, in Frances's memory, seemed to substitute for words unsaid and conversations not had, but which had established an intimacy between them. It had been a part of their good-night ritual, until Frances had reached an age when such rituals had to be abandoned.

As Frances's sobbing subsided, the rubbing stopped. Frances heard her mother push her chair back and get up from the table. When she looked up Aurelia was at the sink. She put on rubber gloves and turned on the faucet to do the dishes.

"I'm sorry," Frances said.

Aurelia did not turn around. "It's hard to watch you in such pain."

Frances sat for a moment, watching her mother scrape the plates, rinse them quickly, and load them into the dishwasher. Her head was pounding. "Do you have any aspirin?"

"Check my medicine cabinet. There should be something."

Frances helped herself up and slowly worked her way down the hall to the bathroom at the end. The door was slightly ajar. She pushed it all the way open. Sunlight through the window filled the white-tiled room. Frances turned and stood facing the mirrored cabinet. In her reflection, the shower curtain behind her provided a colorful floral background to frame her red, swollen face. She reached for the handle and pulled open the medicine cabinet.

Frances took the plastic aspirin bottle off the shelf and shook it gently. Nothing rattled. Empty.

Bending over, she opened the undersink vanity and perused the clutter, rolls of toilet paper, antacid tablets, cough syrup, antihistamines, disinfectants, and bandages. She pushed aside several bottles, searching for ibuprofen, aspirin, any pain reliever, but found nothing. Then, a single sheet of paper folded multiple times into a one-inch strip caught her eye. She pulled it out.

Her hands shook as she unfolded the paper and stared at the words. *Active Ingredient: Dexedrine.* It was the directions and warnings for the use of Thinline appetite suppressants.

> *Do not take more than one capsule per day. Use of this medication has been associated with strokes,*

seizure, heart attack, arrhythmia, and death. Do not take if you are taking a prescription monoamine oxidase inhibitor for depression.

Phenelzine and Dexedrine, Nardil and Thinline, a fatal combination.

Frances stifled a cry. She found herself gasping and managed to keep herself erect only by leaning against the vanity. Water on the rim of the porcelain basin seeped through the fabric of her shirt.

"Did you find it?"

Frances jumped back at the sound of her mother's voice, dropping the Thinline package insert onto the floor.

"I'm sorry. I didn't mean to startle you." Aurelia's eyes fixed on the paper. She bent and picked it up. "I thought you were interested in aspirin."

"When—when did—you . . . buy Thinline?" Frances stammered.

"Several months ago," Aurelia answered quickly. Her voice was flat, controlled. "They made me so jumpy, I couldn't concentrate. Then I ate to try to calm myself down." She forced a laugh. "These hips will be mine until the day I die. There's nothing I can do to change nature." She patted herself. "Your father used to tell me that he liked voluptuous women. Either he changed his mind later in life, or he lied."

Frances felt her heartbeat quicken. Her mother had been at the Fair Lawn Country Club on July Fourth. She had been with Louise Lewis. She had gone to the bar to say good-bye. She knew what Louise had ordered. "You killed her."

Aurelia squinted at Frances but said nothing.

"Why?"

Aurelia's lower lip began to tremble. She diverted her eyes. Suddenly her legs buckled under her, and she lowered herself to the floor. "Stop, Frances. I didn't do anything. You don't know what you're saying."

"Why did you do it?" Frances repeated. She didn't move.

Aurelia tilted her head back and rested it against the wall. She placed her hand on her neck, fingering her throat. "I don't expect you to understand. You don't have that capacity. You're not a mother. You weren't forced to watch what that woman did to your children, how she made them feel, these young girls, good girls, sweet girls, made to feel bad, monstrous, as if you were undeserving. She wouldn't have come into your existence if it weren't for me, if I hadn't left your father. So it was my responsibility to eliminate her."

Frances's head pounded. "Why now?" Whatever misery Clio had inflicted on Frances and Blair as children, nearly thirty years had passed.

"Why not now? I should have acted sooner. Every time I turn around, she's caused more hurt. Your sister was going to lose her business because of Clio, because she wouldn't allow your father to help out. As if they would even miss the money." Aurelia covered her mouth with her fist and seemed to chew on her fingers. Then she dropped her hand to her lap. "And rather than just tell Blair no, Clio managed to make her feel worthless, incompetent. Your sister has worked extremely hard to build that gallery."

Frances thought of Blair at Clio's memorial service, telling Penny Adler to come visit the Devlin Gallery's new space. Blair, so animated about the discovery of Marco, her secret playboy, who within twenty-four hours of Clio's death had managed to turn the bad situation around, to take advantage. Miles had, too. He had jumped on the bandwagon of revelers profiting from Clio's death to cement his Pro-Chem deal.

"Clio kept Henry Lewis out of Fair Lawn. After years of friendship with his in-laws, after Louise and Blair had grown up together as children, she threatened to blackball him. So his daughters, his adorable little girls, will be excluded, treated differently, just like you and Blair were ostracized. You two didn't even feel like you had a home. The effect of that woman continues."

Aurelia rubbed her eyes, then wiped her nose with the back of her hand. "I see it every time I look at you. You were the most joyful, trusting child. If you had seen yourself with your father. You sat on his lap every night and told him all the details of your day, what happened to you, what books you read, what games you played. Then she came into his life, and it was as if you were afraid. Your affection withered. Your whole sense of the world, the goodness of the world, changed. I see you alone, because you have no faith in relationships. I see you isolated, because you can't trust anyone enough to get close. I see you unable to love, because you've never understood that you were lovable. And that's because of her."

Frances listened, but only partially heard, as her

mother explained what had happened. The idea had come to her not long ago, after her show at Guild Hall had been a failure. Depressed, she'd thought that a diet and exercise regimen might help her spirits. She'd bought a package of Thinline. The pharmacist had recommended it as the number-one-selling appetite suppressant in the country. After she'd read the package insert, though, she had realized that amphetamines were contraindicated because of her heart condition. Several weeks passed, and she forgot about the pills. She had been caught up in the agonies inflicted by Clio, comforting Blair and Henry, both injured in their own ways by her malevolence. As she was lying in bed one night, unable to sleep, it had occurred to her that her money had not been wasted. The dosage in one box of Thinline was enough to kill Clio. It said so right on the label. Death by overdose of diet pills—the perfect weapon in a society where everyone wanted to be thin. Who would ever suspect murder?

The planning had been relatively simple once she'd made up her mind. She and Louise played tennis. Aurelia had a chance to look over the sign-up sheets at the Fair Lawn Country Club. She could see when Clio's next game was, and Louise was only too happy to play anytime. July Fourth. The tournament. A big day. Aurelia hadn't been sure the opportunity would arise, but it was a good guess.

She had seen Clio seated with the Bancrofts. Louise would be uncomfortable in Clio's presence. When Aurelia found Louise at the bar, she knew that her opportunity had come. Clio had offered to buy the round, and wanted a Perrier for herself, but there was a long line for the bartender. Louise asked that the drinks be brought to their table when the order had been filled.

Aurelia thanked Louise for the match and said good-bye. Louise returned to the porch. But instead of leaving, Aurelia went out to her car, got the Thinline capsules, emptied their contents into the palm of her hand, wrapped the empty capsules in a paper napkin, and slipped back through the crowd to the bar. She dropped the bundled plastic capsules into the waste container on the porch as she made her way back.

Inside the bar, the Pratt order sat on a tray, ready to go. The place was mobbed, people clamoring for drinks, chatting and socializing, oblivious of the single woman with a handful of Dexedrine. Leaning over the bar, she was able to empty her fist into the sparkling water without anyone noticing. Later that night, Malcolm confirmed that her plan had worked.

"Did you know Clio took Nardil?"

"I had no idea," Aurelia responded. The amphetamines were sufficient on their own. That they did it quicker because of the interaction was a fortuity.

"Was winning Malcolm over part of the plan?" Frances searched her mother's face. That she was gazing at a calculating killer seemed impossible.

"It only occurred to me later how much our relationship could protect me. Malcolm trusts me. We've discussed the investigation all week. He kept saying he shouldn't say anything to me, but then he would laugh. 'Who are you gonna tell?' he said. Malcolm would never think of me. Who would? Richard and I have been divorced for more than thirty years. He's been good to me, financially and otherwise. I have no complaints, virtually no dealings with Clio. And I don't belong to Fair Lawn."

And I've protected you, too, Frances thought. Who would look for motive in the psychological impact of Clio's behavior over the years on now grown children, especially when one of them was in the district attorney's office? Aurelia had been safe from detection all along.

Frances felt as if the oxygen had been vacuumed from the room. As she listened to her mother, the caverns of past pains loomed.

"I'd like to tell you I did this for you, for Blair, but it was for myself. I saw what she had done to you girls all your lives, treating you like second-rate citizens, strangers in your own home, the home that belonged to you before she ever set foot in it. I didn't want to be married to your father, but I never expected he would remarry someone so cruel. I never realized that I'd be responsible for causing you all the heartache that you suffered through as a child, all the agony of being a hated stepchild. So I did it for myself."

An effort to purge her own guilt, Frances thought.

Aurelia spoke through tears, choking on her words. "My life hasn't been what I wanted. I'm not what you might call a success. But I've finally done something productive, something proactive to protect the world, or at least the people I care about, from her infection. She'll never hurt anyone again. Not Blair. Not you. Can you understand that? Can you try for a minute to understand?"

Frances looked down at her mother in a heap on the floor. The folds of fabric splayed out around her body.

Her eyes were rimmed in red, and her nose was filled with mucus.

"I feel great about what I've done. It's the only thing I've ever accomplished. If I die tomorrow, I'll die a happy woman." She broke into sobs and covered her face with her hands.

Frances felt strangely detached. Although she heard the words of her mother's confession, they seemed scripted, surreal. Never once, in the sleepless nights of the past week or in her relentless pursuit of the unhappy people whose lives intercepted Clio's, had she suspected her own mother of committing the crime. Now her mind simply did not want to process the information it was receiving.

Aurelia coughed, cleared her throat, and asked, "What will you do?"

Frances didn't know how to respond. What choice did she have? Turn her over to the police and step aside? Watch the system she had recently abandoned go to work prosecuting Aurelia? Let Perry Cogswell destroy her mother? Hope that a jury would be so sympathetic to the tormented Pratt family that they would nullify the murder indictment by deciding that Aurelia couldn't be held accountable for her actions? When that unlikely outcome failed to transpire, watch the bailiff take her away? That was one option.

Frances remembered less than a week earlier, here in the same house, the scenario she had discussed with Aurelia. *What happens if the murderer isn't caught?* Meaty already thought Clio's death was a suicide. So, after a time, with no new leads, the police, the assistant district attorneys, the media, move on to something else. The case gets closed. The file goes to archives. People forget. Could she?

Frances shut her eyes and inhaled deeply. She felt air fill her lungs and then listened to the sound of her breath as she exhaled. She nodded at her mother, unsure of what signal she was sending but unable to formulate words. Silently she stepped across the threshold and back down the hall.

Frances walked along the side of the road, heading in the direction of her father's house. She dreaded telling him the truth of what her mother had done. Aurelia had deserted him decades earlier, and now she had made sure that he would die alone. Because of her, his family had been torn apart twice.

Instead of turning onto Ox Pasture, Frances decided to take a detour, to follow Halsey Neck Lane to the beach and return on First Neck Lane. She lengthened her stride and swung her arms, needing to stretch her limbs.

The grass between the curb and rows of privet was sprinkled with dandelions and other assorted weeds. As she crossed each driveway, Frances looked up at the expansive houses hidden behind the protective fences or hedges. She tried to imagine what lay inside, the differing dynamics of familial emotions. It had always seemed to her that other people's lives were simpler, that they spent summers around picnic tables and winters in front of fireplaces, content in each other's company, but that her family had struggled silently to maintain, at best, neutrality. She had been as wrong about all of these strangers as she had been about the people in her own family.

For all Clio's faults, for all her hostility toward Richard's children, she had protected the people she loved. She had kept her mother safe from the world, pampered and cared for by benevolent professionals. She had made her husband happy and then, since his infirmity, had made him safe, too. She had ensured that his privacy and dignity were intact. She had surrounded him with caregivers. Frances hadn't done that for anyone. She never allowed anyone to depend upon her. She was self-sufficient, and she wanted everyone else to be that way, too. Emotional neediness, attachments, made her want to run.

In an odd way, Aurelia had also tried to protect the people she loved. She seemed to have the very real sense that, with a single act of violence, she could heal the emotional wounds of her daughters, her friends, perhaps, even unknowingly, the women like Beverly Winters whose lives had been affected by Clio's cruelty.

Words she hadn't heard Aurelia say since her childhood flashed into Frances's mind. Each time she had skinned her knee, or stubbed her toe, or scratched her forehead, her mother would rush over, embrace her, and gently, reassuringly, say, "I'll just kiss it and make it better." It had worked. In her memory, the soft touch of her mother's lips on her bloody flesh had eased the pain. She craved that comfort now.

Clouds covered the sky by the time Frances arrived at her father's house. As she turned into the drive, she could see that the front door was open and that her father sat in the threshold, waiting. His hands clasped the metal arms of his wheelchair. She moved toward him, hesitant. When their eyes met she stopped. His dull eyes stared at her.

He knew. Aurelia must have delivered the news herself.

"What should I do?" Frances asked without moving from where she stood several feet shy of the door.

"Nothing," Richard replied. His voice was soft but firm. "I don't want you, or anyone else, to do a thing."

At some level, Frances had known her father would say the words he'd just uttered. Nothing could bring Clio back. A trial of Aurelia would only make matters worse, exposing Clio's secrets, the hidden past that had haunted her. Yet, at the same time, her father's decision surprised her. The woman he loved murdered by the woman he'd once loved. Didn't he want to make Aurelia pay?

"Are you sure that's what you want?"

Richard's head trembled slightly. He seemed to take a moment to mouth his words without uttering a sound, as if to practice formulating the shape of them, but when he finally spoke, his speech was deliberate. "If Justin were alive, I would think differently. But he isn't. When I die, your mother will be the only family you and Blair have left. I won't be responsible for taking her away from you. I won't make you orphans."

But she took you away from us, Frances thought.

"What else is there for me? Revenge? Never a quality I admired in anyone else, I don't intend to indulge it in myself. Besides, revenge for what? Clio's death? Aurelia seeking a divorce to begin with? You girls have been through enough in your lives."

Her father's words seemed to echo in her ears. She felt weak and wanted to cry. Richard was willing to let her mother go unpunished for the most horrendous of crimes because he wanted to protect his daughters. "It's not—not fair to you," she stammered.

"Fairness plays little part in this world. You know that, Fanny. I can't think of anyone who has passed through life getting only what they deserved, no more, no less. Some are lucky. Their lives are unscathed. They don't have to suffer. For the rest of us, the best we can do is try to live through the adversity, to not get bogged down in whether or not what happens to us is fair in some global scheme, and to continue to feel joy in what is good. I've been lucky because I've known what it is to love, both wives, three children, and my work. You need to find some joy, something to live for. Blair has Jake, the gallery. You, Frances, must find your own peace."

"I can't," she said.

Richard seemed not to have heard. He inhaled several times without appearing to exhale and then continued. "I've made a lot of mistakes. I know that. Perhaps I didn't want to see my own shortcomings as I went along, how I failed your mother, and how I failed you."

"That's not true." As she spoke, Frances realized she was lying. She couldn't bear for her father to suffer anything more.

"I think I knew all along that you and Blair were hurt, that I had let you down, but I relied on your silence, especially yours, Fanny. It became my protection. 'They don't seem unhappy,' I could say to myself. 'Look what I've given them. Look at the wonderful times they are having here in my house. Look at all they have because of me.' I needed that to be true."

Frances wanted to placate him, assure him that his memory was exactly right. She could remind him of the special moments in their childhood, nights of bingo with their father, pizza and the movies with friends, days at the beach, playing tennis, riding bicycles, all the activities of childhood transpiring in a beautiful, idyllic setting. It hadn't been bad, Frances wished she could say, but she couldn't deceive him. She hadn't been able to deceive herself. Beneath the facade of the Pratt family was a dark reality, one in which two young girls dreaded returning to a home where they were despised because they were the product of a first wife. And neither their father nor their mother had done anything about it. Until now.

"I look at you, Fanny, my own daughter, who didn't feel safe enough to tell me how she felt. You internalized your emotions, and I let you do it. Now I wonder whether you can really feel, feel deeply, passionately. You'll let me go to my grave without hearing a word of criticism from your lips, and that's the damage I've done."

Frances's arms and legs felt numb. She stood quiet, staring past her father into the foyer beyond. Her reflection in the carved wood mirror looked completely unfamiliar.

"I can't make it up to you. Even if it were possible, there isn't time left in my life. You'll have to help yourself. I can't make you trust. I can't make you safe. But you must never doubt that I loved you."

Frances felt weak, and she eased herself to the ground. She sat on the threshold for a moment and then allowed her head to rest against her father's leg. She closed her eyes. Her stiffness relaxed as Richard's slim fingers, shaking slightly, caressed her cheek.

"Are you wanting to talk, or shall we just sip our Scotch?" Sam asked, gently resting a hand on Frances's shoulder as he settled beside her on the porch steps. She nodded in recognition of his presence but said nothing.

The last several hours had passed in a thick fog through which she remembered calling Sam from Main Street in Southampton. She'd hardly managed to convey where she was, but Sam had somehow found her more than an hour later, leaning against the steps of the white clapboard Methodist church catty-corner from the public telephones. He had helped her into his Jeep Cherokee and tucked an old quilt around her shivering frame. It was possible that she'd fallen asleep on the way home, staring at the underside of the car's canvas roof, but she couldn't be sure. All she knew was that the familiar sight of her farmhouse, the smell of her flower beds, the warmth of her loyal dogs as they scrambled down the steps to greet her, had awoken something inside her. She was home.

Frances turned her head upward and smiled at Sam. "Thank you," she said. Her voice sounded hoarse, a strange gruffness brought on by lack of use.

"I've never seen someone so in need of a ride." Sam shrugged lightheartedly. "A lost orphan," he added, pushing a stray hair off her face with his thumb.

"I'm sorry about dinner last night."

"I don't know what you've been up to the last couple of days, but you don't need to apologize to me. Ever. You should know that by now." He took a sip of his drink. "Nothing like a single-malt to soothe the spirit," he said.

Frances took a sip as well and felt a pleasant burn in the back of her throat. She stared at the whites of his eyes and noticed for the first time that they had a slight tint of blue. "Sam," she said, humming the end of his name.

"Yes?" His quizzical look seemed a mixture of amusement, curiosity, and concern.

"If someone you loved did something terrible, illegal, what would you do?"

Sam furrowed his brow. "What do you mean?"

Frances thought for a moment. Although she trusted Sam, she couldn't share her secret. She couldn't place the burden of her knowledge on his shoulders, but she needed his advice. "Suppose, for example, your wife had told you that she robbed a bank, shot a guard in the course of escaping with the money. You know if you turn her in, she'll spend the rest of her life in jail. Would you do it? Would you tell the police?"

Sam was quiet, perhaps taken aback by the sudden reference to Rose Guff, perhaps pondering the question Frances had posed. When he spoke, his voice was soft. "I don't know. I'd like to think I would, it's probably the right thing to do, but I can't be sure. Really loving someone is rare. It's almost indescribable in its specialness. You feel blessed. Loss of that person is the hardest thing in the world. I've been through that, and I don't think I could live with myself if I had played a part in ruining her life. So I can't say." He paused and looked at Frances. "I guess that's not much help to you with whatever's on your mind."

Frances smiled faintly. "You're wrong." She closed her eyes and leaned toward him until she felt the softness of his lips against hers and she could taste his breath. Their kiss lasted long enough to establish that they both wanted it to happen again.